# ALISTAIR MACLEAN'S
# RED ALERT

Alistair MacLean, who died on 2 February 1987, was the international bestselling author of thirty books, including world-famous novels such as *The Guns of Navarone* and *Where Eagles Dare*. In 1977 he was commissioned by an American film company to write a number of story outlines that could be adapted into a series of movies; two, *Hostage Tower* and *Air Force One is Down*, were, with Alistair MacLean's approval, published as novels by John Denis; these were followed with six by Alastair MacNeill, the highly successful *Death Train*, *Night Watch*, *Red Alert*, *Time of the Assassins*, *Dead Halt* and *Code Breaker*, and two, *Borrowed Time* and *Prime Target*, by Hugh Miller.

*Red Alert* is the fifth title in the UNACO series.

ALASTAIR MACNEILL

*Alistair MacLean's UNACO Red Alert*

HARPER

This novel is entirely a work of fiction.
The names, characters and incidents portrayed in it are
the work of the author's imagination. Any resemblance to
actual persons, living or dead, events or localities is
entirely coincidental.

*Harper*
An imprint of HarperCollins*Publishers*
77–85 Fulham Palace Road,
Hammersmith, London W6 8JB

www.harpercollins.co.uk

This paperback edition 2010
1

First published in Great Britain by
Collins 1990

Copyright © HarperCollins*Publishers* 1990

Alastair MacNeill asserts the moral right to
be identified as the author of this work

UNACO is a registered trademark of HarperCollins*Publishers*

A catalogue record for this book is
available from the British Library

ISBN-13: 978-0-00-617849-1

Typeset in Meridien by Palimpsest Book Production Limited,
Grangemouth, Stirlingshire

**Mixed Sources**
Product group from well-managed
forests and other controlled sources
www.fsc.org  Cert no. SW-COC-1806
© 1996 Forest Stewardship Council

FSC is a non-profit international organisation established
to promote the responsible management of the world's forests.
Products carrying the FSC label are independently certified
to assure consumers that they come from forests that are managed
to meet the social, economic and ecological needs
of present and future generations.

Find out more about HarperCollins and the environment at
**www.harpercollins.co.uk/green**

# PROLOGUE

On an undisclosed date in September 1979 the Secretary-General of the United Nations chaired an extraordinary meeting attended by forty-six envoys who, between them, represented virtually every country in the world. There was only one point on the agenda: the escalating tide of international crime. Criminals and terrorists were able to strike in one country then flee to another, but national police forces were prevented from crossing international boundaries without breaching the protocol and sovereignty of other countries. Furthermore, the red tape involved in drafting extradition warrants (for those countries that at least had them) was both costly and time-consuming and many an unscrupulous lawyer had found loopholes in them, resulting in their clients being released unconditionally. A solution had to be found. It was agreed to set up an international strike force to operate under the aegis of the United Nations' Security Council. It would be known as the United Nations Anti-Crime Organization (UNACO). Its objective was to 'avert, neutralize and/or apprehend individuals, or groups engaged in international criminal activities'.* Each of the forty-six envoys was then requested to submit a detailed *curriculum vitae* of a candidate its government considered to be suitable for the position of

* UNACO Charter, Article 1, Paragraph IC.

UNACO Director, with the Secretary-General making the final choice.

UNACO's clandestine existence came into being on 1 March 1980.

# ONE

Neo-Chem Industries' Italian plant was situated near the A24 motorway, halfway between Rome and Tivoli. The complex, hidden from the road by a pine grove planted in the 1950s when the land belonged to the army, was surrounded by a 15-foot perimeter fence and patrolled by armed guards, most of whom were ex-policemen lured away from the Carabinieri by the company's lucrative wage prospects.

Pietro Vannelli was an exception. He had been a security guard all his working life. It was all he knew. He was fifty-three years old and had been with Neo-Chem Industries since the plant had opened eight years earlier. Six months ago he had been transferred from ground patrol to the less demanding graveyard shift at the main gate. At first he had been grateful for the move, only too glad to leave the exercise to the younger men. But he soon grew disillusioned. Nothing ever happened. He missed mingling with his colleagues; the jokes, the shared cigarettes, but most of all the poker games held twice a week in one of the warehouses. All he seemed to do now was sit in the hut and read a succession of cheap paperbacks to pass the time. He had been told there was no chance of getting his old job back, so he had made some discreet enquiries about vacancies for nightwatchmen in the city.

3

It would only be a matter of time before the replies came through the post.

A pair of headlights pierced the darkness beyond the gate. It would either be a member of staff who had forgotten some work or someone seeking directions into Rome. Why else would anyone bother to take the signposted road at that time of night? He picked up his torch, tugged his peaked cap over his thinning grey hair, then opened the door and stepped out into the cold night air. A yellow Fiat Regata stopped in front of the gate. The girl who got out was in her early twenties, the same age as his own daughter, with an attractive figure and long red hair. Her face was bruised and blood seeped from the corner of her mouth. Her faded jeans were smeared with mud and her white sweatshirt was torn at the left shoulder. Tears glistened on her discoloured cheeks. He used a sonic transmitter to open the gate.

'What happened?' he asked in horror.

'Please help me,' she whispered in a barely audible voice. 'They're going to kill me.'

'Who?' he said, shining the torch into the darkness behind her.

Nothing.

She suddenly darted past him and disappeared into the hut. He hurried after her. She was cowering in a corner, her hands clenched tightly under her chin, her eyes wide with fear.

'It's all right, you're safe now,' he said with a comforting smile.

He turned back to the door, intending to close the gate, and found himself facing a silenced L34 A1 Sterling sub-machine-gun. The man holding it was Riccardo Ubrino, a swarthy 34-year-old with greasy black hair and a stubbled chin. The man behind him was similarly armed. Paolo Conte was in his early twenties with curly brown hair and

4

wire-rimmed glasses. He wore a brown uniform identical to Vannelli's.

'Carla, get his gun,' Ubrino ordered, indicating Vannelli's holstered Ruger GP100.

Carla Cassalo scrambled to her feet, unholstered the gun, and gave it to Ubrino. He tucked it into his belt, then unslung a second sub-machine-gun from his shoulder and handed it to her.

'I see you're admiring my handiwork,' Ubrino said to Vannelli and cast a sidelong glance at Carla's face. 'Realistic, isn't it? I used to work in the make-up department at the *Teatro dell'Opera*. You'd be amazed what can be done with a little imagination.'

'Who are you?' Vannelli asked, desperately stalling for time. He had to get to the alarm bell underneath the desk behind him.

'Red Brigades,' Carla told him.

'What do you want?' Vannelli's right hand was now touching the desk, his fingers feeling for the button.

Ubrino pressed the tip of the silencer against Vannelli's face. 'Spare a thought for your family before you raise the alarm. Especially your daughter. She's getting married next month, isn't she? I'd hate anything to happen to her before the wedding.'

Vannelli swallowed and brought his hand back into view.

Ubrino smiled faintly and patted Vannelli's cheek. 'Wise decision. I want you to call your colleague in the reception foyer. Boschetto, isn't it?'

Vannelli merely nodded.

'Tell him about the young woman who's cowering with fear in the corner of the hut. You've already called the police but you'd feel a lot better if she were to wait in the foyer for them.' Ubrino grabbed Vannelli's wrist as he reached for the telephone. 'And remember your daughter when you make the call.'

Vannelli jerked his hand free. 'You won't get away with this.'

'Just call him!' Carla snapped, pressing the Sterling into Vannelli's back.

'Boschetto knows my voice. Kill me and you'll never get inside the building.'

'That's where you're wrong,' Carla said with a sneer. 'Paolo was at drama school with me. He's been studying your voice for the last few weeks. He may not have perfected it but Boschetto wouldn't know the difference over the phone.'

Ubrino pushed Carla's sub-machine-gun away from Vannelli's back. 'She's right. We've each got something to contribute to the mission. The Red Brigades *never* carry passengers. Not that we'll need to use Paolo, will we? I'm sure your daughter will look lovely on her wedding day.'

Vannelli snatched the receiver from Ubrino. He had no difficulty in convincing Boschetto to let him bring the girl to the foyer.

'Bring the car inside,' Ubrino said to Conte after Vannelli had replaced the receiver. 'Then we can close the gate. Hurry.'

Vannelli saw Vittorio Nardi for the first time when he took Conte's place at the door. He immediately remembered Ubrino's words: We've each got something to contribute to the mission. Nardi was the same build and height as Vannelli and, in the brown uniform, could pass for him at a distance. Vannelli knew then he was going to die. He was still reaching for the alarm when Ubrino shot him in the back. The force of the bullet knocked him against the wall and he fell heavily to the floor. Ubrino knelt beside him and checked for a pulse. There wasn't one.

Conte pushed past Nardi into the hut, his eyes wide with horror. 'You said there wouldn't be any killing. You said we'd only have to knock the guards out.'

'You better start growing up, kid—'

6

'Shut up, Nardi!' Ubrino cut in sharply, then led Conte from the hut. 'It's your first mission, isn't it?'

Conte nodded.

'You'll learn that it's one thing to plan a mission on paper but quite another to put it into practice. Things happen that we can't foresee in the planning stage. Vannelli went for the button. If I hadn't shot him he'd have raised the alarm and we'd have had to abort the mission. You can see that, can't you?'

Conte nodded again. 'It's just that . . .' He swallowed hard.

'You've never seen a dead body before? Neither had I until I joined the Red Brigades.' Ubrino patted Conte on the back. 'Come on, they're waiting for us in the car.'

Nardi sat behind the wheel, his peaked cap tilted forward to obscure his face. Carla sat beside him, the Sterling on the floor at her feet. Ubrino and Conte climbed into the back of the Regata and ducked out of sight, just as they all had done when Carla had driven up to the gate. Nardi started the car and drove up the winding approach road leading to the plant's main reception area. There wasn't a guard in sight. It was what they had expected. Sunday nights were always reserved for poker and at that moment two-thirds of the security staff were in one of the warehouses huddled around a makeshift table, consisting of two wooden crates pushed together, playing out their first hand of the night. The games invariably went on until the small hours of the morning. They had made an arrangement that Vannelli and Boschetto would call them if any of the senior management arrived unexpectedly at the plant, as had happened a couple of times in the last month. It cost each player twenty thousand lire for every session (the money being divided equally between Vannelli and Boschetto) but they regarded it as a small price to ensure they weren't caught.

Nardi parked in front of the building and got out of the car. Boschetto opened the glass doors with a transmitter then hurried down the steps to where Nardi was standing with his back to him. Nardi, who had been monitoring Boschetto's approach in the reflection of the driver's window, swung round to face him, Ruger in hand. Boschetto opened his mouth to speak but Nardi motioned him to remain silent. Boschetto's eyes flickered towards the gun but he did as he was told. Carla alerted the others and they scrambled out of the car. Ubrino unclipped the transmitter from Boschetto's belt then hit him on the back of the head with the butt of his Ruger. Nardi caught Boschetto as he slumped forward unconscious. He laid him on the ground then got back into the car and returned to the main gate. Ubrino got Conte to help him carry Boschetto behind a hedge to one side of the steps.

'Let Carla into the foyer,' Ubrino said, handing the transmitter to Conte.

'What about you?'

'I'll be with you in a minute. I thought I heard a noise. I'm going to check it out.'

Conte looked down at Boschetto. 'You don't think he'll wake up—'

'He won't wake up!' Ubrino hissed sharply. 'We'll be long gone by the time he comes round. Now go on, Carla's waiting.'

Ubrino waited until Carla and Conte had entered the foyer before he pressed the Sterling against the back of Boschetto's head and squeezed the trigger. Blood splattered over his shoes. He cursed under his breath, wiped his shoes on Boschetto's jacket, then hurried up the steps into the foyer.

'Did you see anybody?' Conte asked, activating the door behind Ubrino.

'No, just my imagination. You're not the only one suffering from nerves.' Ubrino led Conte behind the reception desk and indicated the row of closed-circuit television screens. 'The first sign of any guards, you call me.'

'I will,' Conte replied quickly.

Ubrino attached an earpiece to the two-way radio on his belt then crossed to where Carla was waiting for him at the top of the stairs, his rubber-soled shoes silent on the black-and-white tiled floor. They descended the stairs and he paused to get his bearings, picturing the architect's blueprint in his mind. He pointed to another flight of stairs at the end of the corridor. It led down to the laboratories. He allowed himself a faint smile of satisfaction when he saw the sign on the wall at the foot of the stairs: ◄── LABORATORIES 1 – 17 LABORATORIES 18 – 40 ──►.

They wanted 27. It turned out to be a white door with the words PROFESSOR DAVID WISEMAN printed across it in black. He paused at the door to wipe the sweat from his forehead. Carla instinctively touched his arm. She had been his lover for the past year. He knew she was in love with him. She had told him enough times but he had reciprocated the sentiments merely because he knew that was what she wanted to hear. She was young and attractive, like many before her, but he would have no qualms about ditching her.

He opened the door without knocking. He had expected to find himself in a laboratory with rows of work-benches and charts plastered across the walls; instead this was an office, neatly furnished with a collection of framed diplomas on the wall. He reminded himself that David Wiseman was the plant's senior scientific adviser: an administrator, not a research chemist. And administrators work in offices.

Wiseman sat behind the desk. He was a 49-year-old American with wiry black hair and a neatly trimmed black beard. His eyes widened in horror when Carla appeared in the room behind Ubrino.

'It's just make-up,' Ubrino assured him.

'Why?' Wiseman asked in Italian.

'That doesn't concern you,' Ubrino retorted, then crossed to the desk. 'Have you got the vial?'

Wiseman took a sealed metal cylinder, the size of a cigar case, from one of the drawers and held it up for Ubrino to see. The vial was inside the cylinder. 'A hundred thousand dollars isn't enough. Not after all the risks I've had to take to produce this for you in secret.'

Carla stepped forward and aimed the Sterling at Wiseman's chest.

Ubrino pushed the barrel away from Wiseman. 'Let him speak. As he said, he was the one who took all the risks.'

'I'll have an antidote ready for this by the end of the week. But it will cost you another hundred thousand, to be paid into my Swiss bank account.'

Ubrino nodded thoughtfully, then took the metal cylinder from Wiseman and checked the serial number. SR4785. It was the same as the number he had been given at the final briefing earlier that day.

'Don't forget. A hundred thousand dollars or no antidote.' Wiseman got to his feet. 'My laboratory's next door. It would be better if you coshed me there. That way it would look as if I'd disturbed you.'

'There's been a change of plan,' Ubrino said with an apologetic smile.

'What?' Wiseman demanded. 'Why wasn't I told about it?'

'I doubt whether you'd have gone along with it. We don't need the antidote.'

'That's madness,' Wiseman retorted. 'If the vial was opened without an antidote the consequences would be catastrophic.'

'And that's what makes it all the more valuable.' Ubrino pocketed the metal cylinder, then glanced at Carla. 'Kill him.'

Wiseman grabbed the ashtray from his desk and threw it at her, catching her painfully on the shoulder. He smashed the safety glass on the wall behind him and hit the alarm bell with the palm of his hand. A high-pierced shrill echoed through the complex. Ubrino shot him twice in the back then grabbed Carla's hand and hurried to the door.

'Call Nardi,' he told her, easing the door open and peering out into the corridor. It was deserted. 'Tell him to wait for us at the steps.'

She unhooked the two-way radio from her belt and called Nardi, who told her he was already on his way. She clipped it back on to her belt and they were about to run for the stairs when they saw the approaching guard.

'Put down your gun,' Ubrino said to Carla.

'What?' she replied in amazement.

'Trust me, *cara*,' he said, then took the Sterling from her and leant it against the wall. 'I've got one of them,' he shouted, emerging into the corridor behind her, using her body to shield the Sterling in his hand.

The guard, seeing the uniform, hurried towards them. Ubrino stepped out from behind Carla and shot the guard in the chest. Carla grabbed her Sterling and covered Ubrino while he sprinted to the stairs. A guard appeared at the top of the stairs and Ubrino swung the Sterling upwards, killing him with a single shot. As he turned back to cover Carla a bullet hit the wall inches from his face. He jerked his head away, his back pressed against the staircase wall. Carla, who was already running for the stairs, turned to face the kneeling guard at the end of the corridor. He shot her twice. The Sterling spun from her hands and she landed heavily at the foot of the stairs, her sweat shirt soaked in blood. Ubrino stared momentarily at her sightless eyes, then darted up the stairs to the next level. It was deserted. He ran to the stairs leading up to the foyer and mounted them cautiously, his back against the wall, the Sterling swinging from side to side. He reached the top of the stairs and dived low on to the foyer floor, the Sterling at the ready. The foyer, too, seemed deserted. But he couldn't see the reception desk from where he lay. He scrambled to his feet and tiptoed past the lift, frequently glancing over his shoulder, then pressed himself against the wall, the Sterling held inches from his sweating face. He flicked the switch from single to rapid fire, then pivoted round to face the reception desk, his finger curled around the trigger.

Paolo Conte stood nervously behind the desk, his eyes wide and fearful. Ubrino knew it was a trap. It made sense. Why hadn't Conte called him on the radio when the alarm went off? Because the guards had got to him first. One or more guards would be crouched behind the desk, willing Conte to lure him into the open. An old trick. But still effective. He had been right all along. Conte would never make a good *Brigatista*. He didn't have the guts. Believing in the cause wasn't enough. He had only been drafted into the team because he could impersonate Vannelli on the telephone. Now he was expendable.

Ubrino strafed the desk with gunfire. Conte was hit several times before he slumped to the floor. Ubrino discarded the empty magazine then pulled a fresh one from his pocket and snapped it into place. He snatched the transmitter off the desk but as he turned towards the door a bullet cracked inches from his ear. He dived to the floor and rolled to safety behind the thick concrete pillar in the middle of the foyer. The bullet had come from the direction of the stairs. A second bullet hit the pillar. He was pinned down. Where the hell was Nardi? Had he been caught? Then Ubrino heard the sound of a car engine above the alarm. He glanced over his shoulder and saw the Regata pull up in front of the steps. He unclipped a smoke grenade from his belt, primed it, and rolled it towards the stairs. He activated the doors, then, using the dense black smoke as a cover, he sprinted down the steps and flung himself through the open passenger door. Nardi threw the main gate transmitter to Ubrino, then accelerated away from the guards, who had stumbled out on to the steps, coughing and spluttering from the effects of the smoke grenade. Ubrino activated the gate when it came into view. The car shot through the narrow aperture and Ubrino immediately closed the gate behind him. He tossed the transmitter on to the dashboard, then sat back and closed his eyes.

'Did you get the vial?' Nardi asked once they were clear of the gates.

Ubrino patted his pocket in answer.

'What happened to Carla and Paolo?'

'Dead.'

'I'm sorry. I know you and Carla were . . .' Nardi trailed off with a shrug.

'She knew the risks,' Ubrino said bluntly.

Nardi swung the car into a side road and pulled up behind the white Fiat Uno Ubrino had parked there earlier that evening. They climbed out of the car and Ubrino came up behind the unsuspecting Nardi and shot him through the back of the head. His orders had been to eliminate the others once he had the vial safely in his possession. He tossed the Sterling into the undergrowth, then crossed to the Fiat Uno and took a holdall from the back seat. It contained a pair of jeans and a grey sweatshirt. He changed into them, then stuffed the brown uniform into the holdall and left it beside Nardi's body.

He drove the Fiat Uno the short distance to join the A24 motorway and headed back towards Rome.

# TWO

*Monday*

Lino Zocchi slipped on a pair of sunglasses then stepped out
into the exercise yard, a burly man on either side of him.
It was a bright cool day, far pleasanter than it would be
once Rome was enveloped by the sweltering heat of summer.
Zocchi looked up at the watchtower, manned by an armed
warder, then dug his hands into his pockets and crossed to
the concrete stand on the other side of the exercise yard.
The two men kept in close attendance.

Zocchi was a short, stocky 43-year-old with a leathery
face and black hair cropped close to his skull. He had grown
up in the slums of Rome, committed to the political ideo-
logies of Engels and Marx, and had been recruited by the
Red Brigades when he was in his early twenties. He had
gone on to spearhead a successful recruitment drive in the
south of the country, mainly on the university campuses,
and was rewarded with a post as one of Rome's senior cell
commanders. Three years later he was promoted to brigade
chief of Rome, a position he still held despite having just
started a ten-year sentence for his part in the attempted
assassination of a leading Italian judge. He still had one
ambition left to fulfil – to become leader of the Red Brigades,
even if it meant running the organization from his prison
cell. He knew he could do it.

He climbed to the top of the stand and sat in the place he always took when the weather was good. His two body-guards, both *Brigatisti* serving life sentences, looked around slowly, then seated themselves on either side of him. He took a cigarette from his pocket and pushed it between his lips. One of the bodyguards lit it for him. He heard the sound of the approaching helicopter and looked up when it came into view. The word POLIZIA, in black letters, was clearly visible against the side of the white fuselage. The prisoners gesticulated angrily at it, their voices carrying as they shouted abuse at the pilot. It hovered over the exercise yard. The cabin door opened fractionally. A moment later a single shot echoed out. The prisoners were still scrambling for safety when it gained height again. The cabin door was flung open and the watchtower raked with gunfire, forcing the warder to dive for cover. By the time he got to his feet the helicopter was already out of firing range. He raised the alarm, then used his binoculars to scan the exercise yard for any casualties. He trained them on a section of the stand where the prisoners were congregating in an ever-widening circle.

Zocchi lay on the top step, the cigarette still smouldering inches away from his outstretched hand. The top of his head had been shot away.

Malcolm Philpott used the miniature transmitter on his desk to close the door after the Secretary-General had left the office, then opened his tobacco pouch and tamped a wad into the mouth of his briar pipe. He lit it carefully then sat back in his chair and stared thoughtfully at the ceiling.

He was a 56-year-old Scot with a gaunt face and red hair who had spent seven years as the head of Scotland Yard's Special Branch before taking up his present post as UNACO Director in 1980. The man with the doleful features and thinning black hair sitting opposite him had been his deputy for the past three years. Sergei Kolchinsky, who was four years younger than Philpott, had been a KGB operative for twenty-five years, sixteen of those as a military attache in the West, before he joined UNACO, replacing a fellow Russian who had been sent back home for spying.

UNACO employed 209 personnel, thirty of those being field operatives who had been siphoned off from law enforcement agencies around the world. They worked in teams of three, each team being denoted by the prefix 'Strike Force', and their intensive training included all forms of unarmed combat and the use of all known firearms (although operatives could choose their own weapons for any assignment). The training took place regularly at UNACO's Test Centre off the Interborough Highway in Queens. The entire complex was housed underground to ensure maximum security.

Philpott reached for his cane and crossed to the window. He limped heavily on his left leg; the result of an injury he had sustained in the last days of the Korean War. His office, situated on the twenty-second floor of the United Nations Secretariat, looked out across the East River.

'In view of the report we received this morning we're going to have to bring in Strike Force Three for this assignment,' Philpott said.

'I agree.' Kolchinsky stubbed out his cigarette and immediately took another one from the packet on the desk and lit it. 'But then I'd have used them anyway.'

'Do I detect a hint of favouritism there, Sergei?' Philpott asked as he returned to his chair and sat down.

'Call it respect. Their track record proves they are the best team we've got.'

Philpott entered a code into his computer, read the information from the screen, then banged his fist angrily on the desk. 'They went on leave last week. As if we didn't have enough problems.' He flicked a switch on his desk. 'Sarah?'

'Yes sir?' came the immediate reply.

'Get hold of Mike, Sabrina and C.W. Top priority.'

'I'll get on to it right away.'

'And Sarah, they're on a Code Red standby. Cancel their leave, effective immediately until further notice.'

Sabrina Carver was UNACO's only female field operative. It had initially caused some resentment amongst some of her more chauvinistic male colleagues when she had been recruited from the FBI, but she had quickly proved that she was more than capable of looking after herself and now, two years on, Mike Graham and C. W. Whitlock were the envy of those same colleagues who had made the mistake of doubting her abilities.

Although she lived in New York she still tried to get down to Miami at least twice a year to visit her parents at their Spanish-style mansion in the affluent Coral Gables suburb overlooking Biscayne Bay. When her leave came through it was already the middle of March and she hadn't seen her mother and father since their annual Christmas pilgrimage to New York. She had decided to spend the first ten days of her leave in Miami before flying out to Switzerland to join some of her friends for a week of skiing. The Miami weather was in the high eighties and she had spent most of her time either lazing by the swimming pool listening to jazz on her portable compact disc player, or else out on Biscayne Bay in her father's 42-foot Maxum speed-boat, the *Port of Call*.

She parked her father's BMW 730i opposite the Marina Park Hotel, close to the entrance of the Miamarina, and smiled to herself as she remembered how she had managed to persuade him to call the speedboat the *Port of Call* after one of her favourite songs by her jazz idol, saxophonist David Sanborn. Heads turned to look at her when she got out of the car. She was a strikingly beautiful 28-year-old with a near perfect figure which she kept in shape by

17

attending aerobics classes three times a week when she wasn't on assignment. Her shoulder-length blonde hair, which she had tinted with auburn highlights, was tucked underneath a New York Yankees baseball cap. Mike Graham, a lifelong Yankees fan, had given it to her after she had turned up at the Test Centre wearing an LA Dodgers cap. She had never worn the Dodgers cap since. She was wearing an emerald bikini underneath a baggy white T-shirt and knew she was attracting the attention of the men she passed on her way to where the *Port of Call* was berthed at the end of the pier. She had come to ignore the salacious looks and wolf-whistles, for she believed to acknowledge them would only be a sign of vanity. And she despised vanity in any form.

She stopped beside the *Dream Merchant*, a 107-foot yacht which belonged to John Bernstein, one of Miami's leading financiers and a close family friend for more years than she could remember. Her father had told her the day before that Bernstein was attending an international monetary conference in Washington and wasn't due back until the following week. So what were the two men in black wetsuits doing in the saloon? She was sure there was a perfectly simple explanation but decided to check it out anyway. The gangway had been pulled in so she jumped on to the deck, landing nimbly on her toes. One of the men saw her and swung round, a Walther P5 in his hand. She flung herself to the deck as he fired. The bullet smashed through the glass door and hit the pier. His colleague shouted at him and they disappeared through a side door. Seconds later she heard the sound of engines and got to her feet in time to see the two men fleeing the yacht on red and white jetskis. She clambered back on to' the pier, shouted at a startled couple on a nearby yacht to call the police, then ran to where the metallic-gold *Port of Call* was moored. She untied it, started the engine, then turned it sharply in the water and headed after the jetskis. The two men saw her and split up, one heading for the busy harbour complex, the other continuing towards Lummus Island. She spun the wheel violently and went after the one making for the harbour. She knew she would lose him if he reached the harbour first. There were too many hiding places for a craft of that size. She accelerated sharply and the speedboat skimmed across the water but although she was closing on the jetski she knew she couldn't catch it. He glanced over his shoulder and made the mistake of thinking she would cut him off before he reached the safety of the docks. He panicked and reached for the Walther in his wetsuit pocket. He lost control of the jetski. It somersaulted, catapulting him into the water. She throttled back the engine and pulled up alongside the man who offered no resistance as she helped him into the speedboat. He slumped dejectedly on to one of the padded seats, his hands over his face. Blood ran down the side of his head from a gash above his eye.

Then she noticed the approaching patrol boat. It drew alongside the speedboat and a painter rope was thrown to her.

'There's another—'

'Just tie the rope to your boat,' a ginger-haired man commanded. He was in his early fifties and wore the insignia of a lieutenant.

She switched off the engine then scrambled on to the bow and threaded the rope through the ring, securing it firmly with an overhand knot. The man was hauled over the patrol boat's low railing and sent below to have his wound treated. Sabrina ignored the extended hands and climbed aboard the patrol boat by herself. She asked about the other jetskier.

'A patrol boat has already intercepted him near Lummus Island.' The lieutenant stared at her, then shook his head slowly to himself. 'You've been watching too much *Miami Vice*, sweetheart.'

'I'm not your *sweetheart*,' she snapped back.

'A New Yorker; I should have guessed,' he muttered and reached for her baseball cap.

'You touch that and you'll be in the water quicker than you can draw breath,' she said icily.

'I'd watch my tongue if I were you,' he shot back, pointing a finger of warning at her. 'What the hell were you doing? You could have got somebody killed at the Miamarina.'

'I didn't know they were armed,' she replied defensively. 'The yacht belongs to a friend of mine who happens to be out of town at the moment. What was I supposed to do? Ignore the fact that two men were acting suspiciously on board?'

'You were supposed to call the police and let them handle it.'

'I'll bear it in mind next time, *if* I can find a policeman to call.'

'I've got a good mind to book you.'

'For what?' she replied in amazement. 'Making a citizen's arrest? You guys must really be having trouble reaching your quota of collars for the month.'

Her bleeper sounded. She unclipped it from the bottom half of her bikini and switched it off. 'I need to call New York urgently.'

'Don't tell me, your boyfriend's missing you,' the lieutenant said sarcastically.

There was a ripple of laughter from the men around them.

She bit back her anger. 'If it'll put your mind at rest, have one of your men radio through to police headquarters and check on the speedboat. The *Port of Call*. You'll find it's registered to George Carver, the former Democratic Congressman and Ambassador to Canada and the United Kingdom. He's my father.'

The lieutenant gestured to the door behind her. 'Make

your call, but you're going to have a lot of explaining to do before we're through here.'

She let him lead the way to his cabin.

'I'll be waiting outside the door,' he told her gruffly.

She closed the door behind her and crossed to the telephone on the desk. She dialled an unlisted number.

'Llewelyn and Lee, good morning,' a female voice answered politely after the first ring.

'Sabrina Carver, ID1730630,' she said, quoting the number on her personnel dossier in Philpott's office.

'Hello, Sabrina, the Colonel wants to speak to you urgently. I'll put you through.'

'Thanks, Sarah.'

There was a click on the other end of the line.

'Sabrina?'

'Yes, sir,' she replied, immediately recognizing Philpott's crisp Celtic accent.

'You're on an immediate Code Red standby. There's a ticket waiting for you at the Continental check-in counter. Your flight leaves in three hours. Briefing is scheduled for three-thirty this afternoon.'

She swore inwardly. 'There's a slight problem, sir,' she said, and went on to tell him what had happened.

'I'll call Miami's Chief of Police and have him clear things with this lieutenant. You say his name's Grady?'

'That's what it says here,' she replied, touching the nameplates on the desk.

'Fine. See you later.'

The line went dead. She replaced the receiver and found Grady waiting in the corridor.

'The Chief of Police?' he said in amazement, when she had told him to expect the call. 'Who *are* you?'

'Just another New Yorker,' she replied, touching her cap. 'See you on deck.'

When he reemerged fifteen minutes later she was busy talking to a couple of the men about the intruder, who had already confessed to attempted theft. They saw it as an open and shut case.

'You're free to go,' Grady told her, barely able to keep the contempt from his voice. 'You'll still need to testify in court.'

'You know where to get hold of me, Lieutenant.'

Sabrina climbed back into the speedboat, untied the rope, then turned the boat around and headed back towards the Miamarina.

'What I'd give for one date with her,' one of the men muttered wistfully.

'I know what your wife would give you,' a voice piped up behind him.

The others laughed.

'Okay, the fun's over,' Grady snapped. 'Let's get that damn jetski out of the water before it drifts any further out to sea.'

Mike Graham's first thought on hearing the gunshots had been for the safety of the small herd of white-tailed deer that lived in the forest near his log cabin on the banks of Lake Champlain in southern Vermont. He had spent his vacations watching them since moving from New York two years earlier and the idea of them being harmed both angered and horrified him. Arming himself with an M21 rifle and a powerful pair of Zeiss binoculars, he had set off in the direction from which the gunshots had originated. Not that he had needed to draw on any of his tracking experience to find the culprits. A ten-year-old could have followed the trail of empty beer cans. The two men were sitting against the side of a white jeep in a clearing by the lake, each with a beer in his hand. They were cooking a rabbit over a crudely constructed fire, occasionally turning it on a makeshift spit. He could smell the meat from where he lay. He could also smell the joint they were sharing.

Graham was a youthfully handsome 37-year-old with tousled collar-length auburn hair and penetrating pale blue eyes who kept himself in shape with a daily pre-dawn run followed by a gruelling workout in the converted mini-gym behind the cabin. His obsession with fitness dated back to his childhood in the Bronx when his only ambition was to wear the famous blue and white uniform of the New York Giants. His ambition was realized when he was signed up as a rookie quarterback after he grad-uated from UCLA with a degree in Political Science. A month later he was drafted into Vietnam where a shoulder injury cut short his promising football career. He joined the CIA to help train Meo tribesmen in Thailand and on his return to the United States he was accepted by the élite anti-terrorist squad, Delta. He was promoted to leader of Squadron-B eleven years later and his first mission was to take a five-man team into Libya to destroy a known terrorist base on the outskirts of Benghazi. He was about to give the order to close in on the base when news reached him that his wife, Carrie, and son, Mike Jnr, had been abducted outside their New York apartment by Arab-speaking gunmen. He refused to abort the mission and the base was destroyed. The FBI launched an inten-sive nationwide search but Carrie and Mike Jnr were never found. He was retired from Delta at his own request three months later but was initially turned down for UNACO by the Secretary-General on the basis of his psychiatric report. Philpott personally overruled the Secretary-General's decision and Graham was accepted as a UNACO field operative, subject to periodic reevaluation tests every year.

The older of the two men, who was wearing a peaked cap over his grey hair, tossed the joint into the fire then got to his feet and helped himself to another beer from the cooler on the passenger seat. He was about to sit down again when a movement caught his eye in the scrub behind the jeep. He tapped his blond-haired companion on the shoulder, gestured for him to be quiet, and pointed towards the scrub. The blond-haired man took a .300 Parker Hale from the back of the jeep, raised it to his shoulder and fired. He shouted in triumph and slapped his friend on the back.

'You only hit it in the leg, Ray,' the grey-haired man chided, then took another mouthful of beer. 'Hell, that deer's big enough to keep us in jerky for the next year.'

'Sure is,' Ray replied with a grin. 'Hey, look at it tryin' to get up. It's not goin' to get far on three legs.'

His companion laughed. 'Shoot it in another leg. I bet you ten dollars you can't.'

'You're on, Sam,' Ray replied and raised the rifle to his shoulder again.

Graham, who had crept up silently behind them, struck Ray in the small of the back with the butt of the M21, slamming him against the side of the jeep. The Parker Hale fell to the ground. Sam made a move towards it.

'If you pick it up, you'd better be prepared to use it,' Graham threatened.

Sam swallowed nervously and stepped away from the Parker Hale. Graham picked it up and threw it into the water.

'Who are you?' Ray demanded, his face still twisted in pain. 'There ain't no law 'gainst us huntin' round here.'

Graham ignored him, then reached inside the jeep and released the handbrake. It rolled towards the lake. Graham hurried over to where the deer lay, its eyes wide and fearful as it struggled to stand up. He tried to comfort it by stroking its head. There was nothing he could do to save it. The leg was shattered. He shot it through the back of the head. Its body jerked, then lay still.

'I hope you're proud of yourself, boy,' Graham snapped at Ray, who had managed to stop the jeep inches away from the water.

'We was only havin' some fun,' came the sullen reply.

'Is that what you call it? Well now, it's my turn to have some fun. Take off your boots, both of you.'

'Go to hell,' Sam snarled. 'You've got no right to threaten us like this. Ray's right, we haven't broken any hunting laws.'

Graham looked out across the lake. 'One of the reasons I came to live out here was because of its seclusion. Hardly anybody comes around these parts. I could kill you both, dump your bodies in the jeep, and drive it into the lake. Your bodies would never be found. And if you don't think I'd do it, call my bluff.'

Ray shook his head nervously. 'We ain't doubtin' you'd do it, mister. If it's money you want—'

'Take off your boots!'

The two men exchanged glances, then untied their boots and kicked them off. Graham threw them as far as he could into the lake, then shot out the jeep's back tyres.

'What the hell are you doing?' Sam shouted, his eyes fixed on the deflated tyres. 'We're only carrying one spare.'

'The nearest town's Burlington. It's about five miles from here. Ask for Charlie, he'll sell you a tyre, if you pay him enough.'

'How we supposed to get there?' Ray wailed, staring at his stockinged feet.

'If you run you should make it by mid-afternoon.' Graham pointed east. 'It's in that direction.'

'We'll cut our feet to pieces,' Sam said, looking around in desperation. 'There's nothing but forest for miles.'

'Yeah, deer country.'

Graham shouldered his M21 and disappeared back into the undergrowth, deaf to the shouted pleas of the men behind him. It took him twenty minutes to get back to his cabin and as he neared the door he could hear his bleeper in the bedroom. He hurried inside and switched it off. The telephone beside the bed started to ring. He sat on the edge of the bed and picked up the receiver.

'Mike?'

'Speaking.'

'It's Sarah, from Llewelyn and Lee.'

'1913204,' Graham quoted his UNACO ID number.

'Finally,' she said, the relief evident in her voice. 'I've been trying to get hold of you for the past two hours. Isn't your bleeper working?'

'I guess not,' Graham replied, turning it around in his hand.

'Bring it in, I'll order a replacement from the Test Centre. Colonel Philpott wants to speak to you urgently. Oh, Mr Kolchinsky's just come in. He wants to speak to you.'

'Michael, what's going on down there?' Kolchinsky barked down the line. 'Why haven't you been answering your bleeper?'

'It must be acting up,' Graham replied dismissively. 'What's the big panic?'

'You're on a Code Red standby. Nash has been waiting for you at the Burlington airstrip for the last hour. Pack some summer clothes, the Mediterranean can be very warm at this time of year.'

'You've whetted my interest already.'

'And don't forget to bring your bleeper with you. We can't have you running around with a faulty one, can we?'

Kolchinsky's sarcasm wasn't lost on him. He smiled to himself, then replaced the receiver and crossed to the cupboard to find his suitcase.

Sabrina found a space for her champagne-coloured Mercedes-Benz 500 SEC in the parking bay next to the United Nations Headquarters, then crossed to the Secretariat Building where she produced a pass to gain her entry into the main foyer. The pass identified her as an interpreter based at the General Assembly, the perfect cover considering her degree in Romance languages and her subsequent postgraduate work at the Sorbonne.

26

She took the lift to the twenty-second floor, then walked to an unmarked door at the end of the corridor and punched a code into the numerical bellpush on the adjacent wall. The door opened on to a small, neatly furnished office. Three of the walls were covered with cream-coloured wallpaper. The fourth wall was constructed of rows of teak slats, incorporated into which were two seamless sliding doors which could only be opened by miniature sonic transmitters. The door on the right led into the soundproofed UNACO Command Centre where teams of analysts, using the latest in high-tech equipment, worked around the clock to keep abreast of the ever-changing developments in world affairs. The door on the left led into Philpott's office and could only be opened by him.

Sarah Thomas looked up from her typewriter and smiled at Sabrina. She was an attractive 31-year-old with short blonde hair who had turned down the possibility of a lucrative career in Hollywood after winning a beauty pageant and gone instead to secretarial college in Chicago. She had been with UNACO for four years and was married to the Test Centre's senior martial arts instructor.

'How was the vacation?' she asked after Sabrina closed the door.

'Short,' Sabrina replied with a grin, then sat down on the couch. 'Am I the first one here?'

Sarah nodded. 'Mr Kolchinsky's gone to fetch Mike at the airport.'

'And C.W.?'

'He's in Paris. Jacques Rust is flying up from Zurich to brief him.'

Sabrina indicated the desk panel. 'Well, you'd better tell His Lordship I'm here.'

Sarah smiled then flicked on the intercom switch. 'Sabrina's here, sir.'

'Send her in,' Philpott replied, and the door slid open.

'Afternoon, sir,' Sabrina said as she entered the office.

'Sit down,' Philpott replied abruptly, activating the transmitter on his desk to close the door behind her.

She sat on the nearest of the two black leather couches.

'I received a call earlier this afternoon from Miami's Chief of Police,' Philpott said, reaching for his pipe. 'It seems you not only went out of your way to embarrass this Lieutenant Grady in front of his own men, you also threatened him with physical violence.'

'The guy was a creep—'

'He's a police officer!' Philpott thundered. 'You were supposed to be on leave. And that meant you didn't have official clearance with any of the local law enforcement agencies. I had to pull a lot of strings to get you out of testifying at the trial. What if the papers had got hold of the story? My God, they would have had a field day. You drew unnecessary attention to this organization and that's something I will not tolerate. Pull another stunt like that and you'll find yourself suspended. Do I make myself understood?'

'Yes, sir,' she muttered through clenched teeth.

Philpott lit his pipe and sat back in his chair. 'This negative side has only surfaced since you teamed up with Graham. It's obvious that some of this contempt he holds for the law has rubbed off on to you. It might be your way of getting him to accept you as an equal, I don't know, but it won't do you any good if you're transferred to another team.'

'I resent that, sir. I've never tried to prove anything to Mike. If he can't accept me for what I am, that's his problem. Not mine.'

The intercom buzzed.

Philpott flicked on the switch. 'Yes?'

'Mr Kolchinsky's here with Mike Graham, sir,' Sarah said.

'Send them in.' Philpott switched the intercom off and activated the door with the transmitter on his desk.

Kolchinsky greeted Sabrina with a quick handshake then sat down and lit a cigarette.

'Afternoon, sir,' Graham said to Philpott, then sat on the couch beside Sabrina. 'How you doing?'

'Good,' she replied with a smile. 'And you?'

'Okay, I guess. Where's C.W.?'

'Paris. Jacques is briefing him.'

'Can we begin?' Philpott asked, and waited until he had their attention before continuing. 'Sergei and I had an hour-long meeting with the Secretary-General this morning about this Code Red you've been assigned to cover. That, in itself, should give you an idea of the severity of the situation. How often does the Secretary-General involve himself personally in a case? Sergei will brief you, he's been monitoring the case from the start. Sergei?'

Kolchinsky stubbed out his cigarette and got to his feet. 'Last night four terrorists from the Red Brigades broke into the Neo-Chem Industries plant outside Rome.'

'I take it this is the same Neo-Chem Industries who own that glass and aluminium monstrosity over on West 57th Street?' Graham asked.

'That "glass and aluminium monstrosity", as you call it, is their international headquarters,' Kolchinsky told him. 'They have fourteen plants outside the United States and are widely regarded as one of the foremost pharmaceutical manufacturers in the world.'

'Pity about their taste in architecture.'

'Let's stick to the briefing, shall we?' Philpott said, eyeing Graham sharply. 'Go on, Sergei.'

'One of those killed during the break-in was the plant's senior scientific adviser, Professor David Wiseman. He'd worked for UNACO in the past as a consultant, which was why we were able to gain access to his personal files within hours of his death. A team of scientists from our Zurich HQ took a complete inventory of his stock but found only one item missing. A vial encased in a metal cylinder identical to this one I got from the Test Centre.'

Sabrina took the metal cylinder from Kolchinsky and turned it around in her fingers. 'And nothing else was taken from any of the other laboratories?'

'All the other laboratories were still locked when our people got there. No, the terrorists knew exactly what they wanted and where to find it.'

'What was in the vial?' Graham asked, taking the metal cylinder from Sabrina.

'I'm coming to that.' Kolchinsky lit another cigarette and dropped the match into the ashtray on Philpott's desk. 'According to the files Wiseman kept in his personal safe he had been working on two projects that hadn't been sanctioned by the company. One was to procure a quantity of sleeping gas for the Rome cell of the Red Brigades.'

'And was the Rome cell behind the break-in?' Sabrina asked.

'Yes,' Kolchinsky replied. 'The second project involved viruses. Six months ago he set out to develop a highly contagious recombinant DNA virus which could potentially kill millions of people if it were ever released into the atmosphere. He completed his work on it a fortnight ago.'

Sabrina sat forward, her arms resting on her knees. 'And the Red Brigades took the wrong vial?'

Kolchinsky nodded grimly. 'Both were stored in metal cylinders. The only way of telling them apart was by their different serial numbers. The vial containing the sleeping gas was found in Wiseman's office.'

'What about the antidote?' Sabrina asked.

'He was still working on it at the time of his death,' Philpott replied.

'But surely if all his work's been documented then our

boffins can come up with an antidote themselves?' Graham said, handing the metal cylinder back to Kolchinsky.

'I don't know how much you know about recombination, Michael, but basically it needs the genes of two virus strains to conjugate for it to be successful. An antidote can only be developed if both strains of the virus are known. In this case both strains were artificially created in his laboratory. He referred to them throughout his files simply as "alpha" and "beta". He was the only person who knew what they were.'

'And now he's dead,' Sabrina muttered, rubbing her hands over her face.

'What if the sleeping gas was just a red herring and the virus was destined for the Red Brigades all along?' Graham said.

'That was my theory, until this arrived on my desk.' Philpott removed a telex from the folder in front of him. 'It's a transcript of a taped message the Italian government received earlier this morning. The voice has been identified as Riccardo Ubrino, one of Rome's senior *Brigatisti*. He's threatened to open the vial at ten o'clock on Thursday morning unless he sees a live telecast of Rome's jailed brigade chief, Lino Zocchi, being put on an aeroplane bound for Cuba. What is significant, though, is that he refers to the contents of the vial as "sleeping gas". Why continue the pretence knowing that the authorities will have already discovered the truth, unless he genuinely believes he has the sleeping gas?'

'I don't get it, sir,' Sabrina said, frowning. 'Have we been called in because the Italian government won't comply with his demands?'

'We've been called in because the Italian government *can't* comply with his demands. Zocchi's dead. He was shot by an unknown gunman an hour after the government received the tape. The authorities have instigated an immediate news blackout on Zocchi's death. The prison itself has been isolated. The authorities have come up with a story that there's a bout of acute conjunctivitis amongst the prisoners so that news of Zocchi's death can't be leaked out to visitors. But it can't remain isolated indefinitely. The vial has to be found. Quickly.'

'Can't the authorities get around the table with senior *Brigatisti* and explain the situation to them?' Sabrina asked.

'They already have,' Kolchinsky replied, resuming his seat. 'Word is that Zocchi masterminded the break-in from his prison cell. It was done without the knowledge of the committee, so none of them know where Ubrino's gone to ground. They have no way of contacting him. And even if they could, who's to say Zocchi didn't give him instructions to open the vial in the event of his death?'

'To make matters worse, the gunman who shot Zocchi was in a police helicopter, or what looked remarkably like one,' Philpott added. 'Put yourself in Ubrino's shoes. An hour after the government receives his demands, Zocchi is killed by a gunman in a police helicopter. Coincidence?'

'It's obviously a set-up, sir,' Sabrina said.

'Try explaining that to the Red Brigades,' Philpott replied.

'But why us, sir?' Graham asked. 'Why haul us back from leave when you could have brought in one of the other Strike Force teams?'

Philpott removed a second telex from the folder. 'This also arrived this morning. It concerns Wiseman's brother. You might remember him. Richard Wiseman. I believe he was one of the more colourful officers in Vietnam.'

'Yeah, I remember him. Lieutenant-Colonel Richard Wiseman, Marine Corps. A damn good soldier.'

'He's now General Wiseman of the First Ranger Battalion. And he's out for revenge. I'm not going to go into detail, it's all in the résumé for you to read on the plane. Basically, he's hiring a gunman and a driver to do the dirty work for him. We can't afford to have them encroaching on the case. There's too much at stake. It seems he's chosen a Jamaican from London as the getaway driver. We're going to put our man in his place. And there's only one field operative who fits the bill.'

'C.W.,' Sabrina said.

'Right,' Philpott replied, handing out two manila envelopes to Graham and Sabrina.

The envelopes contained the résumé, which had to be destroyed after reading; airline tickets; maps of their ultimate destination; written confirmation of hotel accommodation; a brief character sketch of their contact/s (if any) and a sum of money in lire. All field operatives also carried two credit cards for emergencies. There was no limit to the amount of money an operative could use during an assignment but it all had to be accounted for to Kolchinsky, with chits to back up the figurework, when they returned to New York.

'Your flight leaves in two hours. Sergei will be going with you to set up a base in Rome. I'll be joining you as soon as I can. Jacques will run things from Zurich in my absence.' Philpott activated the transmitter on his desk to open the door. 'Mike? Sabrina?'

They paused at the door to look back at him.

'Good luck. I've got a feeling you're going to need it.'

C. W. Whitlock replaced the receiver and looked round at his wife, Carmen, who was standing motionless on the balcony, her hands gripped tightly around the railing, the light evening breeze teasing her shoulder length black hair. She was a tall, slender Puerto Rican with a youthful beauty which belied her true age. She was forty. As he stared at her he realized just how much he loved her. But that wasn't enough to save their crumbling marriage.

'It's beautiful, isn't it?' he said behind her, looking across the Champs de Mars at the brightly lit Eiffel Tower which soared 984 feet into the clear night sky.

'That was Jacques on the phone, wasn't it?' she asked softly.

'Yes, he's on his way up,' he replied, putting an arm around her shoulders.

'Don't.' She shrugged his arm off and returned to the bedroom.

He leaned his arms on the railing and looked down at the passing traffic on the Avenue de Bourdonnais. He was a 44-year-old Kenyan with sharp, angular features tempered by the neat moustache he had worn since his university days. After graduating with a BA (Hons) from Oxford he had returned to Kenya where he spent a short time with the army before joining the Intelligence Corps, remaining there for ten years and rising to the rank of Colonel. He had been one of Philpott's first recruits in 1980.

There was a knock at the door.

'I'll get it,' Carmen said.

Jacques Rust smiled at her when she opened the door. He activated his mechanized wheelchair and entered the room. He handed her the bouquet of red roses he was carrying. 'Freshly picked from the *Jardin du Luxembourg*,' he said with a smile. 'Well, I hope not. I bought them from a vendor I've known for years.'

She kissed him lightly on the cheek, the anger suddenly gone from her eyes. 'Thank you, Jacques, they're beautiful. I'll put them in some water.'

'Where's C.W.?'

'He's on the balcony,' she replied. 'I'll get him for you.'

Rust put his attaché case on the floor. He was a handsome 43-year-old Frenchman with pale blue eyes and short black hair. He had spent fourteen years with the French *Service de Documentation Extérieure et de Contre-Espionage* before joining UNACO in 1980. He and Whitlock had worked as a team until the Secretary-General had given Philpott permission to increase the field operatives from twenty to thirty. Sabrina, because of her age and relative inexperience, had been put with them to form the original Strike Force Three.

A year later he and Sabrina were on a stakeout at the Marseilles docks when they came under fire from the drug smugglers they had been watching. He was hit in the spine, leaving him paralyzed from the waist down. He was given a senior position at the Command Centre after his release from hospital, and was promoted to head the European operation when his predecessor was killed in a car crash. He was widely tipped to become the next UNACO Director when Philpott retired in four years' time. That had already given rise to speculation that Kolchinsky would replace him in Zurich with Whitlock taking over as deputy director when he was retired from the field, also in four years' time.

'Hello, C.W.,' Rust said when Whitlock entered the room.

'Jacques,' Whitlock replied, his handshake formal rather than friendly.

'I'll leave you two to it,' Carmen said, emerging from the kitchen where she had put the roses in some water.

'Where are you going?' Whitlock asked.

'Does it matter?' she retorted.

'Of course it matters,' Whitlock shot back. 'I don't want you walking the streets by yourself at this time of night.'

'He's right, Carmen,' Rust said to her. 'This part of the city's crawling with pickpockets and bag-snatchers.'

'Don't worry, I don't intend to walk the streets by myself.' She looked at Whitlock. 'You know where I'll be. If, of course, you remember our honeymoon.'

'You know where she's going?' Rust asked once Carmen had left the room.

Whitlock nodded. 'There's a small bistro not far from

here on the rue de Grenelle. We ate there most nights when we were here on our honeymoon. It's ironic, isn't it? We started our marriage in this room, now it looks like we're going to end it here as well.'

'Don't talk like that, C.W.—'

'Like what?' Whitlock cut in sharply, his eyes blazing. 'You know damn well why our marriage is in such a mess. She wants me out of the firing line at UNACO, I want to stay because I know I have a future with the organization. We chose Paris as neutral ground. No fights. No UNACO. Three weeks to try and save our marriage. What happens? Three days after we get here you call to say that I'm on a Code Red standby. All leave's been cancelled. She's got every right to be mad, Jacques. Every right.'

Rust nodded sombrely. 'I know what you're saying, C.W., but we have to use Strike Force Three. More to the point, we have to use you.'

Whitlock sighed deeply and patted Rust on the shoulder. 'I'm sorry, Jacques, I didn't mean to fly off the handle at you like that. I know we wouldn't have been recalled unless the situation was critical. It's just so frustrating not being able to make Carmen understand that.'

'I don't like it any more than you do, C.W. You know how fond I am of Carmen. I hate to see the two of you like this.'

'I know,' Whitlock said softly, then sat on the edge of the bed. 'What's the assignment—?'

Rust told him about the break-in at the plant, the stolen vial, Ubrino's demands and the death of Zocchi. 'Mike and Sabrina will be handling that side of the case. You're going undercover. We received a report today to say that Wiseman's brother is out for revenge. He's already hired a gunman to find his brother's killer.' He took a blue folder from his attaché case, opened it, and handed a photograph to Whitlock. 'That's the wheelman he wants to use. His name's

Reuben Alexander, a Londoner of Jamaican extraction. You're going to take his place.'

'But I don't look anything like him. All we've got in common is that we're black.'

'Alexander's camera-shy. In fact, he takes it to extremes. That's why we think you'll be able to pull it off without any hitches. That's a police photograph you've got there. And it's the only one they've got, apart from his official mugshots.'

'I take it Wiseman's never met him?'

Rust shook his head. 'Wiseman only put the scheme together when he heard of his brother's murder. Alexander's been in custody for the past fortnight. He's due in court tomorrow. That's when they intend to spring him.'

'I don't get it, Jacques. Why not just have Wiseman and this gunman picked up until we've recovered the vial?'

'On what charge? All we have is the word of an informer. Richard Wiseman is a three-star general. He also happens to be one of America's most decorated war heroes. If we pulled him in without any evidence we'd have the Pentagon down on us like a ton of bricks. We have to keep this whole thing as quiet as possible. Imagine the pandemonium if word ever got out about the vial. This way we can make sure that Wiseman won't get under our feet. It's imperative that Ubrino's given as wide a berth as possible if we're to have any chance of recovering the vial.'

'Who's the gunman?'

'His name's Vic Young. They served in Vietnam together. That's all we know about him at the moment. We're having him checked out, the information will be waiting for you by the time you reach London.'

Whitlock handed the photograph back to Rust. 'Who's my contact in London?'

'A Major Lonsdale of Scotland Yard's anti-terrorist squad.'

'Aren't we handling the switch ourselves?'

'*Non*, the British authorities wouldn't hear of it. It was either the anti-terrorist squad, or nothing. We had no choice. Lonsdale will brief you further once you get to London.'

'What time's my flight?'

'Ten o'clock.'

Whitlock checked his watch. 'It's gone seven-thirty already. You'll have to excuse me, Jacques, I still have to break the news to Carmen.'

'Go on,' Rust said softly. 'I'll see myself out.'

They shook hands, then Whitlock grabbed the key off the dresser and left the room. He took the lift to the foyer, handed in the key, then emerged out into the cool night air and strode briskly to the bistro a hundred yards away on the rue de Grenelle. It was exactly as he remembered it. The whitewashed exterior walls, the green and white awning over the entrance and the umbrella-shaded tables spilling out on to the pavement. He went inside. It was packed. Carmen sat at the counter, tracing her finger absently around the rim of her empty glass.

'Can I buy *madame* another drink?' he asked over her shoulder.

'That's the fourth offer I've had since I came in,' she replied.

'What Frenchman can resist a beautiful woman?' he said, trying to catch the barman's attention.

'What time are you leaving?'

'My flight's at ten o'clock. I'm sorry—'

'Save it, I've heard it all before,' she interceded, snapping her fingers to catch the barman's attention. She asked him to refill her glass.

'*Monsieur*?' the barman asked Whitlock.

'The gentleman was just leaving,' she answered. When the barman had gone she turned to Whitlock. 'Thanks for

38

the second honeymoon, all three days of it. I suppose I should be grateful it lasted that long.'

'Carmen—'

'Leave me alone!'

He kissed her on the cheek. There was nothing he could say.

She stared ahead of her as he left the bistro. She was damned if she would give him the satisfaction of seeing the tears in her eyes.

# THREE

*Tuesday*

The BA 707 touched down at Heathrow at midnight, ten minutes behind schedule. Whitlock took a taxi to the address in East Acton he had been given in his brief. It turned out to be a red-brick bungalow with a low wooden fence running the length of a small, neat garden. The gate squeaked as he opened it. An old intelligence trick. He instinctively looked around. The street was deserted. He took a key from his pocket and unlocked the front door, dumping his overnight bag at the foot of the hallstand. He switched the light on and took in the unobtrusive patterned carpet, the pale-blue walls and the framed photograph of the Queen which hung between the two doors to his right. The first door led into a lounge. The second led into a bedroom. He glanced at his watch. 12.45. He had no idea when the anti-terrorist squad were going to brief him. Tonight? Tomorrow morning? It was up to them to contact him. He certainly wasn't going to wait up for them. He picked up his overnight bag and headed for the bedroom, turning on the light at the wall switch as he went in.

The man in the armchair facing the door was in his mid-thirties with a pale complexion and cropped blond hair. The automatic in his right hand was aimed at the centre of Whitlock's chest.

Whitlock recognized it as a Browning high power, a favourite handgun of the British special forces. He dumped his bag on the bed. 'Are Scotland Yard's anti-terrorist squad always so cordial to foreign visitors, Major Lonsdale?'

The man picked up a photograph of Whitlock from the table beside him, looked at it, then put it down again, laying the Browning on top of it. 'You can never be too careful these days,' he said with a grin, then got to his feet, hand extended. 'George Lonsdale.'

Whitlock shook his hand.

'Your accent intrigues me,' Lonsdale said. 'Eton? Harrow?'

'Nothing so grand, I'm afraid. Radley.'

'Really? I'm an Old Etonian myself.' Lonsdale clapped his hands together. 'Well, how much have you been told about the London operation?'

'Only that you'd be my contact once I got here.'

'I guessed as much. Let's go through to the lounge, we can discuss the details in there.' Lonsdale slipped the Browning into his shoulder holster then picked up a folder from the table and led the way. He switched on the light and indicated the drinks cabinet in the corner of the room. 'What's your poison?'

'I wouldn't say no to a scotch and soda. No ice.'

'Coming up,' Lonsdale replied, crossing to the cabinet. 'We always keep a bit of alcohol in our safe houses. It can get pretty frustrating being cooped up in a place like this for days on end. We find that alcohol helps to relieve the tension.'

'As long as it's taken in moderation.'

'You sound like a commercial for AA,' Lonsdale said with a smile and handed Whitlock his drink. He raised his own glass. 'Here's to a successful operation.'

'I'll drink to that,' Whitlock replied, taking a sip of his whisky.

Lonsdale sat down facing him. 'How much do you know about Alexander?'

'I read his background history on the plane. What I don't know about him isn't worth finding out. One thing does puzzle me, though. If Wiseman doesn't know what Alexander looks like, how can this Young be sure he's springing the real Alexander from the prison van?'

'Young's hired a couple of locals who've worked with Alexander in the past. It's Young's insurance against snatching the wrong man. One of them, Dave Humphries, is on our payroll. It was him who tipped us off about Young in the first place.'

'But if they both know what Alexander looks like, where does that leave me?'

'It's all been taken care of, don't worry. Humphries has agreed to identify you as Alexander in exchange for a small financial incentive.'

'What about the other man?'

'He won't be there. In fact, he's sitting in a police cell right now. And he'll remain there on suspicion of some trumped-up charge until after the breakout in the morning. It's too late for Young to draft in a new accomplice so it will just be the two of them.' Lonsdale removed a silver cigarette case from his inside jacket pocket and offered it to Whitlock, who declined with a raised hand. Lonsdale lit one for himself and pocketed the case again. 'Our original idea was to change vans en route to the Old Bailey but the problem is, we don't know where Young intends to spring you. It could be at any point along the way. We're going to have to be there from the start.'

'How many men in the van?'

'Two of us up front. We're also using our own men to act as your fellow prisoners. The last thing we need is a mass breakout.'

'What time are we due out of the police station?'

'The hearing's scheduled for two. I haven't finalized the exact time of departure with the station commander yet but it should be around eleven-thirty.'

'What about Alexander?'

'He'll be our guest for a few days. We'll hand him back to the prison authorities when we get the nod from your chaps.'

'How have they taken it?'

Lonsdale chuckled. 'They're well pissed off, because it's going to look like they lost Alexander. Too bad, it's something they'll have to accept.'

Whitlock pointed to the folder. 'Has anything come through on Young?'

Lonsdale nodded. 'I read it while I was waiting for you. Some partner you've got there. Seems he ran with a New York gang until he was eighteen when he was drafted into Vietnam. He turned out to be an exceptional soldier, and after the US pulled out in '75 he joined the French Foreign Legion. Spent eight years with them, then deserted and went to Central America to fight against the Sandinistas. He now works with the death squads in El Salvador.' He handed the fax from the Command Centre to Whitlock, then stood up and moved to the window He turned back to Whitlock. 'Married?'

Whitlock's fingers instinctively tightened around his glass. He put it down on the table, hoping Lonsdale hadn't noticed. 'For six years.'

'What does your wife do?'

'She's a paediatrician. How about you?'

'I've been married for eleven years. Cathy used to be a teacher, but now she's a full-time mother. Jill's nine, Holly's five. Cathy's expecting again in October. We already know it's going to be a boy this time. Quite a relief, I'm beginning to get outvoted on everything at home. At least we men will be able to stick together. Have you any children?'

Whitlock shook his head. Just as well, he thought to himself. 'What time will you be here?' he asked.

'About ten. That will give us plenty of time to get to the police station.' Lonsdale drank down the rest of his Scotch in one gulp. 'I'll leave the folder with you and pick it up in the morning. I'll see myself out. Good night.'

Whitlock returned to the bedroom after Lonsdale had left the house. He thought about Carmen as he got ready for bed. He had an insane impulse to ring her but he quickly talked himself out of it. He switched off the light and climbed into bed, pulling the sheets up to his chin. What was going to happen to them? He knew he would lose her if he stayed with UNACO. It was inevitable. She was always worried about him when he was on assignment: worry which was affecting her work. Or so she claimed. But what was the alternative? Leave UNACO to set up some security consultancy that advised Fifth Avenue boutique owners how best to protect their premises? That wasn't for him. He loved the challenge of his work. He only wished he knew how to convince Carmen. He stifled a yawn, turned over, and closed his eyes. Within minutes he was asleep.

The streets of Rome were still quiet when Kolchinsky parked the hired Peugeot 405 in front of a small cafeteria on the via Nazionale.

Sabrina looked through the passenger window. '*Calzone Caffe*, that's it all right.'

Graham, who was seated in the back, glanced at his watch. 'Two minutes to seven. Perfect timing.'

Kolchinsky switched off the engine. They got out and locked the doors behind them. The card hanging in the window read *Chiuso*. Closed. He waited until a couple had walked past then knocked sharply on the door. A corner of the red curtain which spanned the window was pulled back and a moment later the door was unlocked and opened. It was locked again behind them. Apart from the man who had let them in, there was only one other person in the room. He was seated at one of the tables, a copy of *Paese Sera* spread out in front of him. An empty coffee cup stood on the next table.

'Please, come in,' he said, without looking up from the newspaper.

'Major Paluzzi?' Kolchinsky said, approaching the table.

The man held up his hand, continuing to study the page in front of him. He finally shook his head and sat back in the chair, a bemused smile touching the corners of his wide mouth. 'I hate the stock market. That's the third day in a row that my shares have gone down. I should have listened to my father when he told me to dump them.' He suddenly grinned and got to his feet, pushing back the chair, his hand extended. 'Fabio Paluzzi, *Nucleo Operativo Centrale di Sicurezza*.'

They each shook his hand in turn.

Paluzzi was thirty-six years old with a gaunt, pallid face which, together with his cropped brown hair, made him look more like an emaciated prisoner on a hunger strike than one of the most respected officers in the élite Italian anti-terrorist squad, the *NOCS*, better known as the 'Leatherheads' because of the leather hoods they often wore in combat.

'Please, sit down,' Paluzzi said, indicating the table. 'Have you eaten this morning?'

'We had dinner on the plane,' Kolchinsky replied, pulling up a chair.

'You mean breakfast?'

'Dinner, breakfast, it's the same thing. We're six hours behind you in New York.' Sabrina stifled a yawn as if to make her point. 'It's really disorientating.'

'I can believe it. How about some coffee?'

'The magic word,' Kolchinsky replied. 'We checked into the Quirinale Hotel, dumped our things, and dashed over here. Not even time for a coffee.'

'That's easily rectified,' Paluzzi said, and signalled to the man who had let them in. He held up three fingers. '*Tre tazze di caffè.*'

The man pointed to Paluzzi's empty cup.

'*Si, grazie,*' Paluzzi said, nodding his head. He gestured after the retreating man. 'Giancarlo's completely deaf. He used to be with the *NOCS*. His eardrums were shattered in a freak accident when a limpet mine detonated prematurely during an underwater exercise. He bought the café when he was discharged from hospital. I thought it would be the perfect place for us to meet. He can lip-read, but don't worry, he can't understand a word of English. We can talk freely in front of him.'

'Where did you learn to speak English?' Sabrina asked.

'My mother's English,' Paluzzi replied. He took a telex from his pocket and gave it to Kolchinsky. 'Your Colonel Philpott asked me to give you this. It came through about four hours ago.'

Kolchinsky unfolded the telex and read it.

Have held further discussions with the Secretary-General and the Italian Ambassador to the UN. It has been agreed, in view of the gravity of the situation, that the Red Brigades should be given the facts about the missing vial. I have asked Major Paluzzi to make the necessary arrangements.

Philpott

Sabrina read it, then handed it to Graham.

'But this is playing straight into their hands,' Graham said, tapping the paper with his finger. 'Once they know what's *really* in the vial it could push it even further underground. Who knows what they might use it for in the future?'

'I think we should hear what Major Paluzzi has to say before we start jumping to conclusions,' Kolchinsky said.

Paluzzi waited until Giancarlo had deposited the four cups of coffee on the table. 'I've already spoken to Nicola Pisani, the leader of the Red Brigades. He's agreed to cooperate fully with us.'

'And you believe him?' Graham asked incredulously.

'How much do you know about the Red Brigades, Mr Graham?'

'Enough to know that I wouldn't trust the bastards an inch.'

'I know them inside out. I should do after eight years. It was my idea in the first place to contact Pisani.' Paluzzi held up his hand when Graham opened his mouth to speak. 'Give me a chance and I'll explain to you why I did it. We have a senior *Brigatista* on our payroll. A brigade chief, to be exact. He gets to attend all the executive committee meetings. He told us that Pisani called an emergency meeting yesterday. It turned out that the break-in hadn't been sanctioned by the committee. In fact, the first Pisani knew about it was when he turned on his radio yesterday morning and heard that the Red Brigades had claimed responsibility for it. It was obvious that Zocchi was behind it—'

'Why?' Graham challenged.

'Two reasons. Firstly, because Riccardo Ubrino was involved. He's been Zocchi's right-hand man for the last six years. They were inseparable.'

'Couldn't Ubrino have pulled it off by himself?' Kolchinsky asked.

Paluzzi shook his head. 'It was too well planned. Ubrino's a hatchet man, he doesn't have the brains to plan a raid like that. Zocchi did.'

'And the second reason?' Sabrina asked.

'It's a bit more complicated. Pisani found out at the beginning of the year that he had cancer. The doctors doubt he'll see out the year. This has naturally sparked a bitter power struggle amongst the brigade chiefs to appoint his successor. It came down to two men: Zocchi and Tonino Calvieri, Milan's brigade chief. Calvieri is a so-called "moderate". He has the unanimous support of the other brigade chiefs. He's been Pisani's blue-eyed boy for years. But Zocchi had the money behind him. The Rome cell is wealthier than all the other cells put together. And that meant he had the backing of many of the rich irregulars.'

'Irregulars?' Kolchinski asked.

'It's what the *Brigatisti* call sympathizers. They don't have a say at committee level but they can easily make their presence felt by withholding donations if they don't agree with committee policy. And if enough donations are withheld, it would cripple the organization financially.'

'Was this happening?' Kolchinsky asked.

'It was being threatened. And that was something Pisani had to take into consideration when choosing his successor. Then Zocchi was arrested for his part in the attempted murder of a Rome judge. The other brigade chiefs were only too pleased to see the prison gates close behind him. They certainly wouldn't have wanted to spring him. Which leaves Zocchi himself.'

'I still don't see why Pisani has agreed to co-operate with us,' Sabrina said.

'Because the vial could end up being used against him, and the committee, forcing them to concede power to the Rome cell.' Paluzzi held out his hand towards Graham. 'As you said, who knows what use they might find for it in the future.'

'But Zocchi's dead,' Sabrina said.

'But Ubrino isn't, and the Rome cell regard him as Zocchi's natural successor. That frightens Pisani and his brigade chiefs enough for them to agree to help us get the vial back.'

'Surely they could negotiate with him themselves? Then, once they had the vial, they could kill him and install this Calvieri.'

'Nice scenario, Mr Graham, but you're overlooking a couple of points. Firstly, they don't know where Ubrino is, that much we do know from our mole. And secondly, by killing him, the donations from foreign irregulars could dry up. But if we were to kill him, or jail him, for that matter, they would have neatly sidestepped the responsibility.

48

As far as they're concerned, the vial's a small price to pay if it means keeping the Red Brigades intact.'

Graham drank the remainder of his coffee and replaced the cup in the saucer. 'I've got to hand it to you, Paluzzi, you know your business.'

'That's why I was assigned to help you. I know how their devious minds work. And Pisani's sending us their most devious mind of all to help us find the vial. Calvieri.'

'I thought you said he was a moderate?'

'He is, Miss Carver, and that's what makes him all the more dangerous. He and Zocchi were like chalk and cheese. Zocchi, the brash, arrogant radical who used violence against anyone opposing the cause. And Calvieri, the polite, mild-mannered intellectual. He speaks five languages fluently and has been in charge of their PR department for the past four years. At least with Zocchi you knew what to expect. But not with Calvieri. It's impossible to know what's going on in his mind. It's no wonder he's held in such high regard in the Brigades.'

'When do we meet him?' Kolchinsky asked.

'Eight o'clock at the Quirinale.'

Kolchinsky finished his coffee. 'Any news of the helicopter that was used by Zocchi's killers?'

'Still nothing. But we are certain it wasn't a genuine police helicopter. The markings on the fuselage were false.'

'What about the wounded terrorist?' Kolchinsky asked.

'Conte? He's still in a critical condition in hospital. The doctors removed eight bullets from his body. It's a miracle he's still alive.' Paluzzi took another sheet of paper from his pocket and handed it to Kolchinsky. 'The ballistics report on the bullets taken from Conte and Nardi. They all came from the sub-machine-gun found next to Nardi's body. It was clean, so we can only presume that Ubrino had instructions to kill his team once he had the vial in his possession.'

'What can you tell us about Ubrino?' Sabrina asked. 'We don't have much on him at the Command Centre.'

'Grew up in the same slums as Zocchi. Believed passionately in the cause from an early age. Zocchi recruited him. He started out as Zocchi's personal bodyguard but slowly worked his way up through the ranks to his present position of senior cell commander. That meant he was only answerable to Zocchi. We know he's been personally responsible for at least four murders and countless kneecappings here in Rome but we've never had enough evidence to make it stick. He's always had Zocchi to bail him out of trouble.' Paluzzi glanced at his watch. 'I think we should go if we're going to make the Quirinale by eight.'

Kolchinsky was the first on his feet and he led the way out to the Peugeot.

A receptionist at the Quirinale Hotel told them that Calvieri had checked in less than half an hour earlier. She gave them his room number and they rode the lift to the third floor where Paluzzi rapped sharply on the bedroom door.

Calvieri opened it and gestured for them to enter his room. He was a handsome 41-year-old with finely chiselled features, piercing blue eyes and a neatly trimmed brown moustache. His long dark brown hair was combed away from his forehead and secured in a ponytail behind his head.

He closed the door after them and stopped in front of Paluzzi. They each tried to stare the other out like two boxers before a big fight, both oblivious to those around them. Kolchinsky was about to speak but Graham put a hand on his arm to silence him. The movement broke Paluzzi's concentration and he turned away sharply, furious with himself for allowing his feelings to surface so easily. He introduced them to Calvieri. Kolchinsky and Sabrina shook Calvieri's extended hand. Graham refused.

'What organization do you work for?'

'That doesn't concern you, Mr Calvieri,' Kolchinsky replied as he crossed to one of the armchairs and sat down.

'Let's just say we're working with Major Paluzzi and leave it at that.'

'Very well,' Calvieri replied, the resentment obvious in his face.

Kolchinsky took a pack of cigarettes from his pocket and offered one to Paluzzi, who refused with a quick shake of his head. Calvieri took one. Kolchinsky lit it for him, then his own, and discarded the match in the ashtray beside him.

'Has Pisani briefed you?' Paluzzi asked, sitting on the bed beside Graham.

Calvieri nodded. 'I called him when I got here. He wanted to be here in person but he wasn't up to it. He's deteriorating fast. The doctors are doubtful he'll see out the year. At this rate he won't see out the summer. You did tell them about him?'

'They know,' Paluzzi replied.

'He asked me to put myself completely at your disposal. We're just as concerned as you are about getting the vial back safely.'

'That's good coming from you,' Graham snapped. 'It's a bit late to lock the stable door. The horse bolted two days ago.'

'It was an unauthorized operation, Mr Graham. The committee didn't know anything about it until the following day.'

'And that's your excuse? Your organization is in such a shambles that the right hand doesn't know what the left hand is doing any more?'

Calvieri inhaled deeply on the cigarette and moved to the window. A school bus had stopped on the other side of the street. He could see several of the children inside laughing as they play-fought on the back seat. How many of them would die if the virus were to be released into the atmosphere? He turned away, unable to look at their innocent faces.

'Where do you think Ubrino's hiding?' Kolchinsky asked Calvieri.

'I'd say he is still in Rome. His friends are here. They'll shield him. Unfortunately the Rome cell has always been the maverick in the organization. That's how someone like Zocchi became their brigade chief. It could never have happened in any of the other cities.'

'He could also be in Venice,' Paluzzi said.

'Venice?' Calvieri asked in surprise.

'He was posted up there for a few months a couple of years ago. It's about the only time he and Zocchi were ever apart.'

'I didn't know he was ever in Venice. It proves how mysterious the man can be.'

'I doubt he'd have gone to Venice, though,' Paluzzi concluded after a moment's thought. 'It's a moderate stronghold, that's why he didn't last there very long. No, I'd have to go along with Calvieri. He's almost certainly still here in Rome.'

'I used to be the senior cell commander here twelve years ago,' Calvieri said. 'I've still got contacts in the city. I've already told them to find out what they can. If Ubrino's here, they'll pass the information on to me. The problem will be trying to pin him down. He knows he'll have to keep moving to stay one step ahead of us.'

'I suggest you split up into teams,' Kolchinsky said. 'Sabrina, you work with Calvieri. And stick to him like a leech.'

Calvieri shrugged. 'That's fine by me.'

'Her Italian's as good as your English, that's why I've paired her with you.' Kolchinsky turned to Graham. 'You work with Major Paluzzi.'

'How's your Italian?' Paluzzi asked Graham.

'Non-existent.'

'We'll manage,' Paluzzi said with a smile.

Kolchinsky picked up his attaché case and got to his feet. 'You'll have to excuse me. I have several phone calls to make.'

'So have I,' Calvieri said. 'Hopefully one of my contacts will have come up with something by now.'

'Where do we start?' Graham asked Paluzzi.

'Neo-Chem Industries. My men have been there all night. I think it's time to see what they've found.'

Paluzzi parked his white Alfa Romeo Lusso in the car-park opposite the plant's main entrance. They got out and he used a transmitter to lock the doors behind them.

They crossed the car-park and mounted the steps leading into the foyer. The front of the reception desk had been boarded up to hide the bullet holes. The wall behind it had already been redecorated. In fact, the only sign of the break-in was the chipped pillar in the middle of the foyer. Paluzzi identified himself to the receptionist and asked her to have his deputy report to the foyer. He then crossed to where Graham was standing beside the pillar.

'What were your men doing here last night?' Graham asked.

'Trying to find out who was paying Wiseman for the virus. They concealed themselves in the building late yesterday afternoon and waited until the management team had left before going through each of their offices in turn.'

'How did they get past the closed-circuit television cameras?'

Paluzzi gave him a knowing smile. 'Some of these systems can go on the blink at the most inopportune moments.'

'Point taken.'

'We're sure to take some flak when the MD finds out what's happened but we'll weather the storm. We always do.'

The lift doors opened and a tall, dark-haired man emerged into the foyer. Graham doubted he was much older than Sabrina. Paluzzi introduced him as Lieutenant Angelo Marco, his personal adjutant for the past seven months.

'Pleased to meet you, sir,' Marco said, shaking Graham's hand.

'Call me Mike,' Graham told him.

'Well, did you find anything?' Paluzzi asked.

'Yes, sir, but we're going to have a job proving it.' Marco jabbed his thumb upwards. 'We've got a more immediate problem on our hands. The MD's been ranting and raging at me ever since he got here an hour ago. He said he wanted to see you the moment you arrived.'

'What did you find?'

Marco pushed the button for the lift. 'The senior sales manager has received four payments of eighty million lire in the past year. And each time he withdrew sixty-four million lire, in cash, on the same day that the cheques were cleared through his account.'

The lift arrived.

'How much is eighty million lire in dollars?' Graham asked.

'It's about twenty-five thousand dollars,' Marco said, pressing the button for the top floor. He looked at Paluzzi. 'The cheques were all issued by Nikki Karos.'

'Karos?' Paluzzi said thoughtfully. 'That's interesting.'

'Who's this Karos?' Graham asked.

'One of the wealthiest arms dealers in the Aegean,' Paluzzi replied. 'He does most of his business in the Middle East.'

'So if this sales manager was the middleman between Karos and Wiseman, who's to say Karos wasn't acting on behalf of a Middle Eastern client? Iran? Iraq? One of the Lebanese factions? The list's endless.'

'That's what we've got to find out,' Paluzzi replied. 'But first we've got to pacify an angry MD.'

The doors parted and they emerged into a beige-carpeted corridor. Marco led them to a door and entered without knocking. The secretary looked up from her typewriter. Her smile faltered when she saw Marco. Paluzzi rapped loudly on one of the double doors and entered the inner office without waiting for a reply.

The managing director sat behind a large oak desk. The nameplate identified him as Daniel Chidenko.

'I'm Major Paluzzi, I believe you wanted to see me?'

The secretary hurried into the room. 'I'm sorry, Mr Chidenko, they just walked in—'

'It's okay, Margarita,' Chidenko cut in, his hand raised. 'It's not your fault.'

The secretary left the room, closing the door behind her.

'You don't have to speak English to me, Major. I may be American but I am fluent in your language.'

'Mr Graham here doesn't speak Italian.'

Chidenko removed a cigarette from the silver box on his desk and lit it. 'Mike Graham. Our head office in New York told me you were coming.'

'I'm impressed,' Graham replied. 'At least there's one efficient employee in the company. You should have them transferred out here.'

Chidenko ignored Graham's sarcasm and looked at Paluzzi. 'I want to know on whose authority your men broke into the seven offices on this floor, including my own, and went through the contents of the wallsafes?'

'Mine,' Paluzzi replied.

'May I see a search warrant?'

'I don't need one,' Paluzzi replied defiantly.

'Really?' Chidenko tapped the ash from his cigarette into the glass ashtray on his desk. 'You've been trying to link one, or more, of my management team to Wiseman ever since you took charge of this case instead of getting out there and finding the vial. Well, this time you've gone too far. You've broken the law and I'll see to it that you're taken off the case and replaced with someone who's prepared to get his priorities right.'

'Before you do that, Lieutenant Marco has something to show you.'

Marco took the papers he had found in the senior sales manager's wallsafe and handed them to Chidenko.

'They're bank statements,' Chidenko said.

'They're also evidence linking Vittore Dragotti to Wiseman and the virus,' Marco said.

'Show me,' Chidenko said, holding up the papers.

'These payments have been traced to Nikki Karos,' Marco said, pointing out the relevant entries on each of the bank statements.

'And who's Nikki Karos?'

'An arms dealer with powerful connections in the Middle East,' Paluzzi replied.

'So Vittore did some business with him,' Chidenko said, hands outstretched. 'What does that prove?'

'The money was deposited in his private account,' Marco stressed.

'A gift. It happens all the time in this business.'

'We think it was a payoff.'

'So arrest him,'. Chidenko challenged. 'Then let's see what a court will make of your "evidence".'

'No one's going to be arrested yet. All we want to do is talk to him,' Paluzzi said.

'Fine, I'll have one of our lawyers come over.'

'No lawyers,' Paluzzi replied.

Chidenko's hand rested lightly on the receiver. 'You certainly believe in flouting the law, Major. First your men break in here without a search warrant and now you want to interrogate one of my managers but refuse to allow him access to a lawyer. I know his rights, and that means having a lawyer present when you confront him with this flimsy evidence of yours.'

Paluzzi crossed to the desk. 'Get him a lawyer, but I promise you every national paper will carry a front-page story tomorrow morning linking a senior manager at Neo-Chem Industries to an arms dealer whose past deals involving Sarin and Tabun have left hundreds of thousands dead in the Gulf War. It won't look very good coming so soon after the break-in, will it?'

Chidenko sat back in his chair. 'Is Vittore here yet?'

'Not yet, but one of my men is waiting for him in his office.'

The telephone rang.

Chidenko grabbed the receiver, listened momentarily, then held it out towards Graham. 'It's for you.'

'Graham speaking.'

'Mike, it's Sabrina. Calvieri's got word from one of his contacts that Ubrino's been seen in Venice. We're going up there to check it out. I'll see you back at the hotel.'

'Okay. But Sabrina—' Graham struggled to find the words to express himself. 'Take every precaution,' he said finally in a gruff voice. 'I don't trust that bastard an inch.'

'I will. See you later. Bye.'

Graham replaced the receiver and almost immediately the telephone rang again.

Chidenko picked up the receiver again, his eyes darting around the room as he listened in silence. He put his hand over the mouthpiece. 'Vittore's here.'

'We're on our way,' Paluzzi said.

Chidenko passed on the message and had to restrain himself from slamming the handset back into the cradle. He stood up and brushed an imaginary fleck of dust from his jacket. 'Let's get this over with, shall we? Then I'm going to make sure you're kicked off the case.'

'You're not coming with us, if that's what you think,' Paluzzi shot back.

'I've had about all I can take from you, Paluzzi—'

'I don't like pulling rank, but you're forcing my hand,' Paluzzi cut in sharply. He took an envelope from his pocket and slapped it down on the desk. 'Read that.'

'What is it?' Chidenko demanded.

'Read it and you'll find out.'

Chidenko removed a sheet of paper from the envelope and read it. He looked up once, then sank slowly into his chair.

'There's a telephone number at the top of the page if you want to take the matter any further. If not, I've got work to do.'

Chidenko replaced the paper inside the envelope and handed it silently back to Paluzzi.

Graham followed Paluzzi into the corridor. 'What the hell's in the envelope?'

'A letter, signed by the Prime Minister, which, roughly translated, gives me *carte blanche* to use any methods I deem necessary to recover the vial. It also says that any complaints about my methods should be reported to him in person.'

'So why didn't you show it to Chidenko straight away? It would have saved us all a lot of trouble.'

'I don't like to tempt fate. That's why I only use it as a last resort.'

Graham stopped in the middle of the corridor. 'What do you mean, you don't like to tempt fate?'

'It's a forgery. The notepaper's genuine, we get that from a mole inside the Prime Minister's office. We write the text ourselves, depending on the nature of the assignment.'

'And you do it for every assignment?'

'Every difficult assignment. And let's face it, they don't come much more difficult than this one. As I said, it's only used as a last resort.'

'Has anyone ever challenged its authenticity?'

'Not up to now. But I'm sure there will be a first time. That's when I'll start thinking about writing my memoirs.'

'I like it,' Graham muttered thoughtfully. 'I wonder how I can get hold of some White House stationery?'

Marco looked out from a doorway. 'Are you coming, sir?'

Paluzzi patted Graham on the shoulder. 'Come on, Mike.'

Dragotti was standing in front of his open wallsafe, checking through his personal papers, when Graham and Paluzzi entered the room.

'Looking for these?' Paluzzi asked, holding up the bank statements.

Dragotti looked round, momentarily startled by Paluzzi's use of English. He closed the safe and approached Paluzzi. 'Who are you?'

Paluzzi introduced himself and said that Graham was from the company's headquarters in New York, sent out to help with the investigation. Marco spoke softly to Paluzzi, then left the room, closing the door behind him.

'Where's Signore Chidenko?'

'Busy,' Paluzzi replied. 'Now sit down, we've got some questions to ask you.'

'I'm not answering any of your questions until I know why my wallsafe was opened last night. It's an outrage.'

'Call Chidenko, he knows what's going on.'

Dragotti picked up the receiver hesitantly and rang Chidenko's office. He turned away from them as he spoke softly into the mouthpiece.

'What did Chidenko say?' Paluzzi asked once Dragotti had finished his conversation.

'He told me to cooperate with you. What do you want to know?'

'Why has Nikki Karos been paying eighty million lire into your account every month for the past four months?' Paluzzi demanded, dropping the bank statements on the desk in front of Dragotti. 'And why did you withdraw eighty per cent of the money in cash on the same day that each of the cheques was cleared?'

'We had a business deal,' Dragotti replied, fingering the nearest bank statement nervously. 'I should have known it would backfire on me. I told him to pay me in cash but he wouldn't hear of it. He insisted on payment by cheque.'

'Karos never deals in currency,' Paluzzi told Graham. 'It's an idiosyncrasy that's lost him a lot of business in the past.' He turned back to Dragotti. 'So you kept twenty per cent as a commission and paid the balance to Wiseman in cash?'

'Wiseman?' Dragotti replied in surprise. 'I had nothing to do with Wiseman.'

'Don't lie!' Paluzzi snapped.

'I'm not lying. Have you ever heard of phosgene?'

'Of course,' Paluzzi replied. 'It's a nerve gas made up from a mixture of chlorine and phosphorus.'

Dragotti nodded. 'Karos was put in touch with me because he needed large quantities of chlorine for one of his clients so that they could make phosgene themselves.'

'Who?' Graham demanded.

'He never told me. All I knew was that he had a source for phosphorus and he needed the chlorine to complete the deal. I have a reliable contact who could supply him with as much chlorine as he needed, at a knockdown price. That's what he paid me for.'

There was a tap on the door and Marco entered. He spoke softly to Paluzzi, then took up a position by the door.

Paluzzi crossed to the desk, picked up the bank statements and pocketed them. 'It's over, Dragotti. Karos has confessed.'

'To what?' Dragotti asked apprehensively.

'To paying you to act as the middleman between Wiseman and himself.'

'That's ridiculous,' Dragotti retorted.

'We had him picked up earlier this morning. He held out for the first hour but he finally agreed to talk in exchange for a reduced sentence. And from what he's said about you, I doubt you'll get out of jail before you're sixty.'

'You're lying,' Dragotti said, a desperation already beginning to creep into his voice.

'We're prepared to offer you the same deal.' Paluzzi glanced at Marco. 'Read him his rights.'

Dragotti yanked open the middle drawer of his desk and pulled out an RF83 revolver, but when he looked up he found Paluzzi and Marco aiming their Berettas at him.

'Drop the gun,' Paluzzi ordered, his finger tightening on the trigger. 'Drop it!'

Dragotti's plan had backfired. He hadn't known that they would be armed. There was no escape, not now.

'Drop it,' Paluzzi repeated.

'Then what?' Dragotti said in a hollow voice. 'Thirty years inside?'

'Karos hasn't confessed to anything. We haven't even arrested him. It was a trick to try and make you confess,' Paluzzi told him.

'I don't believe you,' Dragotti said, shaking his head slowly.

'Put down the gun, Vittore, and we'll talk,' Paluzzi said.

Dragotti gave Paluzzi a half-smile, then pushed the barrel of the revolver against the roof of his mouth and pulled the trigger. Blood splattered across the window behind the desk and Dragotti slumped to the floor. Paluzzi hurried across to where he lay and felt for a pulse. There wasn't one. He looked up at Graham and Marco and shook his head, then, taking off his jacket, he placed it over Dragotti's mutilated face.

Chidenko and several of his managers burst into the office.

'What happened?' Chidenko demanded, staring at Dragotti's body.

'He shot himself,' Graham replied.

'This isn't some sort of sideshow!' Paluzzi shouted angrily. 'Go back to your offices.'

Chidenko persuaded his colleagues to leave, then crossed to where Dragotti lay and reached down to lift the jacket.

'You don't want to look,' Graham said, grabbing his wrist.

Chidenko jerked his hand free and lifted the cloth. Stumbling backwards a few feet, he clasped his hand over his mouth in a struggle to keep himself from vomiting. When he finally turned back to Graham his face was pale. 'I never realized a handgun could cause so much damage.'

'It can if it's loaded with .38 slugs.'

Marco returned to the office. 'The ambulance is on its way.'

'What now?' Graham asked Paluzzi.

'I'll get hold of the local carabinieri. If we can hand over the suicide to them without too many hitches we should be in Corfu by mid-afternoon.'

'What's in Corfu?'

'Not what. Who. Nikki Karos.'

# FOUR

Mary Robson had always dreamed of becoming a professional dancer ever since she was eight years old. She took up ballet at school but her real love was disco dancing and when, at the age of seventeen, she won a national competition in her home town of Newcastle a theatrical agent offered her a small part in a leading West End musical. Her parents refused to give their consent, arguing that they wanted her to finish her education first. Six months later she ran away to London, certain she would land a part in another West End show, but when she got there she found that she was just one of hundreds, many of whom were better dancers. She took a job in a Soho strip club to make ends meet and it was there that she met Wendell Johnson, a West Indian with a long criminal record. Three months after moving in with him she discovered she was pregnant. She was only nineteen when their son, Bernard, was born. The dream was over.

She was now twenty-two years old, overweight and unemployed. Wendell was in prison, where he had already served ten months of a seven-year sentence for burglary. She would wait for him. Her parents couldn't understand how she could love a man like him. Neither could they understand that she wanted her son to have a father, even if he was a criminal. Not that she saw much of them anyway. She would bring up her son in her own way and to hell with what anyone else thought. And that included her parents.

She finished drying the dishes then stood looking out of the window over the sink at the row of bleak terraced houses on the opposite side of the street. It was a mirror image of all the streets in the neighbourhood. She hated Brixton: it was so depressing. Wendell liked it, because all his friends were there. She had tried to persuade him to put his name down for a council house in Streatham but he had always refused to budge on the issue. They would stay in Brixton.

A police car pulled up in front of the house. Inside were two policemen. The driver got out of the car and approached the front door. Mary discarded her apron and hurried into the hallway. The doorbell rang. Her mind raced as she fumbled to unlock the door. It had to be about Wendell. She pulled open the door, her eyes wide with anxiety.

'Are you Miss Mary Robson?' the policeman asked.

'Yes,' she stammered. 'Something's happened to Wendell, hasn't it?'

The policeman nodded. 'He was stabbed in a fight at the prison. Don't worry though, he'll be all right.'

'Where is he now?'

'He's been taken to the Greenwich District Hospital.'

'Can I see him?'

'That's why we're here,' the policeman replied with a reassuring smile.

'I won't be a minute, I just have to get my son.'

He waited until she was out of sight then looked back at the police car and nodded to his colleague.

The man in the passenger seat removed his peaked cap and raked his fingers through his thick black hair. The black moustache gave a sinister edge to his youthful features. Even so he looked nearer twenty-five than his real age of thirty-seven. His name was Victor Young.

He smiled to himself as Dave Humphries led Mary Robson

and her son towards the police car. It was all going according to plan.

Whitlock and Lonsdale arrived at Brixton police station at eleven o'clock and were immediately ushered into the station commander's office. Chief Inspector Roger Pugh was a tall man in his late forties with silver-grey hair and an easy manner which helped to put them at their ease. He shook hands with them and indicated the two chairs in front of his desk.

'What time are we due out?' Whitlock asked, sitting down. 'Major Lonsdale wasn't sure whether it would be eleven-thirty or twelve.'

'Eleven-thirty,' Pugh replied.

There was a knock at the door.

'Come in,' Pugh called.

The man who entered was in his late twenties with short black hair and a stocky physique. He was wearing the uniform of a warder. Lonsdale introduced him to Whitlock as Sergeant Don Harrison who would be driving the police van. Harrison handed Lonsdale a uniform identical to the one he was wearing.

'There's a changing room down the hall,' Pugh said. 'The desk sergeant will show you the way.'

'I might as well change in here,' Lonsdale replied, giving Pugh a mock suspicious look. 'You're not expecting any WPCs, are you?'

'Not today, I'm afraid,' Pugh said with a smile.

'How did things go with Alexander?' Lonsdale asked Harrison as he started to undress.

'He kicked up a bit of a fuss so we had to drug him. No trouble after that. He's sleeping it off at the safe house.' Harrison took a pair of sunglasses from his pocket and handed them to Whitlock. 'Alexander was wearing these.'

'Thanks,' Whitlock said, slipping them on.

'Are the men ready?' Lonsdale asked.

'Yes sir,' Harrison replied. 'They're waiting at the van.'

'Put them into the cages, we'll be along in a minute.

Harrison left the room.

Lonsdale finished dressing, then picked up his clothes from the floor. 'You don't mind if I leave these here, do you?'

'Not at all. Put them on the chair.' Pugh got to his feet and extended his hand towards Whitlock. 'Good luck.'

'Thanks for all your help,' Whitlock said, shaking Pugh's hand.

'Glad to be of service. Major, I'll speak to you later.'

Lonsdale nodded then left the room with Whitlock. They made their way out into the courtyard where the pale-blue police van was parked. Harrison led them round to the back of the van. The doors were open. Inside was a narrow corridor with three cells on either side of it. Harrison unlocked one of the cells, removed a pair of handcuffs from his belt and snapped them around Whitlock's wrists. Whitlock entered the cell and Harrison locked it behind him. Harrison climbed out of the van and locked the doors. He handed the keys to Lonsdale. They got into the cab and Harrison started the engine.

'Ready, sir?' Harrison asked, his hand resting lightly on the gear lever.

'Let's go.'

Harrison engaged the gears and drove out into Brixton Road, the A23. He kept the speed steady, his eyes continually flickering towards the side mirror.

'What are you looking for, Sergeant? They're hardly going to advertise themselves, are they?'

Harrison smiled ruefully but said nothing. They reached the top of Brixton Road and he was about to turn the van into Kennington Park Road when he heard the police car coming up fast behind them. He automatically touched the brake pedal and pulled over to give the police car the right of way. The police car passed them then immediately slowed and the driver indicated for them to stop.

'What the hell does he want?' Harrison hissed angrily, pulling up behind the red and white Rover.

'Whitlock, probably,' Lonsdale replied, his body tensing as the policeman in the passenger seat got out of the car ahead.

'You think . . . ?' Harrison trailed off and nodded to himself. 'Of course, what could be more natural than a police car and a police van pulled up at the side of the road? Nobody would think of questioning it.'

The policeman knocked on the driver's window.

Harrison opened it. 'What's wrong? We've got five prisoners in the back who are due at the Old Bailey at twelve o'clock.'

'You see the woman and the kid in the back of the police car?' Young asked, making no attempt to disguise his American accent.

'Yes,' Harrison replied hesitantly. 'What about them?'

'They're both unconscious. My colleague has a gun trained on them.' Young put a two-way radio to his lips. 'Show them the gun.'

Humphries raised the automatic momentarily, then ducked it back out of sight.

'If you don't do exactly as I say, he'll kill them both. Starting with the kid.'

'What the hell is—'

'Shut up!' Young cut sharply across Harrison's outburst. 'Switch off the engine.'

'Do it,' Lonsdale said softly.

Harrison did as he was told.

'I'm in charge here,' Lonsdale said to Young. 'I demand to know what's going on.'

'You will. Now give me the keys,' Young said, holding out a black-gloved hand.

Harrison looked at Lonsdale, who nodded. He gave them to Young.

'Get out of the van, both of you,' Young said, stepping away from the driver's door.

Again Lonsdale nodded to Harrison, and they got out of the van. Young led Harrison round to where Lonsdale was standing, his eyes riveted on the woman and her son in the back of the police car. He hated any form of hostage-taking, especially when children were involved. He suddenly thought of his own five-year-old daughter, Holly. It only made him more frustrated. He felt so damn helpless. There were times when he really hated the job . . .

'Who's got the keys to the back of the van?' Young demanded.

'I have,' Lonsdale replied.

'Open the doors.' Young pointed to Harrison. 'You, walk beside him. And remember, any heroics and the kid dies.'

Young followed the two men to the back of the van and watched as Lonsdale unlocked the doors and opened them. The men inside the cages began to shout abuse, demanding to know what was happening. Lonsdale had told them to make their performances as realistic as possible: Young mustn't suspect a thing. Young motioned Lonsdale and Harrison into the back of the van and then climbed in after them.

'Where's Alexander?'

'So that's what it's all about,' Lonsdale said, eyeing Young with disdain.

'Where is he?'

Lonsdale indicated Whitlock's cell.

'Open it.'

Lonsdale and Harrison exchanged glances.

'I said open it. Unless you want the kid to die.'

Lonsdale took the keys from his pocket, selected one, and unlocked the cell.

'What's going on?' Whitlock snapped as Lonsdale pulled open the door.

'You're being sprung,' Young told him. 'Now get out of there.'

Whitlock stared at Young with mock disbelief. 'Who are you?'

'I'm not a cop, that's all you need to know for the moment.'

Whitlock pushed past Lonsdale, then extended his manacled hands towards him. 'You've got the key, screw. Uncuff me.'

Young took the key for the handcuffs from Lonsdale, pocketed it, then shoved Harrison and Lonsdale into the empty cell and locked it. He grabbed Whitlock by the arm and led him out of the van, locking the doors behind him.

'You can uncuff me now,' Whitlock said, nudging Young with his elbow.

'Shut up,' Young snapped, then led Whitlock to the police car. He opened the back door and peered in at Humphries. 'Is this him?'

Humphries nodded. 'That's Reuben all right.'

'Get in,' Young said, bundling Whitlock into the back of the police car beside the unconscious Mary Robson. Hurriedly he got into the passenger seat beside Humphries. 'Let's get out of here. Fast.'

'Dave, what's going on?' Whitlock asked Humphries. 'What the hell is going on?'

'I told you to shut up,' Young said to Whitlock as Humphries swung the police car back out into the road.

'I want to know what's going on!' Whitlock demanded. 'And who's the woman and the kid?'

'Quit with the questions, okay?' Young snapped, glaring at Whitlock.

'I've got a right to know—'

'You say another word and you'll get the same treatment as those two next to you,' Young threatened.

Whitlock slumped back in the seat and said nothing further.

Humphries continued up Kennington Park Road for another six hundred yards then turned right into Braganza

Street where he slowed down before swinging the police car into a double garage and stopping beside a lime-green Fiat Uno. He picked up a remote control from the dashboard and used it to close the garage door.

'Get the lights,' Young said to Humphries.

Humphries got out of the car and crossed to the light switch. He flicked it on then turned back to the car. His eyes registered sudden alarm. Young was out of the car and holding a silenced Heckler & Koch P7 in his hand, aimed at Humphries. He fired twice. Humphries was thrown back against the wall then his body slid lifelessly to the concrete floor. Whitlock struggled to get out of the car, hindered by the handcuffs. When he did manage to straighten up he found himself staring at the silenced automatic in Young's hand.

'I didn't go to all that trouble just to kill you,' Young assured him, reaching slowly through the open window and opening the glove compartment, his eyes never leaving Whitlock's face.

'There was no reason to kill him,' Whitlock said, staring at the body slumped against the wall. 'Why did you do it?'

Young's fingers curled around the tranquillizer gun in the glove compartment and as he withdrew it a faint smile touched the corners of his mouth. In one quick movement he raised the tranquillizer gun and fired. Whitlock winced as the dart hit him in the neck. The garage began to distort into a kaleidoscope of colours. The floor swayed beneath him. He stumbled to one side, bumping heavily against the wall, his legs losing all sense of balance. He felt himself fall forward. Young caught him before he hit the side of the car.

Then everything went black.

*La Serenissima*. Sabrina agreed completely with the name the Venetians had given to their city. It *was* serene. A city with a complex labyrinth of *rii*, canals, and *calli*, narrow streets, supported on piles of Istrian pine which had been driven down twenty-five feet into a solid bed of compressed sand, clay and limestone. She loved it most for its architecture. The Piazza San Marco, dominated by the Basilica with its façade of arches and loggias; the Palazzo Ducale, the seat of power for the past nine hundred years; Santa Maria della Salute, the white octagonal church built after the plague of 1390 which claimed nearly a third of the population. As far as she was concerned, Venice was the most beautiful city in the world.

They had arrived at Marco Polo Airport aboard a UNACO Cessna at midday. Sabrina had picked up a Beretta from a locker in the terminal (the key had been left for her at the information desk by a UNACO contact) and then they had managed to hire a motorboat taxi, agreeing the fare in advance, to take them to the Rio Baglioni, a small canal near the Rialto Bridge, where Calvieri claimed his contact had seen Ubrino earlier that morning.

'The helmsman says we'll be there in another five minutes,' Calvieri said, resuming his seat on the padded bench beside Sabrina.

She merely nodded, looking across at the Ca'd'Oro, a magnificent palace with a Gothic façade which was once lavishly adorned with gold and now housed the acclaimed Franchetti collection of Renaissance art.

'The Ca' do Mosto,' Calvieri said, pointing to the thirteenth-century Byzantine palace a hundred yards further on from the Ca' d'Oro.

She had seen it on her previous visits to Venice but had never found out its name.

'It was originally owned by Alvise de Mosto,' Calvieri shouted above the noise of a passing *vaporetto*, a waterbus, packed with tourists. 'He was an explorer who discovered the Cape Verde Islands off the African west coast.'

'You seem to know a lot about Venice,' Sabrina said, turning to face him.

'It's my favourite retreat,' Calvieri replied with a smile. 'I have many friends up here. It's the most liberal *Brigatista* stronghold in Italy.'

Sabrina glanced at the helmsman, who had his back to them, then leaned forward, her arms resting on her knees. 'So why would Ubrino come back? Paluzzi said he'd been hounded out because he was too radical.'

'I know it doesn't make any sense,' Calvieri agreed. 'But my contact has never let me down in the past.'

'So you said on the plane. I still think it's a trap. It's too easy.'

The helmsman blew the speedboat's horn as he turned the blind corner under the white Rialto Bridge, then swung the wheel deftly to avoid an approaching gondola. He finally stopped the speedboat at one of the landing stages on the Riva del Carbon and tossed the mooring rope to a teenager on the jetty.

'You said you'd take us to the Rio Baglioni,' Sabrina said, getting to her feet.

'That's it, the second canal down,' the helmsman replied, pointing it out. 'You tell me how I'm going to get in there!'

An unoccupied blue and white speedboat was moored in the entrance to the narrow canal, blocking it to traffic.

'Some people have no consideration,' the helmsman muttered, staring at the speedboat.

Sabrina paid him, then scrambled on to the jetty, ignoring Calvieri's extended hand. 'Still so sure it's not a trap?'

Calvieri raised his hands defensively. 'I never said it wasn't. But why would my contact want to set me up? We've been friends for years. As I've said before—'

'I know, he's never let you down in the past,' Sabrina cut in. 'There's always a first time. Come on, I want to take a closer look at the speedboat before we go to that address he gave to you.'

It took them a couple of minutes to reach the Rio Baglioni. It was about seven feet wide, half the size of the average canal, and ended in a cul-de-sac. The perfect setting for a trap. Sabrina crouched down beside the speedboat. A canvas tarpaulin lay in the back. It was covering something. She transferred the Beretta from the holster at the back of her jeans to the pocket of her blouson then reached over and pulled back the tarpaulin. Underneath was a cardboard box with the word 'Valpolicella' stencilled on the side. Calvieri got down on his haunches beside her.

'What the hell do you think you're doing?'

They looked round, startled by the voice behind them. The man was in his mid-twenties. He wore loud checked trousers and a windcheater.

Calvieri got to his feet and eyed the man with obvious contempt. 'Is this your boat?'

'Yeah. Why?' the man muttered in a distinctly American accent.

'I might have guessed. Only a foreigner would moor a boat here. We live down there. How do you expect us to get our boat past yours?'

'Where's your boat?' the man asked, looking round him.

'Moored illegally at the Riva del Carbon. Have some consideration, will you?'

The American had the grace to look apologetic. 'I'll get the keys,' he offered, then headed back towards his hotel.

'False alarm,' Calvieri said once the man was out of earshot.

'What's the address you were given?'

Calvieri took a slip of paper from his pocket. 'Calle Baglioni 17.'

They moved along the footpath beside the canal, until they reached the house. It was a red-brick building with black shutters covering the four windows and an *altana*, a wooden terrace, on the roof. He tried the door. It was locked. He glanced the length of the deserted pathway then took a set of skeleton keys from his pocket and unlocked the door on the fourth attempt. He pocketed the keys but Sabrina grabbed his arm before he could open the door.

'I'm the one with the gun, remember?'

She pushed open the door then pivoted around into the hallway, Beretta extended. Everything was covered in a thick layer of dust.

'Your contact was right about one thing. Nobody's lived here for years.'

'Including Ubrino,' Calvieri said, joining her in the hallway. 'A wild-goose chase.'

'Or a trap.'

They both heard the noise. It came from above. Sabrina led the way up the wooden staircase, wincing every time she stood on a creaky board. A bronze cross, tarnished from years of neglect, was mounted on the wall at the top of the stairs. Calvieri pointed to the door at the end of the corridor, which was ajar. Sabrina nodded, certain the noise had come from inside the room. She kicked open the door then dropped to one knee, the Beretta trained on the figure crouched in the corner. The boy was no older than ten and his eyes were wide with fear. She holstered the Beretta and crossed to where he was huddled against the wall.

'What's your name?' she asked softly in Italian.

'Marcello,' the boy replied, staring at Calvieri. 'Are you the police?'

'Ever seen a policeman with one of these?' Calvieri replied, flicking his ponytail.

Marcello shook his head. 'Are you from the orphanage?'

'No,' Sabrina replied. 'How long have you been here?'

Marcello shrugged. 'A week. Ten days. I don't know.'

'How do you live?' she asked.

'There are many tourists, even in March. I learned how to pick pockets at the orphanage.'

'How did you get up here?' Calvieri asked.

Marcello led them to a single window, opened it, and

pointed to the trellis against the side of the house. 'I never use any other part of the house. That way there's no footprints in the dust to give me away.'

'You've certainly got it all worked out,' Sabrina said.

'I don't want to go back to the orphanage. You won't tell them where I am, will you?'

'No,' Calvieri said before Sabrina could answer. 'Has anyone else been here in the last couple of days?'

'Nobody. You're the only people who know about my hideout.'

Calvieri ruffled Marcello's hair. 'Don't worry, your secret's safe with us.'

Sabrina took Calvieri out on to the landing and shut the door. 'How long do you think he'll last on the streets before the police pick him up?'

'A lot longer than you think. Give him a chance, Sabrina.'

'What chance has he got living like this? He'll probably have a police record before the year's out.'

'Have you stopped to think why he ran away from the orphanage? I know *Brigatisti* who grew up in orphanages and, much as I hate the law, I'd rather see him in a detention centre than having to put up with the abuse that they went through.'

'You're talking about isolated incidents. The vast majority of orphanages look after their children.'

'Are you so sure? And are you prepared to take that chance on his behalf?'

Her brow creased with concern. Taking out the Beretta again she completed the search, by climbing another set of stairs up to the *altana*. The bolt on the door at the top of the stairs had rusted with age. She struggled to draw it back, then pulling the door open, she stepped outside. It was covered with weeds. She checked to see if any of the weeds had been recently disturbed. None had.

Calvieri was waiting for her in the hall. 'Find anything?'

She shook her head and walked back outside on to the

canal path. Calvieri followed her, securing the front door behind him.

'So much for your contact,' she said contemptuously as they made their way back to the canal entrance.

'I'll be taking the matter up with him, you can be sure of that.'

The American had moved the speedboat from the mouth of the canal and was busy mooring it fifteen yards away when he saw them approaching. 'You can get through now!' he said, reaching for the mooring rope in the back of the boat.

Calvieri was about to reply when he saw the white speedboat dart out from behind a row of *vaporetti* moored at the Riva del Carbon. He couldn't make out the pilot's features but there was no mistaking the stumpy Uzi clenched in his right hand. He knocked Sabrina to the ground and flung himself after her seconds before a fusillade of bullets peppered the wall behind them. Sabrina was the first to her feet and ran to the blue and white speedboat.

'What the hell's going on?' the American hissed, staring after the retreating white speedboat.

'I'm taking your boat,' Sabrina said, jumping into the speedboat beside him.

'Like hell you are,' the American retorted, stepping in front of the wheel.

She glanced despairingly at the white speedboat. She had to catch it before it turned up one of the side canals. There was no time to lose. She unholstered her Beretta and levelled it at the American. 'Get out!'

'Jesus, you're crazy,' the American stammered in disbelief, his eyes riveted on the Beretta in her hand.

'Out!' she snapped.

The American swallowed nervously then scrambled up on to the jetty. She swung the speedboat round, and headed after the fleeing gunman. The Grand Canal was teeming with an assortment of craft at that time of the afternoon and the gunman used this to his advantage, weaving in and out of the traffic with the consummate ease of a seasoned helmsman. There were *vaporetti* and *motoscafi*, water taxis, packed with sightseers; *traghetti*, two-man gondolas, ferrying shoppers from one side of the canal to the other in search of bargains at the numerous waterside markets; barges laden with fresh produce destined for the luxury hotels; speed-boats of all shapes and sizes, careful to keep within the strictly enforced speed limits; and the full-size gondolas transporting the wealthy tourists to and from their hotels which lined both sides of the canal.

She lost sight of the white speedboat and cut across the bow of an approaching *vaporetto* – much to the anger of the helmsman who shook his fist at her – to see if the gunman was heading for the other side of the canal. He wasn't there. She slowed the speedboat to a crawl in order to take a closer look around her. Where the hell had the other boat gone? It had weaved between a couple of barges, then – nothing. She accelerated until she reached the spot where she thought it had disappeared. She looked right, then left. Nothing. She looked to her right again. There was another canal leading off from the Grand Canal about twenty yards further on. He could never have reached it in such a short time. Or could he? She slowed the speedboat on reaching the offshoot. The white speedboat wasn't there. She hailed a youth on the pathway who was unloading crates of fresh fruit from a barge and asked him whether a white speed-boat had passed him in the last couple of minutes. He crouched at the edge of the path, his eyes running the length of her body.

'Nice,' he muttered. 'Very nice.'

'Did you see a speedboat or not?' she asked angrily.

He scratched his head. 'Maybe. What's in it for me?'

'Forget it,' she snapped, turning back to the wheel.

Her path was blocked. The mooring rope holding the stern of the barge had been untied and the barge now stood at a forty-five-degree angle to the canal path. It would be impossible to squeeze the speedboat past it. Another youth appeared, holding a gaff. The first youth jumped into the speedboat but before she could react she felt the tip of a switchblade against her ribs.

'Switch off the engine,' he ordered. 'And don't try to reverse.'

She did as she was told.

'I'm sure you're armed,' he said with a sneer, then reached out a hand to search her.

She raised her hands then brought her elbow up sharply under his chin, rocking his head backwards. She twisted his arm savagely behind his back, disarmed him, then jerked his neck back and pressed the blade against his exposed throat. The second youth approached the speedboat cautiously.

'Throw it into the water,' she shouted, indicating the gaff in his hand.

He hesitated and she pressed the blade into the first youth's throat. A trickle of blood ran down the side of his neck.

'Do it, Antonio,' the first youth screamed.

Antonio threw the gaff into the water.

'Now move the barge,' she snapped.

Antonio nodded nervously and ran back to the barge.

She tightened her grip on the youth's hair and pressed the blade harder against his skin. Another trickle of blood seeped from the wound. 'I want some answers. And if I haven't got them by the time your friend's moved the barge I'm going to cut your throat. It might make him a little more cooperative.'

'What do you want to know?' the youth gasped.

'Who hired you?'

'I don't know his name.'

She dug the tip of the blade further into his skin.

'I don't know his name!' he screamed. 'Please believe me. He approached us in a bar last night and offered us each half a million lire to make sure he wasn't followed up here today. We were only to frighten you, that's all.'

'Me in particular?'

'No. Whoever followed him in here.'

'Describe him.'

'Tall. Suntanned. Collar-length black hair. And a mole on his right cheek.'

'Where does this canal lead to?'

'Back to the Grand Canal. It's U-shaped.'

Antonio had managed to manoeuvre the barge against the side of the canal. Sabrina pushed the youth away from her and he immediately scrambled back up on to the pathway. She started up the engine, dropped the switch-blade into the water and eased the speedboat past the barge. Suddenly she smelt petrol. A slick had formed on the water in front of the speedboat. And the pathway beyond the barge looked like it had been hosed down. A man appeared from behind a wall at the end of the path, his suntan and black hair corresponding exactly to the teenager's description. All Sabrina's senses were instantly alert. He acknowledged her with a faint smile and a slight inclination of his head. There was no sign of the Uzi. He was now holding two lighted sticks of rolled-up newspaper in his hands. Her first thought was to shoot him. But even if she were to hit him there was still a danger that the fuel would be ignited. And she wouldn't have time to escape the flames.

She slammed the speedboat into reverse. He tossed one of the sticks of newspaper into the water then dropped the other on to the canal path. A second later he had dis-appeared behind the wall. Flames shot towards the bow of the speedboat. She managed to reverse into the Grand Canal, escaping the fire by a matter of feet. The barge was ablaze within seconds. There was a piercing scream from behind the wall of flames. Sabrina felt completely helpless. There was nothing she could do to save the two youths who must have been caught in the fire.

As she turned her boat round she saw the white speed-boat shoot out from a side canal two hundred yards upriver. She unholstered her Beretta, opened the throttle, and gave chase. The white speedboat began to weave in and out of the congested traffic again but this time she kept on its tail. She heard sirens in the distance and looked round to see a patrol boat closing in on her. When she turned back to the wheel the white speedboat had disappeared. She cursed angrily at herself. Twice she had lost him.

As she passed a *vaporetto* the white speedboat shot out from its blind side and the gunman fired a short burst at her with the Uzi, forcing her to duck low as the bullets chewed across the bow. The tourists aboard the *vaporetto* screamed in terror and the helmsman immediately headed for the nearest landing stage. She raised the Beretta as the white speedboat drew abreast but it buffeted the side of her boat, causing her to fire wide. The gunman peeled away sharply and disappeared behind a passing *vaporetto*. By the time she had regained control of her boat the gunman had disappeared. She hit the dashboard angrily with her fist then glanced behind her at the patrol boat which was now less than a hundred yards away. Then she saw Calvieri signalling to her from a nearby wharf. She went to pick him up.

'Let me take the wheel,' he said, climbing into the boat beside her. 'I know my way around these waters and the first thing we have to do is dump the boat in one of the side canals.'

She gave a resigned nod and switched places with him.

'Are you all right?'

'Sure, apart from my pride.' She shook her head, disgusted with herself. 'I can't believe I let him get the better of me.'

'Come on, Sabrina, don't be so hard on yourself. You're only human—'

'And so is he,' she snapped. 'But why didn't he kill me when he had the chance?'

'I'd say he made a pretty good attempt back there,' Calvieri said, turning the speedboat up the Rio San Polo, one of the largest canals leading off from the Grand Canal.

'He could have shot me when he came out from behind the *vaporetto*. Instead he fired into the bow. It doesn't make sense.'

'You should just be glad you're still alive.' Calvieri moored the boat in a narrow canal off the Rio San Polo then pointed to a house with whitewashed walls at the end of the pathway. 'It belongs to a friend of mine. We can hide there until the police are gone.'

They scrambled up on to the side of the canal.

'Tonino?'

He looked round at her in surprise. It was the first time she had used his first name. 'Tony, please. The last person who called me Tonino was my headmaster.'

'Thanks,' she said softly.

'Strange, isn't it? This time I saved your life. Another time it might be me in that boat trying to kill you.'

'Or me trying to kill you,' she replied, holding his stare.

'Sure, why not?' He gave a nervous laugh, then walked towards the house.

*La Serenissima*. So much for the serenity. Venice would never again be the same for her.

# FIVE

Whitlock woke with a splitting headache. He opened his eyes and looked around him slowly. He was lying on a brown leather couch, a pillow under his head, in an aeroplane. A private aeroplane, judging by the plush furnishings. He tried to sit up but a bolt of pain shot through his head. Instead he lay back and massaged his temples gingerly with the tips of his fingers.

'Take these. We use them in the army.'

Whitlock saw a pair of black-gloved hands out of the corner of his eye. In one hand were two white tablets, in the other a glass of water. Young had worn black gloves. But the voice was different. Older, more distinguished. And, unlike Young's voice, it wasn't discernibly American. It had to be Wiseman. He took the tablets from the palm of the outstretched hand and put one of them into his mouth. It tasted bitter. The glass was put to his lips. He took a mouthful of water and washed the tablet down, followed by the second tablet with another gulp. He placed the glass on the floor and lay back against the pillow, his eyes closed.

It was another five minutes before he tried to sit up again. He lifted his head off the pillow, swung his legs off the couch then sat up and rubbed his eyes. He was beginning to feel human again.

'How's the head?'

Whitlock looked the length of the cabin at the man

seated a few feet away from the cockpit door. He recognized him as Richard Wiseman from the photograph Rust had included in the assignment dossier. The photograph showed him in the uniform of a three-star general. Now he was wearing a light grey suit, white shirt and blue tie. He looked to be in his mid-fifties with a rugged, weather-beaten face, a neatly trimmed black moustache and black hair going grey at the temples. Wiseman repeated the question without looking up from the game of solitaire he was playing.

Whitlock looked at his watch. He had been asleep for four hours. He crossed to the table and sat down opposite Wiseman. 'This has gone far enough. I demand to know what's going on.'

Wiseman nodded as he studied the cards in front of him, and finally sat back, resting his elbows on the arms of the chair. 'What do you want to know?'

'For a start, who are you?'

Wiseman told him.

'Where the hell are we?'

'In my private jet, about thirty-five thousand feet over France. ETA in Rome is twenty-five minutes.'

'Rome?' Whitlock replied, feigning bewilderment. 'Why are you taking me there?'

Wiseman was about to answer when the bathroom door opened at the other end of the cabin. His eyes flickered past Whitlock and he smiled at the approaching figure. 'Back to your old self again, I see. Mr Alexander, you've met Vic Young.'

Whitlock's eyes widened in surprise when he saw Young. The black hair and moustache were gone. Now he was blond and clean shaven.

'I was wearing a wig,' Young said, running his fingers through his thick blond hair. He crossed to the drinks cabinet, poured out two measures of bourbon, and handed one of the glasses to Wiseman. 'What you are drinking, Alexander?'

'Nothing,' Whitlock retorted, eyeing Young coldly. 'Where are the woman and the boy?'

Young shrugged. 'I left them in the police car. They were only drugged.'

'You killed Dave—'

'He knew too much,' Young cut in quickly.

Whitlock shook his head as if in despair. 'I would have got five years, maximum, for the job I did. I'd have been out in three. Now I'm facing a fifteen-year stretch as an accessory to murder.'

Young picked up a card from the floor, dropped it on to the table, then sat down. 'You'll be facing a murder rap if the police find the gun.'

'What are you talking about?' Whitlock said in amazement. 'Murder? I didn't kill him.'

'Didn't you?' Young replied. 'There's only one set of fingerprints on the gun. Yours.'

'That's ridiculous, you pulled the trigger.'

'But I was wearing gloves, remember? I put your prints on the gun while you were unconscious.'

'Where's the gun now?'

'Safe,' Young replied.

'Call it an insurance policy,' Wiseman said.

Young smiled at Wiseman's choice of phrase.

'Insurance against what?' Whitlock asked suspiciously.

'You running out on us before the two of you have finished what you're going to Rome to do,' Wiseman answered.

'Then, when it's over, you hand the gun over to the police?'

'On the contrary. It'll be handed over to you, along with a hundred thousand pounds in cash.'

'And you honestly expect me to believe that?'

'I don't see why not,' Wiseman said, shrugging his shoulders. 'You won't be able to tie Vic in with Humphries' death. He's got half a dozen witnesses lined up who'd swear, in court if necessary, that he was with them in another country at the time of the shooting. I admit I was in London this morning. At the Court of St James. The American Ambassador and I go back a long way.'

'You've got it all worked out, haven't you?' Whitlock said. 'So whatever way you look at it, I've been set up to take the fall.'

'Not if you're smart and do as you're told,' Wiseman replied.

'So why exactly are we going to Rome?' Whitlock asked at length.

'To find my brother's killer,' Wiseman said.

'To find him, or to kill him?'

'It amounts to the same thing,' Wiseman said.

'It gets better by the minute. I suppose my prints will be found on that murder weapon as well?'

'Officially, neither of you is in Italy. You'll both be travelling on false passports. Vic, get his passport.'

Young crossed to an attaché case, took out a passport, and tossed it on to the table in front of Whitlock.

Whitlock picked it up. 'Raymond Anderson?' He opened it and saw the space for the photograph.

'We'll take a Polaroid of you in a moment,' Wiseman said with a shrug, then gestured to Young. 'Vic's travelling as Vincent Yardley. Remember the name.'

'What about you?' Whitlock asked Wiseman.

'I'm going to Rome to collect my brother's body. And that's not a cover story.'

'What happened to him?'

Wiseman picked up a folder from the floor beside his chair and handed it to Whitlock. 'It's all in there. Newspaper clippings, American mostly.'

Whitlock opened the folder. He had already seen many of the clippings, which had been included in his dossier. He leafed through them, pausing occasionally to read something that caught his eye. 'Why did the Red Brigades shoot him?'

'That's what I want to find out,' Wiseman replied, his jaw hardening. 'He'd never harmed anyone in his life. All he cared about was his work. I could have understood it if they had come after me. A decorated soldier with strong NATO connections. I know I'm a target in their eyes. But why David? What really got to me was that the bastards actually gloated about it publicly. That was a mistake. A big mistake.'

Whitlock closed the folder and handed it back to Wiseman. 'I'm sorry about your brother. But I don't see where I fit in.'

'You were recommended to me as the best wheelman either side of the Atlantic,' Wiseman said. 'Vic may need you for a fast getaway. It all depends on where and when the hits take place.'

'Hits? You said your brother's killer, not killers. How many hits are there going to be?'

'Two at least. The gunman, and the person who authorized the killing. And if it turns out that others are involved, they too will be targeted. I want justice, Mr Alexander, no matter what it takes.'

'Why this personal vendetta? Why don't you leave it to the police and let them bring the killers in?'

'I'm a soldier, Mr Alexander. The Red Brigades are the enemy. And I've been taught to kill the enemy.'

'So why don't you, instead of hiring us to do your dirty work for you?' Whitlock's expression was challenging.

Wiseman removed his gloves and held up his hands. Both index fingers were missing. 'The Vietcong cut them off in '69 when they found out I was a sniper. I was one of the lucky ones. I'm still alive. I've had several rifles made for me since then, all with the trigger housed in the butt. They're no substitute for the real thing, though. I only use them for game shooting now. If I don't kill a deer with my first shot I can always rely on a second shot to finish it off. It would be another matter if I could only wound a human target, especially one that was armed. It's not that I'm scared of dying, Mr Alexander, I just want to be sure that the job's done properly. That's why I chose the two of you. Vic was in my platoon in Vietnam. He's still one of the best snipers in the business. And as I said earlier, you're regarded as the best wheelman around. I don't see how the two of you can fail.'

'It's decision time, Alexander. Are you in or out?'

'I didn't realize I had a choice,' Whitlock countered sarcastically.

'It's very simple,' Young said. 'If you're in, you'll be paid forty thousand pounds up front. If you're out, the door's behind you.'

'That's some choice. I'm in, for what it's worth.'

'Excellent,' Wiseman said. He removed an envelope from his pocket and handed it to Whitlock. 'Twenty thousand pounds sterling. You'll be paid the balance on completion of the job.' He noticed the uncertainty in Whitlock's eyes. 'One thing you'll learn about me, Mr Alexander, is that I never renege on a business deal. I pride myself on my honesty. You'll be paid, in full, when it's over.'

Whitlock opened the envelope and looked inside. The money was in used fifty-pound notes.

Young took an eight-inch oblong box from his inside jacket pocket and placed it on the table in front of Whitlock. 'Open it.'

Whitlock picked up the box and removed the lid. Inside was a watch lying on a bed of cotton wool. He took it out, turned it around in his fingers, then looked up questioningly at Young.

'Put it on,' Young said.

'Why? I've already got a watch.'

'Put it on,' Young repeated.

'What's the catch?'

'It's another little insurance policy against you running out on me now that you've got the money,' Young told him. 'It has a small homing device built into it. I have the receiver in my pocket.'

'In other words, I'm being tagged?'

'As a precaution, that's all,' Wiseman said. 'Forty thousand pounds is a lot of money, Mr Alexander. We don't want you to be tempted into doing something you'll regret.'

'And if I refuse?'

Young smiled. 'Then the gun will be left in a convenient place for the police to find. And you'll be handed over to the authorities when we reach Rome. A stowaway.'

Whitlock unstrapped his own watch and snapped the other watch over his wrist.

Young took a miniature black transmitter from his jacket pocket and placed it on the table. 'The back of the watch has been packed with a highly concentrated plastic explosive. It works in conjunction with the transmitter. It can be triggered in three different ways. Firstly, by attempting to remove the watch from your wrist. Secondly, if the button on the transmitter is depressed. And thirdly, if the watch and the transmitter are ever more than three miles apart. The charge is certainly big enough to blow off part of your arm. Potentially it could kill you, depending on where your wrist was at the time of the explosion.'

'I don't believe this . . .' Whitlock trailed off, his eyes blazing.

'I can understand your resentment, Mr Alexander—'

'No you can't,' Whitlock interceded angrily. 'You can't begin to understand it. I've been abducted, drugged, framed, threatened and now tricked into wearing some booby-trapped wristwatch. I've agreed to go along with you – what more do you want from me? If you want me to drive for you, Young, you neutralize this device first.'

Young shook his head. 'It stays on until this is over. And as I'm the one who set the charge, I'm the only one who knows how to neutralize it. You're stuck with it, Alexander. At least for the time being.'

'And you go along with that?' Whitlock asked Wiseman.

Wiseman nodded. 'If that's what Vic wants. It's his operation, he calls the shots. I'll merely be an observer, that's all.'

'I don't trust you, Alexander. But at least this way I know I can depend on you to be where I want you when I want you. Unless, of course, you're willing to lose your arm for the sake of forty thousand pounds. Personally I credit you with a bit more intelligence than that.'

The pilot's voice came over the intercom asking them to fasten their seatbelts as he was about to start the final descent into Rome.

Whitlock snapped the belt shut across him then stared at the watch. They had him exactly where they wanted him. At least for the time being . . .

Philpott answered the telephone on his desk.

'I've got a Major Lonsdale from Scotland Yard's anti-terrorist squad on the line, sir,' Sarah told him.

'Put him through.'

She connected them, then replaced her receiver.

'Colonel Philpott?'

'Speaking. I've been expecting a call from you for the past two hours. What happened? Did C.W. get away all right?'

'That all went fine. He should be touching down in Rome about now.'

'So why the delay?' Philpott asked.

Lonsdale explained what had happened, including the discovery of Humphries' body by the local CID in Stoke Newington.

'Are the boy and his mother all right?' Philpott asked anxiously.

'They're both fine.'

'Why did Young pick them?'

'Harris knows the boy's father, Wendell Johnson—'

'Who's Harris?' Philpott cut in.

'He was the other man Young hired to help him spring Alexander.'

'The one you picked up yesterday?'

'That's right,' Lonsdale replied. 'It seems Young wanted a hostage to force the police guards to release Alexander. But he knew abducting someone in the street would be too dangerous. That's when Harris came up with Mary Robson and her boy.'

'Did Harris tell you this?'

'Yes.'

'How did Young get hold of the police car and the uniforms?'

'He hired the uniforms from a theatrical company. He made a bogus call to the police to lure the police car on to a housing estate in Lambeth. The two of them overpowered the driver and left him tied up in an empty flat on the estate. Whitlock was sprung half an hour later.'

'How did they get C.W. on to the plane?'

'Wiseman's private Lear jet was parked at an American airbase. The sentry on duty at the gate is certain there were only two men in Wiseman's official car when it arrived at the base. Wiseman and the driver.'

'Who must have been Young?'

'The description certainly matches the American who helped spring Whitlock from the police van. We didn't push it any further in case word got back to Wiseman. The logical conclusion is that Whitlock was in the boot, unconscious, when the car arrived at the base.'

'I appreciate your help, Major Lonsdale.'

'Not at all.'

'I'll call you to tell you when you can release Alexander back into the custody of the police.'

'Fine. We'll keep him entertained until then.'

Philpott hung up, then asked Sarah to get him Kolchinsky's hotel in Rome.

\* \* \*

Paluzzi had called Nikki Karos from Rome to find out whether he would be able to see them that afternoon. He had refused to elaborate further over the telephone and Karos had told him they were welcome to fly to the island to see him, though he doubted he would be of much assistance to them.

They had flown in a *NOCS* Cessna as far as the capital, Corfu, where they had transferred to an Alouette helicopter and completed the twelve miles to Karos's mansion on the slopes of Mount Aji Deka, arriving mid-afternoon.

Marco executed a perfect landing within a few feet of the white Mercedes parked on the edge of the helipad. The driver stood beside it, a holstered Bernadelli visible on his belt. Graham and Paluzzi alighted from the helicopter. The driver took their Berettas, saying they would be returned when they left the island. He ushered them into the car, then got behind the wheel and drove the five hundred yards to the Spanish-style mansion which was set against the side of the mountain and supported by four thick concrete pylons driven down forty feet into the base of the rock. A butler, complete with white gloves, accompanied them to a glass-walled lift which ran up the end wall of the building. He pressed a button and they were transported to the roof. The doors opened on to a spacious terrace dominated by an Olympic-size swimming pool. The butler retreated to bring drinks, and they crossed to a railing which ran the length of the terrace to examine the breathtaking view. The village and the tranquil Khalikiopoulos Lagoon stood in the foreground, with Mount Pandokrator, the island's highest mountain, and the rugged Albanian ranges in the distance. It all seemed very peaceful.

Graham moved to the swimming pool and tested the water with his fingertips. It was warm. Then, as he stood up, he noticed the row of glass tanks built into the wall to the left of the lift. Each of the six tanks contained a pair of snakes. A plaque attached to each tank identified the species:

Bushmaster, Eastern Diamondback Rattlesnake, Green Mamba, Gabon Viper, King Cobra and Saw-scaled Adder. Six of the most deadly species known to man.

'Beautiful, aren't they?'

Graham swung round to face the man who had emerged silently from the lift behind him. He was in his fifties with a large nose prominent in an asymmetrical face. He was dressed in a white suit with a panama tugged over his grey hair.

'Karos. Nikki Karos,' the man said, extending a hand towards Graham. 'Paluzzi?'

'Graham. State Department.'

'Ah, the American,' Karos replied, shaking Graham's hand.

Paluzzi crossed to where they were standing and shook Karos's hand.

'The great survivors,' Karos said, looking at the snakes. 'Reptiles have been on this earth, in one form or another, for three hundred million years. From them came the dinosaur, the ichthyosaur, the plesiosaur and all the rest of those magnificent prehistoric creatures. From those proto-types came the mammals and the birds. And when man does finally destroy himself, the reptiles will still be here to start the evolutionary process all over again.'

'Why snakes? Why not crocodiles or lizards?'

'Where's the beauty in the lumbering crocodile, Mr Graham? Or the scurrying lizard? There is, however, immense beauty in the snake. The sleek, streamlined body. The speed with which it strikes its prey. I sit out here for hours watching them.' Karos smiled. 'I'm sorry, I know you didn't come all this way to discuss snakes. Please, won't you sit down.'

They crossed to a table beside the pool and each took a chair. It was pleasantly warm in the thin March sun. The butler returned with a tray and deposited their drinks on the table, along with a plate of *loukanika*, small spicy sausages. It was only when Graham glanced after his retreating figure that he saw a second man standing by the lift, his arms folded across his chest. He was black and a muscular six-foot-five, with a shaven head and a gold sleeper in his left ear. He reminded Graham of an extra from one of Errol Flynn's buccaneering films.

Karos followed Graham's eyes. 'Don't worry about Boudien. He's been my personal bodyguard for the past five years. He's an Algerian. He doesn't say much, but when he does speak, people tend to listen to him.'

'I'm not surprised,' Graham replied, then drank a mouthful of the cordial the butler had brought for him.

'Well, gentlemen, what can I do for you? I must say I'm a little intrigued as to why the State Department should send someone out here to see me. I have no business interests in your country, Mr Graham.'

'It's got nothing to do with my country. What can you tell us about Vittore Dragotti?'

Graham and Paluzzi watched Karos closely, hoping to see a flicker of recognition in his eyes. There was nothing. Not that it surprised them. Karos was very much the professional.

Karos took a sip of his iced tea then shook his head. 'Sorry, I can't say I know the name.'

Paluzzi then put into action the plan they had devised on the plane. He took the bank statements from his jacket pocket and extended them towards Karos. 'These were found in Dragotti's wallsafe. Four of the payments have been traced to you. Perhaps you can explain that?'

Frowning, Karos took the statements from Paluzzi and laid them out neatly on the table in front of him. He removed a pair of reading glasses from his pocket and slipped them on. Having studied the entries Paluzzi had marked in red, he looked up and shrugged. 'It's certainly a mystery to me. I've never done any business with him. Am I allowed to know what he does, or where he works?'

'He's the sales manager at Neo-Chem Industries in Rome,' Paluzzi said.

'Neo-Chem? That's the pharmaceutical company.' Karos smiled faintly. 'We're hardly in the same line of business, are we? All I can suggest is that one of my associates has been doing some business with him—'

'You can cut the act, Karos,' Paluzzi snapped. 'I know for a fact that no payment is authorized without your signature. If one of your associates had been doing business with him, you'd have known about it.'

'Come on, Fabio, stop treating the guy with kid gloves,' Graham said, bringing the next bit of the plan into play. 'Why waste time? Tell him that Dragotti's confessed.'

'Let me handle it my way, okay?' Paluzzi retorted.

Graham turned to Karos. 'Let's cut the crap. We've already seen Dragotti this morning. He agreed to co-operate with us in return for a shorter sentence. He's admitted being the middleman between you and Wiseman. How do you think we got hold of those bank statements?'

A drop of sweat ran down the side of Karos's face. He wiped it away quickly then looked round at the approaching Boudien who had been alerted by the raised voices. He shook his head and waved him away.

'We've got the confession all neatly documented back in Rome,' Graham said. 'It's enough to put you away for twenty years.'

'I'll make a deal with you,' Karos said, once Boudien had disappeared into the lift.

'You're in no position to make deals, Karos,' Graham retorted.

'I can't go to jail, I've got too many enemies there.'

'You should have thought about that before you got involved,' Graham said.

Karos crossed to the railing and looked across the Khalikiopoulos Lagoon. 'I'll take you to Ubrino. In return you give me a twelve-hour head start once the vial's been recovered. It's a small price to pay with so much at stake.'

Graham looked at Paluzzi. 'What do you think?'

Paluzzi stared at his empty glass and finally nodded. He looked at Karos. 'It's a deal. When can you take us to him?'

'Tonight. I'm meeting him outside Sant'Ivo in Rome at eight o'clock.'

'And he'll have the vial with him?' Paluzzi asked, making notes on the pad he had taken from his pocket.

'I can only presume so. He was told never to let it out of his sight.'

'You know this place?' Graham asked Paluzzi.

Paluzzi nodded. 'It's a church near the Pantheon.'

'Why are you meeting him there?'

Karos shrugged. 'He was the one who called the meeting. He just said it was important and for me to meet him there.'

Graham eyed Karos suspiciously, then pointed a finger of warning at him. 'You'd better be on the level because if you're leading us on a wild-goose chase you'll be in jail so quickly your feet won't touch the ground.'

'Why should I deceive you? I've got nothing to gain by it. Not now.'

'Who are you working for?' Paluzzi asked, breaking the silence.

'I'm not working for anybody, I'm working *with* Lino Zocchi, head of the Rome cell of the Red Brigades.'

'Why did he come to you?' Paluzzi asked.

'Because he knew the committee wouldn't sanction the operation. And he needed money to finance it. I had the capital.'

'How much was Wiseman paid altogether?' Graham asked.

'A hundred thousand dollars. Chicken feed, really, when you think about what he created. That virus is priceless. Priceless.'

'Whose idea was the sleeping gas?' Paluzzi asked.

'Zocchi's. It was a diversion, nothing more.'

'So Ubrino knows he's got the virus?' Paluzzi said.

'Of course he does. As I said, the sleeping gas was just a red herring.'

'What are you going to get out of this?' Paluzzi asked.

'Twenty million pounds sterling.'

Graham whistled softly. 'Did Zocchi say how he intended to get the money?'

Karos shook his head, then noticed the forty-foot white Gazelle helicopter crossing the lagoon towards the house.

'Are you going to admire the scenery all day?' Graham snapped.

Karos turned to him. 'No, he never said. I just presumed it would be some kind of deal which included his release as well as a sum of money in return for the vial.'

Graham's eyes flickered past Karos. The helicopter was closing in fast. Too fast. Then he saw the two 30 mm cannons mounted on either side of the fuselage. There wasn't even time to shout a warning. He lashed out sideways, knocking Paluzzi and his chair backwards into the swimming pool. He flung himself into the water as the machine-guns opened fire. Karos's body jerked grotesquely and blood spurted from the bullet holes in his immaculate white jacket. He stumbled against the railing, then disappeared over the side. The pilot raked the terrace for another few seconds then banked the helicopter sharply to the left and headed back towards the capital, Corfu.

Graham and Paluzzi held their breath underwater for another ten seconds after the firing had stopped, then swam across the pool to the safety of the steps, where they surfaced, gasping for air. Graham was the first out of the pool and he ran straight to the railing. Paluzzi was close behind him. Karos lay sprawled on the rocks eighty feet below them, his white jacket startling against the grey of the stone. Paluzzi cursed furiously in Italian, then wiped his hand over his face. There was blood on his fingers.

Graham noticed his frown and gestured to his bleeding lip. 'I didn't exactly have time to choose my spot.'

Paluzzi patted Graham lightly on the arm. 'I owe you my life.'

'Forget it,' Graham replied, stripping off his wet shirt. 'You don't owe me anything.'

Boudien emerged from the lift followed by two guards. Both were armed with Spectre sub-machine-guns. They ran to the railing and peered down at Karos on the rocks below. The two guards, glancing repeatedly at Graham and Paluzzi, spoke softly to Boudien.

'They think we set him up,' Paluzzi said, interpreting the Greek for Graham.

Boudien turned to Paluzzi. 'Did you see what kind of helicopter it was?'

'No,' Paluzzi lied. 'All I saw was that it was white with a single figure at the controls.'

'Did you see his face?' Boudien asked.

'You must be joking,' Paluzzi said incredulously. 'A second later I was underwater.'

Boudien gripped the railing tightly and stared out across the Khalikiopoulos Lagoon.

'Who do you think did it?' Paluzzi asked, casting a side-long glance at him.

'Signore Karos had many enemies. It could have been set up by any one of them.'

'How about Lino Zocchi?' Paluzzi asked, watching for a reaction.

Boudien's face remained impassive. 'I don't know him. Signore Karos never discussed his work with me.' He suddenly eyed Paluzzi suspiciously. 'Is that why you and the American came here, to ask Signore Karos about this man Zocchi?'

'He did come into the conversation.'

'The police will be here shortly,' Boudien said. 'You can tell them about it. You can also tell them how the two of you managed to come out of all this unscathed.'

'You think *we* had something to do with Karos's murder?' Paluzzi demanded.

'That's for the police to decide. The two guards will stay here. They have orders to shoot if either of you attempts to escape.'

Paluzzi watched Boudien return to the lift, then turned to Graham and told him what was happening.

'And there is only one way out of here,' Graham said, glancing at the lift.

'Angelo should have heard the gunfire from the helicopter.'

'What can he do?'

'There's a rope ladder attached to the side of the passenger seat. If he dropped it we could conceivably grab hold of it as the helicopter passed overhead. I know it's a long shot but it's our only real chance.'

Graham looked at his watch. 'It's 4.17. We'll give him until 4.20. No longer. Then we'll have to take our chances with the lift. We have to be out of here before the cops arrive, especially if they are already in Karos's back pocket.'

'What about the guards? We'd be dead before we got anywhere near the lift.'

'We'd be dead before we got anywhere near the rope ladder as well. We've got to take them out, whatever happens.' Graham shaded his eyes as he looked up at the approaching helicopter. 'Looks like the cavalry's just arrived.'

Paluzzi followed his gaze. 'What about the guards?'

'Let them come to us. They're bound to be suspicious of the helicopter. You take the short one on the left. I'll take his friend.'

The guards moved towards them. The short guard gestured for them to move away from the railing. Paluzzi and Graham stepped back, their hands raised above their heads. The second guard crossed to the railing, the Spectre gripped in both hands, waiting for the helicopter to come into firing range. The lift began to descend from the terraces.

Boudien had seen the helicopter and was sending up more guards to deal with it. Graham and Paluzzi exchanged glances. There was no time to lose. Paluzzi lunged at the short guard, parrying the Spectre with his left arm, and brought his knee up savagely into the guard's groin. The Spectre slipped from his fingers. Graham picked it up and shot the second guard even as he turned, gun raised, to fire. Paluzzi grabbed the second Spectre and turned towards the lift, waiting for the other guards to arrive.

The helicopter banked slowly two hundred yards from the terrace then dived towards them, the rope ladder hanging from the passenger door.

'You go first,' Graham shouted above the noise of the helicopter's rotors.

Paluzzi shook his head. 'I owe you—'

'You don't owe me anything,' Graham snapped back. 'Go first, no arguments.'

Paluzzi nodded, his eyes darting between the lift and the helicopter. The thirty-foot ladder brushed the railing and trailed across the terrace towards them. Paluzzi grabbed hold of one of the rungs halfway up with his left hand, the Spectre still clenched tightly in his right. The helicopter began to climb, lifting Paluzzi away from the terrace. Graham fired a burst at the lift as it came into view then jumped up to grab the last rung of the ladder as the helicopter rose away and started to turn towards the lagoon. The Spectre spun from his hand and he was flung against the railing. He caught the side of his head on one of the metal struts before he was pulled up over the railing into the air.

Two guards sprinted from the lift and fired at the retreating helicopter but within seconds it was out of range, leaving them cursing at the railing.

Blood streamed down the side of Graham's face and he had to use all his willpower to stave off the unconsciousness that threatened to overpower him. His left hand slipped and for one terrifying moment all that prevented him from falling the three hundred feet down on to the rocks below was the strength of his right hand on the last rung of the ladder. His body swung precariously from side to side and his head was shaken violently. With a supreme effort he reached up with his left hand and clamped it around the bottom rung again. He tried to pull himself up but it was no good, he just didn't have the energy. He closed his eyes, hoping that might stop his head spinning. It only seemed to make it worse. His fingers were slipping on the ladder. He gritted his teeth and dug his fingers into the rope. It was no good. He was going to fall. His left hand began to slip from the ladder again. As it did a hand clasped his left wrist. He lifted his head painfully and saw Paluzzi above him. Paluzzi was shouting to him. He couldn't hear what he was saying. He gripped more tightly with his right hand and closed his eyes, the pain now unbearable in his head. He felt himself drifting into unconsciousness. His feet touched water. Then his ankles. Then his legs. He opened his eyes. He was being dragged through the water. Paluzzi shook Graham's wrist and mouthed the word 'jump'. Graham let himself fall backwards into the sea. Paluzzi dived in after him. He grabbed Graham under the arms to prevent his head from dipping under the water. Graham opened his mouth to speak, then sagged forward, unconscious, against Paluzzi.

The *NOCS* headquarters in Rome was a large grey building on the via Po, close to the grounds of the West German consulate. It was officially listed as an archive for the Ministry of Defence.

Paluzzi and Marco entered the building through the revolving door in the main entrance and walked to an unmarked door at the end of the long, cavernous hallway. They went inside and Paluzzi locked the door behind them. The room was lined with rows of shelving stacked with cardboard boxes full of old files and dossiers. They crossed to the far wall and Marco activated the façade with a transmitter he had unclipped from his belt. The wall slid back to reveal a soundproof metal door. Marco punched an access code into the bellpush and the door slid open revealing a blue-carpeted corridor. He closed it again behind them, using a second combination which caused the outside wall to slide back into place as well. Paluzzi sent Marco to the computer suite to get a background on Boudien, then went to his office and listened to the messages on his answering machine. One was from Brigadier Michele Pesco, the unit's commander-in-chief, requesting that he report to his office as soon as he arrived. Paluzzi switched the machine off and went straight to Pesco's office.

Pesco was a tall man in his mid-forties whose cropped black hair surmounted cold blue eyes. He had been with the *Brigate Cadore*, one of the Italian army's five crack Alpine brigades, before his promotion to the *NOCS* to take over from his predecessor who had been killed while on a training exercise in the mountains of Sicily. His appointment had caused a lot of resentment among the men who had wanted, and expected, Paluzzi to get the post. Pesco had been in the job for three months and was still treated as an intrusive outsider. He and Paluzzi had never got on. Paluzzi resented Pesco's appointment, especially as his new superior had no previous experience with the *NOCS*. And Pesco resented Paluzzi's popularity with the men. They only spoke to each other when necessary. It was a problem known to Italy's joint chiefs-of-staff but they couldn't decide which of them to have transferred to another unit. And neither man was prepared to back down first. It had become a matter of pride.

Paluzzi knocked on Pesco's open door and entered the room. Pesco was smoking his customary cigar, the thick smoke drifting up into the extractor fan on the wall behind him. The two men acknowledged each other with a curt nod then Paluzzi turned to smile at Kolchinsky and Sabrina who were seated on the couch against the wall.

'Where's Mike?' Sabrina asked.

'He's at the San Giovanni Hospital,' Paluzzi replied and immediately raised a hand to allay her anxiety. 'He's okay, don't worry.'

'What happened?' Kolchinsky asked.

Paluzzi recounted the events briefly, culminating in their rescue from the sea by a coastguard helicopter answering Marco's mayday call.

'How bad is the wound?' she asked, the anxiety still on her face.

'He needed fourteen stitches. The doctors were more worried that the blow could have damaged his eyesight but they gave him the all-clear after a series of tests. They want him to remain in hospital overnight, just as a precaution. He wasn't too happy about that.'

'Well, he can just stay there,' Kolchinsky said, and looked at his watch. 'It's gone six-thirty. How long will it take us to get to Sant'Ivo from here?'

'It's about a ten-minute drive,' Paluzzi replied.

'I'll go with Major Paluzzi,' Sabrina offered.

'No you won't,' Kolchinsky replied firmly. 'You're working with Calvieri. I want you at the hotel where you can keep an eye on him. I'll go with the Major.'

Sabrina sat back glumly and folded her arms across her chest.

Pesco stubbed out his cigar and got to his feet. 'Mr Kolchinsky, I'll leave you in Fabio's capable hands. I have a meeting with the joint chiefs-of-staff at eight-thirty.'

Kolchinsky stood up and shook Pesco's hand. 'Thank you for your time, Brigadier.'

'Glad to be of help.' Pesco smiled at Sabrina. 'A pleasure meeting you, Miss Carver.'

She smiled back.

Pesco acknowledged Paluzzi with another nod and left the room.

'I presume from that show of affection there's little love

lost between the two of you,' Sabrina said, looking at Paluzzi.

'Sabrina, that's enough!' Kolchinsky chided her sharply.

'It's no secret,' Paluzzi told them. 'He's about as popular here as a pit viper in a rabbit hutch. He's never tried to fit in with the rest of us. Giuseppe Camerallo, his predecessor, was an inspiration to us. He led by example. He wouldn't expect us to do anything he wasn't prepared to do himself. Pesco hasn't even been on a training exercise with us yet. He's a desk man. The men don't want that. They want another Camerallo.'

'So why was he sent here?' Sabrina asked.

'Because he's a desk man. Paperwork was Camerallo's weakness. The auditors found the books in a total shambles when they came here after his death. That's why the top brass sent us Pesco. I was put in charge of field operations so it was only natural that the men looked to me as their new leader. Pesco can't accept that. He wants that respect himself. But he won't get it by sitting behind a desk all day. That's why he resents me so much.' Paluzzi sat on the edge of the desk. 'How was the trip to Venice?'

Sabrina told him what had happened.

'Have you identified the man who fired at you?'

'Brigadier Pesco sent my description of the man through to the computer suite ten minutes ago. There hasn't been any feedback yet.'

Paluzzi was about to ring through when Marco apeared at the door, a folder in his hand.

'I've got the information you wanted on Boudien. He seems—' Marco paused when he noticed Kolchinsky and Sabrina. 'Sorry, sir. I didn't realize you had company.'

'Come in, Angelo,' Paluzzi said, beckoning him into the room. 'This is Sergei Kolchinsky, deputy director at UNACO, and Sabrina Carver, Mike's partner. Lieutenant Angelo Marco, my right-hand man.'

Marco shook hands with them, then handed the folder to Paluzzi.

'Do me a favour, Angelo, see what's happened to the description Miss Carver sent through to be analysed in the identograph. It doesn't take ten minutes to come up with a name.'

Marco nodded and left the room.

Paluzzi tapped the folder. 'This is the info on Philippe Boudien, Karos's personal bodyguard. I'll have copies of it made for you before you leave.'

'Is he under surveillance?' Kolchinsky asked.

'Twenty-four-hour surveillance. And the phone line's been tapped. So far nothing.' Paluzzi moved round to Pesco's chair and sat down. 'Any news from your other operative? Whitlock, is it?'

Kolchinsky lit a cigarette and nodded. 'I got a call from him this afternoon. He and Young have booked into a boarding house in the city. Wiseman's staying at the Hassler-Villa Medici.'

Paluzzi whistled softly. 'He must have money to blow. That's one of the most expensive hotels in Rome.'

'His ex-wife inherited the Whiting shipyard outside New York. She sold it five years ago for close on a hundred million dollars. He got to keep the Lear jet, the ranch in Colorado and an estimated ten million when they were divorced last year.'

'Ten million and he's still drawing an army salary? I certainly wouldn't be slogging my guts out for the state if I had that kind of money in the bank.'

'The money isn't important to him. He's a soldier, first and foremost. And a good one, by all accounts.'

The telephone rang. Paluzzi answered it and punched a code into Pesco's desk computer as he listened to what Marco was saying.

'Any luck?' Sabrina asked once Paluzzi had replaced the receiver.

Paluzzi nodded then pressed a 'print' button on the console. A facsimile of the two faces on the screen slid out from a narrow aperture in the side of the computer. He handed it to Sabrina.

'That's him all right,' she announced, handing the facsimile to Kolchinsky. 'But why two pictures?'

'Identical twins,' Paluzzi said. 'One has a mole on his right cheek. The other doesn't. That's the only way of telling them apart.'

Sabrina sat down beside Kolchinsky and looked at the facsimile again. 'You're right. It's uncanny.'

'Do you know which one you saw in Venice?' Paluzzi asked.

'The one with the mole on his cheek. I won't forget him in a hurry. Who are they?'

'Carlo and Tommaso Francia.'

'Who's who?' she asked.

'Carlo's the one you saw in Venice.' Paluzzi stared at the VDU. 'Which means Tommaso was the one in Corfu.'

'I thought you said you didn't see his face,' Kolchinsky said.

'I didn't, but they always work on the same assignments.'

'What does it say about them?' Kolchinsky asked, gesturing to the VDU.

Paluzzi pressed another button and the text came up on the screen. He read it through, translating it into English in his head. He finally looked up at them. 'They were born in Salerno in 1956 and orphaned at an early age. Both excelled as sportsmen and by their teens they were skiing in professional tournaments. Carlo specialized in downhill racing, Tommaso in the slalom. They were chosen for the Italian team for the '76 Winter Olympics but both failed a drugs test on the day before they were due to compete. The FIS banned them for life. They worked as stuntmen for a time before drifting into crime in their late twenties. They now work as freelance enforcers in Italy and Greece.'

'Have you ever come across them?' Kolchinsky asked.

'Not personally, but I know of them.'

'Do they have any sympathies with the Red Brigades?'

'Their sympathies lie with whoever's paying them, Miss Carver. And they don't come cheap. They can afford to name their price. They're probably the best freelance team in the Mediterranean.'

'It's pretty ironic, isn't it?' Sabrina said thoughtfully. 'Karos financed his own death.'

'It certainly looks that way,' Paluzzi replied.

'What about their present whereabouts?' Kolchinsky asked.

'Unknown. They're nomadic. They do have a summer villa at Frezene, a beach resort about twelve miles from here, but neither of them has been seen there in the last year. Naturally I'll have it staked out but I don't see us coming up with anything. We're dealing with professionals.'

'What about the helicopter?' Kolchinsky asked. 'That could be a clue in itself. A white Gazelle with mounted 30 mm cannons. You don't see them every day.'

'I've already got a team working on that but I doubt we'll come up with anything there either. They could have hidden it anywhere.'

'It's hardly the easiest of things to conceal,' Kolchinsky said.

'I agree, but where do we start looking? Italy? Greece? Corfu? Sardinia? Sicily? The list's endless and we don't have the time.'

'Unless, of course, we manage to recover the vial tonight,' Kolchinsky said optimistically.

'Don't hold your breath,' Paluzzi replied. 'This operation's been planned down to the last detail. You can be sure that Ubrino won't venture out into the open unless he knows it's safe.'

'You think it's a trap?' Kolchinsky asked.

'I didn't initially when Karos told us about the meeting.

106

He would have been with us and it would have been too dangerous to hit Mike and me without endangering his own life. It was only after his death that another possibility came to mind. What if the trap had been set for *him*? He knows too much, so Ubrino might have planned to draw him out into the open and have him killed. Except, when we linked him to the missing vial the plan was brought forward, to silence him before he could tell us anything.'

'But Tommaso Francia was too late to silence him before you and Mike got to Corfu so he tried to kill all three of you?' Kolchinsky concluded.

Paluzzi shook his head. 'I don't go along with that. He could have killed us when we were in the pool. We were sitting ducks. It was obvious he was only after Karos.'

'It's like what happened in Venice,' Sabrina said to Kolchinsky. 'It's as if they *wanted* us to escape.'

'It doesn't make any sense,' Kolchinsky muttered, then stubbed out his cigarette and got to his feet. 'It's seven o'clock. I want to see Michael before we go to Sant'Ivo.'

'I'll get these dossiers on Boudien and the Francia brothers translated into English for you.'

'I can do that,' Sabrina said, scowling at Kolchinsky. 'It's not as if I'll have much else to do in my room, is it?'

Kolchinsky took the two folders from Paluzzi and handed them to Sabrina. Paluzzi gave her a sympathetic smile, then phoned Marco to say that he and Kolchinsky were on their way to Sant'Ivo, and that Marco was to go home and get some sleep. He replaced the receiver and got to his feet.

'Are you armed?' he asked Kolchinsky.

Kolchinsky shook his head.

'Take my Beretta,' Sabrina said. She unholstered it from the back of her jeans and offered it to Kolchinsky.

'You hold on to that, Miss Carver. I'll draw a handgun from the armoury for Mr Kolchinsky.'

She reholstered the Beretta. 'Can we drop the Miss Carver bit? You make me feel like an old spinster. It's Sabrina.'

'And I'm Sergei,' Kolchinsky added.

Paluzzi smiled. 'What type of gun do you use, Sergei?'

'Tokarev T-33, but I can make do with whatever you've got.'

'I can get you a Tokarev, no problem,' Paluzzi assured him, and immediately called the armoury to arrange for one to be sent to the office. 'It'll be up in a minute,' he said, coming round from behind the desk.

Marco appeared in the doorway. 'Are you sure you don't want me to come with you to Sant'Ivo, sir?'

'No. Now go and get some rest. I'll call you if I need you, you can be sure of that.'

'Can you let me out?' Sabrina asked Marco. 'I'd better get back to the hotel and see what Calvieri's come up with while I've been here.'

'And don't forget to tell the switchboard to put any calls from C.W. through to you until I get back,' Kolchinsky reminded her.

'I won't,' she replied, following Marco out of the room.

Paluzzi signed for the Tokarev pistol when it was brought to the office, then they left the building and drove to the San Giovanni Hospital on the via d'Amba Aradam opposite San Giovanni in Laterano, the basilica which is the cathedral of Rome. In the hospital foyer Paluzzi approached the reception desk to ask for directions to Graham's private ward. It was on the third floor overlooking the Villa Celimontana, a park bordering the Colosseum.

Kolchinsky knocked and entered.

Graham was sitting up against the headboard, a pillow cushioning his back. He immediately folded the copy of the *International Daily News* he had been reading and tossed it on to the chair beside the bed. The discoloured bruise on the left-hand side of his face was partially hidden by the thick dressing protecting the stitches close to his eye.

'How are you feeling, Michael?' Kolchinsky asked, brushing

the newspaper from the chair as he sat down, his eyes fixed on Graham's face.

'I'm fine, honestly,' Graham replied, pushing back the sheets. He was dressed in his jeans and the clean white T-shirt Paluzzi had got from the hotel for him. 'I'm ready. I've just got to put on my shoes.'

'Ready for what?' Kolchinsky asked sharply.

'Didn't Fabio tell you about Sant'Ivo?'

'Of course he told me,' Kolchinsky retorted. 'You're not going, if that's what you think. You're staying right where you are, at least until tomorrow morning.'

'There's nothing wrong with me, Sergei!' Graham snapped angrily.

Kolchinsky sighed deeply. 'Why must you always fight authority? The doctors wouldn't have asked you to stay here overnight unless they thought it was necessary. Strange as it may seem, Michael, they do know what's best for you under the circumstances.'

'Oh yeah? That's exactly what those psychiatrists said after Carrie and Mikey were kidnapped. *We know what's best for you, Mr Graham*. Like hell they did. They didn't know a damn thing. To them I was just another numbered dossier that was opened when they got to work in the morning and closed again when they went home at night. They didn't have to live with the guilt twenty-four hours a day. I did. They didn't understand what I was going through. They just *thought* they did. If they could have produced a psychiatrist who had lost his family under similar circum- stances to mine then I'd have been quite prepared to listen to him because he would have known what I was going through. It's exactly the same here. Let them produce a doctor who's had a similar injury to mine and I'll listen to him. Damnit, Sergei, who the hell do they think they are, saying they know what's best for me? It's my body. It's my mind. And I know I'm okay.'

Kolchinsky rubbed his face wearily. 'Then discharge

yourself. But that doesn't mean you're coming with us. Go back to the hotel. Sabrina's there.'

'Wonderful,' Graham muttered. 'She'll be mothering me the moment I walk through the door.'

'It's her way of showing that she cares about you,' Kolchinsky said, pushing the chair back angrily and getting to his feet. 'We'll see you back at the hotel.'

Paluzzi followed Kolchinsky into the corridor and closed the door behind him. 'I hope I'm not being intrusive, but what exactly happened to his family?'

Kolchinsky explained about the kidnapping as they walked back to the car.

'And they were never found?' Paluzzi asked.

Kolchinsky shook his head.

'And he's never cracked?' Paluzzi asked as Kolchinsky settled himself into the passenger seat.

'He won't crack. Not Michael. He's far too professional to ever let that happen.'

Paluzzi started the engine. 'I don't know what I'd do if that ever happened to my family.'

'How can you know, unless, God forbid, it ever did happen.'

'True enough,' Paluzzi agreed thoughtfully, as they left the car-park.

'How many children have you got?' Kolchinsky asked, breaking the sudden silence.

'Just the one. Dario. He's eight months old. He's already quite a handful.'

'I can believe that. What does your wife do?'

'Nothing at the moment. Dario's proving to be a full-time job for her. She used to be a stewardess with Air France.' Paluzzi pointed out the floodlit Colosseum as they passed it on their right. 'Have you ever seen it from the inside?'

'Several times. I lived here for eighteen months.'

'You never told me that,' Paluzzi replied in surprise.

'It was when I was with the KGB. I was a military attaché here. It's a good ten years ago now.'

'Do you miss Russia?'

'I don't miss the winters,' Kolchinsky said with a smile, then stared thoughtfully at the passing traffic. 'I like to try and get back at least once a year to see my family and friends. It's when I'm with them that I realize just how much I do miss the country. I intend to retire there when I leave UNACO.'

'Then you'll realize just how much you miss the West,' Paluzzi said with a grin.

'That's true. Have you ever been to the Soviet Union?'

'I haven't,' Paluzzi replied apologetically. 'Claudine, my wife, has been there several times. She says it's a beautiful country. I certainly want to go. It's just a matter of finding the time.'

Paluzzi drove past San Marco, one of the oldest churches in Rome, and continued along Corso Vittorio Emanuele flanked by its impressive collection of Baroque and Renaissance monuments and pulled up opposite Sant'Andrea della Valle, a large sixteenth-century Baroque church. Kolchinsky checked his Tokarev pistol, then pushed it back into his jacket pocket and got out of the car. Paluzzi used the transmitter to lock the doors behind them.

They crossed the road to Sant'Andrea della Valle and Paluzzi pointed out the dome towering behind the Valle Theatre on the left-hand side of the street. Sant'Ivo. They looked around carefully, both with the same apprehensive thought. There were too many people about. It was the perfect setting for a trap. If they were ambushed they couldn't return fire for fear of hitting some innocent bystander. Kolchinsky paused in front of a confectionery shop, using the window as a mirror to scan the road behind him. He couldn't see anything suspicious. Not that he knew what to expect. Paluzzi tapped him on the arm and indicated that they should move on. There was no safety in numbers, not when the Red Brigades were involved. They had no qualms about killing innocent people if it meant hitting back at the authorities they detested so much. He had seen it happen all too often in the past.

A burst of gunfire shattered the confectioner's window into a starburst of tiny fragments of flying glass. Kolchinsky flung himself to the ground. When he raised his head he saw a middle-aged woman sprawled across the pavement in front of the window, her white blouse stained with blood. She was dead. The street emptied as panic-stricken bystanders fled, screaming. The gunman was in the back of a black Mercedes. Kolchinsky crawled to where Paluzzi was crouched behind a silver BMW, the Beretta gripped tightly in his hand.

'He missed you by inches,' Paluzzi whispered. 'Did you see who it was?'

Kolchinsky nodded grimly.

Tommaso Francia brought the black Mercedes level with the BMW. He glanced at Carlo in the rearview mirror. They smiled at each other. Carlo stroked the Uzi's trigger with his gloved finger. He had them. They couldn't get away, not without him seeing them. He could wait. There was no rush.

Graham had followed Kolchinsky and Paluzzi into the hospital car-park where he had hailed a taxi and promised the driver a handsome reward if he managed to tail Paluzzi's Alfa Romeo Lusso without being seen. The driver had grinned like an excited schoolboy and given Graham a thumbs-up sign, relishing the challenge.

The driver had slammed on his brakes to prevent the taxi from ploughing into the back of a Fiat Tipo when it braked sharply behind the black Mercedes. He couldn't reverse, there was a tailback of cars behind the taxi. He was stuck. And very frightened.

Graham leapt from the back seat of the taxi, yanked open

the front door, and hauled the startled driver out into the road. Then, climbing behind the wheel, he slipped the taxi into gear and swung out from behind the Fiat Tipo. There was a gap of ten yards between the Fiat and the Mercedes. Graham rammed the taxi into the back of the Mercedes. The momentum of the impact propelled Tommaso against the steering wheel. The engine stalled. Graham rammed the Mercedes again. Tommaso cursed angrily as he struggled to restart the engine. The engine came to life and the tyres shrieked in protest as the car pulled away, heading for the Vittorio Emanuele Bridge. Graham gave chase. Carlo fired a burst at the taxi. Graham ducked sideways as the bullets hit the windscreen, pockmarking the glass. He hit the windscreen frantically with his forearm, but it wouldn't budge.

Carlo fired again, scoring hits on both the front tyres. The taxi spun out of control and smashed into the side of a parked car, hammering Graham's head against the steering wheel. He immediately felt the blood seeping out from under the dressing and down the side of his face. He unbuckled his safety belt and reached groggily for the door handle. The door was pulled open from the outside and anxious passersby peered in at him. He didn't understand what they were saying. A hand reached out to help him but he shrugged it off and sat back, his eyes closed. It felt as if hundreds of ballbearings were ricocheting around inside his head. The pain was unbelievable. Eventually he opened his eyes, wiped the blood from the side of his face with the back of his hand, and gingerly eased himself out of the car. His legs were unsteady and he had to grab on to the open door to support himself.

Kolchinsky and Paluzzi pushed their way through the crowd to where Graham was standing.

'Are you all right?' Paluzzi asked anxiously.

Graham nodded.

'What the hell were you doing?' Kolchinsky demanded.

'Saving your ass, in case you didn't notice,' Graham

retorted, his face screwed up with the pain throbbing inside his head.

'We were perfectly safe where we were.'

'Not from where I was sitting. What if he'd shot at the petrol tank? You guys wouldn't have known anything about it.' Graham's eyes flickered past Kolchinsky as the taxi driver reached the front of the crowd. 'Now this *is* trouble.'

The driver clasped his hands to his head as he stared in horror at the taxi's crumpled bonnet. A police car pulled up and two carabinieri got out. One of them immediately cleared the crowd of onlookers from the road and began to direct the tailback of congested traffic which had built up on both sides of the road. The second policeman, wearing the insignia of a sergeant, approached the taxi but held up his hand when the driver tried to speak to him. He stared at the bullet holes, the buckled hood and the shredded tyres before finally turning to the driver and asking if it was his car. The driver admitted it was but went on to explain volubly what had happened. The sergeant listened attentively, occasionally nodding his head, then told the driver to wait. He crossed to where Graham was leaning against the side of the taxi, a handkerchief pressed against the wound on his face. Paluzzi cut in front of the sergeant before he could speak and held up his ID card. The sergeant looked at it, then gestured to Graham and asked Paluzzi if he was also with the NOCS.

Paluzzi shook his head. 'He's an American, working with us. That's all you need to know.'

The sergeant glared at Paluzzi. 'We'll see about that. You think you're above the law, don't you?'

'Spare me the lecture,' Paluzzi said, pocketing his ID. 'You don't have the necessary clearance to be told what's going on.'

'I don't give a damn about your clearance,' the sergeant snapped, glancing across at Graham. 'He could have killed someone. That concerns me. And that's why I'm taking him in for questioning.'

'How old are you, sergeant?'

'Twenty-eight. Why?'

'You've got your whole career ahead of you. Don't screw it up by getting involved in something that's way over your head.'

'Is that a threat?' the sergeant hissed under his breath.

Paluzzi looked around him as he considered the question. He finally met the sergeant's eyes again. 'Let me put it another way. You take the American in and I'll see to it personally that you lose your stripes.'

'For doing my job? You'll have to do better than that.'

Paluzzi took the fake Prime Minister's letter from his pocket and handed it to the sergeant. 'I don't think I have to do much better than *that*, do you?'

The sergeant read the letter, refolded it and handed it back to Paluzzi. 'I don't seem to have any choice, Major. What happens now?'

'I'm taking him to hospital. He needs that cut treated. I'll get a full statement from him and have it sent to you first thing in the morning.'

'That's against regulations.'

'I'll get it cleared with your superiors, you don't have to worry about that.'

'And the taxi driver?'

'He'll be compensated in full.' Paluzzi handed the sergeant a business card. 'Any problems, call me.'

The sergeant pocketed the card, eyed Paluzzi contemptuously, then pushed past him to supervise the arrival of the tow truck.

Kolchinsky looked round as Paluzzi approached them. 'Any trouble?'

'Nothing serious.'

'What about the woman back there?' Graham asked.

'She's dead. I'm going back there now to straighten things out with the carabinieri.' Paluzzi handed the car keys to Kolchinsky. 'You drive. Drop me off at the Piazza, then take Mike to the hospital.'

'Do you want me to come back for you?'

'No, I'll get one of my night staff to fetch me. I'll see you at the hotel.'

'Fine.' Kolchinsky opened the driver's door and looked across the car roof at Paluzzi. 'Sabrina should be at the hotel if we're not back by the time you get there.'

Paluzzi nodded and got into the back of the car.

Graham climbed in beside Kolchinsky. 'Still mad at me, *tovarishch*?'

Kolchinsky sighed deeply and shook his head slowly to himself. He put the car into gear and pulled away from the kerb.

# SIX

Whitlock stared distastefully at the takeaway in front of him that he had sent out for. It was supposed to be *bistecca alla pizzaiola*, steak in a tomato and herb sauce. More like *bistecca al'olio*. It was swimming in oil. He prodded the steak with the fork and shook his head in disgust. His stomach grumbled. He was hungry, he had to admit it. The alternative was eating with Young in the dining-room. Suddenly the steak looked appetizing. He opened the second carton, containing peas and courgettes, and tipped them into the first beside the steak. As he ate his mind wandered back over the hours since his arrival in Rome.

Wiseman had been met unexpectedly at the airport by a senior officer from his old unit, the 1st Marine Division, which was stationed at NATO's southern command in Verona. He had told Wiseman that a staff car, and driver, would be at his disposal for the duration of his stay in Rome. Wiseman had declined the offer, saying he was in Italy as a civilian, not as a soldier. He had accepted the offer of a lift to the Hassler-Villa Medici Hotel where, after thanking the officer for his kindness, he had hired a car for himself, then retired to his suite. The officer had taken the hint and discreetly withdrawn.

That was the gist of what Young had told him when he called Wiseman to report that they had checked into the boarding house. Whitlock hated the place. It was small, dirty and smelly. He could hear the incessant blare of a radio in one of the adjoining rooms and he was sure that a woman he had passed on the landing was a prostitute. She was certainly dressed like one. Not that he cared. He was only interested in Carmen. He had rung the hotel in Paris that afternoon, only to be told that she had checked out the previous evening. He had then called the apartment in New York but the telephone had just rung. He even tried her work number but there had been no reply there either. He rang her sister in New York. She hadn't seen Carmen since she and C.W. had left for Paris. She had a lot of friends in New York but they would be the last people she would turn to at a time like this. She was like him in that respect, she kept her personal problems to herself. What if she had packed her things and left the apartment? The idea had certainly crossed his mind but he had rejected it along with all his other little theories. It wasn't in her nature to do that. She knew he would only worry if he couldn't contact her, even if she didn't want to speak to him. So where was she . . . ?

'Alexander?'

Whitlock looked round, startled by the voice behind him. Young stood in the doorway.

'Try knocking next time,' Whitlock snapped, turning back to his food.

'I did, but you didn't respond,' Young said, closing the door behind him. He sat on the edge of the bed and gestured to the takeaway on the table. 'Why didn't you eat downstairs? The food's a lot better than that.'

'I'd say that depends on the company,' Whitlock retorted, cutting the last piece of steak in half.

'I'd watch my mouth if I were you, Alexander.'

Whitlock finished eating, then twisted his chair round to face Young. 'What do you want?'

Young stood up and handed the keys to the hired Seat Ibiza to Whitlock. 'We're going out.'

'Where?'

'The underground car-park on the via Marmorata.'

'Who are we meeting?'

'That doesn't concern you,' Young spat.

'I'm up to my neck in this thing, thanks to you. The least you can do is let me know what's going on.'

Young grabbed Whitlock by his shirt, hauled him to his feet and slammed him against the wall. Whitlock resisted the temptation to break the grip and put Young on his back. He had to let Young believe he had the upper hand.

'Let's get something straight from the start, Alexander. I didn't ask for you. It was the General's idea to bring you in on this, not mine. He was the one who thought I should have a getaway driver. So don't think you're indispensable, because you're not. I can do this with or without you. It makes no difference to me one way or the other.'

'It's nice to know you're wanted,' Whitlock muttered.

'Just remember, I'm the one with the transmitter. You step out of line and I'll use it,' Young snarled, pushing Whitlock away from him.

Whitlock bit back his anger and followed Young into the corridor. They descended the stairs into the foyer. The plump receptionist smiled at them as they passed then returned to her knitting. The red Seat Ibiza was parked directly outside, and Whitlock unlocked the driver's door, got in, then leaned over and unlocked the passenger door for Young. On a map he took from his inside pocket Young pointed out the route he had already outlined in red pen.

Whitlock followed directions and they reached the via Marmorata within ten minutes. Young pointed out the illuminated sign, PARCHEGGIO, and Whitlock swung the car into the entrance, coming to a stop in front of the barrier. Whitlock took a ticket from the machine and the boomgate lifted. Young told him to drive to Level C. Whitlock negotiated the spiralling ramp cautiously and braked on reaching Level C.

'Who, or what, are we looking for?' he asked.

Young pointed to a white Fiat Uno parked beside one of the thick concrete pillars. Whitlock pulled up behind it.

'That's it,' Young said, noticing a copy of the *Daily American* in the back of the car. 'I won't be long. Drive around in circles, I'll signal when I'm ready.'

Whitlock watched Young get out of the car. The gunman was playing it close to the chest. Too close for his liking. He had already assumed that Young was meeting someone who had information on the Wiseman murder – but what good would Whitlock be to UNACO touring around in the car waiting for Young to finish? He had to know what Young was planning. There was only one option open to him: he must bug Young's room. He already had the bug, it was just a matter of planting it . . .

'I told you to drive around the level, I'll signal you when I'm ready.'

Whitlock put the car into gear and drove off. Young pulled on a pair of black gloves as he stared after the car. How many times had he tried to dissuade Wiseman from recruiting Alexander? The hell he needed a wheelman. He could easily have incorporated both jobs into one. And be £100,000 richer into the bargain. But Wiseman had been adamant. Alexander was a necessary back-up. Typical, Wiseman thinking like a soldier. Young didn't like the cocky Englishman but he had no choice but to put up with him for the duration of the assignment. Wiseman's assignment. But once it was over he still had his ace to play. The booby-trapped watch. He smiled to himself. What a tragedy if it happened to detonate accidentally . . .

'Do you have a cigarette?'

Young turned to the man who had emerged from the shadows behind the Fiat Uno. He was in his mid-twenties with long, ragged black hair and a sallow, acne-scarred face. His name was Johnny Ramona. Young took a pack of cigarettes from his pocket and extended it towards him.

Ramona took one and Young lit it for him. 'I would pay you, but I only have this,' he said, taking half a five-hundred-lire note from his jeans pocket.

Young took the note and checked it against the half he had on him. They matched. 'Did you get the information I wanted?'

Ramona nodded and gestured to the Fiat. 'It's safer if we talk inside.'

Young got into the passenger seat and immediately tilted the rearview mirror until he could see behind him.

Ramona got behind the wheel. 'A cautious man, I see.'

'It's one way of staying alive. Well, what have you got for me?'

'You have the money?'

Young took an envelope from his pocket, opened it to reveal the money, but jerked it away from Ramona's grasping hand. 'You'll be paid when I have the information.'

Ramona gave him a twisted smile, sat back and took another drag on the cigarette. 'The Red Brigades were behind the break-in at the plant.'

'Try telling me something I don't know,' Young retorted sarcastically, then glanced in the rearview mirror as Whitlock drove past.

'It was carried out by the Rome cell. The team leader was Riccardo Ubrino, one of the two senior cell commanders.'

'Where's this Ubrino now?'

Ramona shrugged. 'Nobody knows. It is as if he has disappeared off the face of the earth. The only person who might know is Lino Zocchi, but there is no way of confirming that.'

'Who is Zocchi?'

'The brigade chief here in Rome. He is in prison but he cannot be contacted. There has been an outbreak of conjunctivitis there and all visits have been cancelled until further notice.'

'You say this Ubrino is one of two senior cell commanders. Who's the other one?'

'Luigi Rocca.'

'Would he know where Ubrino's gone?'

Ramona shook his head. 'He is as much in the dark as everyone else. And he is the acting brigade chief until Zocchi can be contacted again.'

'So Ubrino's answerable to Zocchi. Who's Zocchi answerable to?'

'Nicola Pisani, leader of the Red Brigades.' Ramona took an envelope from his pocket and removed a sheet of paper from inside it. 'This is the committee structure of the Red Brigades. Pisani is at the top. Zocchi and Calvieri are immediately beneath him—'

'Who's Calvieri?' Young cut in quickly. 'I'm sure I've heard that name before.'

'He is the spokesman for the Red Brigades. He appears regularly on Italian television.'

'Would he know where to find Ubrino?'

'I doubt it. Ubrino is from Rome. Calvieri is brigade chief in Milan. They are two different factions within the Red Brigades. And there is no love lost between the two cities. Zocchi is a hardliner, Calvieri a moderate.'

'But it's possible?'

'It is possible, but most unlikely.' Ramona flicked the cigarette butt out of the window. 'Well, now you have the information you wanted. The money?'

'There's something you didn't tell me.'

Ramona frowned. 'What?'

'That you're also a member of the Red Brigades.'

Ramona chuckled nervously. 'Whoever told you this has got his facts wrong. I have never been with the Red Brigades.'

Young looked in the rearview mirror as Whitlock passed again, then turned back to Ramona. 'No wonder you were so eager to help me. I get the information I want and at the same time the Red Brigades get to keep tabs on me.'

Ramona shook his head. 'Honestly, mister. I have no ties—'

Young palmed a switchblade from his pocket and rammed it into Ramona's ribs, twisting the blade violently up into the heart. He caught Ramona as he fell forward and pushed him back against the seat. He wiped the blade on Ramona's sleeve, then pocketed the knife and got out of the car. He looked around slowly. There wasn't anyone in sight. He took the envelope from Ramona's hand and closed the door. He removed his gloves, folded them over, and slipped them into his jacket pocket.

At a signal, Whitlock picked him up and drove to the exit. He paid the attendant, then swung the car out into the road and returned to the hotel, remembering the route. Young would expect that of him. He parked in the same spot outside the boarding house.

'Want a drink?' Young asked, locking the door behind him.

'I don't drink.'

'That's right, you don't,' Young muttered. 'I remember some of your buddies in London telling me that. So what's wrong, why don't you drink?'

Whitlock paused on the top step and looked down at Young. 'My parents were alcoholics. Drink killed them. Does that answer your question?'

'Suit yourself,' Young replied with an indifferent shrug. 'There's a bar on the end of the block. I'm going to get myself a couple of beers. I'll be back in twenty minutes.'

'Then what?'

'We go out again. Just be sure you're ready.'

Whitlock watched Young walk off towards the bar, then looked at the booby-trapped watch. He had fifteen minutes to plant the bug in Young's room. He hurried up to his own room, locking the door behind him, then took a suitcase from the cupboard and placed it on the bed. He had bought the suitcase, as well as two changes of clothing,

123

that afternoon with some of the expenses money Wiseman had given him. He unzipped it and took out a canvas toilet bag. Inside were two microphones, a radio receiver, a micro-cassette player and a pair of small headphones. He had picked up the toilet bag from a contact that afternoon. He checked the microphones. One was a radio microphone. The other was a 'spike mike'. He would need to get into Young's room to plant the radio microphone. It was too risky. Which left him with the spike mike. It was nine inches long (the actual microphone was only two inches in length) with a thin, metallic spike which could be inserted into a wall or window frame and any noises from the bugged room would then vibrate against the spike and pass through it to the microphone. He moved to the window and checked the distance between it and the adjoining window. Young's room. Ten feet. Maybe twelve. But there was no way across to it. Then he noticed the steel ladder on the far side of Young's window. He presumed it went all the way to the roof because he couldn't see anything in the darkness above him. It would have to be checked out.

He put the spike mike in his pocket and left the room, locking the door behind him. The fire stairs to the roof were at the end of the corridor. He took them two at a time and climbed out of the hatch on to the flat roof. The top of the ladder was visible from where he stood. He crossed to it and peered down into the alleyway below. It was deserted. He gripped the ladder in both hands and shook it violently. It held firm. He then clamped the spike mike between his teeth and descended the ladder to what was, he calculated, Young's window. The ladder was further away from the window than he had initially thought. Probably to dissuade burglars. He reached out towards the window. The frame was just in reach. That was enough. He locked one arm around the ladder then leaned across and tried to push the tip of the microphone into the wood. He was hoping it would be old and brittle, but his hopes were dashed.

The wood was hard. He wiped the sweat from his face, then leaned over again and began to screw the spike into the wood. His arm was aching by the time the microphone was secure. He looked at his watch. He still had eight minutes to spare.

The window was suddenly pushed up. He pressed himself tightly against the ladder, not daring to move in case the slightest noise carried into the bedroom. Young rested his hands on the frame. He had been gone only a few minutes. Why had he returned? Then Whitlock noticed a woman in the alleyway beneath him. It looked like the prostitute he had seen earlier in the boarding house. Young leaned out of the window as she passed, his face turned away from Whitlock. He whistled at her. Whitlock held his breath, knowing he would be spotted if she looked up at Young. She didn't. Instead she held up her middle finger, then disappeared out into the street. Young laughed and ducked his head back into the room, closing the window. Whitlock exhaled deeply. He couldn't believe his luck. But he didn't intend to push it. He climbed back up to the roof, pausing a bare minute to wipe the sweat from his face with a handkerchief before returning to his room and locking the door behind him. He set up the apparatus but used only one of the headphones to see if the microphone was actually working. Silence. He checked the receiver unit. It was definitely working. He sat on the edge of the bed and stared at the wall, willing Young to make some kind of noise. Still silence. He wiped his face again and tossed the handkerchief onto the bed. There was a sudden metallic click in the headphone. He frowned, then smiled to himself when he realized what had made the noise. Young had opened a can of beer. So that was why he had come back early. He had decided to drink in his room. Then he heard the familiar sound of the telephone being picked up. He positioned a pillow behind him, then sat back against the headboard and slipped both headphones over his ears.

'Yes, good evening. Richard Wiseman, please.'

The reception was excellent. It was almost as if Young was in the same room.

'Good evening, sir,' Young said. There was a pause while Wiseman spoke. 'Yes sir, I met with the informer. I got all the information I need from him.' Pause. 'Including the name of the man who pulled the trigger. He's called Ubrino, he's a senior *Brigatista* here in Rome.' Pause. 'No, sir, he seems to have vanished. But I don't anticipate any problems tracking him down.' Longer pause. 'The other three members the informer mentioned were Pisani, head of the Red Brigades, and his two deputies, Zocchi and Calvieri. They're both brigade chiefs. Zocchi here in Rome and Calvieri in Milan. Zocchi's in jail so we won't be able to get to him, at least not straight away.' Pause. 'No sir, Alexander doesn't know the names. I thought it best to tell him as little as possible. I still say he's a liability.' Pause. 'I'd prefer to see him dead. He already knows too much.' Longer pause. 'I appreciate that, sir. I'll call you again in the morning. Good night, sir.' The receiver was replaced.

Whitlock removed the headphones, then put the apparatus back in the suitcase and locked the cupboard door. He sat on the bed again, his mind racing. Were all four *Brigatisti* now on Young's hit list? Including Calvieri? He had to pass the information on to Kolchinsky but there would be no time before they went out again. And where were they going? Was Young going to make his first hit? If so, who was his intended target? He knew Young wouldn't tell him anything. That much was evident. And what had Young meant by, 'I appreciate that, sir'? Appreciate that Wiseman was in charge and that he wanted Young to leave Alexander alone? Or did he appreciate the chance to kill Alexander? Whitlock cursed softly to himself. If only he could have heard what Wiseman had said. He wanted to arm himself. He felt naked without his Browning. But Alexander *never* used firearms. And Young would know that. He couldn't afford to take that chance, it could blow his cover. His wits against Young's firepower. He didn't fancy the odds, not one little bit . . .

There was a knock at the door.

Whitlock answered it.

Young stood in the doorway, the can of beer in his hand. 'Let's go.'

'Where are we going?'

'Don't worry, I'll direct you there.'

Whitlock slammed the door angrily behind him and headed for the stairs. Young took another mouthful of beer, then left the can by the door and hurried after Whitlock.

Sabrina closed *La Repubblica*, got to her feet and moved to the window where she looked out across the brightly-lit city, evoking memories of her previous visits to Rome. The first visit was the one she remembered best, mainly because it was a painful reminder of the way she used to be. The plane ticket had been a twenty-first birthday present from her parents and she had gone with three of her girlfriends from the Sorbonne, where she had been doing her postgraduate degree. She didn't see any of the city's heritage in those two weeks. Their nights were spent at clubs and discos and their days in bed recovering from the night before. And then there were the one-night stands . . .

She turned away from the window and shook her head slowly to herself. It was hard for her to believe that she had once been so immature. Not that it had ended there. After leaving the Sorbonne she had become one of the most sought-after débutantes in Europe. She had attended all the exclusive parties, rubbing shoulders with the rich and famous, and regularly had to fend off proposals of marriage from men old enough to be her grandfather. Then, when she tired of the parties, she found herself another passion: motor racing. It came to a head when she crashed her Porsche at Le Mans. She had severe bone fractures and a punctured lung. She spent the next four months in the American Hospital of Paris and came to realize that her life was going nowhere. She needed purpose and direction. She had joined the FBI on her release from hospital and it had given her the maturity she needed to make the transition to UNACO. *You've come a long way*, she thought to herself, and when she caught sight of her reflection in the mirror she noticed the faint smile of satisfaction on her face.

There was a knock at the door. She peered through the spyhole. It was Paluzzi. She opened the door and invited him in.

He looked around the room. 'Mike and Sergei not back, then?'

She closed the door. 'I thought they were with you.'

He recounted the evening's events. 'I knocked on their doors but there was no reply. I thought they might be with you.'

'I haven't heard from them. I presume they must still be at the hospital.'

Paluzzi nodded, then indicated the armchair by the window. 'May I?'

'Of course,' she replied with a sheepish grin. 'Sorry, my mind was elsewhere. Can I get you a drink?'

'A soft drink, perhaps. Soda water?'

She took a bottle of soda water from the fridge.

He told her not to bother with a glass and took a long swallow from the bottle, then wiped the back of his hand across his mouth. 'That's better. It's been quite a day.'

'But hardly constructive,' she replied, sitting on the bed. 'We're just clutching at straws, aren't we? What chance have we got realistically of finding Ubrino before the deadline on Thursday?'

'Not much, I'm afraid. We could certainly do with a bit of luck.' Paluzzi took a sip, then pointed the neck of the bottle at Sabrina. 'Conte's our only hope now. The doctors are confident he'll regain consciousness. It's just a matter of when.'

'And you think he knows where Ubrino's hiding?'

'It's obvious that Ubrino's orders were to kill the rest of his team once he had the vial. That's borne out by Nardi's murder as well as the attempt to try and kill Conte. Why else would he have been told to kill them, unless they already knew too much about the operation?'

'I see your point. It's still a long shot, though.'

'I agree. But as you said, what chance have we got of finding Ubrino before Thursday? We have to bank on long shots now.'

They lapsed into a thoughtful silence which was interrupted moments later by the telephone ringing. Sabrina answered it. Paluzzi crossed to the window while she talked.

'That was Calvieri,' she said, replacing the receiver. 'He's had another tip-off. This time in Rome.'

'Did he think it was genuine?'

'All he said was that it was an anonymous call. It certainly smells like a trap.' She shrugged. 'It's got to be checked out anyway.'

The telephone rang again.

'That's probably for me,' he said as she picked up the handset.

She listened momentarily, then nodded and passed the receiver to him. She went to the cupboard to get her Beretta and shoulder holster.

'Calvieri did receive an anonymous call,' he said, hanging up.

She looked round at him as she strapped the holster over her T-shirt. 'Who was that?'

'One of the men in the van.'

'What van?'

He jabbed his thumb towards the window. 'I've got two men out there monitoring all Calvieri's calls. I told you about it at HQ.'

'No you didn't,' she replied, shaking her head.

'Sorry, I thought I'd told you. We put a tap on his phone and planted a couple of bugs in his room while the two of you were in Venice. I'm sure he suspects he's being bugged but it's worth a try anyway.'

She pulled on a jacket. 'Is he being tailed?'

'When he goes out by himself.'

'And?'

'Nothing.'

There was a knock at the door. She answered it and ushered Calvieri into the room.

'Evening, Paluzzi. I presume Sabrina's told you about the tip-off.'

'Anonymous, I believe? How original.'

'All I was told was that he's been spotted at one of the safe houses here in Rome.'

'Do you think it's a trap?' Paluzzi asked.

'It's possible. As you know, I'm not very popular any more with the *Brigatisti* here in Rome. Most of them would gladly put a gun to my head and pull the trigger.'

'Do you want back-up?' Paluzzi asked.

'No, definitely not,' Calvieri insisted. 'The last thing we need is a gun battle in the street.'

'Are you armed?' Sabrina asked.

Calvieri nodded.

'A Heckler & Koch P7,' Paluzzi said, looking at Sabrina. 'But don't rely on him to cover your back. He never uses it.'

'I've never been *known* to use it. There is a difference.'

There was an uneasy silence as the two men stared contemptuously at each other.

'Fabio, you're welcome to wait here for Mike and Sergei,' Sabrina said, deliberately stepping between them. 'They should be back any time now.'

'Thanks,' Paluzzi replied. 'I will. Take care of yourself.'

She smiled reassuringly and followed Calvieri from the room.

\* \* \*

The small red-brick house, bordered by a neatly trimmed hedge, was a typical example of a Red Brigades safe house. An inconspicuous building in the heart of suburbia.

Calvieri pulled up opposite the house and killed the engine. He looked at it. A paved footpath, flanked by well-tended flowerbeds, led up to the front door which was illuminated by a subtle entrance light. The only other light came from behind the drawn curtains in the room to the left of the door. He checked out the garage to the right of the house. An Alfa Romeo Alfetta stood in the drive in front of the closed garage door.

'Why didn't you just ring ahead and tell them we were coming?' Sabrina said sarcastically beside him.

'What do you mean?'

'Whoever's in there will have seen the car the moment we pulled up. Why didn't you park at the end of the street? At least then we would have had the option of using either the front or the back of the house to gain entry. Now we've lost the element of surprise.'

'There is no back.'

'How do you know?' she asked suspiciously.

'I've used this house before when I was stationed here. It backs on to the house directly behind it. The only way in from the street is through the front door. The only other way out is through the garage. So you see, we don't have any option. We have to use the front door.'

'And get shot before we're halfway up the garden path?'

'A bit melodramatic, don't you think?' He got out of the car and made a sweeping gesture with his arm. 'This is suburbia. Anything suspicious and the police would be here in a flash. And that would mean the discovery of the safe house. So what use would it be? No, if they're going to spring a trap it will be inside the house, away from prying eyes.'

'What do you suggest we do?'

'Use the front door, what else? I have my skeleton keys

with me, one of them is sure to fit the lock. If Ubrino is in there his only way out will be through the garage. You wait out here in case he shows.'

'Why don't I go in and you wait out here?'

'I know the house, Sabrina. It's got several places where someone could hide in an emergency. You don't know where they are.'

'Then we go in together.' She noticed the uncertainty in his eyes. 'Let me put it another way for you. Either I go in with you or else I call Paluzzi and have his men go in with me. The choice is yours.'

'Some choice.' He opened the gate and looked at the garage. 'He couldn't get out there anyway.'

'Why not?'

'The car's parked against the garage door. He'd have to use the front door.'

They approached the front door cautiously, their hands holding the guns in their pockets. The door was ajar. They exchanged wary glances. Calvieri ran his fingers lightly down the jamb to check for any booby-trapped wires. Nothing. He eased the door open with his fingertips. The hallway was deserted. She took the Beretta from her pocket and slipped past him into the hallway. He closed the door behind them and followed her. She pointed to the first door on the left. He nodded and took the Heckler & Koch P7 from his pocket, his eye continually darting towards the other closed doors leading off from the hallway. She pressed herself against the wall and indicated that he should do the same on the other side of the door.

'I'll go in first,' she whispered.

He nodded reluctantly.

She curled her fingers around the handle then shoved open the door and dived low into the room, fanning it with her Beretta. There was only one man in the room. He was seated in an armchair facing the door. It wasn't Ubrino.

He was a heavyset man in his forties with black hair slicked back from a craggy face.

She got up on to one knee, the Beretta aimed at his chest. 'On your feet, very slowly. And keep your hands where I can see them.'

He looked past her and smiled when Calvieri appeared in the doorway. 'I'm impressed, Tony. Your new bodyguard?'

Calvieri lowered his gun. 'I might have guessed. What are you doing here, Luigi?'

'You know him?' Sabrina asked.

'Unfortunately, yes. Luigi Rocca, one of Zocchi's more repulsive puppets.'

'I'd mind my tongue if I were you, Tony. My men don't take too kindly to me being insulted by someone like you. Look behind you.'

Calvieri looked round slowly, his nerves taut. Two men had emerged from the opposite room. Both were armed with AK-74 assault rifles.

'Drop the gun, Tony.' Rocca looked at Sabrina. 'You too, *bella*.'

Calvieri let the P7 fall from his fingers. One of the men retrieved it. Sabrina stared at the two Kalashnikovs pointing at her and reluctantly tossed her gun on to the floor. The same man picked it up.

'You never answered my question, Luigi,' Calvieri said, coming into the room.

'I will, in time. Aren't you going to introduce me to your beautiful companion?'

'Her name's Sabrina Trestelli. She's a graduate of Trento University.'

'Beauty *and* brains. Pity you chose to join the wrong cell, *bella*.' Rocca beckoned the two men forward. 'Entertain the lady while I talk to Signore Calvieri.'

'Whatever you have to say to me can be said in front of her,' Calvieri said, looking round as the two men approached her.

The first man grabbed her arm. She brought her knee up sharply into his groin. He shrieked in pain and crumpled to the floor.

'Touch me and I'll break your arm,' she snarled menacingly at the second man.

He looked hesitantly to Rocca for instructions.

'Leave her,' Rocca said, then gestured dismissively at the man gasping on the floor. 'Take him away. Wait outside for me. I'll call if I need you.'

The man helped his colleague from the room and closed the door behind them.

Rocca got to his feet and crossed to a side table. They both refused his offer of a drink. He poured himself a whisky, then resumed his seat and pointed to the couch behind them. Obediently they both sat down.

'This has gone far enough, Luigi. What do you want?'

'Answers,' Rocca replied, and took a sip of whisky.

'Answers to what?' Calvieri demanded.

Rocca ran his palm over his greasy hair. 'I'm in charge now that Signore Zocchi and Ubrino are *allegedly* indisposed. I use the word "allegedly" because the city's been rife with rumours, counter-rumours and accusations ever since the break-in at the Neo-Chem plant on Sunday night. I have to reassure my *Brigatisti*, Tony, that's why I lured you out here. I need answers, and I need them quickly.'

'Then I suggest you make an appointment to see Signore Pisani and discuss your problems with him.'

'Credit me with some intelligence, Tony. Pisani's dying. He's nothing more than a figurehead now. You've been running the show for the past few months, not him.'

'Who told you that? Zocchi?' Calvieri could see he was right by the look in Rocca's eyes. 'I thought as much. And you're the one complaining about rumours? Signore Pisani is dying, we all know that, but to say that he doesn't play an active part in the running of the Red Brigades any more is complete nonsense. Who do you think sent me to Rome

134

to find Ubrino? I certainly didn't send myself. I'm here on his specific instructions. Signore Pisani will tell us when he wants to stand down. But until then he is still our leader. So that's one rumour quashed already.'

'What about the rumour that Zocchi's dead?' Rocca said, then drank down the rest of his whisky. 'That's why the prison's been sealed off.'

'The prison's been sealed off because of an outbreak of acute conjunctivitis. I know for a fact that Signore Pisani spoke with one of the doctors who went to treat the prisoners. He saw Zocchi. That was yesterday afternoon. It's possible that Zocchi could have been killed since then, we've no way of confirming or denying that. But look at it logically. If something had happened to him, I think the committee would have heard about it by now.'

'What's the doctor's name?'

'Are you questioning Signore Pisani's word?' Calvieri demanded angrily.

'I just want to talk to the doctor myself,' Rocca said defensively.

'So you're calling him a liar.'

'Of course not, but how can I be expected to answer these rumours unless I have the facts at my disposal?'

'I've told you already, call a meeting with Signore Pisani. He'll understand your predicament.' Calvieri stood up. 'If that's all, I've got a busy day ahead of me.'

'Why are you looking for Ubrino?' Rocca asked suddenly. 'What did he take from the plant?'

'That doesn't concern you.'

'I have a right to know!' Rocca snapped, banging his fist angrily on the arm of the chair. He waved the guard away when the door opened. 'You're in my city, Tony. That makes it my concern.'

'Signore Pisani will call a committee meeting early next week to discuss the implications of the Neo-Chem affair. I'm not at liberty to say anything until then.'

'If you survive that long.' Rocca reached for his cigarettes on the table and lit one. 'There's a lot of ill-feeling among the younger *Brigatisti* who resent the way you're hunting down Ubrino like some wild animal. A contract's been put out on you. I can't guarantee your safety here in Rome any more.'

'So that's what this is all about. You can't control your minions and you're scared that if anything were to happen to me before contact's made with Zocchi, it could jeopardize your chances of ever reaching brigade chief.'

'It's got nothing to do with that!' Rocca snapped indignantly. 'I'm warning you. Get out of Rome, you're not welcome here any more.'

'I'll get out when I know Ubrino's not here. Not before.' Calvieri paused at the door and looked back at Rocca. 'I'm right, though. If something were to happen to me it would reflect very badly on you. You'd never make brigade chief. You'd be lucky to remain a cell commander.'

Rocca waited until Calvieri and Sabrina had left, then stubbed out his cigarette angrily and reached for the telephone.

The armed guard approached the fifteen-foot wrought-iron gate and shone his torch through the bars at the Alfa Romeo Alfetta outside. Rocca made no attempt to shield his eyes from the glare of the torch, and activating the driver's window, he shouted to the guard that he had an appointment to see Nicola Pisani. The guard contacted the house on his two-way radio to confirm the appointment then used a remote control to open the gates. Rocca drove through and the guard immediately closed the gates behind him.

Whitlock and Young had seen the Alfa Romeo Alfetta enter the grounds from their Seat Ibiza parked at the end of the street.

'What now?' Whitlock asked.

'It doesn't change anything,' Young replied, stubbing out his cigarette among the half-dozen butts already in the ashtray. 'I'm still going in.'

Whitlock stared ahead of him. Whose house was it? Young had refused to tell him anything, saying the less he knew, the better it would be for him. He could only assume the house belonged to a senior *Brigatista*. Possibly even Pisani. But he couldn't be sure. It left him feeling helpless and frustrated. And he still hadn't managed to contact Kolchinsky. That worried him. What if Young was about to blunder in on Ubrino's hideout? Not that he could do anything about it, not without compromising his own cover.

'Let's go,' Young said, getting out of the car.

Whitlock climbed out from behind the wheel and pocketed the keys. He looked at Young who was dressed completely in black, a sinister figure. Young pulled a black balaclava over his head then took a silenced Heckler & Koch MP5 sub-machine-gun from the back of the car and slung it over his shoulder. Whitlock followed him to the eight-foot-high perimeter wall and after glancing the length of the deserted street he cupped his hands together to give him a foothold to reach the top of the wall. Young hauled himself up on to the wall, careful to avoid the tripwire alarm, and looked down into the garden, choosing the spot where he wanted to land. He dropped the sub-machine-gun over, then jumped nimbly into the garden, rolling with the fall as he hit the ground. He retrieved the gun and sprinted to the nearest tree where he paused to catch his breath. Then, taking a night-vision scope from the pouch on his belt, he surveyed the house and its surroundings. Where were the guards? A moment later he spotted one close to the house, an Alsatian at his side. Young moved forward cautiously, darting from tree to tree, until he was within twenty yards of the house. The dog suddenly stopped and looked towards him. Had it sensed him? He screwed up his face as the sweat burnt into his eyes but he made no attempt to wipe it away. Any sudden movement would certainly alert the dog. The guard looked from the dog to the trees but was unable to see anything in the darkness. He spoke softly to the Alsatian then reached down and unleashed it.

Young unslung the sub-machine-gun as the dog bore down on him. He swallowed nervously and curled his finger around the trigger. It wasn't so much killing the dog as stopping it. Even if he did kill it, its momentum could carry it forward on to him. He could be knocked out. Stunned, certainly, and that would give the guard time to open fire. He aimed low, taking out the dog's front legs. It yelped in agony as it fell, face first, to the ground. The guard was still raising his Kalashnikov when Young shot him twice in the chest, knocking him back into the flowerbed bordering the porch. The dog was trying pitifully to stand up, its bloodied legs buckled grotesquely underneath its chest. He shot it through the head. Its body jerked, then it fell heavily on to its side. He remained on one knee, waiting for any sign of the other guards. When none appeared he got to his feet and dragged the dog behind the nearest tree. He crossed to where the guard lay and picked up the Kalashnikov, ejected the clip, and tossed them both into a bush. He rolled the guard underneath the steps, then tiptoed up on to the porch. He crouched beside the window and peered discreetly through the net curtains. The television set was on but the room was empty.

'*Si alzi!*' a voice barked behind him, telling him to get up.

Young shifted uncertainly on his haunches, not understanding the order. He tightened his grip on ˌthe sub-machine-gun as he monitored the guard's movements in the reflection of the window. The guard stepped forward and prodded Young in the back with his rifle. Young launched himself backwards, knocking the guard off-balance. He landed on his back, then rolled sideways and shot the guard through the head. The guard's body hit the wooden railing, which broke under his weight and he fell off the porch into the flowerbed. Young cursed silently. He had no time to hide the body for the other guards would certainly have been alerted by the sound of breaking wood. He moved to the door and tried the handle. The door swung open. He locked it behind him, then moved cautiously up the hallway, swivelling round to face each door, the sub-machine-gun gripped tightly in both hands.

Then he was aware of a movement at the top of the stairs. The driver of the Alfa Romeo Alfetta. Rocca got off a single shot before Young returned fire. Rocca's shot was off target. Young's burst peppered the wall inches from where Rocca was standing. Rocca dived to the ground. Young, sensing the advantage, hurried up the stairs but when he reached the top and swivelled round to fan the hallway Rocca was already gone.

He knew he didn't have time to waste. He had to find Pisani before any more guards arrived. But where was he? He could be anywhere in the house. What if he had been moved when the shooting started? Young knew there was only one way of finding out. He pressed himself against the wall beside the first door then reached out and opened it. Nothing. He swivelled round and fanned the room with his sub-machine-gun. An empty bathroom. He moved to the second door and opened it. A bedroom. Again, empty. He looked round anxiously when he heard the sound of banging on the reinforced front door. Then he heard the sound of breaking glass. A window? He had been sure all the ground-floor windows would be protected with burglar alarms. Had the guards found another way in? How many of them were there? He turned his attention back to the third door and pushed it open.

Two bullets echoed out, slamming harmlessly into the wall. Young flung himself low through the doorway, already firing before he hit the carpet. One of the bullets took Rocca high in the shoulder. The Bernadelli spun from his hand. Young glanced at the ashen-faced man sitting in the corner of the room with a blanket around his legs. Pisani. He recognized him from one of the photographs in the envelope he had taken from Ramona. He kicked the Bernadelli underneath the bed then reached behind him and locked the door without taking his eyes off either man. Pisani remained motionless in his chair, his eyes riveted on Young. Rocca stood in the middle of the room, his left hand clutching his right shoulder. His fingers were covered in blood. Young shot him through the head. Rocca fell back against the wall and slid lifelessly to the floor, his hand leaving a smear of blood on the white embossed wallpaper. Young trained the sub-machine-gun on Pisani.

'I am glad to see that you are a professional,' Pisani said softly, then coughed violently, his face clenched against the agonizing pain. He wiped the spittle from his lips with the back of his hand. 'The doctors have given me two months to live, three at the most.'

'How did you know I spoke English?'

'Word gets around when a foreigner asks delicate questions about the Red Brigades. We are a very close family, especially here in Rome. Unfortunately Johnny Ramona defied my instructions and passed certain information on to you. He always was greedy. At least you saved us the trouble of disciplining him.'

The door handle was tried from the outside. A voice called out in Italian. Still smiling at Young, Pisani slipped his hand deftly underneath the blanket. Young reacted faster, and shot him through the head. Pisani slumped back in the chair, a trickle of blood running down the bridge of his nose and on to his pallid cheek. The blanket slipped from his legs. Young was momentarily puzzled. There had been no weapon secreted beneath it. Then it suddenly made sense. Pisani had wanted to die, it was an escape from the agony of his cancer. He had tricked Young, knowing that as a professional he would kill him. He hadn't wanted the guards to save him.

Young ran to the window and pushed it open. The roof sloped at a forty-five-degree angle with a twelve-foot drop to the garden. A bullet splintered the door behind him. Then another. He scrambled out on to the sill and a bullet cracked inches from his head. He overbalanced, slid down the roof, catching his elbow painfully on the gutter, and landed heavily on the grass. He remained on his back, winded by the fall. The guard who had shot at him appeared over him, the AK-47 gripped tightly in his hands. He was barely out of his teens, and he was nervous. Young glanced towards his own sub-machine-gun. It was out of reach. He still had an ace to play: the switchblade strapped to his left wrist.

He struggled to sit up, then clutched his wrist, feigning a look of intense pain, and had successfully palmed the switchblade by the time the youth prodded him with the Kalashnikov, telling him to stand up. A face appeared at the bedroom window. The youth instinctively looked up. Young lunged at him, springing the blade in the second before he drove it into the unprotected body. He grabbed the Kalashnikov from the youth's hands and sprayed the windows with gunfire, forcing the guard to dive for cover. He discarded the Kalashnikov, picked up his own sub-machine-gun and sprinted to the temporary sanctuary of the trees, where he unclipped a two-way radio from his belt and told Whitlock that he was on his way. He looked back towards the house. Nothing moved. He made his way through the trees until he saw the main gates ahead of him. Although he could see the small hut beside it, he couldn't tell if there was anyone inside. He inched his way forward. Then he saw the guard standing outside the gate. The remote control to activate the gates was clipped to his belt. Young cursed angrily under his breath. He was trapped. He only had one option open to him. He reluctantly unclipped his two-way radio and called Whitlock again.

\*    \*    \*

Whitlock put the two-way radio back on to the dashboard, got out of the car and walked slowly down the street, his hands dug into his pockets. The guard saw him but made no attempt to conceal his Kalashnikov.

Whitlock smiled at him in greeting, then took Young's cigarettes from his pocket and pushed one between his lips. He made a show of patting pockets for matches, then crossed the road to where the guard was standing. '*Ha da accendere*?' he asked, using his limited Italian.

The guard shook his head and waved him away from the gates. Whitlock feigned to his left then pivoted round and caught the guard on the chin with a perfectly timed haymaker. The guard was unconscious before he hit the ground. Whitlock winced as he flexed his hand painfully. He removed the remote control from the guard's belt and opened the gates. Young slipped out into the street and Whitlock immediately closed the gates behind him. Young took the remote control from Whitlock, wiped it clean of fingerprints, then tossed it down the nearest drain. They ran back to the car. Whitlock started the engine and pulled out into the road. Young removed his gloves, balaclava and sweatshirt then reached behind him for a holdall from which he took a white T-shirt and pulled it on, tucking it into his trousers. He stuffed the gloves, balaclava, sweatshirt and the sub-machine-gun into the holdall then ruffled his blond hair and picked up his cigarettes from the dashboard.

'Seems like you needed me after all,' Whitlock said with evident satisfaction.

Young inhaled deeply on the cigarette but remained silent.

'Can I at least know *now* who you hit?' Whitlock bit back his anger when Young continued to say nothing. 'It's going to be in all the papers tomorrow.'

'So ask the receptionist to reserve you a couple.' Young wiped his forearm across his sweating face. 'We have to dump the car. We can drop it off at the rental agency and get another one on the way back to the hotel.'

'That's too obvious. If the police do get a description of the car they're sure to check with the rental agencies. Taking it back to the rental agency so soon after the crime would certainly arouse suspicion. I say we dump it in a car-park and hire a new one from a different agency in the morning.'

Young nodded in agreement and flicked his half-smoked cigarette out of the window. He closed his eyes and remained silent for the rest of the journey back to the boarding house.

Sabrina and Calvieri returned to the hotel and went straight to her room. Kolchinsky answered the door.

'How's Mike?' she asked before Kolchinsky could say anything.

'Ask him yourself,' Kolchinsky said, gesturing behind him.

She winced at the discoloured bruise on the side of Graham's face as she crossed to the bed and sat down beside him. 'How are you feeling?'

'I'm okay,' he replied dismissively. 'How did you get on?'

'We didn't,' she replied, despondent, and told them what had happened.

'Is there any chance of this Rocca discovering the truth?' Kolchinsky asked Calvieri.

'No,' Calvieri replied. 'Only Signore Pisani and I know about the vial. And Signore Pisani won't tell him anything.'

'Rocca's not a problem,' Paluzzi said from his chair by the window. 'He couldn't find his way out of a floodlit alley without asking for directions. You have to understand that the entire Rome cell of the Red Brigades was geared around Zocchi. He was the kingpin. The decision-maker, if you like. Ubrino and Rocca are good lieutenants in that they were able to see that Zocchi's orders were carried out success-fully. But neither of them is capable of running a cell, least of all the one here in Rome. It's by far the most complex

143

of all the Red Brigades' cells. That's why there are so many rumours around at the moment. Rocca doesn't have the ability or the experience to deal with the situation. Zocchi, on the other hand, would have quashed them within hours.'

'Paluzzi's right,' Calvieri said grudgingly, then sat down in the chair on the other side of the window. 'Zocchi ran Rome as a one-man show. The cell is in chaos now, as Sabrina saw for herself tonight. It's going to take a lot of hard work to pull it round again.'

'At least something good has come out of all this,' Graham said, eyeing Calvieri coldly.

'Sabrina tells me you knew Nikki Karos,' Kolchinsky said, breaking the lingering silence.

Calvieri nodded. 'I've had dealings with him in the past. Strictly on a business level. His sort are anathema to me. Capitalists, driven by greed and power. The very basis of corruption in our so-called "free society".'

'Spare us the lecture, Calvieri,' Graham snapped. 'What about the Francia brothers? Do you know them as well? Strictly on a business level, of course.'

Calvieri smiled faintly at Graham's irony. 'I know of them. But I've never met them, if that's what you mean.'

The telephone rang.

Sabrina answered it, then put her hand over the mouthpiece. 'Tony, it's for you.'

Calvieri took the receiver from her. He was pale with shock when he replaced it a minute later.

'What's wrong?' Kolchinsky asked.

'Signore Pisani's dead,' Calvieri replied softly. 'He was shot.'

'What happened?' Sabrina asked.

'The details are still sketchy at the moment. All I know is that a masked gunman got into Signore Pisani's house and shot him, Rocca and four other *Brigatisti*. The only clue we have is that the gunman's accomplice was black.' Calvieri shook his head in disbelief. 'I only spoke to Signore Pisani a couple of hours ago. You'll have to excuse me. I must get over there straight away to initiate our own investigation.' He noticed the uncertainty in Kolchinsky's eyes. 'I'll still be working with you. That hasn't changed. It's what Signore Pisani would have wanted. I'll arrange for one of the other brigade chiefs to take charge but I need to be there until he arrives.'

'Any idea when you'll be back?' Kolchinsky asked.

'Hopefully by the morning.' Calvieri took a notebook from his pocket, wrote down Pisani's telephone number, and handed the sheet of paper to Kolchinsky. 'I'll be there if you need me.'

Kolchinsky waited until Calvieri had closed the door behind him, then slumped into the vacant chair beside the window. 'Black accomplice. No prizes for guessing who that was.'

'But why Pisani?' Paluzzi said with a frown. 'He knew nothing about the break-in until it was broadcast on the radio the next day.'

'Young wouldn't have known that,' Sabrina replied. 'To him Pisani was a legitimate target.'

'If that's the case then he could be intent on wiping out the entire committee,' Paluzzi said. 'That's the last thing we need.'

'I don't understand your concern,' Graham said to Paluzzi. 'Young would be doing you a favour by wiping out this committee, as you call it. It would throw the Red Brigades into total chaos.'

'God forbid. I know these committee members inside out. Bring in a load of new faces and all that painstaking work's gone out of the window. I'd have to start the whole process again from scratch. We'd also lose our mole. And there'd be no way we could replace him. Not at that level.'

Graham stood up. He crossed to the door then swung round to face Paluzzi, his eyes blazing. 'It's the same old story, isn't it? Better the devil you know! Instead of trying

145

to smash the backbone of this committee you take the easy way out and leave them where they are because that way you can keep tabs on them and rap them on the knuckles when they step out of line. That makes you an accomplice, Fabio. You're no better than they are.'

'I can understand your bitterness, Mike—'

'Can you really?' Graham cut in with biting sarcasm. 'Your family hasn't been butchered by terrorists in the name of some cause the anarchistic bastards don't even understand.'

'Mike—'

'Stay out of this, Sabrina,' Graham snarled, without taking his eyes off Paluzzi.

'You just can't accept what you did in Libya, can you?' Sabrina stood up and approached Graham. 'And because of that you'll find any excuse to attack others for what you regard as your own mistakes.'

'Sit down, Sabrina,' Graham whispered in a threatening tone.

'No, not this time. This needs to be said. It's long overdue.' She held his withering stare. 'You knew the risks when you joined Delta. So did Carrie. That's why she asked you to get a desk job. You refused because you knew you wouldn't last five minutes closed up in some office. You're a field operative. One of the best. It's where you belong. She knew that too. She may have never said it but deep down inside she knew you were right. Why else do you think she stood by you? And that's what made your decision in Libya the right one. It's what she would have wanted you to do. Why don't you let yourself see that, Mike? Why?'

Graham's fists were clenched tightly at his sides. She thought for a moment that he was going to hit her. Then he spun round and left the room, slamming the door behind him.

Kolchinsky shook his head despairingly, then rubbed his hands over his face. 'Well done, Sabrina. You know exactly what he's like when he gets into one of his moods. That's all we need at a time like this.'

'It had to be said, Sergei,' Sabrina replied.

'Don't you think your timing could have been a little better? We've got thirty-six hours left before the deadline. This was supposed to be a briefing.' Kolchinsky banged his fist angrily on the arm of the chair. 'Next time you want to stir up his memories, try to be a bit more subtle about it. You, of all people, should know how touchy he is about Carrie and little Mikey.'

'Precisely,' she shot back. 'Whenever their names are mentioned everyone clears their throats and someone quickly changes the subject. What good can that do him? It can only make him feel even more guilty than he already feels. The only way to help him is to make him confront the guilt that's eating away inside him.'

Kolchinsky sighed deeply, then gestured to the telephone. 'Just order some coffee, will you?'

She sat on the bed and picked up the receiver. 'Fabio?'

'Coffee would be good, thank you. And something to eat, if possible. I'm famished.'

She ordered three coffees and some sandwiches from room service, then hung up and turned back to Kolchinsky. 'You know I'm right, Sergei.'

'Let's drop the subject, shall we?'

There was a knock at the door. Sabrina answered it. She had never seen the man before. He asked to speak to Paluzzi. The two men spoke in the doorway for several minutes and when Paluzzi returned to his chair he was carrying a folder.

'What was all that about?' Kolchinsky asked.

'It was one of the men from HQ,' Paluzzi replied, sitting down and opening the file. 'I've had several teams working on the case from different angles. These are their reports.'

'Have they come up with anything?' Sabrina asked, as he sorted through the sheets of paper.

'The warder at the prison was shown a picture of a Gazelle

147

similar to the one Tommaso Francia used on Corfu. He's positive that it's the same make of helicopter used in the Zocchi murder.'

'This case gets more baffling by the minute,' Kolchinsky said with a weary sigh. 'Zocchi and Karos hire the Francia brothers. Then they're killed by them. It doesn't make sense.'

'Perhaps there's a third party involved,' Sabrina ventured.

Paluzzi shook his head. 'I can't see it. I'm sure Karos would have told us if there were.'

'But he was killed before you had a chance to question him fully,' Sabrina said.

'True, but he was quick to finger Zocchi. Why not finger the third party as well, if one was involved?'

'Perhaps too quick?' Kolchinsky mused thoughtfully.

Sabrina looked at Kolchinsky. 'You think Karos fingered Zocchi deliberately to throw us off the scent of his real partner? It would certainly account for the murders.'

'Fabio, what do you think?'

Paluzzi shook his head.

'Why?' Sabrina asked.

'It all comes back to Ubrino. He was totally dependent on Zocchi. He never did anything without first consulting him. No, Zocchi had to be involved somewhere along the line.'

'What else did your men come up with?' Kolchinsky asked, breaking the sudden silence.

'It seems Vittore Dragotti, the sales manager at Neo-Chem Industries, was in serious financial difficulty at the time of his death. That would explain why he was acting as the middleman between Karos and Wiseman.'

'And still no sign of the money Karos paid to Wiseman?' Kolchinsky asked.

'His bank accounts have been turned inside out. Both here and in America. Nothing. It's probably stuck away in some numbered Swiss account.'

There was another knock at the door. Sabrina answered it again, this time admitting the waiter with the tray, which he deposited on the table between Kolchinsky and Paluzzi.

Sabrina poured out three cups of coffee, added a dash of milk to her own, then retreated to the bed.

'Aren't you eating?' Paluzzi asked her.

'I ate earlier. And anyway, it's white bread. I never touch it.' She smiled wryly. 'I have enough trouble as it is keeping in shape.'

'There I have to disagree,' Paluzzi said gallantly.

'Have you finished translating those dossiers on Boudien and the Francia brothers?' Kolchinsky interrupted, selecting a sandwich from the pile on the plate.

She nodded and pulled the dossiers out from the bedside cabinet. She returned them to Paluzzi and handed a photocopy of her translation to Kolchinsky.

'I'll give Mike his when I see him again.'

'You'll give it to him tonight. He has to be kept up to date.'

'Thanks,' she replied, screwing up her face.

'It's your fault he stormed out in the first place. And get your act together. Both of you. There's no room for personal squabbles at a time like this. We have to pull together as a team. If either of you can't accept that, I'll have you replaced.'

She nodded sombrely. 'I'll tell him.'

Kolchinsky finished his coffee, then looked at Paluzzi. 'Is there anything else?'

'No, I don't think so,' Paluzzi replied, scanning the reports. 'There's been no change in Paolo Conte's condition. I'll be told the moment he regains consciousness.'

'And you contact me,' Kolchinsky told him. 'I don't care what time it is.'

'That goes without saying,' Paluzzi assured him, then stood up and stifled a yawn. 'I'd better be on my way. My wife hasn't seen me for days.' He looked down at Kolchinsky.

'I'll have a full report for you on the Pisani murder first thing in the morning.'

'I'd appreciate that.'

Paluzzi said good night and left the room.

'I've still got some paperwork to complete before I turn in,' Kolchinsky announced. He crossed to the door and paused to look back at Sabrina. 'I meant what I said about you and Michael.'

'I'll talk to him, Sergei, I said I would,' she replied with a hint of irritation in her voice.

Kolchinsky disappeared out into the corridor, closing the door behind him. Sabrina waited until she was sure he had gone, then collected the photocopy from the bed and went to Graham's room at the far end of the corridor. She knocked. No reply. She knocked harder. Still no reply. She cursed softly to herself. Where was he?

'Looking for me?'

She spun round, startled by Graham's voice, then let out a deep sigh and clasped her hand to her chest. 'God, you gave me a fright. Where did you come from?'

He indicated the stairs beside the lift, then turned back to her. 'Sergei sent you, didn't he?'

'I'd have come anyway. We need to talk.'

He unlocked the door, switched on the light, then removed a cigar humidor from his suitcase and opened it to reveal a B405 Surveillance System, standard issue for all UNACO field operatives, and used it to check that his room hadn't been bugged in his absence. The room was clean. He replaced the humidor in his suitcase, then took a bottle of Perrier water from the fridge and opened it.

'You want something to drink?'

'No thanks, I've just had coffee.' She sat in one of the armchairs by the window.

'What's that?' he asked, pointing to the paper in her hand.

She gave it to him then updated him on the points made by Paluzzi after Graham had left. He listened carefully, then put the photocopy on the bedside table to read later in more detail.

'I didn't mean to upset you earlier,' she said. 'I just felt it needed to be said.'

She tensed herself for the rebuke. It was always the same when someone tried to raise the subject of his family. He would only talk about them *on his terms*. It was a deep, personal grief and he had never let anyone past the barriers he had built around himself since the tragedy.

'You're probably right,' he muttered at length, his hands clenched tightly around the bottle.

His reply caught her off-guard. He looked up slowly at her. The cynicism had gone from his eyes, and he suddenly looked vulnerable. It was a side of him she had never seen before. She said nothing. It was up to him to break the silence. *On his terms.*

'What you said in your room hurt me,' he said softly, his eyes never leaving her face. 'That's why I stormed out. I needed to go for a walk and clear my head. My anger was initially aimed at you. But the more I thought about it, the more I realized that I was angry with myself. You're the only person who's ever tried to help me overcome the grief, or perhaps I should call it bitterness, that's built up inside me since I lost Carrie and Mikey. Everyone else tiptoes around it as if it doesn't exist. And I've always resented you for it. That's why I've knocked you whenever I could. It was my way of getting back at you. You hurt me, I hurt you. Pretty pathetic when you think about it. Some partner I've turned out to be.'

Sabrina still said nothing, but her face showed her sympathetic concern.

'There's something I want to tell you. It might give you a better understanding of what's going on up here,' he said, tapping his head. 'I've never told this to anybody before. Not even my mother. And I'm closer to her than I am to anyone.' He placed the bottle on the carpet between his feet and ran his fingers through his hair, struggling to marshal his thoughts. He finally looked up at her. 'I was going to resign my post at Delta after I got back from Libya.'

'Did Carrie know?' Sabrina asked softly.

He shook his head. 'She found out she was pregnant two days before I left for Libya. That's when I made my decision to quit, but the crisis was already brewing in Libya and I didn't get a chance to do anything about it. We were going to throw a party when I got back to announce her pregnancy to our family and friends. I thought that would be the perfect time to tell her.' He smiled sadly. 'You can't imagine how happy that would have made her.'

'But would you have been happy?' she asked.

'It wasn't a decision I took lightly, believe me. And I wouldn't have done it unless I was absolutely certain in my own mind that it was the right thing to do. At the time I thought it was.' He picked up the bottle and turned it around slowly in his hands. 'Without sounding vain, I could have walked into any number of jobs. Instructor, supervisor, consultant. And none of them would have been desk jobs. I would have been still in the field and I would have had my family around me. It's exactly what Carrie would have wanted.' His gaze moved around the room. 'You can't imagine how I felt when I heard about the kidnapping. I was gutted. My first reaction was to call off the mission. That way I would have been reunited with Carrie and Mikey when I got back home. At least in theory. But the more I thought about it, the more I realized I just couldn't do it. It would have been the coward's way out. How could I have ever looked them in the face again? There was only one decision I could take. Maybe now you can appreciate the hell I've been going through these past fourteen months.'

'I think I can,' she said quietly.

He stood up. 'We've got a big day ahead of us tomorrow.

I'm going to have a bath, then get some sleep. Who knows what time we'll be woken in the morning.'

'Thanks for talking to me, Mike.'

'Sure,' he muttered.

She hugged him to her, then quickly left the room.

# SEVEN

*Wednesday*

The telephone rang.

Kolchinsky rolled over in bed and reached out a hand to feel for the receiver. He knocked his watch and cigarettes off the bedside table, then, opening one eye, he saw that the telephone was still a foot away from his outstretched fingers. He struggled to sit up in bed and lifted the receiver to his ear.

'Sergei?'

'Speaking,' Kolchinsky replied, then reached down to pick up his cigarettes and watch from the floor. He squinted at the time. 7.04 a.m. He yawned.

'It's Fabio. Paolo Conte's regained consciousness.'

Kolchinsky lit a cigarette, then dropped the packet on the table. 'Have any of your men had a chance to speak to him?'

'Not yet. I'm on my way to the hospital now.'

'I'll meet you there in thirty minutes,' Kolchinsky said, then put his hand over the mouthpiece and coughed violently.

'Are you all right?' Paluzzi asked.

'Fine,' Kolchinsky said, eyeing the cigarette with distaste. 'I'll tell the others.'

'What about Calvieri?'

'He'll have to be told,' Kolchinsky said.

'I'll leave that to you. See you at the hospital in thirty minutes.'

Kolchinsky replaced the receiver, then took another drag on the cigarette. Why did he persist in smoking? It wasn't as if he even enjoyed it any more. It had just become a costly, addictive habit. He stubbed out the cigarette, then called Graham and Sabrina in their rooms. He then rang Calvieri's room. No reply. He dialled the number Calvieri had given to him the previous evening. It was answered immediately.

'*Posso parlare con Tony Culvieri?*' Kolchinsky asked.

'*Resti in linea,*' came the reply, and Kolchinsky heard the receiver being placed on a hard surface, probably a table.

It was picked up moments later. '*Pronto, sono Tony Calvieri.*'

'It's Kolchinsky. Conte's regained consciousness. We're meeting Paluzzi at the hospital in thirty minutes.'

'I'll be there as soon as I can.'

'Any luck with the investigation?'

Calvieri sighed. 'Not really, I'm afraid. I'll fill you in when I see you. Thanks for letting me know about Conte.'

Kolchinsky met up with Graham and Sabrina ten minutes later outside the hotel and they drove to the Santo Spirito Hospital in the heart of the city. Paluzzi was waiting for them in the foyer.

'Have you spoken to Conte?' Kolchinsky asked.

'I haven't had a chance. I've only just got here myself.' Paluzzi waited until a nurse had passed out of earshot then asked, 'Where's Calvieri?'

'He was still at Pisani's house when I called. He said he would be here as soon as he could.'

'That suits me fine,' Paluzzi said, leading them to the lift. 'I don't want him around until we've finished questioning Conte.'

'Why?' Sabrina asked.

Paluzzi got into the lift last and pressed the button for the third floor. 'It's psychological. Ubrino tried to kill him. We have to play on that if we're going to get him into our confidence. If we're seen to be working with the Red Brigades it could undermine our position. We can't afford to take that chance.'

They got out on the third floor. Paluzzi indicated the two uniformed carabinieri sitting outside the private ward at the end of the corridor. They approached the two men and Paluzzi identified himself.

'Who are the others?' one of the policemen asked.

'They're with me, that's all you need to know. Is Conte still conscious?'

'Yes, sir,' the policeman answered.

Paluzzi took Graham to one side. 'I'm sending these two for an early breakfast. I'd like you to wait out here for Calvieri. Whatever you do, don't let him come in.'

'Got you,' Graham replied.

Paluzzi spoke to the two policemen and they headed off for a welcome bite to eat. He opened the door and a third policeman, sitting beside the door, immediately got to his feet and challenged him. Paluzzi showed him his ID and asked him to join his colleagues in the cafeteria. The policeman left the room. Kolchinsky and Sabrina went inside and she closed the door silently behind her.

Conte lay motionless on the bed. His face was sallow, his bloodshot eyes watching their every move. He tried to speak, but his throat was dry. Sabrina poured some water from the jug on the bedside table into a tumbler and tilted his head forward so he could take a drink. He coughed as the water ran down his throat.

'*Grazie*,' he said in a barely audible whisper.

'*Prego*,' she replied, putting the tumbler back on the table.

She was amazed at how young he looked. The UNACO

156

dossier had given his age as twenty-two. He looked more like a schoolboy. Sixteen, seventeen at most. What had motivated him to join the Red Brigades when he had his whole life ahead of him? It seemed such a waste. Why couldn't he see that? Perhaps now he would realize the futility of it all. The dream had become a nightmare.

Graham peered around the door. 'Fabio, you'd better get out here.'

Paluzzi crossed to the door. 'What is it? Has Calvieri arrived?'

'Calvieri I can handle.' Graham stabbed a thumb over his shoulder. 'There's a doctor out there who's pretty pissed off with you. He says you were supposed to call him when you got here. Know anything about it?'

Paluzzi nodded and stepped out into the corridor.

The man was in his thirties with black hair and a neatly trimmed black beard.

'Doctor Marchetta?' Paluzzi asked.

'*Si*,' came the curt response.

Paluzzi introduced himself in English and held up his ID card.

'And who is he?' Marchetta gestured to Graham. 'I take offence to being bullied by some foreigner.'

'He's a security consultant with Neo-Chem Industries. He was sent over here from the United States to help with the investigation.'

Marchetta glared at Graham, then turned back to Paluzzi. 'We agreed over the phone that you would contact me when you arrived at the hospital,' he said, switching to Italian to exclude Graham from the conversation.

'I tried to contact you but you were unavailable at the time.'

'Then you should have waited until I was available!' Marchetta snapped angrily.

'I'm conducting a serious criminal investigation, Doctor. I don't have time to wait about for you or anybody else.

157

Surely you have an assistant? Why couldn't you have sent him to meet me?'

'The reason why I wanted to speak to you personally was to tell you about Conte's condition. He's very weak right now. It's only to be expected after being in a coma for the past forty-eight hours. I can't let you talk to him for more than five minutes. You'll be able to question him further this afternoon, depending of course on his condition.'

'I don't have time to question him in instalments,' Paluzzi said sharply. 'I need answers *now*.'

'It's out of the question. He's in no condition to be interrogated. Five minutes, that's all.'

'I'm not asking you, Doctor, I'm telling you. I'm not leaving here until I have the answers I want.'

'Major, your jurisdiction's out there,' Marchetta said, gesturing towards the window with a sweep of his arm. 'But your authority ended when you entered the hospital. This is my jurisdiction. And what I say goes.'

'Four guards were killed during the break-in.' Paluzzi pointed to the door. 'He is one of the men responsible—'

'I hate the Red Brigades just as much as the next man, Major, but I'd be failing in my duty as a doctor if I didn't do everything in my power to nurse him back to health. Then he can stand trial and I hope he spends the rest of his life in jail for what he's done. But in this hospital he's a patient, not a terrorist. And he'll be treated as such.'

'Ten minutes,' Paluzzi said. 'And before you launch into another speech, spare a thought for the victims' families.'

'I can't risk it, Major. Not at this stage. The matron will be up in exactly five minutes' time to administer his medication.' Marchetta spun on his heels and strode to the lift.

'What was all that about?' Graham asked.

'I was buying some time for Sergei and Sabrina. I only hope they used it.'

Graham frowned, then took his seat again opposite the door.

Paluzzi went back into the ward. Kolchinsky, standing by the window, immediately put a finger to his lips and motioned to him to remain at the door. Paluzzi nodded then looked at Sabrina who was sitting by the bed, her back to him, a micro-cassette player in her hand. Kolchinsky tiptoed across to Paluzzi and indicated that they should leave the room.

'What's wrong?' Graham asked as they emerged into the corridor.

'Nothing,' Kolchinsky said, easing himself on to the chair beside Graham. 'Sabrina's managed to get him talking. I don't want them interrupted until she's finished.'

'She's got about four minutes left,' Paluzzi said, and recounted his conversation with Marchetta.

'And what if she's not through by the time the matron arrives?' Graham asked.

'Then we come back later,' Paluzzi answered.

'What?' Graham stared at Paluzzi in disbelief. 'This could be the breakthrough and you talk about coming back later? The deadline's tomorrow morning, in case you've forgotten.'

'I don't have any authority in here, Mike. If we start throwing our weight around we're going to be out on the street before we know what's hit us. And knowing the sort of person Marchetta is, he'll block any further visits until he's sure Conte's up to them. And he'd be perfectly in his rights to do so. We've got no option, we have to play it by the rules.'

Graham was about to speak but thought better of it. What was the use? Paluzzi was right.

'We've got company,' Paluzzi said as Calvieri emerged from the lift.

'Just what the doctor ordered,' Graham muttered.

'Morning,' Calvieri called out, then gestured towards the door. 'What have you got from Conte?'

159

'Nothing yet,' Kolchinsky said. 'Sabrina's still in there with him.'

'Let me speak to him,' Calvieri said, making for the door.

Paluzzi blocked his path. 'Not until we know what Sabrina's found out. You walk in there now and you could blow any chance we have of cracking the case.'

Calvieri moved to the window and watched a barge laden with crates of fresh produce negotiate its way under the Vittorio Emanuele Bridge and disappear around a sharp bend in the river.

'What's the latest on the Pisani murder?' Kolchinsky asked.

Calvieri turned away from the window. 'Five dead. Signore Pisani; Rocca, the man Sabrina and I saw last night; and three *Brigatisti* who were guarding the house.'

'Any clues, other than that one of the assailants was black?' Kolchinsky pressed.

'None so far. It was obviously a professional hit. Even the number plates on the getaway car were blacked out with masking tape.'

'Who do you suspect?' Kolchinsky continued.

Calvieri shrugged. 'We have a lot of enemies but as I said, this was certainly a professional hit. That rules out the vast majority of fascist groups. Most of them wouldn't have the imagination to hire an outside man, let alone have the money to pay him.'

'So you think it was carried out by a contract killer?' Kolchinsky said.

'That's my guess, yes.' Calvieri bit his lower lip pensively. 'He probably flew in last night, did the job, then flew out again this morning. Our best lead is this black accomplice of his. If we can find him we could identify the hit man.'

Graham and Kolchinsky exchanged glances.

'So you think his accomplice is a local?' Graham asked.

'That's the assumption we're working on at the moment. I'm confident we'll find him before the police do.'

'Then what? Thumbscrews and electric shocks?'

'We have our methods, Mr Graham, just like you.'

The door opened and Sabrina emerged into the corridor. 'I thought I heard your voice, Tony. Conte wants to see you.'

'I thought he might,' Calvieri said, smiling triumphantly at Paluzzi.

She grabbed Calvieri's arm when he tried to get past her. 'I'm Sabrina Trestelli, your assistant from Milan. It's the only way I could get him to talk.'

'Of course,' Calvieri said, and followed her into the ward.

'Have you had a chance to talk to your man, Whitlock, since the hit last night?' Paluzzi asked Kolchinsky.

'No, he hasn't contacted me.'

'And you've got no way of contacting him?'

Kolchinsky shook his head. 'It would be too dangerous. He'll call when he can.'

'We've got to warn him, Sergei,' Graham said. 'What chance has he got if Calvieri's thugs catch him unawares?'

'We can't, Michael, you know that. We could blow his cover.'

'I can put a tail on him. No *Brigatista* will get near him.'

'And what if Young smells a rat? We're dealing with a professional, Fabio, not some two-bit Chicago hood.' Graham looked at Kolchinsky. 'We've got to warn him, Sergei.'

'Let's play it by ear, shall we?' Kolchinsky said defensively, knowing Graham was right. But it was neither the time nor the place to discuss it.

'It's throwing-out time,' Paluzzi said, indicating the matron at the end of the corridor.

Kolchinsky stood up. 'I hope Sabrina's got everything

she can out of Conte. We can't be coming and going for snippets of information every few hours.'

The matron greeted them with a smile and disappeared into the ward. Calvieri and Sabrina emerged moments later.

'Well, what have you found out?' Kolchinsky asked anxiously.

'I'll tell you on the way back to the hotel,' Sabrina replied, holding up the micro-cassette player in her hand. 'It's all on here.'


'That's it,' Sabrina said, switching off the micro-cassette player. She got up from the armchair in Kolchinsky's room and helped herself to a roll from the breakfast tray which he had ordered.

'Good God,' Kolchinsky muttered, then placed his empty cup and saucer on the table beside him, his mind still reeling from Sabrina's translation of the dialogue on the tape.

'Let me get this straight,' Graham said, looking at Sabrina. 'Ubrino intends to open the vial at ten o'clock tomorrow morning at the Offenbach Centre in Berne, Switzerland, to coincide with the start of the summit of European leaders being held there, unless he sees a live telecast of Zocchi being put aboard an aeroplane bound for Cuba within the next twenty-five hours.'

'That's it,' she replied grimly.

'And he's got no idea where Ubrino might be hiding out until then,' Kolchinsky added. 'Calvieri, you know him better than the rest of us. Where do you think he is?'

'I don't know him that well. I would say he was still in Rome. It's what I'd do if I were in his position. Stick with the people I can trust.'

'But you haven't had one positive sighting of him here in Rome since the break-in,' Graham said. 'He could already be in Switzerland.'

'Of course he could,' Calvieri replied. 'But I still think he'd want to stay in an area where he knew he would be safe. And that has to be Rome. We do have sympathizers in Switzerland but very few of them share the radical views of the Rome cell. I'm sure if Paluzzi and I put our heads together we could come up with a list of names of Swiss sympathizers who could be hiding him. But I still say he's in Rome.'

'Fabio, I want you and Calvieri to put that list together,' Kolchinsky said.

'We can get on to it right away.'

'Give me an hour,' Calvieri said, getting to his feet. 'Bettinga's coming down from Genoa to take charge of the investigation at Signore Pisani's house. He should be there by now. Once I've briefed him I'll be completely at your disposal.'

'Well, the sooner you go, the sooner you'll be back,' Kolchinsky said, then jabbed his finger towards the door. 'Go on. And for God's sake, hurry up.'

'You can count on it.'

'Do you go along with his Rome theory?' Graham asked Paluzzi after Calvieri had closed the door.

'It makes sense, let's put it that way. And if he's right, we've got more chance of finding Lord Lucan here in Rome than we do of finding Ubrino. Even as the acting leader of the Red Brigades, Calvieri still won't hold much sway here. Pisani didn't, and he was more radical than Calvieri. As I've told you before, the Rome cell is a law unto itself.'

'So what's our best bet?' Kolchinsky asked. 'To try and catch him at the Offenbach Centre?'

'I wish it were,' Paluzzi replied. 'He was a make-up artist at the *Teatro dell'Opera* some years back. And a damn good one by all accounts. He's used a variety of disguises in the past and you can be sure he'll use another one to get into the Offenbach Centre.'

163

Kolchinsky rubbed his hands wearily over his face. 'Some breakthrough this is turning out to be.'

The telephone rang.

'That could be C.W.,' Sabrina said, jumping up to answer it.

'Sabrina?'

She immediately recognized Philpott's voice.

'Morning, sir,' she replied in surprise and glanced at her watch. It would be just past 4 a.m. in New York.

'Is Sergei there?'

'Yes sir,' she replied, handing the receiver to Kolchinsky who was already standing at her side.

'Morning, Malcolm,' Kolchinsky said, gesturing to Sabrina to pass him his cigarettes and matches. 'I wasn't expecting to hear from you until this afternoon.'

'Bad news, I'm afraid,' Philpott answered. 'I've just had a call from Major Lonsdale of Scotland Yard's anti-terrorist squad. Alexander's escaped.'

Kolchinsky sat on the edge of the bed and dropped his unlit cigarette into the ashtray. 'That's all we need.'

'Lonsdale's confident that he'll be re-arrested if he tries to leave the country but I still think C.W. should be told in case he does manage to slip through the net.'

'I'll get a message to him as soon as possible.'

'Any new developments since I last spoke to you?'

Kolchinsky told him briefly what Sabrina had found out from Conte earlier that morning.

'I'll call Reinhardt Kuhlmann, the Swiss police commissioner. We go back a long way. I'll tell him to expect a call from you this morning. You can fill him in on the details when you talk to him. I know he'll give you his full cooperation. And you better get hold of Jacques in Zurich and tell him the news as well. He can always liaise with Reinhardt until you get to Switzerland.'

Kolchinsky promised to call Philpott later in the morning, then hung up and told the others about Alexander's escape.

'But how are you going to warn him without blowing his cover?' Paluzzi asked.

'I wish I knew.' Kolchinsky looked at Graham and Sabrina. 'Well, any suggestions?'

'Yeah,' Graham announced. 'It involves Sabrina.'

'I might have guessed,' she said, eyeing Graham suspiciously. 'Well, what wonderful scheme have you come up with this time?'

Graham held out his empty cup towards her. 'How about a refill before I start?'

'That's where C.W.'s staying,' Graham said, pointing out the boarding house to Sabrina as they passed it in the car. He drove around the corner then pulled into the first available parking space he saw and killed the engine.

'This had better work,' she muttered, reaching down for her bag.

He looked at her and smiled to himself. She was dressed in a tight-fitting white blouse, a black leather mini-skirt, black stockings and black shoes with three-inch stiletto heels. Her hair was loose on her shoulders and she had purposely overdone the make-up, marring her naturally fine features. It had to be realistic, much as she hated the idea of impersonating a prostitute.

'I'm glad to see you find it funny,' she said sharply, reaching behind her for the black leather jacket on the back seat.

'You look great,' he said with a grin.

'You would think so. You're a man.' She opened the door. 'I'll see you back at the hotel.'

'Sabrina?'

She looked back at him.

'Good luck.'

'Who needs luck dressed like this?'

'You've got a point there,' he replied, then started up the car and drove away.

She took a deep breath as she walked towards the boarding house, well aware of the attention she was attracting from passing male motorists. She ignored the wolf-whistles even though she knew a real prostitute would have gladly stopped to trade insults with her leering admirers. It would only have made her feel even cheaper than she already felt. She was the first to admit she enjoyed wearing eye-catching clothes, but she *always* dressed for herself, not for anyone else. With these clothes she felt as if she was dressed for every man in the city. She hated the feeling. It was degrading.

She reached the boarding house and climbed the steps to the open door leading into the foyer. The receptionist gave her an indifferent look as if she'd seen it all before and returned to her knitting. Sabrina climbed the stairs to the first floor where she paused to get her bearings from the directional board on the wall. A door opened and an elderly couple emerged from their room. They eyed her disapprovingly as they walked to the stairs. She waited until they had laboriously descended, then pushed a stick of gum into her mouth and made her way to Whitlock's room, where she rapped loudly on the door.

The door was opened. It was Young. What was he doing there? Had Paluzzi's men got the two room numbers mixed up?

'I look for Signore Anderson,' she said in a strong Italian accent. 'You Anderson?'

'Hell, no,' Young replied, then ran his eyes the length of her body and whistled softly to himself. 'But right now I wish I was. Anderson, you've got company.'

Whitlock's eyes widened in amazement when he saw Sabrina but he quickly checked himself and approached the door, waiting for her to give him a cue.

'You call agency and ask for girl who speak English,' she said, chewing methodically on the gum. 'But who your friend? You say nothing about friend on phone. It cost more.'

Young grinned at Whitlock. 'Well, I'll be damned. When did you reserve this little beauty?'

'Last night, after we got back. I fancied a bit of company but they told me none of the English-speaking girls were available until this morning.'

'Company, is that what you call it?' Young ran his fingers through her hair. 'You're something else, sweet-heart.'

'You touch, you pay,' she said sharply.

'Some other time,' Young said with a sneer. He slapped Whitlock on the arm. 'I'll see you later.'

Whitlock waited until Young had disappeared down the stairs, then closed the door and crossed to the bedside table and switched on the radio. He found a music channel and beckoned Sabrina towards him.

'Is the place wired?' she whispered, dropping the gum into the ashtray.

He shook his head. 'No, I checked it this morning. It's the walls. They're paper thin. If Young comes back I wouldn't put it past him to try and listen through the wall. The radio will drown out any noises we're supposed to be making.'

'That's a relief,' she said with a wry smile.

'Whose idea was it for you to dress up like this?'

'Mike's, naturally. I picked up the clothes on approval from a boutique half an hour ago. They're going straight back again this afternoon, believe me.' She sat down on a wooden chair and put her bag on the dressing-table behind her. 'It worked, though, just as he predicted it would. It was the one sure way of seeing you alone.'

'How long have I been under surveillance?'

She smiled. 'How did you know that?'

'How else would you have known I was in?'

'A couple of Fabio's men have had the boarding house

under surveillance since the hit last night. I hear you've already changed getaway cars?'

'I did it first thing this morning. We couldn't be sure whether it was spotted or not last night.'

'Not according to the police report Fabio got through this morning. But whether the Red Brigades know is another matter altogether. Calvieri's being very secretive.'

'Wouldn't you if you were in his position?'

'I suppose so. That's one of the reasons I'm here.' She went on to explain first about Alexander's escape from custody, then about Calvieri's theory about the gunman's black accomplice.

'And Calvieri's sure to have a better description of me than the police if it came from that guard I knocked out,' he said once Sabrina had finished speaking.

'They're looking for a local,' she reminded him.

'That's according to Calvieri. And now with Alexander on the loose I'm going to have to keep one eye open for him and the other open for some Red Brigades hit squad that could come knocking on my door at any moment. How the hell am I supposed to concentrate on Young with all this going on around me?'

She took a Browning Mk2 from her bag and offered it to him. 'I know,' she said. 'You may need this.'

'And how would I explain it to Young? Alexander never uses guns. No, I daren't risk it.'

'You may have to use it on Young, especially if Calvieri's his next target.' She explained briefly what Conte had told her. 'We can't afford any slip-ups at this stage of the operation. And any attempt to hit Calvieri would certainly throw us off-balance. He's our only hope if we need to negotiate with Ubrino. We'd be lost without him. Take the gun, C.W. Please.'

Whitlock took the Browning from her and slipped it into the bedside table drawer. He glanced at the booby-trapped watch but decided against telling her about it. The others had enough to worry about as it was. He would deal with it himself.

'I don't know exactly when we're leaving for Berne,' she said, breaking the sudden silence. 'Probably some time in the next few hours. There isn't much else we can do here. You're to liaise with Jacques from now on. He'll pass your reports on to Sergei.'

Whitlock nodded.

'I'd better be going,' she said, getting to her feet and smoothing down her mini-skirt. 'I'm dying to get out of these clothes and scrape the make-up off my face. I don't know how these girls can put up with the discomfort every time they go out on the streets. It's revolting.'

'It's a living, I guess,' he replied and walked with her to the door. 'Thanks for coming over, Sabrina. I appreciate it.'

She hugged him. 'Take care of yourself.'

'And you,' he replied, then closed the door after her.

She hailed the first taxi she saw outside the boarding house. It stopped beside her. Had she been dressed differently the driver would probably have ignored her. Not that it bothered her. She was just glad to be heading back to the hotel.

Calvieri found a parking space on the busy Corso Vittorio Emanuele and walked the two blocks to *La Sfera di Cristallo*, a small, inexpensive restaurant which had been there for as long as he could remember. It had only ever had one owner, a fat, balding man now in his mid-sixties with a liking for the music of Berlioz.

He went inside. Nothing had changed since he had been there last, when he had been a Rome cell commander. And that included the music. He recognized the piece immediately: 'The Hungarian March' from *The Damnation of Faust*. He had heard it enough times in the past.

'A table for one?' a female voice inquired behind him.

He turned round and smiled at the teenage waitress. 'Thank you, no. I'm looking for Signore Castellano. He's expecting me. The name's Calvieri.'

'I know who you are,' she said with a quick smile. 'I've seen you on television. What you say makes a lot of sense.'

'Thank you.'

'I'll call . . .' she trailed off when she caught sight of the eighteen-stone Castellano approaching them.

'Tony,' Castellano called out in his gravelly voice and clasped Calvieri in a bear-like grip, kissing him on both cheeks. 'You're looking well, my friend.'

'And you're looking well fed,' Calvieri countered, patting Castellano's stomach.

Castellano chuckled but his face quickly became serious and he pressed his fist against his chest. 'My heart is heavy today, Tony. Signore Pisani was a great man. But I know you won't fail us as our new leader.'

'I'm just deputizing until the committee meets next week to vote for a new leader.'

'You're too modest, Tony. You can't lose. There's nobody to touch you.'

'I'm sure Zocchi would have something to say about that.'

'Ah, Zocchi. He's a pig. He's where he belongs. In jail.' Castellano put an arm around Calvieri's shoulders and led him through the packed restaurant to a door beside the swing doors leading into the kitchen. It was marked: DIRETTORE. 'Signore Bettinga's waiting for you in there. Can I get you something to eat? A small pizza napoletana? That was always your favourite.'

'I've eaten, thank you. But I wouldn't say no to one of your famous cappuccini.'

'Coming up,' Castellano replied and disappeared into the kitchen.

Calvieri entered the office and closed the door behind him. Luigi Bettinga sat behind Castellano's desk absently paging through a culinary magazine. He was a small, dapper man in his late thirties with beady eyes and prematurely grey hair. He always reminded Calvieri of an accountant. They had been close friends for years and Calvieri saw him as an integral part of the new committee under his leadership.

'*Ciao*, Tony,' Bettinga said and came round to the front of the desk to shake hands with Calvieri. 'I'm sorry I wasn't at the house this morning. The plane was delayed in Genoa. I must have got there just after you left.'

'You're here now, that's the main thing,' Calvieri said, helping himself to a cigarette from the pack on Castellano's desk. 'Your phone call intrigued me. Why did you want to meet me away from the house?'

'The house and the grounds are still crawling with police. I couldn't take the chance of letting them overhear what I'm going to tell you.'

'You've come up with something already, haven't you?'

Bettinga nodded. 'Yes, but I can hardly take the credit. I only took over from where you left off.'

'So what is it?'

There was a knock at the door and Castellano came in with the cappuccino. He put it on the table and withdrew discreetly, closing the door carefully behind him.

'Well?' Calvieri prompted.

'We know the identity of the gunman's accomplice.'

'That's excellent news.' Calvieri picked up the coffee cup and sat down in the leather armchair against the wall. 'Is he a local?'

Bettinga shook his head. 'The name on the passport is Raymond Anderson. It's sure to be false.'

'Where's he staying?'

'A boarding house on the via Marche near the Villa Borghese.'

'What about the gunman?' Calvieri asked, wiping the froth from his moustache. 'Any clues to his identity?'

'Not yet. But we do have a description of him. We got it from the receptionist at the car hire company who told us about Anderson. Blond. Good-looking. American accent.'

'An American?' Calvieri mused thoughtfully.

'The boarding house is under surveillance. What do you want done?'

'The American *must* be taken alive. We have to find out who he's working for. Who knows, one of us could be his next target.'

'And Anderson?'

'He's not so important. It's the American I want.' Calvieri took another sip of the cappuccino. 'This has to be a low-key affair, Luigi. The police mustn't suspect anything. If they found out we had the American they would raid every safe house in the country looking for him. There's only one man I'd trust to handle this kind of job.'

'Escoletti?'

'Right. Giancarlo Escoletti. Get him on the next flight to Rome. We can't afford to waste any more time.'

'I'm way ahead of you, Tony. I've got Escoletti on standby at the Condotti Hotel. I sent for him as soon as I got your call last night.'

'Mister Efficiency himself. Next you'll be challenging me for the leadership.'

'It never crossed my mind, Tony,' Bettinga replied indignantly, then noticed the smile on Calvieri's face. 'Your little joke, right?'

Calvieri had always maintained that Bettinga would have made a perfect poker-faced comedian. He never smiled. Irony was totally lost on him.

'Call Escoletti and tell him to bring the American in.' Calvieri finished his cappuccino and got to his feet. 'I've got to get back to the hotel.'

'What did Ubrino steal from the plant? Signore Pisani

wouldn't have asked you to help the authorities unless it was something pretty important.'

'I can't say anything at the moment, Luigi. I promise I'll give the committee a full report at next week's meeting.'

'Do you think there could be a connection between the break-in at the plant and the hit on Signore Pisani?'

'That's what I hope to find out from the American.'

Bettinga sat down behind the desk after Calvieri had left the room and dialled the number of the Condotti Hotel. He asked for Escoletti's room.

'Hello?' a voice answered.

'Escoletti?'

'Speaking.'

'It's Bettinga. I've spoken to Signore Calvieri. He wants the American brought in alive.'

'What about Anderson?'

'He's not important. You can kill him if you have to. You know where to take the American. Call me when it's done. And Escoletti, don't risk anything that could alert the authorities. Signore Calvieri was quite insistent about that.'

'Leave it to me. The authorities won't suspect a thing.'

Bettinga replaced the receiver, then took a couple of peppermints from the bowl on the table and thoughtfully put them into his mouth.

'Where have you been?' Kolchinsky demanded once he had let Calvieri into his room.

'I'm sure you know that already,' Calvieri replied. 'Paluzzi's men have been tailing me ever since I arrived in Rome. But to answer your question, I was called out unexpectedly to deal with some Red Brigades business.'

'We had an agreement, Calvieri. You work with us until the vial's been recovered. And that means staying on call, like the rest of us. So next time you get an unexpected call, send one of your associates to deal with the problem. Isn't that what leadership's all about? Delegation?'

'I'll bear it in mind, *next time*,' Calvieri retorted sarcastically.

'You do that. But right now you'd better start packing.' Kolchinsky handed Calvieri an airline ticket. 'Flight 340 to Berne. It leaves Rome at twelve-twenty. That's in less than two hours' time. And you *will* be on the plane with the rest of us, that I promise you.'

Escoletti parked the hired Fiat Regata a block away from the boarding house, took the black doctor's bag from the back seat and got out of the car, locking the door behind him.

He was a tall, distinguished-looking man in his late forties with thick black hair which was beginning to grey in streaks at the temples. He had once been a doctor but had been struck off the medical register for attempting to rape one of his patients. On his release from jail he had drifted into a life of crime and joined the Red Brigades in '84 after meeting Calvieri at a recruitment party in Milan. His expertise with firearms (he had been a crack shot since his early teens) together with his extensive medical knowledge had made him one of the most in-demand assassins in the organization. In '87 he had been promoted on to the committee as a senior security consultant, a position he still held, which entailed him advising the different cells on the feasibility of their intended terror campaigns across the country. He still worked in the field, but only on those assignments sanctioned at the highest level of the committee. He was known as 'the Specialist'. Just like a doctor.

He walked past the boarding house to the narrow alleyway which ran parallel to the side of the building. He picked his way with distaste through the overflowing dustbins and paused at the foot of the fire escape. Anderson and Yardley were in Rooms 15 and 16. First floor. That's what the receptionist told him when he had called the boarding house from the hotel. He climbed the metal stairs to the first floor and pulled open the door. The corridor was deserted. His plan was simple. He would immobilize both men with the dart gun in his overcoat pocket then withdraw back down the fire escape and make his way round to the reception where he would say that they had called him earlier complaining of upset stomachs. He would then go to their rooms, call the bogus ambulance which was on standby not far from the boarding house, and tell the receptionist that he had diagnosed food poisoning in both cases. They would then be taken away on stretchers, 'under sedation', and driven in the ambulance to a safe house on the outskirts of the city. The manager of the boarding house would play down the incident, desperate to avoid any adverse publicity, and by the time the authorities did latch on to the deception the committee would have the answers they wanted and the two men would be dead. He had used the plan in the past to kidnap targets selected by the committee. It had never failed.

He stopped outside Anderson's room. Certainly the lesser of two evils. He curled a gloved hand around the dart gun in his pocket and rapped sharply on the door. Silence. He knocked on Yardley's door. Again, silence. He cursed under his breath. It was what he had been dreading. The boarding house had only been under surveillance for the past forty minutes. They must have gone out before that. On foot. The Volkswagen Jetta Anderson had hired that morning was still parked out in the street. They could be back at any time. He decided to check the rooms for any clues to their real identities. Not that he held out much hope. They were professionals. Well, the one calling himself Yardley certainly was. But he would talk, like the others before him. Escoletti had his methods. He was a doctor. A specialist.

He would search Anderson's room first. Then Yardley's room. Then he would wait.

Whitlock had left the boarding house soon after Sabrina. He had needed to clear his thoughts. He had gone for a walk, careful to keep easily within a mile radius of the bar at the end of the block where Young was drinking.

What if Calvieri was the next hit on Young's list? He would have to stop Young if he did get too close to Calvieri. What about the transmitter? He was suddenly glad of the Browning Sabrina had given to him. He had no qualms about killing Young, especially with the threat of the transmitter ever present in his mind. To hell with Philpott's orders in the dossier to bring Young in alive. He would do what *he* thought best under the circumstances. And that meant killing Young.

What about Alexander? He doubted he would have to deal with him. How could Alexander possibly trace him? Young wouldn't have used his real name in London. And there was no record of their departure at any of the airports. An American airbase would be the last place he would think of checking. And even if he did, how far would he get? No, Alexander didn't worry him.

What did worry him was a revenge attack by the Red Brigades. It had been a mistake to approach the guard so openly outside Pisani's house. But what choice did he have? He had to get Young out, if only because of the transmitter in his pocket. Had he driven the car up to the gate the guard would have opened fire. Not that he could say anything to Young about Sabrina's warning. His only hope was if Calvieri went to Switzerland. They would surely follow him. And that would take the heat off them, at least for the time being . . .

He finished his espresso at the small coffee bar, paid for it, and walked the short distance back to the boarding house. The receptionist handed him his room key, then returned to her knitting. He froze halfway up the stairs when he saw Escoletti using one of the skeleton keys to open Young's door. He pressed himself against the wall when Escoletti looked round furtively before picking up his black bag and disappearing into Young's room. Whitlock's mind was racing. Who was he? A detective? A *Brigatista*? Did he have any accomplices? Was the boarding house being watched? He looked down into the foyer. It was deserted. He retraced his steps down the stairs and went out into the street. He looked around slowly, careful not to arouse any suspicion. He couldn't see anything untoward. Not that he had any idea who, or what, he was looking for. He had to warn Young. He walked to the bar and pushed open the door. It was a small room with a dozen tables dotted about the floor and a counter running the length of one wall. A propeller fan turned slowly overhead. The five customers all sat at the bar. Nobody spoke.

Young sat at the end of the counter, a bottle of Budweiser in front of him. He was about to take a mouthful when he noticed Whitlock standing by the door. 'Well, how was she?' he called out, then beckoned Whitlock towards him. 'As good as she looked?'

'I've got to talk to you,' Whitlock said, ignoring Young's unpleasant leer.

'So talk,' Young replied, lifting the bottle to his lips.

'Not here,' Whitlock retorted. 'Over there, at one of the tables.'

Young frowned but followed Whitlock to the table furthest away from the counter. Whitlock sat facing the doorway, watching for the tail he was sure had followed him to the bar.

'What is it?' Young demanded.

Whitlock told Young what he had seen at the boarding house.

'And you've never seen this guy before?' Young asked.

Whitlock shook his head. 'He looked like a cop.'

177

Young pushed the bottle away from him. 'We've got to get out of here, fast. If you were followed it'll only be a matter of time before the reinforcements arrive. Wait here.'

'Where are you going?'

Young didn't answer the question and crossed to the counter where he spoke softly to the barman. He then took a wad of notes from his jacket pocket and handed them discreetly to the barman who pocketed them then indicated the door behind him with a vague flick of his hand. Young beckoned Whitlock over.

'What's going on?' Whitlock asked.

'I've just bought us an escape route,' Young replied, then pointed to the entrance. 'We can't get out that way. Not if it's being watched.'

The barman opened the hatch and Whitlock followed Young behind the counter. The barman closed it behind them then led them through the door into the kitchen. A woman looked up from the vegetables she was dicing, smiled fleetingly at the barman, then returned to her work. The barman opened the back door and Young peered out into the alleyway. He gestured for Whitlock to follow him, and the barman closed the door behind them.

'Which way?' Whitlock asked.

Young pointed left. 'According to the barman it comes out in the street at the back of the bar. We'll be able to get a taxi there.'

'How much money have you got on you?'

Young shrugged. 'About forty thousand lire.'

'I've got even less. How far's it going to get us? You'll have to call Wiseman and tell him what happened. We need more money.'

'I'll call him later. First we need to get to the *Stazione Termini*,' Young said as they reached the road. 'Flag down the first taxi you see.'

'Why are we going to the station?' Whitlock demanded. 'We need money before we can go anywhere.'

'That's why we're going to the station. General Wiseman left a holdall in one of the lockers for this kind of emergency. It contains money, new passports and a duplicate set of the weapons I've been using out here. Now let's find a taxi.'

# EIGHT

Reinhardt Kuhlmann had been the Swiss police commissioner for sixteen years. Now, aged sixty-one, he had vowed to make it his last year in office. It would be his third 'retirement' in seven years. On the two previous occasions he had been back behind his desk within months. But, much as he hated the idea, he knew he would have to bow out this time. The pressure from his family was getting to him, especially from his son and daughter-in-law who were continually badgering him to spend more time at home with his wife. They didn't understand. Neither of them was connected with law enforcement. The force was in his blood. It had become an addictive drug over the past forty-two years and his greatest fear was what effect retirement would have on him.

He pushed any thoughts of his impending retirement from his mind. He would have plenty of time to reflect on it in the years to come. He opened his briefcase and took out a folder. There was only one word on it. UNACO. Although he and Malcolm Philpott were old friends he had never attempted to hide his dislike for the organization. The concept of an international strike force appealed to him, but that's where it ended. He argued that their use of blackmail, intimidation and violence, as well as their willingness to bend the law to suit their own needs, made them just like the criminals they had been set up to combat in the first place. But he knew his was a lone voice of protest. There were times when he thought he was something of an anachronism in the contemporary world of law enforcement. He hated guns, and he particularly hated the idea of gun-toting foreigners shooting up his country. It had happened before and he knew it would happen again. It was inevitable.

There was a knock at the door.

He answered it and immediately recognized Kolchinsky from the photograph in the folder lying on the table behind him. They shook hands and then Kuhlmann ushered him in.

'I feel as if I know you already,' Kolchinsky said with a smile. 'Malcolm's told me a lot about you.'

'Nothing bad, I hope. Won't you sit down?' Kuhlmann indicated the two chairs on either side of the window. 'I ordered some coffee when I knew you were on your way up. It should be here any time now. How was your flight?'

'Tedious, but aren't they all? When did you get in from Zurich?'

Kuhlmann sat down. 'A couple of hours ago.'

'And you've been fully briefed?'

Kuhlmann pointed to the folder. 'Your man, Jacques Rust, briefed me over breakfast this morning.'

There was another knock at the door. As Kuhlmann had predicted it was the room service waiter with the coffee. He took the tray from him and set it down on the table beside his chair.

'How do you take your coffee?'

'Milk, one sugar,' Kolchinsky replied.

'Tell me, how did Rust manage to get these rooms at such short notice?' Kuhlmann asked as he poured out the coffee. 'I'm told there isn't a spare hotel bed within a twenty-mile radius of the city for the duration of the summit. I could understand if he'd managed to get one room. But six? And all here at the Metropole. I'm intrigued.'

Kolchinsky refused to rise to the bait. Philpott had

warned him about Kuhlmann's attitude towards UNACO. Kuhlmann was out to prove that Rust had used some underhand method to get the rooms. Kolchinsky was sure Rust *had* used some underhand method – how else would he have got them? But that's what made him such an invaluable asset to UNACO. He was like Philpott in that respect. They played on the indiscretions of others to get what they wanted. Kuhlmann would probably regard it as blackmail. Kolchinsky regarded it as simply good business sense.

'I haven't spoken to Jacques recently so I honestly couldn't tell you how he did it,' Kolchinsky replied truthfully, taking the cup and saucer from Kuhlmann and sitting back in his chair. 'Did Jacques give you a photograph of Ubrino to circulate among your men?'

Kuhlmann nodded. 'It's been faxed through to every police station in the country. I've got teams checking all the hotels, boarding houses and chalets in and around the Berne area. If he's here, we'll find him.'

'He is a master of disguise,' Kolchinsky reminded him.

'Which is why a police artist put the photograph through his computer and came up with a series of different disguises. Seven possibilities in all. They're all being used in the search. We may be a small nation, Mr Kolchinsky, but we do have an effective police force. I see to that.'

'It was an observation, not a criticism.'

'I resent UNACO being here, Mr Kolchinsky. But I especially resent you bringing scum like Calvieri into the country. We can catch Ubrino ourselves. I have some of Europe's finest policemen on the force. Men who use brains, not guns, to bring criminals to justice. We don't need you here.'

'So expel us,' Kolchinsky challenged.

'If it were up to me none of you would have got permission to land here in the first place. Unfortunately my Government views the situation differently.'

'Malcolm told me you disliked UNACO. I never realized how much until now.'

'I make no secret of my opposition to UNACO. It's become too powerful for its own good in the last few years. Your field operatives can literally get away with murder because they know they're immune from prosecution. How can charges be brought against someone working for an organization that doesn't officially exist? UNACO's a law unto itself. That's something I can't accept.' Kolchinsky picked up the folder. 'Don't get me wrong, though. You'll have my full cooperation while you're here in Switzerland. I never allow my personal feelings to interfere with my work. It would amount to professional suicide if I did.'

Professional suicide. Kolchinsky knew all about that. He had spent sixteen years as a military attaché in the West for daring to criticize the draconian methods of the KGB. The irony was that had he kept his mouth shut, like many of his liberal colleagues, he would almost certainly now be a member of the Politburo, or at least a Directorate head in the KGB, heralding in the new era of Soviet politics. But he had done what he had thought right at the time and now he could live with a clear conscience. He had no regrets. Well, almost none . . .

There was a knock at the door.

Kuhlmann answered it. Paluzzi introduced himself and followed the police commissioner into the room.

'Sorry I'm a bit late,' Paluzzi said, giving Kolchinsky an apologetic smile. 'I'd barely got to my room when the phone rang. It was Angelo.' He glanced at Kuhlmann. 'My adjutant, Lieutenant Angelo Marco.'

'Has he come up with something?' Kolchinsky asked.

'Whitlock and Young have disappeared.'

'Disappeared?' Kolchinsky repeated anxiously.

'The Red Brigades are on to them. They obviously realized this and fled the boarding house. They left everything behind. We don't know where they are at the moment.'

'So they could conceivably be in the hands of the Red Brigades?'

'No, they're not,' Paluzzi said, trying to reassure Kolchinsky. 'The Red Brigades have sent their most experienced assassin after them. His name's Giancarlo Escoletti. We bugged his hotel room while he was at the boarding house waiting for them to return. When they didn't show he went back to the hotel and called Luigi Bettinga, Calvieri's new right-hand man, and told him he'd lost them. We're watching his every move. If he does manage to track them down we'll pull him in before he can do anything. He's the least of our worries. It's Young that concerns me. If Calvieri is his next hit it won't be very difficult for Young to trace him to Switzerland. What if they're already here? All Young needs is a sniper rifle and he'll be spoilt for choice when it comes to selecting a time and place for the hit.'

'Have you got photographs of Whitlock and this man Young?' Kuhlmann asked.

'I've got a photograph of Young in the case dossier in my room,' Kolchinsky said. 'It's slightly blurred but it's the only known one on file. I don't have a photo of C.W. with me. There are some on file in New York.'

'Have one faxed through to our Zurich headquarters, then we can circulate them both to all the airports and stations. If they've passed through any of them in the last few hours, we'll know about it.'

'I'll call Jacques right away. May I use your phone?'

'Please do,' Kuhlmann replied.

Kolchinsky explained the situation to Rust who promised to contact Philpott immediately and have a photograph of Whitlock faxed through to Zurich. Kolchinsky had barely hung up when the telephone rang.

'Excuse me,' Kuhlmann said as he answered it. After listening for a few moments he put his hand over the mouthpiece. 'Ubrino's been found.'

Kolchinsky and Paluzzi exchanged excited glances.

Kuhlmann spoke for a minute more and then replaced the receiver. 'An estate agent recognized him from one of the photographs. He came here a month ago and booked a chalet on the outskirts of the city. He picked up the keys from the estate agent on Monday.'

'The son-of-a-bitch,' Paluzzi hissed. 'He's been here all the time. We've been chasing shadows for the past three days.'

'Is the chalet being watched?' Kolchinsky asked.

Kuhlmann nodded. 'There's a couple of plainclothes men up there now. There's no sign of Ubrino but they've reported seeing smoke coming from the chimney. So it's fair to assume he's home.'

'Fabio, call Michael and Sabrina. Tell them to meet us here.'

'And Calvieri?' Paluzzi asked, his hand hovering over the receiver.

'And Calvieri,' Kolchinsky said with a sigh.

The briefing was short. Paluzzi would take Graham and Sabrina to within five hundred yards of the chalet, where they would rendezvous with the two policemen. Then, once they had seen the chalet for themselves, they would decide on the best way to approach Ubrino and recover the vial intact.

'Can you see anything?' Paluzzi asked as the Westland Scout passed over the rendezvous area.

'Not a damn thing,' Graham muttered, then glanced over his shoulder at Sabrina. 'You've got the binoculars. Any sign of those cops?'

'Not yet,' she replied without lowering the binoculars. She continued to scan the desolate white slopes beneath them, hoping to catch a glimpse of movement. Nothing. Not even a deer bounding through the snow in search of shelter from the deafening whirr of the helicopter's rotors.

Was it such godforsaken territory? Ubrino had certainly chosen his hideout well.

A sudden movement caught her eye and she swung the binoculars on to the cluster of pine trees to her left. Had she been wrong? Then she saw it again, the glint of sun on a ski pole. She tapped Paluzzi on the shoulder and pointed in the direction of the trees. A figure in a white camouflage overall emerged from the trees and waved at the helicopter.

'I'll take the helicopter down,' Paluzzi said, his eyes focused on the altimeter. 'I daren't land it, though. I don't know the depth of the snow. Get ready, both of you. I'll give you the signal to deplane.'

Graham and Sabrina were wearing white Goretex overalls and white ski boots lent to them by the local police. The sunglasses were their own. They clambered into the back of the helicopter and retrieved their ski poles and Volkl P99 skis from the rack against the side of the cabin. They were both experienced skiers but, like the other field operatives, they still had to undergo rigorous outdoor training which included skiing, mountaineering and hang gliding at a secret camp in the backwoods of Maine.

Graham pulled open the door and winced as a gust of cold wind whipped through the cabin. After they had snapped on their skis Sabrina kept her eye on Paluzzi, waiting for his signal for them to deplane. Paluzzi continued to press down on the collective-pitch lever to lower the helicopter towards the ground then, when the pads were a couple of feet above the snow, he nodded his head vigorously, the signal to deplane. They launched themselves through the doorway and landed nimbly in the snow, bending their knees to cushion the impact of the fall. The helicopter immediately rose upwards and banked sharply to the left, soon to disappear over the treetops.

The man approaching them was in his late twenties with short blond hair and blue eyes. His goggles were pushed up on to his forehead. 'Mike? Sabrina?' he called out.

'Yeah,' Graham replied and shook the man's outstretched hand.

'Lieutenant Jurgen Stressner,' he said, shaking Sabrina's hand.

'Where's your partner?' Graham asked.

'He's watching the chalet,' Stressner replied, pointing behind him. 'Our orders are to assist you in any way possible. Do you have a plan in mind?'

'Not yet,' Graham replied. 'We'll need to see the chalet first.'

'Of course,' Stressner said, pulling the goggles back over his eyes. 'Follow me.'

Stressner led them down the slope and into a narrow gulley which emerged out on to another slope. Ten yards ahead of them was a dense forest of pine trees. He cut a swath through the trees and came to a sudden halt two hundred yards further on. He pointed to where his partner was crouched behind a rock twenty yards away, a pair of binoculars in his hand.

'Sergeant Marcel Lacombe. He knows this part of the country better than any man I know.'

Lacombe was a middle-aged man of military bearing, with silver-grey hair and a thick grey moustache. He greeted Graham and Sabrina with a nod.

'Still no sign of him?' Stressner asked, taking the binoculars from Lacombe and giving them to Graham.

Lacombe shook his head.

Graham studied the lone chalet, fifty yards away from where they were crouched. 'It's totally exposed out there. He'll see us the moment we show our faces.'

'Can I make a suggestion?' Stressner said.

'Please do,' Graham replied, handing the binoculars to Sabrina.

'There are two doors. Front and back. I suggest we pair

off and approach the doors separately. If he sees two of us coming towards the front of the chalet he's sure to try and make a break for it through the back door.'

'Assuming he doesn't open the vial first,' Graham muttered, his eyes flickering towards Sabrina.

'Vi-al?' Stressner said, frowning. 'What is that?'

'Haven't you been briefed?' Sabrina asked.

'All we know is his name and what he looks like.'

'We have to tell them about the vial,' Sabrina said to Graham. 'They can't be expected to go in there blind.'

Graham nodded in agreement and explained briefly about the contents of the vial.

'And you think he would open this vial if he saw us coming?' Stressner asked anxiously.

'It's possible,' Graham replied, tight-lipped. 'But I think he's more likely to try and make a break for it, especially if he only sees two of us approaching the chalet.'

Sabrina nodded. 'I'd go along with that. So if two of us lie in wait for him at the back of the chalet, out of sight, and he does try to sneak out we'll be able to grab him before he has a chance to open the vial.'

'In theory,' Graham said.

'We have no choice,' Stressner said.

'You've got a point there,' Graham replied. 'It's best if we stick with our original partners. I presume the two of you are armed?'

The question surprised Stressner. 'This is Switzerland, not the backstreets of America. We only use firearms in exceptional circumstances.'

'And this isn't an exceptional circumstance? Ubrino will be armed to the teeth in there, you can be sure of that. Here, take my Beretta.'

Stressner put a restraining hand on Graham's arm. 'I won't need it. Put yourself in Ubrino's position. He doesn't know we're unarmed. He's more likely to try and slip out of the back than engage in a firefight.'

'Or use the vial to effect an escape,' Sabrina said.

'In which case the two of you will be lying in wait for him,' Stressner said. 'You need the guns, not us.'

Graham trained the binoculars on the chalet again. Curtains drawn, overnight snow packed against the foot of the front door and the absence of any ski tracks in front of the chalet gave it an eerie, deserted appearance. He focused the binoculars on the chimney. A steady stream of smoke filtered up into the blue sky. He wondered if Ubrino had left the chalet since he got there on Monday. Why bother?

'How do we get round to the back of the chalet without being seen?' Sabrina asked.

'I'll let Marcel explain. He's the expert.'

'My English not good,' Lacombe said to her. 'I explain better in French. You speak French?'

She nodded, then listened attentively as he told her the best route for them to take to come up behind the chalet unnoticed.

'You have radios?' Stressner asked.

Graham tapped one of the pockets in his overall. 'Kuhlmann got them for us. He had them pre-set to your frequency.'

Stressner looked at his watch. 'It should take you ten minutes at the most to get yourselves into position. Call me when you're ready. Then we can move in.'

Graham nodded, then followed Sabrina back through the trees, into the gulley, and out to the slope where they had deplaned. They traversed the face of the slope, crossing it without losing any height, then skied down a *couloir*, a steep, narrow descent, and emerged on to a flat stretch of the mountain. She stopped and pointed to the sixty-foot ridge on their right. The chalet was directly behind it. They pulled the hoods over their heads to give them added concealment in the snow then made their way slowly up the ridge, crawling the last five feet to the top.

'Look, ski tracks leading from the door,' she whispered.

'Yeah,' he muttered, his eyes screwed up behind his sunglasses as he stared at the single upstairs window facing out on to the ridge. The curtains were drawn.

'Call Stressner, tell him we're in position.'

Graham inched his way backwards until he was out of sight of the chalet, then took the two-way radio from his pocket and called Stressner. He replaced the radio in his pocket when he had finished and gave Sabrina a thumbs-up sign. 'They're going in. I'll move further down the ridge. If Ubrino does try to make a break for it I'll be in a better position to cut him off. You stay here . . .' He trailed off, hearing the sound of a helicopter in the distance. 'What the hell's Paluzzi playing at? I told him I'd radio if we needed assistance.'

'He must have picked up your conversation with Stressner and thought it was meant for him. Get him on the radio, tell him to pull out.'

Graham took the radio from his pocket again. 'Yankee to Leatherhead, come in. Over.'

There was a pause then the crackled reply: 'Leatherhead to Yankee, I read you. Over.'

'What the hell are you doing?' Graham hissed angrily. 'I haven't given the order to move in. Return to base and await further instructions. I repeat, return to base. Over.'

Another pause. 'Leatherhead to Yankee, message unclear. I am at base. Repeat, I am at base. Over.'

Graham was about to speak when the helicopter came into view. It was the white Gazelle Tommaso Francia had used on Corfu. Graham scrambled to the top of the ridge. He had to warn Stressner and Lacombe. They were already clear of the trees. Stressner swung round to face the helicopter as it dived towards them. Tommaso Francia opened fire. Both men were hit by a hail of bullets and the helicopter immediately banked sharply, skimming over the chalet and passing within ten feet of the ridge where Graham and Sabrina lay motionless in the snow.

'Leatherhead to Yankee, I heard gunfire. Are you all right? Do you need assistance? Over.'

Sabrina picked the radio out of the snow. 'Sister to Leatherhead, we've come under fire from the Francias' helicopter. Stressner and Lacombe have been hit. Need assistance. Repeat, need assistance. Over.'

'Message understood. Am on my way. Over and out.'

Graham was the first on to his feet. 'We've got to take cover before it comes back. The chalet's our only chance.'

They approached the chalet cautiously and took up positions on either side of the back door. They took the Berettas from their pockets and Graham indicated for Sabrina to go around the side of the chalet. She nodded then moved apprehensively towards the end of the wall, the Beretta held barrel upwards inches away from her face. Once there she paused to wipe the sweat from her forehead. She glanced over her shoulder but Graham had already disappeared around the other side of the chalet. She swivelled round, Beretta held at arm's length. Nothing. She could see Stressner's body from where she stood. He lay on his back, his white overall saturated with blood. Then she heard the sound of the helicopter's engine behind her. She turned to see the Gazelle rise into view from behind the ridge. She flung herself into the snow a split second before a row of bullets peppered the side of the chalet where she had been standing. The helicopter swivelled fractionally as if on an invisible axis until the 30 mm cannons were aimed at her. She tried desperately to get to her feet. She knew she wouldn't make it before the guns opened fire.

The Westland Scout seemed to appear from nowhere. It shot across the front of the Gazelle and Tommaso Francia recoiled in horror, unconsciously jerking his hands off the controls. The Gazelle bucked sharply and went out of control. It plummeted towards the chalet. He managed to regain control of it at the last moment and it missed the roof by a matter of inches. One of the pads struck the chimney and

Sabrina had to scramble out of the way as bricks and mortar rained down into the snow. The Gazelle levelled out and disappeared over the pine trees in pursuit of the Westland Scout.

'You okay?' Graham asked behind her.

She nodded, then removed her sunglasses and wiped her sleeve across her forehead. 'Now's our chance to get Ubrino, with the helicopter out of the way.'

'You take the back, I'll take the front.'

He moved round to the front of the chalet and ducked as he passed a window, even though earlier the curtains had been drawn, only straightening up again when he was clear of it. He unclipped his skis then pressed himself against the wall and reached out slowly for the door handle. His gloved fingers curled around it and he pushed it down. The door was unlocked. He opened the door and took up a firing stance, Beretta extended, legs bent and apart. He found himself looking down a dimly lit hallway. He stepped inside and his eyes instinctively moved towards the wooden stairs to his right. Was Ubrino at the top, waiting to pick him off the moment he tried to climb them? Or was he hiding in one of the rooms leading off from the hall?

He noticed a movement out of the corner of his eye and spun round to face the open door, the Beretta held at arm's length. Nothing moved. A sprinkling of snow landed in front of the door. *That* was what he had seen. More snow fell to the ground. It couldn't be thawing, the chalet was enveloped in shade. That meant something else was dislodging the snow. Or *someone* else. Ubrino. He waded out into knee-deep snow and as he looked up at the sloping roof Ubrino propelled himself away from the open skylight window. Graham raised his Beretta to fire. Ubrino launched himself off the edge of the roof and caught Graham's wrist with the edge of his ski, knocking the gun from his hand. He landed awkwardly and skidded sideways into the snow. He managed to get to his feet before Graham felled him with a bruising football tackle. Ubrino lashed out with his ski pole, catching Graham painfully on the shoulder. He lashed out again with the ski pole, this time hitting Graham in the face. The basket at the end of the pole ripped open the stitches in the side of Graham's face, spurting blood across the snow. Graham cried out in pain and stumbled backwards, his hand covering the wound as blood streamed down the side of his face. Ubrino scrambled to his feet and set off down the slope.

Sabrina emerged from the chalet and got off three shots at the retreating figure before he disappeared around the shoulder of the mountain. She dug her ski poles into the snow and launched herself after him.

Graham returned to the chalet, where he found a clean towel and pressed it tightly against the wound in an attempt to try and stem the flow of blood. He was about to run some water in the washbasin when he heard the sound of a helicopter engine stuttering in the distance. He went to the front door and looked up into the sky. The Westland Scout was approaching the chalet low over the pine trees, black smoke billowing out from the single turboshaft engine mounted behind the cabin. It managed to avoid the trees and crash-landed thirty yards away from the chalet. The fuel tank was ruptured and a fire started in the tail section. Paluzzi threw open the cockpit door and stumbled towards the chalet. He was only yards away from it when the helicopter exploded, hurling chunks of flaming debris hundreds of feet into the air. He was flattened by the force of the explosion. Graham hurried out to where he lay, helped him to his feet, and led him back to the chalet.

'You okay?' Graham asked anxiously once they were inside the door.

'I'm okay,' Paluzzi replied with a weak smile. 'What happened to you?'

Graham told him about Ubrino.

'I'll go after Sabrina,' Paluzzi said. 'She'll need back-up. I'll take your skis.'

'She's got a radio. She'll call us if she needs back-up.' Graham looked at the twisted remains of the helicopter burning fiercely in the snow. 'What happened to you?'

'I gave Francia a good run for his money but he finally got a direct hit on my engine. I had to limp back here, it's all I could do.'

'Why didn't he follow you in?'

'My guess is he heard my distress call. He peeled off as soon as I started smoking. Kuhlmann's sending a couple of police helicopters but you can be sure that Francia will be long gone by the time they get here.'

'When do you expect them?'

'They should be here in about ten minutes.'

Graham expressed his approval then disappeared back into the bathroom to wash the blood from his face. Paluzzi walked to the front door and stared at the bodies of Stressner and Lacombe lying in the snow. Then he looked down the slope, his thoughts with Sabrina.

Sabrina was gaining rapidly on Ubrino. Then the Gazelle appeared behind them. Tommaso Francia couldn't risk shooting at her in case one of the bullets hit Ubrino.

She looked over her shoulder at the helicopter and saw Carlo Francia standing in the open cabin doorway. He was dressed in skiing gear. Moments later he propelled himself through the doorway, landing with bended knees on the slope twenty yards behind her. The helicopter flew past her and Tommaso Francia threw a rope ladder to Ubrino through the passenger door. Carlo Francia unshouldered his Uzi and fired a burst into the snow behind Sabrina. She veered to the left, giving Ubrino a few valuable seconds to grab hold of the ladder which dangled enticingly in front of him. He discarded one of the ski poles and reached out for the ladder. His fingers found one of the rungs and he clamped

194

his hand around it. Then, discarding his other ski pole, he grabbed the ladder with his other hand. He felt himself being lifted off the slope. Tommaso Francia activated a button on his control panel and the rope ladder began to reel in automatically. The helicopter banked sharply, denying Sabrina a shot at Ubrino. Within seconds it had disappeared from view.

She looked behind her. Carlo Francia was still there, the Uzi in his right hand. He acknowledged her with a faint smile and a slight inclination of his head, just as he had done in Venice. He squeezed the trigger. She curved sharply to avoid the bullets and entered a dense thicket of larch trees. Francia double-angled, forming an inverted 'L' in the snow to change direction, and followed her into the wood. He fired again but the bullets chewed harmlessly into the trees on either side of her. The wood ended abruptly and she found herself beginning a steep, curving descent. She looked behind her. No sign of Francia. She carved the first bend and stopped sharply, coming to a halt out of sight of the trees. It was her only chance. She had to get behind him. But what if he approached the bend firing? She crouched down, the Beretta clenched tightly in her gloved hand.

Francia took the bend wide and only saw her as he shot down the slope. His eyes widened in amazement. How had she stopped so quickly? A bullet cracked inches from his head. Suddenly the hunter had become the hunted. He fired wildly behind him but the bullets went well wide of the mark. He cursed himself for panicking. Then he saw his chance: a ridge directly in front of him. He tucked his body down to increase his speed and as he hit the ridge he pirouetted in mid-air, just one of the freestyle manoeuvres which had brought him such acclaim as a professional skier, and fired at Sabrina on the turn. A bullet ripped through her sleeve, grazing her arm, and she had to call on all her expertise to keep herself from overbalancing and tumbling into the snow.

Francia executed the perfect landing, then looked behind him, the Uzi at the ready for the first sight of Sabrina riding the crest of the ridge. She still hadn't appeared by the time he reached the next bend. Now he could lie in wait for her further down the slope. It would be impossible for him to miss her as she took the bend. He smiled to himself as he leaned into the bend. His smile faltered when he saw the precipice fifteen yards in front of him. He tried to stop but lost control and tumbled down the slope. He came to rest within a few feet of the edge and the Uzi disappeared over it. He raised his head fractionally and looked down into the canyon below him. A sheer drop of eight hundred feet. He reached down to unclip his skis. The sudden movement dislodged a piece of ice behind him. It confirmed his worse fears. He was lying on a cornice, a sheet of ice overhanging the precipice. Any movement could cause it to break off. He swallowed nervously and blinked rapidly as the sweat dripped into his eyes. All he could do was wait for help. But for how long?

Sabrina descended the ridge cautiously, the Beretta held tightly in her hand. Her arm was throbbing. She could feel the blood oozing down the inside of her sleeve and into her glove. Her progress was slow and she paused before reaching the bend in the slope. What if Francia was lying in wait for her around the corner, as she had done to him earlier? An Uzi against a Beretta. She didn't fancy the odds. She wiped the sweat from her face and inadvertently smeared blood across her cheek. She decided to take the bend as wide as she possibly could. At least that way she would be able to see Francia if he had concealed himself on the other side of the bend. She dug her ski poles into the snow and propelled herself forward. She saw the precipice as she took the corner and came to a halt ten feet away from where he lay. For a moment she thought it was a trap. Then she saw the fear in his eyes.

'Help me, please,' he pleaded in English, his eyes riveted on her.

She moved closer, the Beretta still trained on him.

'You help me, I tell you what you want to know,' he said in a breathless voice. 'Please, you must help me.'

'I'm going to extend my ski pole towards you. Grab hold of the basket. Do you understand?'

He nodded.

She lay flat on the hard surface snow and reached out the ski pole towards him. It didn't reach his hand. She inched her way forward, knowing she could also be on the cornice. And it could collapse at any moment. It was impossible to know where the mountain ended and the cornice began. There was a sudden crack and another sheet of ice broke off behind him. He gritted his teeth, not daring to look over his shoulder. He was now barely three feet away from the edge of the precipice. She was at full stretch, not daring to move any closer. The pole was within his reach. His fingers touched the tip and he managed to grab hold of it. She gripped the other end of the pole with both hands, steadying herself. Cracks began to appear in the ice around him and as his fingers curled around the basket a section of ice broke underneath him. He slid backwards, his legs now dangling over the edge of the precipice. She dug her skis into the snow, desperately trying to anchor herself, but she felt herself being dragged towards the precipice as Francia continued to slide further over the edge. In desperation he grabbed the basket with both hands but this only served to pull her even closer to the edge. She knew she couldn't save him and unless she let go of the ski pole she would be dragged over the edge with him. She began to ease the strap off from around her wrist.

'No, please,' he screamed, desperately trying to get a better grip on the basket.

She tugged at the strap until it slid off her hand. For a brief moment he clawed frantically at the ice, then he fell, the wind tearing the scream from his lips. She moved back slowly until she felt she had put enough distance between herself and the edge of the precipice, then got to her feet and wiped her sleeve across her glistening face. What if she had tried to outrun him instead of ducking down behind the slope when she did? What chance would she have had to stop at that speed? She would have been the one who went over the precipice. She shuddered. It had been that close.

She sat down in the snow and leaned back against a large tree. Then, taking the two-way radio from her pocket, she called Graham to arrange for a helicopter to pick her up. She had had enough skiing for one day.

# NINE

'Are you all right?' Kolchinsky asked anxiously when Sabrina entered his hotel room.

'It's just a graze,' she replied, touching his arm reassuringly.

'Where's Michael?'

'He's coming,' she said, gesturing vaguely to the door behind her.

'How is he?'

'I'm okay,' Graham answered from the doorway.

Kolchinsky winced when he looked round at Graham. His left eye was now half-closed and the white dressing secured over his new stitches contrasted vividly with the discoloured bruising on the left-hand side of his face.

'It's not as bad as it looks,' Graham muttered, closing the door behind him.

'You could have fooled me.' Kolchinsky smiled grimly.

'Has Fabio briefed you on what happened this afternoon?' Sabrina asked, pouring out two cups of coffee from the pot on the tray.

'He's told me everything,' Kolchinsky replied. 'I was hoping we could all have a meeting as soon as the two of you got back from the hospital. That won't be possible now. At least not for the time being.'

'Why, what's happened?' Sabrina asked, handing a coffee to Graham.

'Commissioner Kuhlmann received a call half an hour ago to say that the Francias' Gazelle helicopter had been found abandoned in a field on the outskirts of Worb. It's a town about ten miles from here. He's driven out there with Fabio to take a closer look at it.'

'No sign of Ubrino or Tommaso Francia?'

'None at all.'

'Has Carlo Francia's body been found?' Sabrina asked, sitting on the bed.

'What was left of it,' Kolchinsky replied.

'Was anything found at the chalet?' Graham asked.

'The police report hasn't come through yet but you can be sure we'd have been told if they had come up with anything positive.' Kolchinsky shook his head. 'No, we won't have any luck there.'

'That was to be expected really,' Sabrina said with a resigned shrug. 'Ubrino was hardly going to flee the nest without taking the golden egg with him, was he?'

'Which puts us back to square one *again*,' Graham said. 'And we've got less than fifteen hours to go before tomorrow's deadline. Not that that means anything. We haven't got a hope in hell of finding him now.'

'Leaving the Offenbach Centre as our last line of defence,' Sabrina added, looking at Kolchinsky. 'What extra security measures are being taken there tomorrow?'

'Commissioner Kuhlmann has drafted in seventy policemen and thirty policewomen from around the country. They'll all be in plainclothes.'

'Why plainclothes?' Graham said. 'Surely an extra hundred uniforms would be more daunting to someone like Ubrino?'

'And frighten him off?' Kolchinsky replied. 'Remember, he doesn't know that we know the vial is destined for the Offenbach Centre. If the grounds were swamped with uniformed guards he might turn back and make his demands from a hideout anywhere in the country.

Then where would we be? No, we have to play this as covertly as possible. He's sure to have a rough idea of how many security staff are employed by the Offenbach Centre. It's imperative that he isn't suspicious when he gets there. As you said, we won't find him now. Tomorrow's our last chance.'

Graham finished his coffee and got to his feet. 'Are we still going to have this meeting tonight?'

'That all depends on when the two of them get back. Why, is there something on your mind?'

'I've got a few questions to put to Calvieri. I can do it now, or later.'

'Fabio told me about your little theory linking Calvieri to Ubrino. It doesn't hold any water, Michael. You're letting your emotions get the better of you.'

'The fact remains that someone tipped off either Ubrino or the Francia brothers about our movements this afternoon. Who knew we were going to the chalet? You, me, Sabrina, Fabio, Kuhlmann and Calvieri. Who would you suspect?'

'Calvieri never left this room from the time we had our briefing until the time Kuhlmann received Fabio's call requesting back-up. When could Calvieri have warned them? I'm the first to take notice of your hunches, Michael, but this time you're way off the mark.'

'Someone tipped them off, Sergei. There are two bodies in the mortuary to prove it.' Graham glanced at Sabrina. 'And it could so easily have been three.'

'We don't know that they were tipped off, Michael. It's pure speculation.'

'I still want to talk to Calvieri,' Graham said.

'There's enough tension as it is without you adding to it. Leave him alone. And that's my final word on the subject.'

Graham threw up his hands in frustration and sat on the edge of the bed. The telephone rang.

Kolchinsky answered it.

'Sergei, it's C.W.,' Whitlock said at the other end of the line.

'C.W.?' Kolchinsky replied in surprise. 'How did you know we were here?'

'Jacques told me. I can't talk for long. Young and I are here in Berne.'

'I know.'

'You know?' It was Whitlock's turn to be surprised.

'I had a photograph of you sent out from New York. You were recognized by one of the staff at the airport. Where are you staying?'

'That doesn't matter at the moment. Young's setting up a hit on Calvieri.'

'When?'

'Now. This is the first chance I've had to call you since we got here. Young picked up a case from a locker at the airport. It has to be a high-powered rifle.'

'Where are you calling from?'

'A callbox opposite your hotel. Young went into the building behind me a couple of minutes ago. It's my guess he'll lure Calvieri out to the front of the hotel. What do you want me to do?'

'Stop him. It's gone far enough. Are you armed?'

'I wish I was. I had to leave the Browning behind when we fled the boarding house in Rome.'

'Do you want back-up?'

'No back-up, thanks. If Young suspects for one moment that I've double-crossed him he'll use the transmitter to detonate the watch. I'll get him myself.'

'How?'

'You let me worry about that. Keep an eye on Calvieri all the same. Try and keep him in the hotel. I'll call you back later.'

'C.W., be careful.'

'You can count on it,' Whitlock said and hung up.

Kolchinsky recounted the conversation to Graham and

Sabrina. He thought for a moment, then said, 'Sabrina, I want you to go down to the foyer. If Calvieri does show his face I want you to keep him occupied until I give you the all-clear sign.'

'How am I supposed to keep him occupied?'

'I'm sure you'll think of something,' Kolchinsky said, opening the door. 'Now go on, you're wasting time.'

'I still say C.W. needs back-up,' Graham said, after Kolchinsky had closed the door.

'No back-up.'

'He's unarmed—'

'Michael!' Kolchinsky snapped. 'I'm as worried about him as you are but he specifically said no back-up. All we can do is wait for his call.'

'All we can do is *hope* for his call,' Graham muttered, then crossed to the tray to pour himself another cup of coffee.

Whitlock emerged from the callbox and looked up at the building behind him. Three floors. Several of the third-floor windows were illuminated. The rest of the building was in darkness. Young wouldn't risk using the third floor. And the first floor was also out. He wouldn't get the right angle on his shot from there. Which left the second floor. Whitlock glanced at his watch. Young already had a five-minute headstart. Whitlock walked towards the alley at the side of the building. He suddenly froze mid-step and the woman behind him stumbled against his arm. He muttered an apology without taking his eyes off the man in the fawn trenchcoat who was standing at the entrance to the alley. He held a black doctor's bag in his gloved hand. It was the same man Whitlock had seen at the boarding house in Rome. Escoletti looked about him casually, then disappeared into the alley. Whitlock continued to stare at the spot where Escoletti had been standing. How had he found them so quickly? What if he managed to overpower Young and take him away for questioning? What about the transmitter?

Whitlock moved cautiously towards the alley, intent on following Escoletti at a distance.

As Whitlock had predicted, Young had chosen the second floor for the hit. Getting into the building had been easy. The door leading into the alley was unlocked. Once inside he had discovered that the building was some kind of youth centre. According to the bulletin board, the first floor housed an arts and crafts workshop, the second floor a martial arts club and the third floor a discothèque. And only the discothèque was open that evening. The noise would provide the perfect cover for the hit. Nobody in the building would hear the gunshot.

He had passed a couple of teenagers on the stairs between the first and second floors but neither of them had given him a second glance as they made their way to the exit. The double doors were padlocked on the second floor. It took him a few seconds to pick the lock, then he eased one of the doors open and went inside. The street light shone dimly through the Venetian blinds. He could see the padded mats laid out neatly across the wooden floorboards. Then he noticed the two glass cabinets against the wall. He whistled softly to himself as he stared at their contents. One of the cabinets contained a pair of sheathed *tachi*, the Japanese sword traditionally worn suspended from the belt. The second cabinet contained ninja weaponry: *kama*, the sickle used for cutting corn, which doubles as a lethal weapon; *kusari-gama*, a sickle attached to a lead ball with a chain; *nunchaku*, the corn-beater, consisting of two short lengths of wood joined by a chain; *sai*, an iron dagger protected by two lateral hooks which is used to check, or deflect, the *tachi*; *shuriken*, the small, iron projectile with sharp, serrated edges; and the *tonfa*, a twenty-inch oak rod with a cylindrical handle fixed three-quarters of the way along its stem.

Young stared, fascinated, at the assortment of weaponry until a loud hornblast from a taxi in the street below brought him sharply back to his senses. He crossed to the venetian blinds where he opened his slim, black case and carefully removed the sections of the specially designed detachable Mauser SP66 sniper rifle which he had asked Wiseman to get for him. He screwed on the Zeiss 1.5–6 × 42 zoom telescopic lens then reached through the venetian blinds and opened the window. He had a perfect view of the main entrance to the Metropole Hotel. He took a cordless phone from the case and rang the hotel. It was answered by one of the switchboard operators and he asked for Calvieri's room.

'*Pronto*, Tony Calvieri.'

'You want to know who killed Pisani, don't you?'

'Who is this?'

'I'll meet you outside the hotel in two minutes. If you're not there, I'll assume you're not interested and leave. Two minutes.'

'How will I recognize you?'

'I'll recognize you.'

Young disconnected the line and replaced the phone in the case. He picked up the sniper rifle and leaned the barrel lightly on the window frame. He adjusted the sights until he had a perfect image of the doorman's head in the crosshairs. Then, curling his finger around the trigger, he squeezed it gently. Click. He selected a 7.62 mm semi-jacketed soft point bullet from the case and fed it into the breech. Like any good sniper, he only needed one bullet. He rested the rifle on the window frame again and waited for Calvieri to appear.

A smile touched the corners of his mouth when, a minute later, the electronic doors parted and Calvieri emerged into the street. He tightened his grip on the rifle then lined up Calvieri's forehead in the crosshairs. His finger rested lightly on the trigger but he held back from firing when Calvieri suddenly swung round towards the doors behind him. He looked to see who had distracted Calvieri's attention. It couldn't be. It was a woman, dressed differently, but closely resembling the prostitute he had seen in Whitlock's room in Rome. His mind raced. Who was she? Was she a *Brigatista*? Why was she in Berne? What was her relationship with Calvieri? More to the point, what was her relationship with Alexander? Was Alexander working with Calvieri? Had Alexander compromised the assignment? Alexander had a lot of explaining to do. Then Young would kill him. He couldn't afford to take any chances. But he had some unfinished business to attend to first. He lined up Calvieri's forehead in the sights again. He slowly tightened his finger on the trigger.

The room was suddenly flooded with light.

'Drop the gun,' Escoletti ordered from the doorway.

Young used the reflections in the window to watch the figure behind him. He had two options. Try and shoot him on the turn. Or throw down the rifle and take his chances from there. It was obvious that the gunman wanted him alive, otherwise he would already have put a bullet in his back. He laid the rifle down carefully in front of him then turned round slowly to face his assailant. He looked from the Bernadelli in Escoletti's hand to the black bag on the floor beside him. It had to be the man Alexander had seen at the boarding house. A sudden thought crossed his mind. What if Alexander was working in league with him?

'Who are you?' Young asked. 'Red Brigades?'

'That's right,' Escoletti replied. 'You should have quit while you were ahead. But, like so many before you, you underestimated the Red Brigades. We're not the disjointed, ramshackle organization our Government would have the world believe. How do you think we were able to track you down to that boarding house in Rome? How do you think I was able to trace you here so quickly?'

'So what happens now?'

'You will be taken back to Italy and tried by a people's court.'

'And submitted to your proletarian justice, no doubt?' Young said with a sneer. 'You sound just like the Vietcong I was fighting eighteen years ago. Unenlightened, uneducated, red scum.'

'Who brought your country to its knees,' Escoletti said with evident satisfaction. 'The people triumphed over the *fascisti*, one of the greatest victories in socialist history.'

Whitlock appeared in the doorway behind Escoletti, a 5-inch length of lead piping in his hand. He pressed it into Escoletti's back and told him to drop the gun. Escoletti stiffened but made no move to drop the Bernadelli. Whitlock's heart was racing. If Escoletti called his bluff and turned on him he would be dead. It was as simple as that. Escoletti finally let the Bernadelli fall to the floor. Young picked it up before Whitlock had a chance to get to it. Escoletti looked round at Whitlock, his eyes lingering on the lead piping in his hand. His face remained expressionless.

'I'll spare you the kangaroo court,' Young said to Escoletti, and shot him through the head.

'You didn't have to kill him!' Whitlock exclaimed, staring at the body sprawled at his feet.

'That's right,' Young replied. 'Close the door.'

Whitlock closed the door behind him and when he turned back to Young he found the Bernadelli trained on him.

'I never did trust you,' Young said, taking a step towards Whitlock. 'As I said to you in Rome, it was General Wiseman who wanted you in on the operation. Not me. I could have handled it by myself, no trouble.'

'I can see that,' Whitlock said sarcastically. 'You needed me to save your arse at Pisani's house. And you needed me to save it again tonight.'

'For which I'll be eternally grateful,' Young replied with

equal sarcasm. His eyes narrowed. 'Who was the woman with Calvieri?'

Whitlock frowned. 'What woman? What are you talking about?'

'That so-called prostitute who came to your room in Rome was out there talking to Calvieri not five minutes ago. Who is she?'

'Is that what all this is about?' Whitlock said, gesturing to the Bernadelli in Young's hand. 'You see a woman who *looks* like an Italian prostitute talking to Calvieri and you immediately jump to conclusions.'

'They were one and the same, I'm sure of it. I'm hardly likely to forget a face or a figure like that in a hurry.'

'What possible reason would that prostitute have for coming up here to Berne? It makes no sense at all. And if you thought about it logically, you'd agree.'

'You're good, I'll grant you that. But you're not good enough. If you haven't told me who she is in five seconds' time I'll put a bullet in your left kneecap. I'm told the pain is unbearable. Another five seconds and I'll put a bullet in your right kneecap. Then, if you still won't talk, I'll resort to the transmitter. I'm dying to try it out. It's the first of its kind. If it's any good I might just patent it. I'm sure the CIA would be interested.'

'You're mad,' Whitlock said, staring at the glazed expression in Young's eyes.

'Five seconds. Starting now.'

'Look, I don't know who she is,' Whitlock said in desperation, his eyes flickering towards the glass cabinets on the wall. They were out of reach. Even if he could have reached them, he would have had to smash the glass to get to the weapons. Young would have shot him long before he got there.

'Two seconds,' Young said, reaching his left hand into his jacket pocket for the transmitter.

Whitlock saw his chance. He lunged at Young, bringing

208

the lead piping down across the back of his gun hand. Young cried out in pain and the Bernadelli fell to the floor. Whitlock grabbed Young's wrist as he pulled the transmitter from his pocket and ran him backwards into the cabinet containing the two ceremonial *tachi*. The glass shattered and Whitlock slammed the back of Young's hand against the shards still embedded in the frame. A piece of glass sliced across the back of Young's hand and in his haste to pull away from the searing pain the transmitter slipped from his bloodied fingers. Whitlock made the mistake of taking his eyes off Young for a split second to kick the transmitter out of the way. Young butted Whitlock savagely in the face and followed through with two hammering body punches, dropping Whitlock to his knees. Young grabbed the nearest *tachi*, wrenched it out of its sheath, and, using both hands to grip the hilt, lashed out at Whitlock, who managed to hurl himself sideways a split second before the blade, missing him by inches, sliced through the mat where he had been kneeling. Whitlock brought his foot up sharply into Young's midriff then, springing to his feet, he managed to draw the second *tachi* from its sheath before Young had time to catch his breath.

They circled each other warily, the *tachi* held away from their bodies, neither of them prepared to make the first move. Young suddenly gripped the hilt firmly in both hands and scythed the blade at Whitlock, who parried the blow with the blunt edge of his *tachi*. Young lashed out again but this time Whitlock managed to evade the blade, which smashed into the second cabinet, spilling several of the ninja weapons on the floor around them. Young swivelled round as Whitlock aimed a thrust at his midriff and blocked the attempt. The two blades locked and Whitlock shoved Young against the wall, his arm shaking as he forced the two blades ever closer to Young's face. Young lashed out with his foot, catching Whitlock on the knee.

Whitlock stumbled back in pain, lost his footing on one of the mats, and fell to the floor. Young noticed the transmitter lying beside the door. He discarded the *tachi* and made a grab for it.

Whitlock knew he wouldn't be able to reach Young before he pressed the button. He looked around in desperation for the Bernadelli. It was out of reach. His fingers touched something cold on the floor beside him. An eight-sided *shuriken*. It was his only chance. Young uncapped the transmitter's protective seal and looked up triumphantly. Whitlock flung the *shuriken*. It struck Young high in the forehead, spraying blood across the wall behind him. The transmitter slipped from Young's hand and the astonishment was still mirrored in his eyes when he fell forward on to the floor.

Whitlock got to his feet gingerly and retrieved the transmitter, which lay next to Young's body. He secured the protective cap over the button again then crossed to the case by the window and used the cordless telephone to call Kolchinsky and tell him what had happened. Kolchinsky told him to go back to the boarding house where he was staying and he would arrange for a scientist to be sent down from Zurich to defuse the booby-trapped watch. Whitlock replaced the telephone in the case and walked to the door, where he paused to pick up the Bernadelli. It could come in useful. He pocketed it then looked around slowly at the havoc before closing the door behind him and padlocking it again.

Kolchinsky replaced the receiver and told Graham what had happened.

'Is he all right?' Graham asked once Kolchinsky had finished speaking.

'Mercifully yes. I told him to go back to the boarding house.'

'Surely he'd be of more use to us here?'

'And let Calvieri see him?'

'That's being a bit overcautious, isn't it?'

'I don't think so. Remember, the Red Brigades have got a good description of C.W. I'm not saying Calvieri would link him to the hit but it's not worth taking that chance. It's best if we keep him in the wings until we need him.'

'I see your point,' Graham admitted.

'I want you to go down to the foyer and tell Sabrina what's happened. I'll let you know when Fabio and Commissioner Kuhlmann get back from Worb.'

'What do you want us to do until they get back?'

'There isn't much you can do.'

'What are you going to do about the bodies across the road?'

'I'll have to discuss that with Commissioner Kuhlmann when he gets back.'

'And Wiseman?' Graham asked, as Kolchinsky led him to the door.

'That's up to the Colonel. I'm going to call him now.' Kolchinsky opened the door. 'And Michael, leave Calvieri alone.'

'When have I ever disobeyed an order, Sergei?' Graham asked, feigning a look of innocence.

'Frequently,' Kolchinsky replied, closing the door.

Heads turned when Graham emerged from the lift but he ignored the curious looks as he scanned the foyer for Sabrina. She wasn't there. He sighed irritably, then crossed to the reception desk and asked for her to be paged. She arrived at the desk within seconds of the call being made.

'Where have you been?' Graham asked, leading her away from the desk.

'I was in the bar,' she replied, 'having a drink with Calvieri.'

'Sounds cosy,' he muttered.

She ignored the sarcasm. 'Any news of C.W.?'

He told her briefly what had happened.

'That's a relief,' she said. 'I almost missed Calvieri when he came down here.'

'What do you mean?'

'Well, I had this plan to call the switchboard from a house phone the moment I saw Calvieri and have him paged to the reception desk. I would have pretended to have been an anonymous caller with information on the Pisani murder. I could have kept him talking on the phone long enough for C.W. to deal with Young.'

'So what went wrong?'

'I was watching the lift. Calvieri must have used the stairs. You can't see them from the house phones. I only saw him as he was about to leave the hotel.'

'How did you get him back inside?' Graham asked, glancing at the electronic doors.

'How could I, without arousing suspicion? Fortunately he came back in when he saw me. It must have been close.' She gestured in the direction of the bar lounge. 'I'd better get back. Why not join us?'

'No thanks, I'm pretty selective about who I drink with.'

'And I'm not, is that it?'

'I don't drink with terrorists,' he said sharply.

'This is business, Mike, just remember that.'

'Oh yeah?'

'What's that supposed to mean?' An elderly couple looked at them, startled by her raised voice.

'Is there a problem?' Graham asked, staring at them coldly. They moved away.

'I'm not going to have a slanging match with you out here, Mike. If you don't want to come for a drink, that's fine by me. I just wanted . . .' she trailed off with a shrug and turned to leave.

He grabbed her arm. 'You just wanted what?'

'It doesn't matter,' she retorted, then shrugged off his hand and strode back into the bar.

Graham exhaled deeply, then went after her. They were seated at a table in the corner of the room.

Calvieri saw him and beckoned him over. He pulled out a chair for Graham to sit down. 'Mike! Come and join us. What will you have to drink?'

'The coldest bottle of Perrier you've got,' Graham said, glancing up at the waiter.

'I see you changed your mind,' Sabrina said, eyeing Graham sharply.

'Yeah,' Graham muttered, then sat back and looked distantly around the packed room.

The waiter returned with the Perrier water and a glass filled with ice. He placed them on the table in front of Graham.

'Please, this is on me,' Calvieri said, reaching out for the chit.

Quickly Graham grabbed the chit from the table and signed it. He looked across at Calvieri after the waiter had left. 'You buy your own drinks. I'll buy mine. That way there can be no misunderstanding.'

'Ever since we met you've gone out of your way to condemn me for my beliefs. What makes you so sure you're right?'

'That's a question you should put to the families of all those people the Red Brigades have murdered in the past twenty years,' Graham replied, holding Calvieri's gaze. 'You might just learn something.'

'We only hit legitimate targets, Mr Graham. Politicians like Moro and Tarantelli. Or soldiers like General Giorgieri or your own Leamon Hunt, the director general of the Sinai Peacekeeping Forces we assassinated in 1984. *Fascisti.*'

Graham drank a mouthful of Perrier and sat forward, his arms resting on the table. 'What about all those innocent bystanders, caught in the crossfire of your so-called fight against fascism? Are they also legitimate targets?'

'It's regrettable, but there will always be innocent casualties in this kind of conflict.'

Graham shook his head in disgust. 'The standard terrorist reply. You know you can't possibly condone it, so you evade the question.'

'The Red Brigades don't kill senselessly, Mr Graham. There's always a reason for our actions.' Calvieri took a sip of brandy, then placed his glass on the coaster in front of him. 'You may think we're just a group of terrorists out to spread anarchy and revolution. It's not the case. We have aims and ambitions like any other political organization. We have a strong following, especially amongst the working classes.'

'You did, until you killed Aldo Moro in '78,' Sabrina cut in quickly. 'You've never managed to regain that level of support since.'

'Granted, killing Moro was a mistake. It gave the authorities a martyr and we lost an important hostage who could have brought us a lot of money. But that was a long time ago. We have won back that support, irrespective of what the Government would lead the world to believe.

'This country has had to endure an endless succession of inept, corrupt governments, none more so than the present communist government under Enzo Bellini. The balance of payments is the worst in living memory, unemployment is up fifteen per cent and tens of thousands of Italians are living below the poverty line.'

'The perfect climate for revolution,' Graham said.

'The perfect climate for change,' Calvieri retorted. 'The people have lost faith in the politicians; both the Christian Democrats and the PCI, the Communist Party. It's time to brush aside the dead wood and replace it with a new, dynamic force in politics capable of putting this country back on its feet again.'

'In other words, the Red Brigades,' Sabrina concluded.

'Not necessarily, no.' Calvieri watched the puzzlement in

their expressions. 'Of course there are those *Brigatisti* who won't settle for anything less than the overthrow of the democratically elected government, in the blinkered belief that the Red Brigades could seize power in the ensuing confusion.'

'Like Zocchi?' Sabrina said.

'He was the worst. But there are others, some even on the committee. And these are the ones the authorities highlight in the media, making us all out to be bloodthirsty, revolutionary anarchists whose only law comes from the barrel of a gun.'

'You're their spokesman, surely that gives you a platform for your own views?' Sabrina said.

'I wish it were that simple. The Red Brigades only make the news when they fall foul of the law. That's the only time the media want to know me. Of course I try to put across the other side of the story, but once the interview gets back to the studio it's butchered by the editors and by the time it reaches the television news I've been quoted completely out of context. The media depend on viewing figures to survive, and sensationalism seems to be the way to achieve them. I can't win.'

'So what *are* your aims, if not the violent overthrow of the government?' Graham asked.

'Don't get me wrong, I'm not opposed to the violent overthrow of the government. Especially this government. If a volunteer was needed to put Bellini out of Italy's misery I'd be glad to put the gun to his head and pull the trigger. It's just not a viable proposition, not here in Europe. That's where the militants and I disagree. Are the armed forces and the police just going to stand by and let us topple the government in a blaze of gunfire? Of course not. We have to be realistic. The answer is a coalition.'

Graham sat back and folded his arms across his chest. 'Tell us about it.'

'We want the working classes to have a say in the running

of the country. At the moment they don't, which is why there is such an unacceptably high level of unemployment. What I'd like to see in the foreseeable future is for the PCI to take on board two, maybe three, *Brigatisti* and give them a portfolio in the government.'

'With an eye on the Red Brigades finally running the country?' Graham said.

'It's a nice thought but we just don't have the experience to run the country by ourselves. Again, that's where the militants and I disagree. I think it would work. The PCI have the experience and we have the input of ideas which have been sadly lacking in the past few governments.'

'You're overlooking one point,' Sabrina said. 'Some years back the PCI denounced you as "common terrorists". What makes you think they would agree to a coalition?'

'The Christian Democrats are currently ahead in the polls because of the way the PCI have wrecked the economy. At this rate the PCI don't stand a chance of being returned to power at the next election. But with the support we have amongst the working classes we could not only win them the next election, but the one after that as well. That's not something to be taken lightly.' Calvieri finished his brandy. 'It's all hypothetical at the moment. We do have contacts inside the PCI but the final decision would lie with Bellini and his senior ministers.'

'And if they don't agree to your terms they'll become "legitimate targets" like Moro and Tarantelli?'

Calvieri smiled at Graham. 'They're already legitimate targets. So you see, the sooner they agree to meet us, the better it will be for all concerned.'

'Blackmail,' Graham muttered. 'I might have guessed.'

'I prefer to call it common sense,' Calvieri replied.

Over the loudspeakers came the request that Michael Graham contact the switchboard immediately. He crossed to the house phone at the end of the bar. The call was from Kolchinsky.

'Commissioner Kuhlmann and Major Paluzzi have just got back,' Kolchinsky told him. 'We'll have that meeting now.'

'Your room?'

'Yes. Is Sabrina with you?'

'Yeah. And Calvieri.'

'I told you to leave Calvieri alone,' Kolchinsky said sharply.

'Sabrina was having a drink with him. What was I supposed to do, sit at the next table?' Graham raked his fingers through his hair. 'Do you want us to bring him along?'

'No, just the two of you. We won't be able to talk freely if he's there. Sabrina can brief him later.'

'Okay. We'll be up in a couple of minutes,' Graham said, then replaced the receiver and returned to the table.

'Sergei?' Sabrina asked, looking up at him.

'Yeah, he wants to see us right away.'

'Does that include me?' Calvieri asked.

'No. Sabrina will brief you later if there's anything you need to know.'

'It's so refreshing to work in an atmosphere of trust and cooperation,' Calvieri said bitterly.

'I'd prefer to call it common sense,' Graham replied with a forced smile.

They took the lift to the third floor and walked the short distance to Kolchinsky's room. Sabrina knocked. Kolchinsky opened the door and ushered them inside.

'I hear you've been drinking with the enemy,' Paluzzi said with a smile.

'Not by choice, believe me.' Graham went on to explain what Calvieri had told them about the possible coalition between the Red Brigades and the PCI.

'I've never heard about it before,' Kuhlmann said.

'I'm not surprised,' Paluzzi replied. 'It's not exactly something the PCI want the world to know about. At least not yet.'

'So you're saying there *will* be a PCI – Red Brigades coalition at the next election?' Graham said in amazement.

'It's certainly a possibility. As Calvieri said, the PCI don't stand a chance of being returned to power. They need the extra votes. And the Red Brigades are capable, in theory, of giving them those extra votes.'

'But surely the Italian people wouldn't accept the coalition?' Sabrina said.

'I don't have to tell you how bad our economy is at the moment. And it's getting worse by the day. The people have lost faith in the politicians. Can you honestly blame them? They want hope for the future. And if a PCI – Red Brigades coalition can offer them that hope, they'll be voted into power.'

'So what's stopping the coalition happening?' Kolchinsky asked.

'In a word, Bellini. He's totally opposed to the idea.'

'At least someone's got some scruples.'

Paluzzi laughed and patted Graham on the shoulder. 'You obviously don't know about Enzo Bellini, Mike. He'd make a pact with the devil if he thought it would keep him in power. It's not the coalition that bothers him. It's the idea that he could lose the Prime Ministership and all the privileges that go with the job.'

'Would he be deposed?' Sabrina asked.

'Undoubtedly. Along with most of his cabinet. Especially his senior ministers, who are all loyal to him. Although I don't vote for the PCI, I have to admit that they do have several up and coming politicians who could work wonders for the country. They all back the coalition. And that's why none of them have been given posts in the government.'

Kolchinsky turned away from the window, his eyebrows furrowed thoughtfully. 'What if the vial was going to be used not only to free Zocchi but also to force Bellini to step down as Prime Minister so that these coalition talks could take place?'

Paluzzi shook his head. 'Opposition to the coalition isn't just confined to the PCI. The Red Brigades also have their dissenters. And Zocchi was the loudest of them. He was a militant who wouldn't settle for anything less than the violent overthrow of the government in power. Negotiations between the PCI and the Red Brigades were out of the question as far as he was concerned. And that went for the Rome cell in general. The idea of the coalition was drafted by Pisani, Calvieri and Luigi Bettinga, Genoa's brigade chief, the three so-called "moderates" on the committee. Had any of them been involved in the theft of the vial I'd have said you had a valid point. But not with Zocchi and Ubrino.'

There was a knock at the door and Paluzzi answered it. He stepped aside to let the two waiters enter and Kolchinsky told them to leave the trays on the dressing-table. Sabrina signed the chit and they left the room.

'There's tea, coffee and sandwiches,' Kolchinsky said, gesturing towards the trays. 'Help yourselves.'

Paluzzi poured himself a coffee then used his teaspoon to lift the edges of the bread to see what the sandwiches contained.

'I ordered you egg mayonnaise and cheese salad,' Kolchinsky said behind him.

Paluzzi looked round in surprise. 'How did you know I was a vegetarian?'

'It's in your file at UNACO,' Kolchinsky said, helping himself to a couple.

'You've got a file on me at UNACO?' Paluzzi exclaimed, looking from Kolchinsky to Sabrina.

Graham put a hand on Paluzzi's shoulder as he reached over for a sandwich. 'Thing is, Fabio, you just can't be too careful when it comes to differentiating between friend and foe. One day friend, next day foe.'

'Like Calvieri?' Paluzzi said.

'No, he'll always be foe,' Graham replied.

Sabrina took a cup of coffee to Kuhlmann who was seated by the window. 'Did you come across anything in the helicopter?'

'Nothing. I've got a team of forensic scientists going over it now but I can't see them coming up with much.'

'There wasn't a single fingerprint on it,' Paluzzi said, looking across at Sabrina. 'Not one.'

'What about Ubrino and Francia?' Graham asked. 'Surely the locals must have seen them?'

'Someone gave two men fitting their descriptions a lift to the railway station,' Kuhlmann said. 'They seem to have disappeared into thin air after that.'

'They must have bought tickets. Surely somebody must remember them?'

'The staff at the station were questioned thoroughly, Mr Graham. None could recall them.'

'What if they never boarded the train but slipped back into town?'

'We thought of that, Miss Carver,' Kuhlmann said. 'All accommodation centres have been checked. Nothing. I've also instigated the surveillance of all known terrorist sympathizers in Switzerland. If Ubrino or Francia are staying with any of them, we'll know about it.'

'There isn't much else we can do, except wait,' Paluzzi said, sitting down next to Graham.

'Have you spoken to the Colonel, Sergei?' Graham asked.

Kolchinsky nodded. 'He's flying out to Switzerland tonight. I'm picking him up at the airport tomorrow morning.'

'What did he say about Wiseman?'

'He's gone to ground. His present whereabouts are unknown.'

'And Alexander?' Sabrina asked.

'He was spotted at a tube station in London this morning.

Scotland Yard are confident of picking him up within the next couple of days.'

'The ambulances have arrived,' Paluzzi said, peering down into the street.

'What ambulances?' Sabrina asked, craning her neck to look over Paluzzi's shoulder.

'To take away the bodies of Young and Escoletti,' Paluzzi replied, then stood aside to give her a better view of what was happening in the street below them.

'Escoletti?' Graham said, crossing to the window.

'Giancarlo Escoletti, the Red Brigades' most senior hitman,' Paluzzi told him. 'Just the sort of person to be sent after Pisani's killers.'

'How do you know it was Escoletti?' Sabrina asked. 'Have you been over there?'

Paluzzi shook his head. 'I knew who it was when Sergei mentioned the black doctor's bag found beside the body. It was Escoletti's trademark.'

'C.W. won't be implicated, will he?' Graham asked, turning to Kolchinsky.

'I cleared that with the Commissioner as soon as he arrived,' Kolchinsky replied, indicating Kuhlmann. 'It'll be an open and shut case. Escoletti surprised Young, a fight ensued, and they killed each other. At least that's the story that will appear in the morning papers.'

Graham put his empty cup on the tray. 'Talking about the morning, hadn't we better get on with the briefing?'

'Quite right, Michael. Commissioner Kuhlmann and I will meet the Colonel's plane at seven-thirty then the three of us all go directly to the Offenbach Centre for a meeting with representatives of those countries taking part in the summit.'

'Have they already been briefed about the vial?' Sabrina asked.

Kolchinsky nodded. 'The Colonel told the sixteen Ambassadors at the United Nations as soon as we knew that Ubrino's final destination was the Offenbach Centre. They've been kept up to date on all the latest developments.'

'What about us?' Graham asked. 'What will we be doing?'

'You three, plus Calvieri, will be in a car parked a few hundred yards away from the Offenbach Centre. You'll be in constant radio contact with me.'

'What use will we be there?' Graham exclaimed in disbelief. 'We know what Ubrino looks like. We should be working with the security guards, not sitting in some damn car.'

Kolchinsky studied the remaining sandwiches on the plate then selected one and turned back to Graham. 'Ubrino also knows what you look like. All of you. And if he sees any of you at the Offenbach Centre he's likely to smell a rat and take off. Then what? We wouldn't know where to start looking for him. At least this way we can pin him down to one place. And as I told you earlier, an extra hundred policemen and women have been drafted in to help look for him.'

'Chances are he'll wear a disguise,' Paluzzi said, looking at Kuhlmann. 'And if he does, I guarantee that none of your people will recognize him. He's a master of deception.'

'I've heard about these disguises,' Kuhlmann replied. 'That's why everyone entering the building will be subjected to a body search. We also have X-ray machines at all entrances to check bags and briefcases. He may be able to disguise himself, but he won't be able to disguise the vial. He won't get into the building undetected, of that I'm certain.'

'I wish I could share your confidence,' Paluzzi said, then turned to Kolchinsky. 'Do you need me for anything else? I've some calls to make before I go to bed.'

'No, I don't think so,' Kolchinsky replied.

'What time do you want us in position, Sergei?' Sabrina asked.

'I'll be there from eight o'clock. Any time after that.' Kolchinsky took a map of Berne from under a dossier on the bedside table and handed it to her. 'I've marked the street with a cross where I want the four of you to wait. It's close to the highway.'

'What about radios?' Graham asked.

'Fabio's got one. It's all you'll need.' Kolchinsky shot Graham a hard look. 'As long as everyone obeys orders and stays together.'

'Yeah, sure,' Graham muttered, then stood up and stifled a yawn. 'It's been a long day and I, for one, am shattered.'

'You're not the only one,' Sabrina agreed, getting to her feet.

'Not so fast, young lady,' Kolchinsky said. 'You've still got to brief Calvieri before you go to bed.'

'You're all heart, Sergei,' she replied with a grimace.

Kolchinsky saw Kuhlmann and Paluzzi to the door then turned back to Graham and Sabrina. 'Strange how the human mind works. There we all were, tiptoeing about as if this wasn't really a crisis. But behind the façade of professional detachment we were all asking ourselves the same questions. What if Ubrino slips the net and opens the vial? How many millions will die before an antidote is found? And we'd be among the first to be contaminated. Yet none of us has voiced our anxieties, myself included. Strange, isn't it?'

'That's what I like about you, Sergei,' Graham said, patting Kolchinsky on the back. 'Your unfailing optimism.'

Kolchinsky smiled fleetingly, then exhaled deeply. 'It's going to be a long night. I know I'm not going to get any sleep.'

Sabrina glanced at Graham and noticed the uncertainty in his eyes. A mirror image of her own? Kolchinsky was right. None of them wanted to address the issue head on. Not even Graham. The most vociferous amongst them.

'None of us will, Sergei, you can be sure of that,' Graham said then disappeared out into the corridor.

Sabrina looked across at Kolchinsky who was standing with his back to her at the window then turned and left the room, closing the door quietly behind her.


Whitlock stared at the food in front of him. *Choucroute garnie*, sauerkraut with boiled ham and Vienna sausages. One of his favourite dishes. He had bought it on the way back to the boarding house but when he had opened the carton in his room his appetite seemed to vanish. He just wasn't hungry. He had prodded the food absently with his fork for the last hour without making any attempt to eat it. Now it was cold and unappetizing. He suddenly stabbed the fork into one of the sausages and pushed the carton away from him. He glanced at his watch. 10.40 p.m. What did time matter? He stood up and crossed to the telephone on the bedside table. He picked up the receiver and rang the apartment in New York. He let it ring for a minute. No reply. How many times had he rung the number in the last hour? Ten? More like fifteen. And each time the same. He had rung Carmen's work number half a dozen times as well, with the same result. He replaced the receiver, then walked to the window and looked down into the alley below him. A teenage couple were kissing in the shadows of a doorway. He turned away angrily and sat down again. He was out of his mind with worry. Where was Carmen? Her sister hadn't seen her. Her friends hadn't seen her. It was completely out of character for her to act like this. He had called all the main hospitals in New York but none of them had any record of her admittance. He had even contacted the city mortuaries but again his enquiries had drawn a blank. He was desperate to talk to her. He suddenly banged his fist angrily on the table. He had to stop dwelling on Carmen's disappearance and concentrate on the assignment.

Damn his selfishness. He had to pull himself together. Quickly.

He picked up one of the keys on the table. It was for Young's room. He had been meaning to search the room ever since he got back to the boarding house. Now was a perfect time. It would help him to take his mind off Carmen. Well, he could try. He left his room, looked the length of the deserted corridor, then moved to the adjacent door, unlocked it, and slipped inside. He closed the door behind him and switched on the light. The room was identical to his own. A double bed, a table, a chair, a chest of drawers and a washbasin beside the window. Even the garish wallpaper was the same. He searched the chest of drawers and found a passport in the bottom drawer in the name of Vincent Yannick. A Walther P5 lay beside the passport. It was a good, reliable handgun, used mainly by the West German and Dutch police forces and exported extensively to both North and South America. He still preferred the Browning for accuracy. Not that he had much choice. The Browning Sabrina had given to him in Rome was in the hands of the *NOCS*. As was everything else they had left behind at the boarding house. He looked under the bed and pulled out the pale-blue holdall Young had taken from the locker at Berne's Belpmoos Airport. He unzipped it. Inside were bundles of Swiss francs, all in used notes. He would give the money to Kolchinsky to hand over to UNICEF.

He looked around sharply when he heard the noise. It came from next door, from within his own room. He immediately thought of the scientist being sent from Zurich to de-activate the booby-trapped watch. But there was another possibility. A Red Brigades assassin. He peered out into the corridor. It was still empty. He closed the door silently behind him and approached his own room cautiously, the Walther gripped tightly in his hand. The door was ajar. He kicked it open and dropped to one knee, training the Walther on the figure standing by the window. The man was in his forties with short blond hair and wire-rimmed glasses. He raised his hands slowly.

'Who are you?' Whitlock demanded.

'My name is Dr Hans Gottfried,' came the nervous reply. 'Monsieur Rust sent me. I did knock on the door but there was no reply. That is why I came inside.'

Whitlock got to his feet and tucked the Walther into his belt. 'I'm sorry if I startled you but I couldn't afford to take any chances.'

Gottfried lowered his hands. 'I quite understand.'

'Can I get you something to drink? Tea? Coffee? That's about all they serve here.'

'Nothing, thank you. May I see the watch?'

Whitlock held out his arm. Gottfried studied the watch for some time, then asked to see the transmitter. He turned it around in his hand then undid the protective cap to expose the detonator button.

'Don't touch that!' Whitlock shouted, his eyes wide in horror.

Gottfried smiled gently. 'I do not intend to, I assure you. I was just looking at the design.'

Whitlock slumped on to the bed. 'I'm sorry, I'm just on edge. I've been like this ever since I was tricked into wearing this damn thing. What if the strap came loose while I was asleep? What if Young went on drinking and inadvertently strayed more than three miles away from the boarding house? You could count the number of hours' sleep I've had since Monday on one hand. I'm exhausted.'

'I can well imagine,' Gottfried said, picking up an attaché case from beside the bed. 'You will sleep well tonight, I promise you that.'

How the hell could he sleep well not knowing where Carmen was? He stifled a yawn, then forced a quick smile when he noticed that Gottfried was watching him.

'Do you know anything about the origins of the device?' Gottfried asked, placing the case on the table.

'He did say it was the first of its kind and he had this insane idea to patent it if it proved successful.'

'Homemade. I thought as much. That means the transmitter could also be booby-trapped.'

'Wonderful,' Whitlock muttered, then crossed to the window and sat on the edge of the sill. 'What's the next move?'

Gottfried patted the attaché case. 'This contains a portable scanner we developed last year. It works on the same principle as the X-ray machines used at airports to check suitcases. We will be able to see if the transmitter is booby-trapped.'

'And if it is? What then?'

'That would depend on the nature of the device,' Gottfried replied, opening the case and starting to piece together the machine. 'If it is a tricky operation we will have to fly back to Zurich and defuse it in the laboratory. And if something were to go wrong, God forbid, there would be a medical team on standby to give you immediate assistance.'

'That's comforting to know,' Whitlock replied, grim faced.

'We have to accept that possibility,' Gottfried said, glancing up at Whitlock. 'The only way to de-activate this device is by cutting it off at the power source. That means opening the casing. And if this man Young knew anything about booby-traps, he could have made the job very difficult indeed.'

Whitlock wiped the back of his hand across his clammy forehead.

Gottfried removed a length of flex from the case and held up the plug which was attached to the end of it. 'Where is the nearest socket?'

'By the bed. Here, I'll plug it in for you.'

'Thank you,' Gottfried said, handing the flex to Whitlock.

227

'Okay?'

'*Ja*, it is working.'

Whitlock took up a position behind Gottfried's chair and looked more closely at the apparatus inside the attaché case: a twelve-inch fold-up square box, with protective curtains at each end, a compact control console and a monitor which was built into the lid of the case. Gottfried placed the transmitter inside the chamber, then pressed a series of keys on the console in front of him. An image of the transmitter's components appeared on the screen.

'The normal two wires connected to the detonator cap,' Gottfried said, pointing them out with the tip of his pen. 'Nothing unusual there.'

'What about the sides of the case? He could have set a hair-trigger device which would detonate the watch if any attempt was made to open the transmitter.'

Gottfried enlarged each side of the transmitter in turn but there were no strands of wire crossing the joins between the two halves of the case.

'There is another possibility,' Gottfried said at length. 'A light-emitting diode. It is a tiny photocell incorporated into the circuit which would trigger off the explosive charge the moment it came into contact with a light source.'

'In other words, when you removed the back of the transmitter.'

'Exactly. But there is a way of getting round it. Infra-red light.'

'Does that mean I'm going to have to fly back to Zurich with you?' Whitlock asked.

'That is up to you. There is an infra-red light built into this system but if you would prefer to go to Zurich—'

'Not if we can do it here,' Whitlock cut in. 'I'm on standby. My colleagues may need me at any time.'

'Very well. Will you switch off the light and close the curtains, please? The infra-red light can only work in complete darkness.'

Whitlock did as he was asked. Gottfried activated the infra-red, which was built into the lid of the case, then switched off the scanner and removed the transmitter from the chamber. He placed it face down on the table then selected a screwdriver from the miniature tool kit he had taken from his pocket and began to unscrew the first of the four screws holding the two halves of the case together. Whitlock remained motionless behind him, his breathing shallow and ragged. He wiped the sweat from his eyes then bit his lower lip painfully when Gottfried placed the fourth screw on the table and gingerly lifted the back off the transmitter. He breathed out deeply and managed a nervous smile when Gottfried held up the back half of the case to show him that it was perfectly harmless. Gottfried took a pair of pliers from the kit and studied the two wires more closely. One blue. One yellow. The standard wiring for a device of that kind. He used the tip of the pliers to look under the wires for any booby-trap that may not have shown up on the monitor. Nothing. He sat back and shook his head slowly.

'What's wrong?' Whitlock asked anxiously.

'I have this feeling that something is not right,' Gottfried replied, staring at the two wires. 'It is almost as if he is inviting us to go ahead and cut the wires. Why go to such lengths to booby-trap the watch but not the transmitter? It makes no sense.'

Whitlock remained silent. Not that he could have spoken anyway. His throat was suddenly dry. Gottfried took a small scalpel from the kit and cut a two-inch gash in the yellow flex. He peeled the plastic back and studied the fine network of wires inside it. He did the same with the blue flex and it was a couple of minutes before he sat back and nodded to himself.

'Well?' Whitlock asked.

'It is booby-trapped.' Gottfried used the scalpel to point out a single strand of wire amongst the network inside the yellow flex. 'There it is.'

Whitlock stared at Gottfried. 'How can you tell? It just looks like another wire to me.'

'It would, to an untrained eye. I have been defusing explosive devices for the past fifteen years. I know what to look for.' Gottfried used the scalpel as a pointer and followed the passage of the wire to the detonator cap. 'If you look closely you will see that this strand was connected separately from the other wires. The perfect booby-trap.'

'Is there one in the blue flex as well?'

Gottfried shook his head. 'It is not necessary. Both lengths of flex have to be cut to defuse the device. He only needed to booby-trap one of them.'

'Thank God for suspicious minds,' Whitlock said, wiping his forearm across his forehead.

'More like devious minds. The only way to beat these kind of people is to think like them.'

Gottfried picked up the pliers and cut through the blue flex. Then, using the tip of the screwdriver to isolate the booby-trap, he cut the remaining wires inside the yellow flex to make safe the transmitter.

'You can take off the watch now.'

Whitlock stared at the watch, an uncertainty in his eyes.

'Trust me, Mr Whitlock, the watch is perfectly safe now.'

'It's not that I don't trust you. It's Young I don't trust.'

Gottfried switched the light on again then turned back to Whitlock. 'You are worried about the booby-trap in the strap, not so?'

Whitlock nodded. 'As I said, I don't trust that bastard an inch. It would be just like him to have the last laugh.'

'The booby-trap needs to work off a power source. The power source has been cut, so the booby-trap cannot work. It is as simple as that.' Gottfried smiled at the doubt in Whitlock's eyes. 'What must I do to convince you?'

Whitlock sat on the edge of the bed and smiled ruefully at Gottfried. 'Nothing. I'm convinced.'

'So take off the watch.'

Whitlock unclipped the strap and let out a deep breath when the watch slipped off his wrist on to the back of his hand. He eased it over his fingers and dropped it on to the bed.

'Thanks,' Whitlock said softly, massaging his wrist where the watch had been pressed against his skin.

'I am glad to be of assistance.' Gottfried pointed to the watch. 'May I take it with me? I would like to examine it more closely in the laboratory.'

'Please, take it,' Whitlock said, handing the watch to Gottfried. 'I never want to see it again.'

Gottfried smiled, then dismantled the X-ray machine.

'Can I at least buy you a drink before you go back to Zurich?' Whitlock asked.

'That is very kind of you but I have to get back as quickly as possible. Yours is not the only such difficulty awaiting my attention, you understand.'

'Of course. I hope it all goes well.'

'I am sure it will.' Gottfried closed the attaché case and locked it. 'Nice to have met you, Mr Whitlock.'

'Likewise,' Whitlock said, shaking Gottfried's hand. 'I just wish it had been under more relaxing conditions.'

'*C'est la vie*,' Gottfried replied with a resigned shrug, then took his leave.

Whitlock closed the door behind him then kicked off his shoes and lay on the bed, his hands clasped behind his head. He knew he should be feeling great relief now that he was rid of the watch. But he only felt empty. It was probably the same feeling the condemned man feels on the eve of his execution. He stifled a yawn. His body was exhausted but his mind was awake. Very awake. He glanced at the telephone and thought about Graham, Sabrina and Kolchinsky. He knew none of them would be sleeping. But at least they had each other for company. He had nobody. Not even his wife. He'd probably get back to the apartment and find the divorce papers in the post.

*If* he got back, he reminded himself. That all depended on Ubrino.

He sat up and reached for the telephone. He rang the apartment in New York. He let it ring for the customary minute. No reply. He thought about calling her work number then replaced the receiver and pushed the telephone away from him. Why bother? There would be no reply.

*C'est la vie . . .*

# TEN

'What time is it?' Graham asked.

'Five minutes later than the last time you asked,' Sabrina replied, exasperated. 'And ten minutes later than the time before that. And fifteen—'

'Okay, you've made your point. Ask a civil question and all you get is sarcasm.'

'That's rich coming from you, Mike—'

'Sabrina, please,' Paluzzi interceded quickly, his hands raised defensively. 'We're all on edge, let's not make it any worse than it already is.'

Paluzzi sat behind the wheel of the white BMW 735i that Kuhlmann had had delivered to the hotel for them that morning. Graham sat beside him. Sabrina and Calvieri were in the back. They had been parked in the street that overlooked the Offenbach Centre for the past forty minutes, waiting for Kolchinsky to call them on the two-way radio lying on the dashboard. So far only silence. Paluzzi stared at the building in the distance. He remembered the official opening earlier in the year when one critic had called it 'a monstrous glass and aluminium bandbox, without the ribbons'. He could see what the critic had meant. There was nothing appealing about it. A ten-storey building, cylindrical in shape, with a glass and aluminium exterior and a flat roof to accommodate a helipad. Helicopters had been landing and departing regularly in the last forty minutes and he was sure the traffic would get busier as the day wore on.

'What's the time?' Graham asked, nudging Paluzzi's arm.

Paluzzi pulled back his sleeve to reveal his gold Cartier watch. 'Nine twenty-four. Where's your watch?'

'It got bust on the mountain yesterday. I'll send it to the jeweller's when I get back to New York. It's pretty special to me.'

'Was it a present from your wife?'

'Yeah,' Graham muttered, then lapsed into silence.

Paluzzi turned his attention back to the Offenbach Centre. The more he looked at it, the more he came to agree with the critic. Berne, a beautiful, medieval city, had always rebuffed the advances of modern development, and planning permission had been granted to Jacob Offenbach, the Swiss multimillionaire, only on condition that the Centre was built on the outskirts of the city, away from the charm of the Old Town district. The people of Berne had never taken it to their hearts, calling it the *Raumschiff*, the spaceship, because of its futuristic appearance and design. It would never be accepted by the locals, and he could see why.

'Does anyone mind if I smoke?' Calvieri asked, breaking the silence.

'Yeah, I mind,' Graham bit back, then threw up his hands dismissively. 'What the hell, I'm going for a walk. Do what you want.'

'Don't go far,' Paluzzi said. 'Sergei could call at any moment.'

'Stop panicking, I'm only going to that fruit and vegetable shop over there.'

Graham forced himself not to slam the door behind him. Sliding on his dark glasses, and then thrusting his hands into his pockets, he walked the length of the narrow street to the shop. He crouched in front of the display outside, which was shaded from the sun by a white canopy, and tested the apples for their ripeness. He suddenly became aware that he was being watched. He looked up. A five-year-old boy stood in the doorway, pointing a toy gun straight at him. Graham feigned a look of surprise and slowly raised his hands. The boy glanced with alarm at Graham's chest. Graham looked down. His holstered Beretta was visible. He immediately got to his feet and covered the holster with his jacket. The boy stared fearfully at him, then ran into the shop. Graham cursed himself but a hand grabbed his arm before he could go after the boy. He spun round to find Sabrina behind him.

'What happened?' she asked, then glanced towards the doorway after he had told her. 'I'll talk to him. He's hardly going to understand you, is he?'

Graham nodded and she disappeared into the shop. She emerged a minute later with a brown-paper bag in her hand. The boy was with her.

'Magnum!' the boy shouted with a wide grin, then pretended to shoot at Graham before hurrying up the street and disappearing into one of the houses.

'He thinks I'm Magnum?' Graham asked in amazement.

'I told him you were a real-life Magnum. It certainly appealed to him.' She took an apple from the bag and tossed it to Graham.

They crossed the street to the site of a demolished house and sat on what remained of the front wall.

'I'm sorry I snapped at you in the car,' she said at length. 'I had a pretty rough night. I don't know how much sleep I actually got. About two hours, probably.'

'That much?' Graham replied, turning the apple in his hands. 'I doubt I even got an hour.'

'How did you pass the time?'

'I watched television, there wasn't much else to do.'

She sat forward, her elbows resting on her knees. 'I tried to but I found I couldn't concentrate for more than a few minutes at a time. In the end I was just glad of the background noise. I don't think I could have coped with the silence.'

'I know what you mean. There was a soccer match on one of the channels. I stayed with it for the whole game but I still couldn't tell you the score. Hell, I couldn't even tell you who was playing.' He tugged back her sleeve to check the time: 9.37. 'Twenty-three minutes left. And here we are sitting around waiting to die.'

She put a hand lightly on his arm. 'I hate this waiting as much as you do, but you know that Sergei's right. If Ubrino did see us, he'd be sure to bolt. Then what?'

Paluzzi jabbed the horn and, climbing out of the car, beckoned them frantically to him. They ran to the car.

'What is it?' Graham asked breathlessly.

'Sergei's just been on the radio. Ubrino's been caught inside the building but he won't say anything unless Calvieri's there.'

'Did he have the vial on him?' Sabrina asked, getting into the back.

Paluzzi glanced at her in the rear-view mirror and shook his head. 'He's been searched from head to toe. It wasn't on him.'

'Was he wearing a disguise?' Graham asked.

'Not when he was caught,' Paluzzi replied, starting the engine. 'But he must have worn one to get into the building. How else would he have got past the guards?'

'It doesn't make any sense!' Sabrina exclaimed, looking at Calvieri. 'Why would he take off the disguise once he was inside the building? It's almost as if he wanted to get caught.'

Calvieri shrugged. 'We'll find out soon enough. The main thing is he's been caught.'

Paluzzi put a siren on the roof and drove the short distance to the N12 southbound motorway. He took the turn-off for the Offenbach Centre and came to a stop three hundred yards further on in front of a red and white boom-gate. An armed guard approached the car. Paluzzi produced the pass provided by Kuhlmann and, after checking it, the guard gave him directions to a side entrance where Kolchinsky would be waiting. The guard then gave the order to lift the boomgate. Paluzzi slid the car into gear and drove into the grounds.

Pantechnicons of varying shapes and sizes, covered with the logos of the world's media, lined the sides of the road and spilled over into the massive car-park which had been designed to take two thousand cars. There wasn't a space available. Paluzzi drove around the perimeter then turned into the alley indicated by the guard and stopped beside a fire escape. Kolchinsky, who had been standing by the door, hurried forward to meet them.

'Why all this cloak and dagger stuff?' Calvieri asked, climbing from the back of the car. 'Why can't we use the main entrance like everyone else?'

'Because we're armed,' Sabrina answered, patting her holstered Beretta hidden discreetly beneath her beige jacket. 'If we used the main entrance the X-ray machines would go berserk.'

'Have you managed to get anything out of Ubrino yet, Sergei?' Graham asked as they followed Kolchinsky to the door.

'He refuses to say anything until he's seen Calvieri.'

The guard at the door stood aside to let them pass then closed it again behind them. They were in the main foyer, which bustled with activity as journalists sought last-minute interviews with the politicians as they made their way towards the lifts. Kolchinsky took four ID passes from his pocket and handed them out.

Graham clipped his to his jacket pocket. 'Where did you get the passport photographs from?'

'The Colonel brought them with him,' Kolchinsky replied as they walked towards the lifts.

They took the lift to the fifth floor where Ubrino was being held in one of the conference rooms. Kolchinsky stopped outside an ornately carved oak door and knocked twice, paused, then knocked twice more. The armed guard inside peered through the spyhole, then unlocked the door to admit them. The room was small and windowless, with a rectangular mahogany table and fourteen matching chairs around it. Kuhlmann dismissed the guard and Kolchinsky introduced Paluzzi and Calvieri to Philpott.

Philpott turned to Ubrino. 'Well, Calvieri's here now. Where have you hidden the vial?'

Ubrino merely shrugged his shoulders.

'I'll find out,' Graham hissed angrily.

Philpott put a hand lightly on Graham's arm, then looked at Calvieri. 'Talk to him. Maybe you can coax it out of him.'

Calvieri crossed to where Ubrino was sitting and patted him on the shoulder. 'He doesn't know where it is.'

'How do you know that? You haven't even asked him yet,' Kolchinsky said.

Calvieri took a small transmitter from his pocket and held it up for them to see. It was the size of a cigarette lighter. 'He doesn't know because I never told him.'

Paluzzi stared at Calvieri in horror. 'You've been behind this all along. And we've played straight into your hands.'

Graham slid his hand behind his back, feeling for his holstered Beretta.

Calvieri touched the detonator with his forefinger. 'The transmitter's linked to a small charge of plastic explosive attached to the side of the cylinder. It's powerful enough to break both the cylinder and the vial in half. Question is, Mr Graham, can you draw your gun and kill me before I push the button?'

'Let it go, Mike,' Philpott said without looking at Graham.

Graham's hand dropped to his side.

'Now, I want you each to remove your handguns and place them on the table. One at a time. Ladies first.'

Sabrina removed her Beretta, using her thumb and fore-finger, and put it on the table. Graham and Paluzzi did the same.

'You won't get away with this, Calvieri,' Kuhlmann rasped sharply.

'Get away with what? You don't even know what I want yet.'

'What *do* you want?' Philpott asked.

'All in good time, Colonel. In the meantime, would you put the key for Riccardo's handcuffs on the table next to the guns.'

'I don't have it. The guard took it with him.'

'I wouldn't insult the intelligence of the UNACO Director. Please don't insult mine.' Calvieri smiled at their startled expressions. 'Oh yes, I know who you work for. When you refused to tell me I did a little investigative digging of my own. It took a while but I got there in the end.'

'How did you find out?' Philpott demanded.

'I have my sources, let's leave it at that. Now, the key.'

Philpott put the key on the table, then turned back to Calvieri. 'You killed Zocchi, didn't you?'

'Had him killed,' Calvieri corrected, then picked up the key and unlocked one of the cuffs. He gave the key to Ubrino to unlock the second one himself. 'I must say all your little theories about Zocchi certainly kept me amused these past few days. I knew that with him dead the authorities would have no option but to call us in to help them find the vial. And I was the only *Brigatista* Signore Pisani would trust with such a delicate task. That's how the plan came into being in the first place. And as you said, Paluzzi, you played straight into my hands. Riccardo didn't have the vial on him when he got here, that would have been too dangerous. I had it with me. I knew we wouldn't be searched when we entered the building. I passed it on to a sympathizer in the foyer. It's already been secreted somewhere in the building. So I have you to thank for helping me smuggle it past the guards.'

Ubrino tossed the handcuffs on to the chair then collected the handguns from the table. He handed two to Calvieri and tucked the other into his belt.

'Where does he fit into all this?' Paluzzi asked, indicating Ubrino.

'He's been my inside man in Rome for the past six years. I knew you would immediately suspect Zocchi if Riccardo was involved in the break-in at the plant.'

'How did you get in?' Kuhlmann demanded of Ubrino.

'I pose as maintenance engineer,' Ubrino replied in a thick Italian accent. 'Nino Ferzetti, that is his name. We have the same build and height. He wear the beard and glasses. It is an easy . . .' he trailed off and looked at Calvieri. '*Travestire*?'

'Disguise,' Calvieri answered.

'*Si*, it is an easy disguise for me. I carry his pass so the guard do not stop me.'

'Where's the real Ferzetti?' Philpott asked.

'At home, sleeping off the effects of a spiked drink he had last night.' Calvieri pointed to the door behind them. 'I think you've taken up enough of my time as it is. Colonel, call me when you have a number where I can contact you. And make it soon. The longer you delay, the less time there will be to process my demands.'

'One last question, Calvieri,' Paluzzi said. 'Why the Offenbach Centre?'

'It's quite simple. The summit is being covered by journalists from all over the world. You can't do anything overt without alerting them. I'm sure you all know what happened in 1938 when Orson Welles narrated *The War of the Worlds* on American radio. There was unprecedented panic across the country. Can you imagine that on a global scale?'

'I'll call you in a few minutes,' Philpott said brusquely, then walked to the door.

'There is one more thing,' Calvieri said. 'Sabrina stays with us.'

'Like hell she does,' Graham snapped.

'I was talking to Colonel Philpott.' Calvieri retorted, then whispered to Ubrino, who immediately drew the Beretta from his belt and aimed it at Kuhlmann. 'You have five seconds to comply otherwise Kuhlmann will be shot. Then Kolchinsky—'

'Okay, you've made your point,' Philpott cut in. He turned to Sabrina. 'We'll have to do as he says.'

'I understand, sir,' she replied with a quick smile.

'What the hell do you need her for?' Graham demanded. 'You've got the detonator, isn't that enough?'

'I'll only use the detonator as a last resort. In other words, if my demands are not met. Sabrina's the deterrent to stop you and Paluzzi from getting any heroic ideas about storming the room like a couple of over-enthusiastic schoolboys.'

'I'm going to come after you when this is over, Calvieri,' Graham said menacingly. 'I don't care where you go, I'll find you. That's a promise.'

'In that case I look forward to seeing you again, Mr Graham. Please close the door on your way out.'

Ubrino waited until they had left, then locked and bolted the door behind them and handed the key to Calvieri.

Sabrina sat down and looked up at Calvieri. 'Are your demands really worth the lives of millions of innocent people?'

'Don't try to play on my emotions, Sabrina, it won't work.'

'I didn't know you had any,' Sabrina shot back.

'*Manette*,' Calvieri said to Ubrino and pointed to the hand-cuffs.

Ubrino pulled Sabrina's hands behind her back and snapped the handcuffs over her wrists. He grinned at her, then reached out to touch her face. She kicked at him savagely, catching him full on the shinbone.

'Tell your poodle to keep his hands off me,' she snapped, her eyes blazing at Calvieri.

'I'm sure he's learnt his lesson,' Calvieri replied, casting a disdainful glance towards Ubrino. He took the Beretta from Ubrino's hand, ejected the clip, pocketed it, then threw the gun on to the table. 'Leave her alone. She isn't one of your wide-eyed recruits. She'd kill you without batting an eyelid.'

'Nobody does that to me, especially not a woman,' Ubrino hissed through his clenched teeth.

'You just won't learn, will you?' Calvieri pointed a finger of warning at him. 'I won't tell you again. Leave her alone.'

The telephone rang. Calvieri answered it.

'It's Philpott. I've set up a base in the manager's office. Extension 257.'

'I'll be in touch.' Calvieri replaced the receiver and looked across at Ubrino. 'We're in business.'


Dieter Vlok was a short, athletically built man in his late forties with black hair and a neatly trimmed black beard. He had been widely regarded in his native West Germany as one of the country's leading hotel managers, first at the Vier Jahreszeiten in Hamburg, then at the Bremner's Park in Baden-Baden, before he went to Switzerland to take up his most challenging post to date, that of general manager of the Offenbach Centre.

His office, situated on the tenth floor, had a breathtaking view of the city spread out in the distance. He stood motionless by the window as Philpott described the latest developments to him. Although he had been briefed that morning, he was still finding it hard to believe that such a catastrophe could be unfolding on his own doorstep.

'As I said this morning, it's imperative that we keep this under wraps,' Philpott said in conclusion, then sat back in the padded chair behind the desk. 'If the press get the slightest whiff of a story, God knows the pandemonium that would result.'

'Of course, I understand,' Vlok replied, turning to face

242

the others. 'I just find it hard to comprehend. This man Calvieri knows what will happen if the vial is opened and yet he says he's quite prepared to do it if his demands are not met.'

'What do you expect? He's a terrorist,' Graham retorted gruffly.

'Even so, what can he hope to achieve?'

'We'll find out soon enough,' Philpott replied. 'That's why we'll need to use your office as a base.'

'It's at your disposal. Any calls for me will be put through to my assistant. Not that I need the room anyway. I'll be down in the conference hall making sure everything runs according to plan for the opening ceremony at eleven o'clock.'

'Do you have an architect's plan of the building?' Philpott asked, tamping a wad of tobacco into the mouth of his pipe.

'Not here. There's one in the safe at reception. I'll have it sent up to you.'

'No, we have to keep our presence here as quiet as possible. Mike will go with you.'

'Of course. I'm sorry, I'm not used to this kind of secrecy.'

'How can we contact you if we need you?' Kolchinsky asked.

Vlok opened his jacket to reveal a bleeper attached to his belt. 'Ask the reception to page me if you need me. Anything at all.'

'I will, you can be sure of that,' Philpott replied.

Vlok looked at his watch. 'I better get down to the conference hall.'

Philpott gestured for Graham to go with Vlok, then sat back in the chair and lit his pipe. He waited until they had left before looking across at Kolchinsky. 'Have you got C.W.'s number? We're going to need him here.'

'I was thinking the same thing.' Kolchinsky took a black notebook from his pocket, opened it at the relevant page, and put it on the desk in front of Philpott.

'When are you going to tell the delegates about Calvieri?' Kuhlmann asked, pacing the floor in front of the desk.

'When we know his demands. There's no use calling meetings every five minutes. And for God's sake, Reinhardt, stop pacing about like an expectant father. It's driving me crazy.'

Kuhlmann sat down beside Kolchinsky on the leather sofa but within seconds he was back on his feet. He crossed to the window. 'I should have barred Calvieri from Switzerland when I had the chance. But no, I let you talk me out of it. Now look what's happened. Why did I listen to you?'

'Barring him wouldn't have solved anything,' Philpott said, reaching for Kolchinsky's black book. 'He'd just have gone somewhere else.'

'But at least he wouldn't be in Switzerland,' Kuhlmann retorted.

'So that's what it's all about,' Philpott snapped, then swivelled round in the chair to face Kuhlmann. 'We have a saying in English, Reinhardt, "If you can't take the heat, get out of the kitchen." Perhaps it's just as well that it's your last year in office. You obviously can't take the heat any more.'

Kuhlmann was silent.

Philpott picked up the receiver and dialled the number of the boarding house where Whitlock was staying.

'C.W.?'

'Yes sir,' Whitlock answered, recognizing Philpott's Scottish brogue.

'I want you to get over to the Offenbach Centre right away. I'll have a security pass waiting for you at the main gate. We're on the tenth floor, the manager's office.'

'I'm on my way, sir,' Whitlock replied.

Philpott replaced the receiver and looked at Kolchinsky. 'We're going to need handguns for Mike and C.W. Major Paluzzi, what weapon do you use?'

'Same as Mike and Sabrina. A Beretta 92.'

Kolchinsky got to his feet. 'So that's two Berettas and a Browning.'

'I want you carrying as well, Sergei.'

Kolchinsky nodded. 'I'll get on to it right away. There's a phone in the outer office I can use.'

'Oh, and Sergei, get a couple of cheap wristwatches for Mike and C.W. as well.'

The telephone rang.

Kolchinsky froze, his hand on the handle of the communicating door.

'Get the guns, Sergei,' Philpott said. He picked up the receiver as Kolchinsky disappeared into the outer office. 'Yes?'

'What's going on up there?' Calvieri demanded. 'I called a minute ago and the line was engaged. Let's get something straight right from the start. That line is to remain open at all times. Is that understood?'

'Perfectly,' Philpott replied.

'I'm going to issue my demands now. Are you ready to write them down?'

'I'm ready.'

'My demands are twofold. Firstly, the Italian Prime Minister, Enzo Bellini, who is attending the summit, will call a special press conference for five o'clock this afternoon at which he will announce that he is stepping down as the leader of our country on the grounds of ill-health. He has had problems with his heart in recent years so this will give credence to his story. I do have a television set in the room, Colonel, so if he doesn't appear at exactly five o'clock I'll press the button. It's that simple.'

'And what do you hope to achieve by getting Bellini to resign?'

'You let me worry about that. You just make sure he gets the message.'

'And the second demand.'

245

'There are sixteen countries represented at this summit. Between them they will pay the sum of a hundred million pounds to the following five revolutionary organizations: *Action Directe* in France, the Red Army Faction in West Germany, the Red Brigades in Italy, *Euskadi ta Askatasuna*, ETA, in Spain, and the Irish Republican Army in Britain. Twenty million each. They have until five o'clock this afternoon to have the money ready for collection.'

'That's impossible. They won't be able to raise that kind of money in seven hours. Make it a more realistic deadline.'

'Six hours and fifty-four minutes to be precise. Once they have seen Bellini resign on television a member of each organization will call the Foreign Office in their particular country with details of where they want the money to be delivered. They will then call me when they have recovered the money. But they will only call when they are sure that they are safe and that no homing devices have been hidden amongst the notes. They each have a special password, known only to the two of us, so don't try anything foolish like using some of your own people to call me pretending to have the money. Then, once I have received all five calls, I'll contact you again to arrange for a helicopter to fly Riccardo and me out of here.'

'What about Sabrina?'

'She'll come with us, at least for part of the way. I'll then call you in the morning to tell you where to find the vial and the transmitter.'

'I've told you, getting hold of that kind of money—'

'If, however, the governments refuse to pay the ransom,' Calvieri cut in, ignoring Philpott's protestations, 'try and stall for more time, or even try to evacuate the building by staging some fake bomb hoax in order to conduct a search, I won't hesitate to press the button.'

'I've told you, Calvieri, they won't be able to raise that sort of money in seven hours.'

'Why do you persist in insulting my intelligence, Colonel?

We both know the leaders of those five countries alone could raise twenty million pounds by making a single phone call. And they could arrange to have the money ready for collection in half the time I've given them. Please call me when you know their decision. They have exactly six hours and fifty minutes left.'

The line went dead.

Philpott replaced the receiver then looked at Kolchinsky who was hovering by the door. 'Have you arranged for the handguns to be brought here?'

'Yes.' Kolchinsky gestured to the pad Philpott had used to jot down the demands. 'What does he want?'

Graham came in before Philpott could reply. He dumped the three rolled-up blueprints on the desk then looked at them both carefully, suspicious of the sudden silence. 'What's wrong?'

'Calvieri's just called the Colonel with his demands,' Kolchinsky replied.

'What are they?' Graham asked Philpott.

'I was about to announce them when you arrived.' Philpott relit his pipe, then recounted the demands.

'I'd say they got off lightly,' Kolchinsky said, then pushed a cigarette between his lips and lit it.

'I agree,' Philpott replied. 'He could have asked for ten times that amount and they would still have had to pay up.'

'What's to say he won't keep the transmitter and ask for another hundred million once his demands have been met?' Graham asked.

'Absolutely nothing.' Philpott looked at Paluzzi who was sitting thoughtfully on the couch. 'What do you make of the Bellini angle?'

'Have you been told about Calvieri's plans to form a coalition between the Red Brigades and the PCI?'

Philpott nodded. 'Sergei briefed me on the phone last night.'

'That's your answer. Without Bellini the coalition would

become a distinct possibility.' Paluzzi got to his feet and crossed to the window. He stared up at the sky, then turned back to them. 'As you know, the *NOCS* have a senior mole on the Red Brigades committee. What I'm about to tell you has to be strictly off the record.'

'We understand,' Philpott replied softly.

'The Red Brigades have infiltrated the PCI. Nothing unusual in that, you might say. It wouldn't be, but their mole is the Deputy Prime Minister, Alberto Vietri.'

'Good God,' Kolchinsky muttered in horror. 'And if Bellini steps down, Vietri takes over as Prime Minister.'

'Leaving the floodgates open for the Red Brigades to overrun the PCI,' Graham added.

'In theory,' Paluzzi replied. 'It's the Red Brigades' most closely guarded secret. Now that Fisani's dead, there are only two committee members left who know about Vietri's duplicity: Calvieri, and our mole. So you see, if it were ever made public the finger of suspicion would immediately point at our mole.'

'Unless something were to happen to Vietri,' Graham said. 'An accident of some kind.'

'It will, believe me,' Paluzzi replied coldly. 'Alberto Vietri will *never* become Prime Minister of Italy.'

'You're proposing . . .' Kuhlmann trailed off as he stared at Paluzzi. 'That would be murder.'

'What do you suggest, Commissioner?' Paluzzi asked, the sarcasm not lost on Kuhlmann.

'Threaten to expose him publicly unless he agrees to resign. Politicians fear scandals more than anything else.'

'It's a nice scenario, Commissioner, but you're over-looking one small point. What if Vietri calls our bluff? We don't have a shred of evidence to back up our accusation. All we have is the word of an informer. And he's hardly going to hand over any incriminating evidence to us, is he? He might as well put a gun to his head and pull the trigger.'

'Why should Vietri—'

'Reinhardt, that's enough!' Philpott reached for his cane and stood up. 'Major Paluzzi doesn't need a lecture from you on how to handle his domestic problems.'

'Are you condoning murder, Malcolm?' Kuhlmann challenged.

'I don't have the time to stand here and argue with you, Reinhardt. Vietri doesn't concern us. Calvieri and Bellini do. I suggest you keep that in mind.' Philpott moved to the door, then turned back to Kolchinsky. 'I'm going to see Bellini before I meet the other leaders. I think it's only right to put Calvieri's demands to him first. I want the four of you to go through the blueprints while I'm gone and make a list of all the places where the vial could be hidden.'

'It'll be like looking for a needle in a haystack.'

'I'm well aware of that, Mike, but it's better than sitting around here for the next seven hours hoping that one of the cleaners will find it.'

Paluzzi waited until Philpott had left the room before crossing to the door. 'I'll be back in a moment. I have to call headquarters in Rome.'

'To arrange for Vietri to meet with an *accident*?' Kuhlmann said.

'To arrange for Calvieri's apartment in Milan to be taken apart, brick by brick if necessary. It might throw up a clue. Satisfied?'

Kuhlmann looked at Kolchinsky after Paluzzi had disappeared into the outer office. 'Perhaps Malcolm was right after all. Perhaps the heat is getting too much for me these days.'

Kolchinsky maintained a diplomatic silence. He picked up the nearest blueprint, sat down and unrolled it across the desk.

Enzo Bellini was a small man in his early sixties with snow-white hair and a craggy face lined from the pressure of years in the forefront of Italian politics. He spoke no English.

Cesare Camillo, a handsome man twenty years his junior, was acting as interpreter. Camillo was one of Bellini's senior aides who was already being tipped as a future PCI leader. He had represented Bellini at the briefing called by Philpott and Kolchinsky that morning.

The two men sat facing Philpott in a small antechamber behind the conference hall. Bellini remained silent as Philpott, through Camillo, explained the first of Calvieri's demands to him. His face was expressionless as he listened to Camillo, his hands gripping the table in front of him tightly.

Philpott waited until Camillo had finished translating his words, then sat back in the chair and stared at Bellini's bowed head. 'I thought I should tell you first rather than just announce it in front of the other leaders.'

Camillo translated. Bellini said nothing.

'I've arranged to meet the others in five minutes' time to put Calvieri's demands to them. I need to know if Signore Bellini is prepared to accede to the demands before I see them.'

Bellini listened silently as Camillo translated Philpott's request, then spoke in a barely audible voice, his eyes never leaving Philpott's face.

'Under the circumstances, Signore Bellini feels he has no alternative but to resign. It is a small price to pay for the safety of Europe and its peoples. I will represent Signore Bellini at this meeting. He feels he has nothing more to contribute.'

'I understand,' Philpott replied softly.

Bellini got to his feet and walked to the door. Philpott stared after him. A broken man. He had merely passed on Calvieri's demand but he still felt a sense of guilt. It was a feeling he couldn't seem to shake off.

Camillo closed the door behind Bellini, then turned to Philpott. 'Calvieri seems to think that by forcing Signore Bellini to step down it will bring the chances of a coalition between the PCI and the Red Brigades that much closer to fruition. He couldn't be more wrong. We may not be a popular government, but we are loyal to each other. And especially to Signore Bellini. We'll close ranks at the top. The Red Brigades won't get a look in. Our deputy Prime Minister, Signore Vietri, will see to that. He hates the Red Brigades more than anyone else in the cabinet. Calvieri's in for a big surprise. A very big surprise.'

Philpott closed the folder in front of him. If it were up to him he would tell Camillo where Vietri's true loyalties lay. But it wasn't. He had already chided Kuhlmann for interfering in Italy's domestic problems. Not that Camillo would believe him anyway. Not without proof. He suddenly remembered Paluzzi's words. *Alberto Vietri will never become Prime Minister of Italy.*

Camillo may yet be right. Calvieri could well be in for a big surprise.

The meeting had been convened in a soundproof room down the corridor from the conference hall. The fifteen leaders were all present, along with the aides who had represented them at the morning briefing (it cut out the need for translators for those leaders who didn't speak English, minimizing the chances of a security leak).

Philpott felt like a headmaster as he stood in front of them detailing the demands he had received from Calvieri. There was a moment's silence after he had finished speaking, then the room was filled with the sound of angry voices as the delegates conferred, outraged at the audacity of Calvieri's demands. Philpott allowed them to let off steam. After all, they were politicians. Finally he clapped his hands, bringing them to order.

'We have to discuss this rationally if we're going to reach any kind of decision.'

'Where is Signore Bellini?' a voice called out.

Philpott looked at Camillo and indicated that he should answer.

'Signore Bellini is meeting the rest of our delegation. He won't be attending the opening ceremony. He feels it would be better if one of his senior ministers was there from the start. I have already informed the chairman.' Camillo gestured to the Swiss President, who nodded in agreement. 'He has asked me to represent him at this meeting.'

Philpott raised his hand before anyone could speak. 'I can understand how you must all feel about the way Signore Bellini has been treated, but it's neither the time nor the place to discuss it. We must address the second of Calvieri's demands, the payment of a hundred million pounds to the five terrorist groups.'

The Dutch Prime Minister raised a hand to catch Philpott's attention. 'Do *you* believe he would press the button if his demands were not met?'

'Yes,' Philpott replied bluntly.

'He's a madman!' someone called out.

There was a murmur of agreement.

Philpott shook his head. 'No madman could have pieced together an operation like this. It's been meticulously planned down to the last detail. Every loophole's been plugged. We're not dealing with some two-bit hoodlum here. He's probably more intelligent than most of us in this room. And that's not something I'd say lightly.'

'Couldn't your people launch a commando-style operation on the room and recover the vial?' the Norwegian Prime Minister asked.

'Out of the question,' Philpott replied. 'The room has no windows. The only way in is through the door. And that would have to be blown. When I left the room Calvieri had his finger on the button. All he would have to do is press it if we made any attempt to storm the room.'

'These questions aren't getting us anywhere,' the British Prime Minister snapped irritably. 'If Colonel Philpott

252

thought there was a chance of recovering the transmitter intact he would have told us already. Obviously there isn't. It's something we have to accept. And the sooner we come to a decision, the sooner the wheels can be set in motion to get the vial back safely.'

Philpott nodded gratefully to the Prime Minister. They went back a long way. One of the Prime Minister's first tasks on coming into office had been to forward Philpott's *curriculum vitae*, together with a personal letter of recommendation, to the Secretary-General of UNACO for consideration as Director. He never knew whether the letter had helped to sway the Secretary-General's decision but he had always been grateful for the Prime Minister's unswerving belief in him. It had made his job that much easier.

'I can only advise you,' Philpott said, looking around slowly at the faces in front of him. 'The final decision rests with you. And as the Prime Minister has said, we don't have much time. It's imperative that you reach your decision as soon as possible.'

'What choice do we have?' the British Prime Minister said. 'It's not as if we're dealing with a hijacked aeroplane or a kidnapped businessman. We're dealing with a lethal virus which could potentially kill millions. A virus without an antidote. If it were just our lives at risk, I'd certainly say we should stand firm against the demands. But it's not. Much as it goes against everything I believe in, I say we pay the ransom.'

'One hundred million pounds in the hands of terrorists,' the Austrian Chancellor said, breaking the sudden silence. 'They will be able to buy enough arms to carry out horrendous attacks across Europe. It will snowball into a bloody conflict, you mark my words.'

'Do you think I want to contribute to their coffers?' The British Prime Minister's eyes were blazing. 'None of you has campaigned more vociferously than I have to unite our countries in the fight against terrorism. It sticks in my throat to have to pay one penny to these murderers, but I don't see that we have any choice.'

'You misunderstand me, Prime Minister,' the Austrian Chancellor said defensively. 'I was not criticizing you, it was merely an observation. In fact, I wholeheartedly agree with what you say.'

'A hundred million is a small price to pay for the safety of our people,' the Swedish Prime Minister added. 'We will pay our share of the ransom.'

'The French Government, too, will pay its share of the ransom,' the aide announced on behalf of the Prime Minister.

Philpott raised his hands as the noise intensified around him. 'It's no use everyone talking at the same time. There's an easy way to settle this. Is there any government who will *not* pay its share of the ransom?'

There was silence.

'I'll pass your decision on to Calvieri. Naturally we'll do everything in our power to find the vial before the deadline but I have to admit our chances of doing so will be remote, to say the least. The search will have to be undertaken in complete secrecy if we're not to alert Calvieri and provoke a catastrophe. It's the only way we can prevent the press from getting hold of the story.'

'We understand that,' the Swiss President said, speaking for the first time. 'The money will be ready for the five o'clock deadline.'

Philpott nodded. 'Naturally I'll keep you all up to date on any developments that may arise during the day. But as I said, I don't hold out much hope of finding the vial before five o'clock.'

'We know you and your team will do your best,' the British Prime Minister said.

'I only hope that will be enough,' Philpott replied.

Whitlock had arrived at the Offenbach Centre while the meeting was in progress and was poring over one of the plans with Graham when Philpott returned to the office. Philpott lit his pipe and recounted briefly what had happened at the meeting.

'At least they've agreed to pay the ransom,' Kolchinsky said.

'As a last resort,' Philpott replied. 'We're going to have to pull out all the stops to find the vial before five o'clock. If the ransom is paid it'll not only be a psychological victory for world terrorism, it'll also leave us with a lot of egg on our faces. It'll be the perfect ammunition for those politicians who'd like nothing better than to see UNACO disbanded. I can just imagine what they'll say. We worked with Calvieri from the start. A known terrorist. We even helped him smuggle the vial into the building.'

'We had no way of knowing he was the mastermind behind the whole thing,' Graham said angrily.

'We know that, but you can be sure our opponents will use it against us. We have to find the vial if we're to save face.' Philpott stabbed the stem of his pipe at the blueprint on the desk. 'Have you compiled the list yet?'

Kolchinsky handed a sheet of foolscap paper to Philpott. 'We're going to have to draft in more personnel, Malcolm. There are over fifty possible hiding places on that list. We'd never be able to cover them all thoroughly by five o'clock.'

'I had the same thought on the way back from the meeting,' Philpott said. 'I don't think I realized just how big the building was until then. It means more people are going to know about the vial. That's something I was hoping to avoid. But it can't be helped. Five extra men, maximum. The search has to be undertaken in secrecy.'

'I've got four men on standby at the airport,' Paluzzi announced. 'I had them flown in this morning in case we needed them. They've been on the case since Monday so there will be no need to waste time briefing them.'

'Get them over here as quickly as possible,' Philpott told him. 'There's no time to lose.'

Paluzzi disappeared into the outer office to use the telephone.

'Michael came up with something while we were going through the plans. What if Calvieri gave the vial to a woman? We don't have Sabrina to check the women's cloakrooms.'

'Good point.' Philpott looked at Kuhlmann. 'We'll need your best policewoman. I'll brief her personally.'

'I'll get on to it right away,' Kuhlmann said, and left the room.

Philpott read through the list. 'You're going to need some kind of cover to make it easy for you to move about the building without drawing unnecessary attention to yourselves.'

'I've already seen to that,' Kolchinsky replied. 'Vlok's bringing up half a dozen maintenance overalls for us to use.'

Paluzzi returned. 'The men should be here in about fifteen minutes. One of my deputies, Captain Molinetti, has taken a team of men to Milan to search Calvieri's apartment. He'll only call if they come up with something important. I've told him to ask for you.'

'I look forward to hearing from him,' Philpott replied, then reached for the receiver to call Calvieri.

Calvieri replaced the handset and gave Ubrino a thumbs-up sign. Ubrino punched the air in delight and grinned at Sabrina, his animosity towards her forgotten in his moment of triumph.

'You haven't won yet,' Sabrina snapped, glaring at Ubrino. 'Five o'clock's still a long way off.'

'It will be for us, stuck in here,' Calvieri said, then sat down opposite Sabrina. The transmitter was still clenched tightly in his left hand. 'I don't think your colleagues would agree with you, though. They have six hours left to find the vial. So much ground to cover and so little time in which to do it. And to make matters worse, they have to conduct the search in complete secrecy. It wouldn't do to alert the media, would it? So many problems to overcome. And even then they still won't find it. All that time and effort wasted.'

'Don't count on it,' she retorted, eyeing him coldly.

'I don't underestimate any of you, believe me. That would be suicidal. I don't expect them to sit around idly waiting for the deadline. Of course they're going to try to find the vial. But I bargained on that when I was planning the operation. That's why I've had it hidden where they'll never find it.'

'Where?'

Calvieri smiled faintly and put his finger to his lips. 'There's a saying in Latin. *Vir sapit qui pauca loquitur.*'

'The man is wise who talks little,' she translated.

'In other words, know when to hold your tongue.'

'You should have borne that in mind yesterday.'

'I don't follow you,' Calvieri said with a frown.

'When you were so quick to tell Mike and me about your plans to put Italy back on its feet again. Now you're threatening to destroy it, along with countless other nations around the world. You can't have it both ways. Question is, which is the truth?'

'I'm sure you're going to tell me,' Calvieri said.

'I don't have to. You answered it yourself when you insisted that I remain here with you.'

'I see what you're getting at,' Calvieri said, keeping up the sarcasm. 'You think I was telling the truth yesterday. And by holding you here I've prevented you from passing information on to the leaders which could have had a bearing on their decision whether or not to pay the ransom.' He chuckled softly to himself. 'It's a fascinating theory but unfortunately there's one major flaw in it. Why didn't I insist on holding Graham and Paluzzi here as well? They know just as much about the coalition as you do.'

'Because they don't know you like I do,' she replied

quickly. 'Fabio knows you, and the other *Brigatisti*, like a teenager knows his favourite band. He knows your family histories, who your associates are and what you've done since joining the Red Brigades. But he doesn't know you as a human being. I got to know you as a person over these past few days. Take that incident in Venice. You treated that runaway as if he were your own son. And it would be the children who would be the first casualties if the virus was ever released into the atmosphere. You know you could no more press that button than send that kid back to the orphanage.'

Calvieri put the transmitter on the table and clapped lightly. 'Bravo. A wonderful speech. So touching.'

Ubrino grinned at Sabrina. 'So much for your theory, *bella*.'

Calvieri held up the transmitter in front of Sabrina. 'It's like nuclear weapons. Are they just a deterrent, or would they be used as a last resort? Bluff and counter-bluff. It's all a game.' He shifted his chair round to face the television screen, then looked back at her, a faint smile on his lips. 'Or is it?'

Philpott arranged for the final briefing to be held at 11.15 in the boardroom on the tenth floor. He was the last to arrive, having left Kuhlmann in Vlok's office to man the telephone. After taking his place at the head of the table he took his pipe and tobacco pouch from his jacket pocket and put them beside the folder he had brought with him. He took a wad of tobacco from the pouch and as he tamped it into the mouth of his pipe he looked around slowly at the faces watching his every move. Paluzzi and his men sat on his left, Kolchinsky, Graham and Whitlock on his right. Sergeant Ingrid Hauser, the policewoman he had briefed only minutes earlier, sat beside Whitlock. She was in her late twenties with a stocky figure and curly black hair. Her confident manner had already impressed him.

'Coffee, sir?' Whitlock asked, indicating the tray in the middle of the table.

Philpott shook his head and carefully lit his pipe. He exhaled the smoke upwards, then opened the folder in front of him. 'I've divided the list into four sections. I want you to work in teams. Two to a team.'

'I'll work with C.W.,' Graham said.

Philpott shook his head. 'Your Italian's non-existent. Sergei's and C.W.'s isn't much better. You'll each be paired off with one of the Italians. They can cover for you.'

'I'll work with Fabio, then,' Graham said.

'I'm keeping you two well apart,' Philpott replied, jabbing the stem of his pipe at each of them in turn. 'I've read the Corfu report. You're a bad influence on each other.'

Graham and Paluzzi grinned like a couple of mischievous schoolboys.

'C.W., you'll work with Major Paluzzi. You'll be Team One.' Philpott looked at Paluzzi. 'I need two men to work with Sergei and Mike. Who would you suggest?'

'Sergeant Visconti can work with Sergei,' Paluzzi replied, patting the arm of the swarthy man sitting beside him.

Philpott jotted down the name. 'You'll be Team Two.'

'Lieutenant Marco can work with Mike. They know each other from Rome. He's also the most level-headed one amongst us. He certainly won't be a bad influence on Mike.'

There was a ripple of laughter from the Italians, which Marco dismissed good-humouredly with a flick of his hand.

'You'll be Team Three. Which leaves you as Team Four,' Philpott said, pointing his pen at the two men sitting between Visconti and Marco.

'Sergeants De Sica and Alberetto,' Paluzzi said.

Philpott wrote the names down, then handed out the four lists. 'Teams One and Two will assume the identity of security agents. Teams Three and Four will be maintenance men. That way you'll be able to gain access to the areas specified on your lists. I've tried to spread the workload evenly throughout the four lists but if a team does fall behind it's up to them to contact me and I'll try and get one of the other teams to help them out.' He turned to Paluzzi. 'I assume your men are armed?'

'Beretta 92s,' Paluzzi replied.

'Good.' Philpott looked at Kolchinsky. 'The handguns you ordered arrived just before I came here. They're in the office.'

'What about the maintenance overalls?' Graham asked.

'They're also in the office,' Philpott answered. 'Dieter Vlok has given me four bleepers which work off the system he has in his office. Each team will carry one. You'll be bleeped only in an emergency so please respond promptly. Call the office from the nearest house phone. The extension number's on each of the lists. And one last point. For God's sake be careful of the metal detectors at the main entrances. You shouldn't need to leave the premises but if you do and you get into any difficulties, call the office. If I'm not there you can speak to Commissioner Kuhlmann. We'll smooth things over. But under no circumstances are you to call on each other for help. I don't want any public confrontations with the security staff. Is that understood?'

There was a murmur of agreement.

'Well, I think that about covers everything,' Philpott concluded, closing the folder. 'All that remains now is for me to wish you luck. You all know what's at stake. That alone should be enough of an incentive.'

Kolchinsky got to his feet, signalling that the briefing was over. The others followed him out of the room.

Philpott remained in his seat after they had gone. He was thinking about Sabrina. Was it any wonder that there was still only one female field operative at UNACO? No one had yet come close to matching her abilities. She was a cut above the rest. And that included the majority of her male colleagues as well. Graham was the exception. The maverick. Philpott regarded him as second only to Jacques

Rust, in his opinion UNACO's best ever field operative. But Graham had only been with them a year. He would become the best, given time, especially if Sabrina remained his partner. Their record was unparalleled. They had solved every case to date. Until now. If only she were there to partner Graham now . . .

He pushed the thought from his mind, reached for his cane and got to his feet. He picked up the folder and pipe and left the room, closing the door behind him.

# ELEVEN

Whitlock checked underneath the last of the tables in his section of the restaurant on the eighth floor, then straightened up and looked across despairingly at Paluzzi.

'Seventeen minutes to one,' Paluzzi muttered, glancing at his watch. 'It's taken us over an hour just to check the kitchen and restaurant. We're never going to finish at this rate.'

Whitlock nodded sombrely. 'Don't remind me. What's next on the list?'

'The foyer.'

'Wonderful. Now we'll be in full glare of the press.'

The bleeper sounded. It was attached to Whitlock's belt. He switched it off and met Paluzzi's questioning look. 'Am I expecting too much?'

'Probably, but there's only one way of finding out.'

Whitlock crossed to the telephone and rang Vlok's office. Philpott answered.

'It's C.W., sir. Has the vial been found?'

'No,' Philpott replied brusquely.

Whitlock shook his head at Paluzzi.

'I might be on to something,' Philpott told him. 'I want the two of you to check it out.'

'What is it?' Whitlock asked eagerly.

'Were you told about Nino Ferzetti?'

'The maintenance worker Ubrino impersonated to get into the building?'

'The same. Well, Commissioner Kuhlmann had the local police go round to Ferzetti's flat to see if he was all right. He was still out cold when they got there. They managed to bring him round and he told them he was drinking with a Vito Cellina last night. He also works in the maintenance department. I called Jacques in Zurich and had him run a check on Cellina. He's clean but it turns out his stepsister, Louisa, had been involved with the Red Brigades before her death from a drugs overdose last year.'

'So Cellina could be Calvieri's contact inside the building?'

'He could be, but I still have my suspicions. It's all too convenient. It's as if Calvieri wanted us to find out about Cellina. Why else would Ubrino have mentioned Ferzetti? I could be wrong, of course. That's why I want the two of you to get on to it right away.'

'Do you know where he is at the moment?'

'In the basement. That's where the maintenance department is housed.'

'We're on our way, sir.'

The lift only went as far as the foyer, but there were stairs leading down to the basement to the right of the reception desk. They ignored the sign on the door, STAFF ONLY, and descended the stairs to a tiled corridor. To their right was a swing door leading into the workshop. To their left was a cream-coloured door with the words ERHALTUNG MANAGER stencilled on it in black. The maintenance manager's office. Paluzzi rapped loudly on the door.

'*Herein*,' a voice called out.

They entered the room. The man behind the desk was heavyset, his face remarkable only for its surly expression and black-framed glasses. The name tag on his grey overall identified him as Hans Kessler. Paluzzi told Kessler in

German that he was a security adviser and asked him where they could find Cellina.

'What's this all about?' Kessler demanded in German, getting to his feet and removing his glasses. 'Vito's a good worker—'

'We don't want a reference,' Paluzzi cut in, 'we want to talk to him. Are you going to take us to him or do I have to call Dieter Vlok and tell him that his maintenance manager is refusing to co-operate with the authorities in a matter of national security?'

Kessler scowled but did as he was told, leading them into the workshop where he identified Cellina as the figure standing with his back to them on the other side of the room.

'We'll take it from here,' Paluzzi said to Kessler. 'Thank you for your help.'

Kessler looked from Paluzzi to Whitlock, then turned and left the room, muttering under his breath. The other five maintenance men in the workshop were watching them. Only Cellina seemed oblivious to their presence. It was not until Paluzzi approached Cellina that he noticed the blowtorch in his hand. He was welding. Paluzzi stopped a few feet away from Cellina, out of range of the blow-torch, and called out to him. At first he thought Cellina hadn't heard him but a moment later he switched off the power and looked around.

'Are you Vito Cellina?' Paluzzi asked in Italian.

Cellina pushed the visor away from his face. He was a gangling man in his thirties with collar-length brown hair and a sallow complexion. 'Yes. Who are you?'

'Security. I'd like to talk to you about a friend of yours. Nino Ferzetti.'

'He's not here,' Cellina said, glancing nervously about him. 'He didn't come in to work this morning.'

'That's because you spiked his drinks last night.'

'I don't know what you're talking about,' Cellina stammered.

Paluzzi ripped the visor from Cellina's face then grabbed him by the front of his overall and slammed him against the workbench. 'I'm in no mood to play games with you. I want some answers and I want them now!'

One of Cellina's colleagues picked up a screwdriver, but when he tried to approach Paluzzi he found his path blocked by Whitlock, who had unfastened his jacket to reveal the holstered Browning. The man took a hesitant step backwards, then tossed the screwdriver on to the workbench. Whitlock ushered the men from the workshop and hovered menacingly at the door to dissuade any of them from returning.

'Now it's just you and me,' Paluzzi hissed, tightening his grip on Cellina's lapels. 'Where's the vial Calvieri gave to you this morning?'

Cellina made a desperate grab for the blowtorch. He managed to curl his fingers around the handle before Paluzzi brought the butt of his Beretta down savagely on the back of his hand. Cellina cried out in pain and jerked his fingers away from the blowtorch, which clattered on to the floor. Paluzzi twisted Cellina's arm behind his back and frog-marched him to the bandsaw in the middle of the room. He switched it on, then forced Cellina's face on to the cold metal workbench. Cellina struggled in vain to break Paluzzi's hold as his face was pushed ever closer towards the serrated blade.

'I'll tell you where it is,' Cellina screamed, his eyes wide with fear. 'Please, no more. I'll tell you.'

'I'm listening,' Paluzzi replied, still pushing Cellina's face towards the blade.

'It's under my workbench,' Cellina shouted breathlessly.

Cellina's face was within inches of the blade when Paluzzi reached down and switched off the machine. Cellina crumpled to the floor, shaking, his face buried in his hands.

Paluzzi hauled him to his feet and shoved him towards the workbench. 'Show me,' he snarled, then unholstered his Beretta and pressed it into Cellina's back. 'And do it slowly.'

Cellina crouched down and pointed a trembling finger at the metal cylinder attached to the underside of the work-bench with masking tape.

'Did he say what was in it?' Paluzzi demanded.

Cellina shook his head. 'He just told me to keep it here in the workshop. Out of sight. That's why I taped it beneath my workbench.'

Whitlock crossed to where they were crouched and peered at the metal cylinder. 'It certainly looks intact.'

Cellina frowned at Whitlock. He spoke no English. Whitlock eased himself into a position where he could study the cylinder more carefully. It wasn't booby trapped. He peeled off the masking tape, then stood up and checked the serial number: SR4785. The same number as on the cylinder stolen from Neo-Chem Industries.

'I'll call the Colonel,' Whitlock said, walking to the wall-phone beside the swing door.

'Did Calvieri say why he wanted you to keep it here?' Paluzzi asked Cellina.

'All he said was that someone would contact me this afternoon and I was to give it to them.'

'Who?'

'I don't know. He said they would identify themselves with a password.'

'What was in it for you?'

Cellina sagged against the workbench and ran his fingers through his hair. 'My stepsister was a *Brigatista* in Milan. She died last year from a drug overdose. Calvieri threat-ened to tell my mother about Louisa. She knew Louisa died from drugs but she didn't know anything about her ties with the Red Brigades. She suffered a heart attack within days of Louisa's death. It nearly finished her off. Another shock like that would surely kill her. I couldn't risk it. You must understand that.'

'And how's she going to react to your arrest? Have you thought about that?'

Cellina buried his face in his hands again.

Paluzzi crossed to where Whitlock was standing by the swing door. 'What did the Colonel say?'

'He wants me to take the cylinder up to the office straight away. It'll have to be sent for analysis. He's arranging for a security guard to take Cellina off our hands but he wants you to wait here until the guard arrives.'

'Sure,' Paluzzi said, then noticed Whitlock's questioning look towards Cellina. 'I'll tell you about it later.'

Whitlock nodded and reached for the swing door. He suddenly turned back to Paluzzi. 'What would you have done if he'd called your bluff?'

'He didn't, did he?' Paluzzi replied, glancing at the bandsaw.

'But what if he had?'

'It could have got a bit messy,' Paluzzi said with an indifferent shrug.

'You would have carved up his face?' Whitlock asked in disbelief.

'What use is a threat unless you're prepared to back it up?'

'Now I see what the Colonel meant,' Whitlock muttered.

'About what?'

'You and Mike being a bad influence on each other,' Whitlock replied, then disappeared out into the corridor.

'I'm not convinced,' Philpott said, turning the cylinder around in his fingers. 'I still say it's a red herring. That's why I don't intend to tell the others until it's been analysed. If they think there's a chance that it's the real vial it could lull them into a false sense of complacency. And that would jeopardize the search.'

'Your confidence in them is touching, sir,' Whitlock said, fighting the anger in his voice.

'I have every confidence in them,' Philpott replied sharply. 'I know they wouldn't let it affect them consciously. But the subconscious plays tricks on us all without us even realizing it.'

The door opened and Kolchinsky entered breathlessly. 'I came as soon as I could. But why the secrecy?'

'Because I'm not convinced this cylinder contains the virus,' Philpott replied, placing it on the table. 'You didn't mention anything to Visconti, did you?'

'I did as you said and told him you needed me back here to help you co-ordinate the search.'

'Good. I've arranged for Ingrid Hauser to join him when she's finished checking her areas.'

Kolchinsky picked up the cylinder. 'The serial number's the same. What makes you think it's a dummy?'

'We found it too easily. Calvieri's planned this operation down to the last detail. I find it inconceivable that he would slip up at this late stage.' Philpott relit his pipe. 'But this is all speculation. We can't possibly know until its contents have been analysed. One of our helicopters is waiting for you on the helipad. The lab technicians in Zurich have been put on immediate standby.'

'I hope you're wrong about this, Malcolm,' Kolchinsky said, holding up the cylinder.

'So do I,' Philpott replied.

Kolchinsky slipped the cylinder into his pocket and left.

Bachstrasse was a gloomy, deserted cul-de-sac off the Utoquai, a wharf on the banks of Lake Zurich. The road was strewn with bricks and masonry. The buildings themselves had been derelict for years. A hoarding at the entrance to the cul-de-sac warned: FALLING MASONRY. CARS PARKED AT OWNERS' RISK. A second hoarding was more ominous: UNSAFE STRUCTURES. DANGEROUS. KEEP OUT!

UNACO owned Bachstrasse. They had erected the hoardings. They had strewn the bricks and masonry on the road to give the impression that the buildings were unsafe. Privacy was essential. Their European Test Centre, housed in a network of soundproofed catacombs, ran the length of the street. The only way into the Test Centre was through the warehouse at the end of the cul-de-sac. It was a rectangular building and, like the other buildings in the street, its windows had long since been vandalized. The battered, corrugated-iron door could be activated electronically from inside the Test Centre, provided the correct password was given. The password itself was changed every day. The roof, like the door, could be opened from inside the Test Centre but, for security reasons, it was only used in emergencies.

The helicopter descended into the deserted warehouse and when it landed on the concrete floor the roof slid back into place. The pilot cut the engine. A circular section of the floor, fifty feet in diameter, which supported the helicopter, was lowered by means of a hydraulic press and locked into place beside a landing stage. The two halves of the floor closed above the helicopter.

Kolchinsky unfastened his safety belt and picked up the small, insulated lead case at his feet. It contained the metal cylinder. He clambered out of the helicopter and made his way down a set of metal stairs to where a white-coated technician was waiting to take the case from him.

'Monsieur Rust is waiting in his office for you,' the technician said politely, then strode with barely contained impatience down one of the corridors leading from the landing stage.

Kolchinsky headed down another corridor and paused outside a door marked: J. RUST – DIRECTEUR. He knocked. An overhead camera panned his face and a moment later there was an electronic click as the door was unlocked. Kolchinsky entered the plush office and the door closed behind him. Rust activated his wheelchair and approached Kolchinsky. They shook hands.

'I think you know Professor Helmut Scheffer, head of our science department,' Rust said, indicating the black-haired man sitting on the sofa against the wall.

'Of course,' Kolchinsky replied. 'How are you, Helmut?'

'Well, thank you,' Scheffer said, getting to his feet to shake Kolchinsky's hand.

'Emile made good time,' Rust said, glancing at his watch. 1.40 p.m. 'It can't have taken him much more than twenty minutes to fly you here from Berne.'

'About that,' Kolchinsky agreed, then sat down in the leather armchair in front of Rust's desk. He looked at Scheffer. 'How long will it take for your people to analyse the contents of the vial?'

'Had it been a glass cylinder, a matter of seconds. We could have used either infra-red spectroscopy or nuclear magnetic resonance. But not with metal. It will have to be cut open inside an isolation chamber.'

'Like a glove box?' Kolchinsky asked.

'Glove boxes have been known to leak. This chamber's windowless. The whole operation will be carried out by means of closed-circuit television cameras using mechanical hands which are operated from outside the chamber. Once the cylinder has been opened a sample can be transferred to a glass vial for analysis. The results will show up as a series of oscillations on a graph which we can use to identify the different components that make up the substance.'

'But how long will it take?' Kolchinsky repeated.

'How long?' Scheffer pouted thoughtfully. 'Anything up to two hours.'

'Two *hours*?' Kolchinsky parroted in disbelief. 'The way you described it, it sounded more like twenty minutes.'

'I only outlined the process for you,' Scheffer said defensively. 'I'd be glad to explain it in more detail if you want.'

'It wouldn't mean anything to me if you did,' Kolchinsky

replied with a quick smile. 'Science was never my strong point.'

Scheffer moved to the door. 'They will be waiting for me in the lab. I'll let you know the moment we've identified the substance in the cylinder.'

Rust activated the door, then closed it again behind Scheffer.

'Two hours!' Kolchinsky exclaimed, getting to his feet. 'I never thought it would take that long.'

'Neither did I.' Rust indicated the armchair in front of his desk. 'Sit down, I'll order us some tea.'

'I can't sit around here for the next two hours. I've got to get back to the Offenbach Centre. There's still so much to do, especially if the cylinder does turn out to be a dummy. You can call Malcolm when the results come through.'

'I'll get hold of Emile for you,' Rust said, reaching for the telephone.

'Two hours?' Philpott said after Kolchinsky had finished briefing him. He took a sip of tea then sat back in his chair. 'Not that it matters. We have to keep searching.'

'Where's Visconti?' Kolchinsky asked, picking up his Beretta from the desk.

'Sit down,' Philpott said, indicating a chair. 'Have some tea and calm down. You're like a hyperactive child at the moment.'

'There isn't time—'

'Sergei,' Philpott cut in, pointing to the chair.

Kolchinsky slipped the Beretta into his shoulder holster and reluctantly sat down.

Philpott poured him a cup of tea. 'Ingrid Hauser's working with Visconti now. I'd rather use you as an auxiliary. That way you can help out if one of the teams falls behind schedule. It will save us having to pull out one of the other teams to help them.'

Kolchinsky nodded and lit a cigarette.

The telephone rang.

Philpott answered it. He listened in silence. 'Thanks for letting me know,' he said at length, and replaced the receiver.

'What is it, Malcolm?' Kolchinsky asked anxiously, noticing the concern on Philpott's face.

'That was Vlok. He has just received a bomb threat.'

Graham and Marco knew their recall had nothing to do with the vial, that much Philpott had told them on the telephone. Apart from that they were just as much in the dark as the other three teams who were already in the office when they got there.

'What's this all about, sir?' Graham asked.

'There's been a bomb threat,' Philpott replied. 'Dieter Vlok took the call. The caller claimed to have planted a bomb somewhere close to the building. It's due to go off at three o'clock.'

'That's in thirty-eight minutes time,' Marco said, looking at his watch.

'Have you told Calvieri?' Whitlock asked.

'I haven't told anybody outside this room. Vlok's the only other person who knows about it. And I've sworn him to secrecy. I haven't even told Commissioner Kuhlmann, and I don't intend to. Strictly speaking, the bomb threat falls under his jurisdiction but knowing him, he'll want to evacuate the building as quickly as possible. And that could make Calvieri panic, especially as he specifically warned us against *staging* a bomb scare.'

'Where is Kuhlmann?' Whitlock asked.

'Interrogating Cellina,' Philpott replied. 'You're going to have to postpone the search for the vial. At least for the time being. We have to find that bomb.'

'If there *is* a bomb,' Graham said.

'I'm not taking any chances, Mike.' Philpott shook his head in desperation. 'If there is a bomb, and it goes off, and it comes out later that we received a warning beforehand there's going to be hell to pay. Heads will roll. Starting with mine.'

'You're going to have to try to reason with Calvieri,' Paluzzi said to Philpott.

'I intend to. I'm sure he won't let us evacuate the building but he might be able to find out if there is a bomb. And if so, where it's hidden.'

'Leaving us to defuse it?'

'Of course I'd rather bring in the bomb squad, Mike, but their first priority would be to evacuate the building. And that would give Calvieri itchy fingers.' Philpott gestured to Kolchinsky. 'Sergei's worked out the areas for each team to cover. I want you to get on to it right away.'

'We're just clutching at straws, sir,' Graham said. 'What chance have we got of finding it?'

'Have you got a better plan, Michael?' Kolchinsky snapped angrily, opening the door leading into the outer office. 'Let's go. The Colonel will bleep us if he gets any positive feedback from Calvieri.'

Philpott waited until they had left then dialled the extension number Calvieri had given him.

Calvieri was watching an interview with the French Prime Minister when the telephone rang. He crossed to the side table and answered it. Philpott told him about the bomb threat.

'The Greek ELA?' Calvieri said.

'That's who the caller claimed to be representing,' Philpott replied. 'We have to evacuate the building. If the bomb—'

'No,' Calvieri cut in angrily. 'I've told you already, I'll push the button if any attempt is made to evacuate the building.'

Philpott exhaled deeply, struggling to control his temper. 'I'm not going to argue with you, Calvieri. There isn't time. If you're not prepared to have the building evacuated then

273

at least find out whether there is a bomb or whether it's just a hoax. You've got the contacts. I don't need to remind you that it's just as much in your interest as it is in ours to get it defused in time.'

'I'll look into it.'

'It's already two twenty-five—'

'I said I'll look into it!' Calvieri replaced the receiver, then spun round and punched the wall furiously.

'What is it?' Ubrino asked anxiously.

'Get Bettinga on the line,' Calvieri said softly.

'Why, what—'

'Just do it!' Calvieri yelled.

Ubrino nodded hesitantly, then picked up the receiver and dialled a number in Rome to find out where he could contact Bettinga.

Calvieri looked down at his hand. The skin around the knuckles was torn and the blood trickled down between his fingers. He noticed Sabrina watching him carefully. He sat down opposite her. 'You think I've finally snapped, don't you?'

'No, but I think you're pretty pissed off about something,' she replied, holding his stare.

'You could say that.' Calvieri winced when he tried to flex his fingers. 'This is going to hurt like hell in the morning.'

'I assume from what you said on the phone that there's been a bomb scare.'

'You're very perceptive,' Calvieri replied, then looked across at Ubrino. 'Well?'

'They are trying to find out where Signore Bettinga is at the moment,' Ubrino said, his hand over the mouthpiece.

'Who are you talking to?'

'Larusso, one of the cell commanders in Rome.'

'I know who he is! Ask him if he's got the number of the ELA headquarters in Athens. That's all I want to know.' Calvieri turned back to Sabrina. 'Yes, there's been a bomb threat. Are you familiar with the ELA?'

She shook her head.

'It stands for *Espanastatikos Laikos Agonas* which, roughly translated, means the People's Revolutionary Struggle. Radical fundamentalists, nothing more.' Calvieri took the transmitter from his pocket and turned it around in his hand. 'I've spent months planning, and perfecting, this operation. And now the ELA are threatening to ruin it all. If the bomb were to go off the whole complex would be evacuated. The perfect opportunity for a search.'

'It sounds like a case of the biter bit. If, of course, there is a bomb.'

'There's a bomb, I'm sure of that. You'll find—'

'I've got the number,' Ubrino called out.

'Call it and ask for Andreas Kozanakis head of the ELA.' Calvieri turned back to Sabrina. 'As I was saying, you'll find that anonymous bomb threats are invariably hoaxes. But if an organization gives its name, that means they're after publicity. And who's going to take them seriously if they're not prepared to back up those threats?'

'The voice of the expert,' Sabrina said with disdain.

Calvieri stood up, pocketed the transmitter, and crossed to where Ubrino was standing. 'Any luck?'

'It's ringing,' Ubrino replied.

The receiver was lifted at the other end of the line.

'Tony,' Ubrino said, extending the receiver towards Calvieri.

'Hello, who's speaking?' Calvieri asked in Greek.

'Andreas Kozanakis. Who is that?'

'Tony Calvieri, Red Brigades.'

'It's an honour—'

'Shove your honour,' Calvieri said tersely. 'I want to know if the ELA have planted an explosive device at the Offenbach Centre due to go off at three o'clock. Yes or no.'

There was silence.

'Answer me!' Calvieri snapped.

'I am not at liberty to discuss that with you,' Kozanakis replied.

'How's Alexis?' Calvieri asked, his voice calm.

'What?' Kozanakis replied, the question catching him off guard.

'Alexis, your daughter. How old is she now? Seventeen? Eighteen? It's her first year at Rome University, isn't it? I believe Lino Zocchi promised to keep an eye on her for you. Pity he's in jail. I'd hate something to happen to her. She's got her whole life ahead of her.'

'Leave Alexis out of this,' Kozanakis said, a note of anxiety creeping into his voice.

'Then tell me about the explosive device.'

Kozanakis exhaled deeply. There was a pause. 'Semtex. Twenty pounds.'

'Nasty,' Calvieri said. 'Where is it?'

'I don't know. One of my aides installed it.'

Calvieri looked at his watch: 2.33. 'You've got exactly twelve minutes to find out where the Semtex has been hidden. If I haven't heard from you by two forty-five then I'll call Rome and have a couple of my *Brigatisti* visit Alexis at her residence. I'm sure she'll amuse them.'

'No!' Kozanakis screamed down the line.

'I know you won't let it come to that, Andreas.' Calvieri gave him the number, and extension, where he could be reached. 'Twelve minutes. Don't let Alexis down.'

'How much lower can you sink?' Sabrina hissed when Calvieri had replaced the receiver.

'I never realized you spoke Greek as well,' Calvieri said. 'You continue to impress me.'

'It's not mutual,' she retorted. 'A seventeen-year-old girl. You disgust me.'

'And how would UNACO have handled the situation?' Calvieri asked, sitting astride the chair at the head of the table, his arms resting on its back.

'We wouldn't have threatened to send round a couple of hatchet men to rape her.'

'Who said anything about rape?' Calvieri exclaimed with a look of feigned disbelief.

'Spare the theatrics, we both know what you meant.'

'He'll call before two forty-five,' Calvieri said.

'And if he doesn't?' she challenged.

'He will, end of subject.' Calvieri looked at the television screen. 'What's happening?'

'The Dutch Prime Minister's making a speech about the need for European unity in 1992,' Ubrino replied.

'Still no sign of Bellini?'

Ubrino shook his head. 'The Foreign Secretary is still representing the Italian Government.'

'Good.' Calvieri watched the screen for a couple of minutes, then got to his feet and took a pack of cigarettes from his pocket. It was empty. He crumpled the pack into a ball and threw it angrily against the wall. 'You got a cigarette?' he asked Ubrino.

'I smoked my last one twenty minutes ago,' Ubrino said with an apologetic shrug.

'Great. We could be here all night and we're already out of cigarettes.' Calvieri crossed to the side table and rifled through the drawers. 'Pens, paper, even peppermints. But no damn cigarettes.'

'What do you expect?' Sabrina said. 'It's a conference room, not a tobacco stall.'

Calvieri closed the bottom drawer, then tugged back his sleeve to look at his watch: 2.39.

'*Tempus fugit*,' Sabrina said, looking at the clock on the wall.

'He's still got six minutes.' Calvieri leaned back against the side table and folded his arms across his chest. 'He'll call. Wouldn't you? Or perhaps you don't think I'd carry out my threat against Alexis, just as you don't think I'd press the button if it came to the crunch.'

'I'm sure you would, under the circumstances.'

277

'And what's that supposed to mean?'

'As you said earlier, who's going to take you seriously unless you're prepared to back up your threats? But I still don't believe you'd push the button, even as a last resort. You'd have so much to lose.'

'If I found myself in a situation where I was forced to press the button, I'd have reached a stage where I had *nothing* left to lose.' Calvieri dismissed the subject with a curt flick of the hand. 'This is all idle speculation. Bellini will resign, the money will be paid and the virus will be returned to the authorities intact.'

'Let's hope the ELA have read the script as well.' Sabrina looked up at the clock. 'Three minutes left. Are you still so sure he's going to call?'

'Of course,' Calvieri replied indifferently.

They lapsed into silence, both caught up in their own thoughts.

She knew he wouldn't push the button. He couldn't. He wasn't the megalomaniac the others believed him to be. She knew him better than them. He had even managed to fool Ubrino – then again, that wouldn't be very difficult. She smiled faintly as she looked at Ubrino, who sat in front of the television set, as enthralled as a child. She had her doubts whether he even understood what was being said at the conference. He was slow, even gullible. But he was also very dangerous. He wouldn't touch her as long as Calvieri needed her. They were sure to use her as a hostage to get clear of the building once the ransom had been paid. Then what? She suddenly realized her life was entirely in Calvieri's hands. There was little comfort in that thought.

Calvieri flexed his fingers and winced as the pain shot through the back of his hand. He took the transmitter from his pocket again and turned it around slowly in his hands. It seemed to ease the pain. Strange. His eyes flickered towards the telephone. Damn the ELA. What if Kozanakis couldn't contact his aide? What if the bomb went off? The building would be evacuated. Then what? He looked at the transmitter. The button. He smiled to himself. Would he press it? Not according to Sabrina. Only he knew the answer. If it did come to the crunch, he –

The telephone rang.

He snatched up the receiver.

'Calvieri?'

'About time,' Calvieri replied, recognizing Kozanakis's voice. He glanced at his watch: 2.44. 'You just made it. What did you find out?'

'The Semtex is in the boot of a white Audi Quattro. It's parked close to the building.'

'Number plate?'

'He doesn't remember,' Kozanakis replied hesitantly.

'Brilliant! Does it have any distinctive features?'

'A plaid rug on the back seat, that's all he can remember.'

'Is the boot booby-trapped?'

'Yes,' came the resigned reply. 'It'll blow if any attempt is made to open it.'

'You've done well, Andreas.'

'What's going on?' Kozanakis demanded. 'I had this number checked with the operator. You're at the Offenbach Centre.'

'That's right,' Calvieri said brusquely.

'The ELA has planned this for months—'

'You're way out of your league,' Calvieri interrupted him sharply. 'The Red Brigades have got something big going down here. It'll be in the news soon enough. But until then you're to keep your mouth shut. If only for Alexis.'

'This is going to cost you, Calvieri.'

'I'm sure we can come to some arrangement.' Calvieri cut the connection and smiled at Sabrina. 'What did I tell you?'

'What did you mean about it being in the news?' she asked

suspiciously. 'I thought the whole point of the exercise was to keep the media in the dark.'

'It is, while we're here. But I intend to hold a press conference once I reach my final destination. I want the world to know what happened here today. And I'll exploit it to the full. The capitulation of the smug Western governments who have always vowed publicly never to bow to so-called terrorism. They will be humiliated and discredited in the eyes of the world. The Red Brigades will become legendary. But more importantly we'll have sent out a message to our revolutionary comrades fighting for justice the world over. And that message will be: we can win. We *will* win.'

'You're deluded,' Sabrina said, shaking her head sadly to herself.

'Am I?' Calvieri said almost to himself, as he picked up the receiver to call Philpott.

Philpott consulted Kolchinsky's list after he had spoken to Calvieri. Teams One and Three were the closest to the building. He bleeped them then chewed the stem of his unlit pipe as he anxiously waited for them to call, his eyes continually flickering towards the desk clock as the seconds slipped away.

Graham and Marco located the white Audi Quattro within a minute of contacting Philpott. It was parked fifty yards away from the building. It had been positioned for maximum effect. A plaid rug lay crumpled on the back seat. It had diplomatic plates which later turned out to be false.

'We need a piece of wire to unlock the door,' Marco said.

'To hell with that,' Graham replied, then picked up a rock from a nearby flowerbed and pitched it through the driver's window. He reached through the broken window to unlock the door, then used the rug to brush the glass from the seat.

Two security guards, who had seen what had happened from their posts at the main gate, sprinted across to the car, batons drawn. One of the guards prodded Graham painfully in the chest with the tip of his baton and ordered him in German to put his hands on the roof of the car. Graham punched him. The guard fell as if poleaxed. The second guard shoved Marco aside but found himself staring down the barrel of Graham's Beretta. Whitlock and Paluzzi arrived breathlessly, having been alerted by the sound of breaking glass. Whitlock immediately pushed Graham's gun hand down to his side. Paluzzi was about to reach for his *NOCS* card when Vlok emerged from the building and ran towards them, shouting at the guard to leave Graham alone. The guard did as he was told. Vlok looked down at the unconscious man, then took the second guard to one side and explained briefly about the bomb. The guard, obeying Vlok's orders, dispersed the small crowd of onlookers, then turned his attention to his colleague sprawled beside the open car door.

'Was that necessary?' Vlok asked, indicating the unconscious guard.

'We'll discuss that later. Right now we've got a bomb here that's due to go off in,' Graham paused to look at his watch, 'eleven minutes.'

'Can't you defuse it?' Vlok asked.

'It's booby-trapped. We don't have the time or the equipment to deal with it,' Whitlock told him. 'We've got to get the car off the premises as quickly as possible.'

Graham slid behind the wheel to hotwire the ignition. 'There must be a secluded spot somewhere around here,' he said without looking up. 'We can leave it there and let it blow.'

'It's too dangerous,' Paluzzi said. 'The vibration could trigger off an avalanche on one of the surrounding mountains. Perhaps more than one avalanche. We can't risk it.'

The engine spluttered then died. Graham cursed angrily,

then reached under the wheel in another attempt to start the car.

'What are we going to do?' Vlok asked anxiously.

'Water, that's the only answer,' Whitlock replied after a moment's thought.

'Water?' Vlok said with a frown.

'A gorge, a lake, even a swimming-pool would do. If we can immerse the car in water, it'll short-circuit the wiring in the bomb and that would stop it from exploding.'

'There is a lake not far from here,' Vlok said. 'It's very small.'

'How far?'

Vlok shrugged helplessly. 'A five-minute drive, about that.'

'Did you hear that?' Whitlock asked Graham.

'I heard. We'll get going as soon as I can get this started.'

The engine coughed into life. Graham revved the engine, then gestured for them to get into the car.

'What have you in mind?' Whitlock asked.

'You'll see. Now get in.' Graham turned to Paluzzi. 'You guys tell the Colonel what's happening.'

'How will you get back?' Marco asked.

'I've got that covered,' Graham replied, closing the door.

'Good luck,' Paluzzi said, hitting the roof with the palm of his hand.

Graham reversed out of the space, then spun the wheel violently and sped towards the red and white boomgate.

'What's the plan?' Whitlock asked from the back seat.

'There's a police car parked outside the main gate. It can give us an escort to the lake. We'll get there in half the time.'

'In theory,' Vlok said.

'What's that supposed to mean?' Graham asked, glancing at Vlok in the rear-view mirror.

'The quickest route to the Lottersee, that's the name of the lake, is on the old Berne–Thun road. It's only used by lorries now that the N6 has been built. It's a narrow, twisting road and overtaking is virtually impossible.'

'It gets better by the minute,' Graham muttered, then trod lightly on the brake as they neared the boomgate.

'I'm not saying we'll encounter any traffic,' Vlok said, trying to appease Graham. 'Most of the lorries use the N6 anyway. But it's best to be warned.'

Graham stopped the car but kept it idling. Vlok told the guard to raise the boomgate. It was raised and Graham drove through. He pulled up beside the police car. Vlok got out, identified himself to the uniformed policeman behind the wheel, and told him about the bomb in the boot of the Quattro. The policeman listened in disbelief, then leaned over and pushed open the passenger door. Vlok got in beside him. The policeman started up the engine.

'Wait,' Graham shouted at the policeman above the drone of the siren. He turned to Whitlock. 'Out. If I'm going to drive this baby into the lake, I don't want to be carrying any passengers.'

Whitlock nodded, then climbed out of the Quattro and got into the police car. Graham gave the policeman a thumbs-up sign. The police car pulled away in a screech of burning rubber. Graham glanced at the dashboard clock. Eight minutes. He put the Quattro into gear and sped after the police car. They joined the N6 and kept to the fast lane, forcing the traffic in front of them to give way. When the police car suddenly swung across into the middle lane Graham was quick to follow it, forcing a Seat Malaga to brake sharply behind him. The driver hooted angrily. The police car then took a gap in the slow lane and indicated that it would be leaving the motorway at the next turn-off. Thirty yards away. Graham cursed under his breath. He couldn't get into the slow lane, there was a tailback of traffic behind the police car. He waited until he was only a few yards away from the turn-off then accelerated sharply and cut across the slow lane into the slip road.

Brakes screeched behind him, followed by the sickening crunch of clashing metal. He didn't look back. The cars hadn't been travelling very fast. There shouldn't be much damage. A crumpled fender. A shattered light. Nothing more. He braked at the end of the turn-off, changed down into second, and followed the police car on to the old Berne–Thun road.

He saw what Vlok had meant about overtaking being virtually impossible. The single lane on each side of the road was narrow, restricting visibility. To the left was a sheer drop of two hundred feet, to the right a towering rockface. He followed the police car around a sharp bend in the road and groaned in dismay at the pantechnicon twenty yards ahead of them. The pantechnicon disappeared around another bend. He glanced anxiously at the clock. He had six minutes left. He wiped the back of his hand across his sweaty forehead and turned the car into the bend. The police car was already sitting on the pantechnicon's tail, waiting for an opportunity to pass. It swayed out from behind the truck but the policeman couldn't risk overtaking on one of the blind corners. Graham bit his lip nervously. They would never reach the lake at this rate. He knew he would have to take the initiative. He had no choice. He gritted his teeth and pulled out from behind the police car. He passed it. Another bend loomed ahead. The police car dropped back, giving him the chance to tuck in behind the pantech-nicon. Graham knew it would only waste more time. He had to get past. The Quattro and the pantechnicon turned into the bend together.

The pantechnicon driver saw the lorry first and desper-ately tried to wave Graham back. Then Graham saw the lorry. He looked behind him. He wouldn't be able to drop back behind the pantechnicon, the distance was too great. It left him with no option. Evasive action. He swung the wheel sharply to the right, missing the lorry by inches. The lorry swerved to the left, clipping the side of the pantechnicon. The Quattro struck the mountain side-on and a protrusion of rock ripped a jagged gash in both doors before Graham managed to swing the car back on to the road. He glanced in his rear-view mirror. Both the lorry and the pantechnicon had stopped. The police car didn't stop.

Graham looked at the clock. Three minutes. And still no sign of the lake. He had already decided to send the car over the edge of the road if he hadn't seen the lake within the next minute. Avalanche or not, he wasn't going to kill himself for some terrorist's bomb. He was already contemplating where to ditch the car when he saw the signpost. LOTTERSEE – EINGANG ½km. It was still going to be tight. Then he saw the lake to his left. Its tranquillity reminded him of Lake Champlain. But it was only a fraction of the size.

The road descended rapidly. He followed another sign-post on to a dirt road which led him to the lake. He couldn't drive the car into the water, there was no guarantee that the boot would be submerged before the bomb detonated. He scanned his surroundings. A wooden jetty fifty yards away. It would be perfect. He spun the wheel violently and drove to the jetty. It was deserted. The whole area seemed to be deserted. The police car appeared in his rear-view mirror. He mounted the jetty carefully, fearful that the wooden boards wouldn't hold the car's weight. They held firm. He checked the time. A minute left. He decided against jumping from the car before it left the jetty, not with so much at stake. He would bail out when it hit the water. It would take several seconds to sink, giving him enough time to swim away.

He pressed the accelerator and the car shot forward. He braced himself as the car launched off the jetty. Then it hit the water, nose first. He immediately unbuckled his seatbelt and pulled on the door handle. The door wouldn't open. The car dipped forward and the cold, murky water flooded in. He tugged desperately at the handle then hit the door with his shoulder. It was jammed. The lock had been damaged when the door had been raked against the mountain. Within seconds the inside of the car was flooded. His only chance was the passenger door. He reached for the handle. The car bucked forward, knocking him against the windscreen. He felt as if his lungs would burst. If only he could get to the passenger door . . .

Whitlock knew something was wrong when he saw Graham struggling with the door handle before the front of the Quattro disappeared. He leapt out of the police car, discarded his jacket and his Browning, and ran to the end of the jetty. He dived into the water just as the last part of the Quattro slid under the water. He took a deep breath and dived. He could see where it had come to rest on its wheels. As he got closer he saw Graham struggling frantically with the passenger door. Whitlock grabbed the handle with both hands and, anchoring his right foot against the back door, he slowly eased it open. Graham pushed desperately from his side until the gap was big enough for him to squeeze through. They imme-diately propelled themselves upwards to the surface where they paused, coughing and spluttering, to catch their breath before swimming quickly to the jetty. Vlok and the policeman hauled them out of the water. Graham slumped down on to the wooden planks and exhaled deeply. It had been close.

Whitlock crouched beside Graham and put a hand lightly on his shoulder. 'Are you okay?'

'Yeah,' Graham replied, then put an arm around Whitlock's shoulders. 'I don't know how much longer I'd have lasted out there if you hadn't showed up when you did. Thanks, buddy.'

Whitlock shrugged it off, then stood up and helped Graham to his feet. 'What we need now is a hot shower and a change of clothing before we catch pneumonia.' He looked up at the policeman. 'Any chance of a lift back to our hotel?'

'You bet,' the policeman replied with a grin.

# TWELVE

Rust sat behind his desk. In front of him was a folder
containing the latest developments of Strike Force Nine's
operation in Paris. He had read it four times already but
his mind refused to take any of it in. All he could think
about was the vial. He looked at his watch: 3.30 p.m. An
hour-and-a-half had elapsed since the cylinder had been
taken away for examination. It could be another thirty
minutes before the results were known. Perhaps longer. The
waiting was killing him. He took a sip of coffee. It was cold.
He spat it back into the cup and was about to make himself
a fresh one when he heard a knock at the door. He looked
at the television monitor on his desk. It was Scheffer.

He activated the door.

Philpott was on the telephone when Graham and Whitlock
entered the office. He gestured for them to take a seat.
'Thanks for letting me know, Jacques,' he said finally then
replaced the receiver and turned to face them. 'The results
have just come through. The vial contained water.'

'I can't say I'm surprised, sir,' Whitlock replied. 'As you
said, it would have been too easy.'

'Has Vlok told you what happened with the car?' Graham
asked.

'Yes. I've notified the bomb squad. It's in their hands
now.' Philpott looked at the desk clock. 'There's less than

ninety minutes left before the deadline. I want you to rejoin your teams and continue the search for the vial.'

'And what if we do find another one?' Graham asked. 'There won't be time to send it to Zurich for analysis.'

'I've asked Jacques to have a carbon-steel-plated Magnox flask sent down here from Zurich. It's similar to the containers that are used for the disposal of highly toxic nuclear waste, only much smaller. The helicopter should get here within the next thirty minutes. Then if the vial is found, it can be sealed inside the flask, rendering it harmless.'

'But what if it's another red herring?' Graham asked.

'Let's find it first,' Philpott replied evasively, then bleeped Paluzzi and Marco to determine their positions so that Whitlock and Graham could rejoin them.

The telephone remained silent for the next twenty minutes. Then it rang twice in the space of five minutes. The first call was from Emile, the helicopter pilot, to say that he had arrived at the Offenbach Centre with the Magnox flask. Philpott told him to remain with the helicopter on the helipad.

The second call was from Michele Molinetti. Philpott couldn't place the name.

'Perhaps I should have said Captain Molinetti of the *NOCS*.'

'Of course,' Philpott replied, now remembering the name. 'You're at Calvieri's flat in Milan, not so?'

'That is correct.'

'Have you found something?' Philpott asked.

'We have found an address book hidden in a secret compartment beneath the floorboards in his bedroom. All the names are of known terrorists here in Italy, except for one. There is no address with the name, just two telephone numbers. One home, one work. I checked the code with the operator, and it's Zurich.'

'Zurich?' Philpott repeated, reaching for his pen. 'I'll get on to it right away.'

'The name is Helga Dannhauser,' Molinetti said, then went on to read out the two telephone numbers. 'We have no record of her here in Italy. She could be linked to one of the other European terrorist groups, but none of us has ever heard of her.'

'I appreciate the call, Captain.'

'I only hope you have more luck than we've had. We had already checked out all the names, even before we found the book. We're satisfied that none of them is linked to the case. Another dead end as far as we're concerned.'

'I'll let you know if we come up with anything. I've got the number of Calvieri's flat here somewhere.'

'Colonel Paluzzi knows it anyway. Goodbye, sir, and good luck.'

Philpott replaced the receiver and immediately bleeped Paluzzi. Whitlock rang the office and Philpott asked him to send Paluzzi up to him straight away. When Paluzzi arrived Philpott told him about Molinetti's call.

'Helga Dannhauser?' Paluzzi said thoughtfully as he stared at the sheet of paper Philpott had given to him. 'The name doesn't mean anything to me either.'

'I want you to ring those numbers using the other phone. I would have done it myself but I think you'll get further with your fluency in German.'

Paluzzi went into the outer office and sat down at the secretary's desk. He called the home number first. He let it ring for a minute but there was no reply. He then called the work number.

'*Guten tag, ZRF,*' a female voice answered.

'Could I speak to Helga Dannhauser, please,' Paluzzi said in German.

'Do you know which department she's in?'

'I don't, I'm sorry. A friend of hers gave me this number

the last time she visited me in Berlin. She told me to look up Helga if I was ever in Zurich. To be honest, I don't even know what ZRF stands for.'

'Zurich Rundfunk Firma. It's an independent television company. I can't say I know any Helga Dannhauser but I'll put you through to the personnel department. She may be new here.'

Paluzzi was put through to the personnel department. He was told that there had never been anybody by that name working at the station. He thanked the assistant and hung up. His body tingled with excitement. He knew he was on to something. He picked up the receiver again and rang police headquarters. He asked them to check the name Helga Dannhauser against the first number he had rung. The name was fed into the central computer and seconds later he was told that the number was registered to a Miss Ute Rietler. He dialled the number of the ZRF station again and asked to speak to Ute Rietler. This time the switchboard operator put him through to the news department. The phone was answered by a gruff male voice.

'Could I speak to Ute Rietler, please?'

'Ute's not here,' came the reply. 'She's in Berne covering the European summit.'

Paluzzi slammed the receiver back into the cradle, then leapt to his feet and raced into the inner office, where he poured out his findings to Philpott.

'There has to be a connection,' Paluzzi said in conclusion. 'It's too much of a coincidence.'

'I agree. It could be a security measure on his part to list her under a false name.' Philpott picked up the receiver and rang the press room. He asked to speak to Ute Rietler.

There was a lengthy pause before the receptionist came back on the line. 'Miss Rietler returned to her hotel about twenty minutes ago. She won't be back for another hour. Would you like to speak to one of her assistants?'

'No, it's a personal matter. Which hotel is she staying at?'

'I don't know, sir.'

'Then find out, lass,' Philpott thundered.

The flustered receptionist came back on the line a few seconds later. 'The Ambassador, on Seftigenstrasse. Do you know where it is?'

'I'll find it, thank you.'

Philpott wrote the name of the hotel and the street on a sheet of paper and handed it to Paluzzi. 'I want you and C.W. to get over there right away. She's our last chance. And for God's sake, hurry. There're only forty minutes left before the deadline.'

Paluzzi stuffed the paper into his jacket pocket and hurried from the room.

Philpott sat back and looked at the telephone. 'I think we've *finally* got you.'

Paluzzi found a parking space a block away from the Ambassador Hotel. They ran to the hotel, mounted the steps two at a time, then strode briskly across to the reception desk.

'Can I help you?' a blonde-haired receptionist asked with a glossy smile.

'Ute Rietler, her room number please?' Paluzzi said.

The receptionist punched the name into the computer. 'Suite 240. I'll tell her you're here. Your names, please?'

'It's okay, we work with her,' Paluzzi replied, forcing a smile. 'She's expecting us.'

'It's on the second floor. Turn right out of the lift.' The receptionist turned her attention to another guest waiting impatiently to check in.

Both lifts were in use. They took the stairs. Whitlock paused on the second floor to look at his watch. There were twenty-one minutes left before Bellini was due to announce his resignation. He followed Paluzzi to Suite 240. Paluzzi rapped loudly on the door. No reply.

'What if she's not here?' Whitlock whispered.

'She's got to be,' Paluzzi replied, and knocked again.

'Who is it?' a female called.

'Police.'

The door was opened on a chain. 'Where's your ID?'

Paluzzi produced a false carabinieri badge and held it up for her to see. Whitlock held up his false Scotland Yard card that had been made at the Test Centre in New York.

'Italian police? British police? You have no jurisdiction here in Switzerland.'

'We're here for the summit. We'd like to ask you some questions, that's all.'

For a moment they thought she would refuse to speak to them. Then the door closed, the chain was removed, and it was opened again to admit them. Ute Rietler was an attractive redhead who looked to be in her late twenties. It was clear, even in the white towelling robe she was wearing, that she had a stunning figure.

'I hope we didn't get you out of the bath,' Paluzzi said.

'I was just getting dried when you knocked,' she replied, closing the door behind them. 'I'm due back at the Offenbach Centre in forty minutes so I'm in a hurry. What is it you wanted to ask me?'

'An old friend of yours,' Paluzzi said, helping himself to a grape from the fruit bowl on the sideboard. 'Tonino Calvieri.'

'Who?' she retorted with a frown.

Whitlock watched her carefully. She hadn't reacted to the name at all. Not even a flicker of the eyes. But then she was *ZRF*'s leading anchorwoman. Philpott had phoned the information through to them on the carphone. And that meant she didn't allow herself to get flustered. An act. And a good one at that.

'You've never heard of Tonino Calvieri?' Paluzzi said, leaning against the sideboard.

She dug her hands into her pockets and chewed her lip thoughtfully. 'No, I don't think so.' She suddenly nodded her head. 'Wait a minute, isn't he that terrorist who's just taken over as the new leader of the Red Brigades? We ran a short item on him a couple of days ago. What has he got to do with me?'

'You tell us, Miss Rietler,' Paluzzi said.

'Tell you what?' she snapped.

'Why your phone number appears in his address book hidden in his apartment in Milan.'

'This is too much—'

'Where is the vial he gave you to hide?' Paluzzi cut in sharply.

'I've had enough of this badgering. I'm calling the hotel security.' She disappeared into the bedroom and snatched up the receiver.

'I'd put that phone down, Miss Rietler,' Paluzzi said from the doorway. 'Or should I call you Miss Dannhauser?'

Her body stiffened and her fingers tightened around the handset. The act was over. She replaced the receiver and sat on the edge of the bed, staring at the carpet.

Paluzzi picked up a framed photograph from the bedside table and his eyes narrowed in sudden comprehension.

'What is it?' Whitlock asked, looking at the freckle-faced boy in the photograph.

'He's the spitting image of his father. And I thought I knew everything about Calvieri.'

'That's Calvieri's son?' Whitlock said in astonishment.

'He couldn't look more like his father if he tried,' Paluzzi said, then looked down at Ute Rietler. 'He gave you the vial, didn't he?'

'I don't know what you're talking about,' she replied, but there was no conviction in her voice.

'Ute, you've got to help us,' Paluzzi said softly.

'I can't.'

'Why?' Paluzzi asked.

'He said he'd expose my past unless I did what he wanted.'

'You're not making any sense, Ute,' Paluzzi said. 'Your past has already been exposed. We know about it. You must cooperate with us, it's your only chance.'

'I can't,' she repeated.

'And what's going to happen to your son when you're jailed for life for conspiring with a terrorist? He'll be taken into care. I doubt you'll ever see him again. Is that what you want?'

There was a long silence. Ute Rietler was struggling with her inner emotions. When she finally spoke, it was in a barely audible voice. 'It's taped underneath the chassis of our outside broadcast van. It's parked near the main gate.'

Whitlock bolted into the adjoining room to call Philpott.

'I don't know what's in it, you must believe me,' she pleaded. 'Tony said it would be picked up by a member of another terrorist group some time today. That's all he told me.'

'When did you meet Tony?'

'Rome, eight years ago. I went there to stay with some friends after my parents were killed in a car crash outside Bonn. I met him at a Red Brigades rally. We fell in love at first sight. At least that's what I thought at the time. I found out later that I was just another in a long line of girlfriends. We'd only been seeing each other for a couple of months when I discovered I was pregnant. That's when I came to my senses. I wanted my child to have a proper family, not be surrounded by anarchists and killers. Tony was very understanding but he refused to leave the Red Brigades. He said his place was with them. I decided then I wanted to start a new life so that Bruno would never have to know about his father. Tony helped me fake my own death, a boating accident in the Adriatic. I was listed as missing, presumed dead. He got me a new passport in the name of Ute Rietler and I decided to start afresh here in Switzerland. I cut my hair, dyed it and took to wearing contact lenses instead of glasses. I got a job with *ZRF*, and the rest I'm sure you know.

'I never saw or heard from him again until he called me last week, asking for my help. I told him I didn't want anything more to do with the Red Brigades but he threatened to splash my past across every tabloid in Europe if I didn't agree to help him. What choice did I have? I went to his hotel last night and picked up a package from the reception desk. His instructions were with the metal cylinder. I never knew what was in it . . .' Her voice faded to nothing and she wiped a tear from the corner of her eye. 'You're going to take Bruno into care, aren't you?'

'No,' Paluzzi replied, and paused in the doorway to look back at her. 'I promise I'll do everything I can to keep your name out of this.'

She smiled weakly, then put her hands over her face and began to cry softly to herself.

In the other room Whitlock was standing by the window, staring absently at the traffic in the street below.

'Ready?' Paluzzi asked.

'Sure.' Whitlock crossed to where Paluzzi was waiting for him at the door. 'What happened in there?'

'I'll tell you about it in the car,' Paluzzi said, opening the door.

Whitlock stepped out into the corridor and instinctively glanced at his watch: 4.46 p.m.

Philpott sent Graham and Marco to get the vial. Vlok had arranged for a maintenance van to be parked at the back of the building for their use. Marco got behind the wheel and started the engine. Graham climbed in beside him. Marco slipped the van into gear and drove to where the dozens of media pantechnicons were parked. He cruised the road leading to the boomgate as they scanned the pantechnicons for the one belonging to *ZRF*. He braked in front of the boomgate – there was no sign of the one they were seeking. A guard approached the driver's window and Marco asked him whether he knew where the *ZRF* vehicle was parked. The guard consulted the clipboard in his hand. He flicked through the sheets of paper, then leaned his arm on the open window and showed Marco its position on a plan he had made of the media vehicles the previous night. It was parked on the grass behind the row of vehicles nearest the road. Marco thanked him, did a U-turn, and drove back ten yards before finding a space between two giant pantechnicons big enough to drive through. He braked immediately. The grass was seething with cables. They would have to continue on foot.

Graham jumped out and picked his way through the cables to a white vehicle with the letters *ZRF* painted in black on either side. Marco went after him and after looking around quickly he slid underneath the pantechnicon where Graham was already feeling around the edges of the chassis for the metal cylinder. Ute Rietler was hardly likely to have crawled right underneath and taped the vial to the centre of the vehicle's underbelly.

They heard voices and tucked their legs out of sight seconds before a couple of engineers approached the back of the pantechnicon and climbed inside, closing the door behind them. Graham indicated for Marco to start at the front and work his way back. He would start from the back. Marco nodded and leopard crawled to the front of the pantechnicon. Graham reached the back section then removed a small torch from his pocket and switched it on. He played the beam across the chassis, concentrating on the edges. The door opened again. He switched off the torch. A man came out and paused at the foot of the steps, inches

away from where Graham lay motionless on the grass. He
shouted something in German and a moment later a packet
of cigarettes was thrown to him. The man didn't catch it
and the packet landed on the middle step. For a horrifying
moment Graham thought it was going to topple off the step
and land next to him. It came to rest on the edge of the
step. A hand appeared and picked it up. The man walked
away from the pantechnicon, and Graham exhaled deeply.
As he switched the torch on again, a hand touched his leg.
He looked round sharply, cracking the back of his head
painfully on the exhaust pipe. Marco held up a hand apologetically then patted the breast pocket of his maintenance
overall.

'You got it?' Graham whispered.

Marco nodded. 'It was taped under the mudguard.'

Graham wriggled his way out and rubbed the back of
his head gingerly. A man suddenly emerged from the back
of the pantechnicon beside the *ZRF* one. He paused on the
bottom step and eyed them suspiciously.

Marco got to his feet, brushed the grass from his overall
and shook his head sadly at the man. 'You wouldn't believe
the amount of rust under there. It's not fit to be on the road.
I'd check under your van if I were you.'

The man watched them get back into the maintenance
van, then shrugged and walked away. Marco started up
the engine and reversed out fast into the road.

'We've got nine minutes left to get the cylinder to the
helicopter,' Graham said. 'Forget about the back entrance,
we'll never make it. Drive to the main entrance, it's our
only chance.'

'We'll never get through without setting off the metal
detector,' Marco replied.

'We've got to do it.'

Marco sped round the perimeter of the car-park and
pulled up in front of the main doors.

'Run like hell,' Graham told him. 'And use the stairs,

they could shut down the lifts before you reach the helipad.'

'What are you going to do?'

'Someone's got to cover your back. Whatever happens to me, don't turn back. Just keep running.'

Marco nodded. Graham patted him on the shoulder and they leapt out of the van. The doors parted electronically in front of them. Marco entered first. The metal detector buzzed. He broke into a run when a guard approached him. The guard shouted at him to stop. Graham shoulder-charged the guard as he reached for his holstered pistol. The pistol spun from his hand. A second guard was instantly on the scene. Graham tackled him, knocking him to the floor. He retrieved both pistols and sprinted after Marco. The two guards radioed for back-up. There wasn't much else they could do. Graham reached the stairs before any of the guards could get to him. Fortunately they hadn't dared to shoot because the foyer was packed. He only paused for breath when he reached the fifth floor. There was still no sign of the guards. It surprised him. He took a deep breath, then bounded up the stairs, two at a time, until he reached the tenth floor landing. Still no guards. What was going on? Were they waiting for him on the helipad? How would they know where he was headed? He pressed himself against the wall and pushed open the door leading out on to the helipad. No gunfire.

'Michael?' a voice called out from the helipad.

Graham recognized Kolchinsky's voice. He was also the only person he knew who called him Michael.

'Michael, is that you?' Kolchinsky called out again.

Graham wiped the sweat from his forehead and stepped out on to the helipad. Vlok stood beside Kolchinsky and Marco, a two-way radio in his hand.

'We thought you two might use the main entrance to save time,' Kolchinsky said. 'So when we heard that two maintenance workers were headed for the stairs we put two and two together and Dieter gave instructions to the guards to give you free passage to the helipad.'

'You sure know how to spoil a guy's fun, Sergei,' Graham said with a half-smile.

Kolchinsky checked his watch. 'You did it with four minutes to spare. You could have taken the lift after all. It would have been far less strenuous.'

Graham smiled as Kolchinsky crossed to the telephone to break the news to Philpott.


'Wouldn't you like to join us?' Calvieri said to Sabrina and indicated the third chair in front of the television set.

'The air's a lot cleaner where I am,' Sabrina retorted sharply.

'Humour, even in defeat. I admire you for that.' Calvieri sat down and rubbed his hands together. 'I've been waiting for this moment ever since the PCI came to power two years ago. The public humiliation of Enzo Bellini.'

'It's five o'clock,' Ubrino said, glancing at his watch. 'He should be arriving any moment now.'

Calvieri nodded. 'All that's missing is a cigarette. I would die for one.'

'Me too,' Ubrino muttered, and helped himself to another peppermint from the packet he had taken from the drawer.

They watched the screen as the Swiss President emerged through a side door and crossed to a table where he sat down and surveyed the dozens of journalists seated in front of him. Cameras flashed incessantly. A journalist shouted out a question but the Swiss President immediately raised a hand for silence.

'Ladies and gentlemen, thank you for coming here tonight,' the President said in English. 'I called this press conference to deal with the rumours that the Italian Prime Minister, Signore Enzo Bellini, is to step down through ill-health. It is true that he was taken ill this morning, which is when the rumours began, but I am glad to report that it is nothing more serious than influenza. I have just seen Signore Bellini and he has asked me to assure you that he will *not* be standing down, either today or at any time in the foreseeable future . . .'

'What are you talking about?' Calvieri shouted at the screen. He rubbed the back of his hand nervously across his mouth. 'It's part of the deal. Bellini must resign.'

The telephone rang.

Calvieri knocked over his chair in his haste to answer it.

'I thought you'd like to see the start of the press conference before I called you,' Philpott said.

'What are you playing at, Philpott?' Calvieri snarled, his breathing ragged. 'I told you what would happen if either of my demands weren't met. You've just made a very big mistake—'

'We've found the vial.'

Calvieri's eyes narrowed with uncertainty. 'Where?'

'In the workshop.'

Calvieri burst out laughing, such was his relief.

'But we expected a red herring,' Philpott continued. 'That's why we carried on with the search even after it had been found. Miss Rietler was very helpful when it came to finding the real vial. Or should I call her Miss Dannhauser? After all, that was the name in the address book we found under the floorboards in your flat.'

Calvieri's face went pale. He fumbled for a chair and sat down slowly.

'The lab results came through fifteen minutes ago,' Philpott said, knowing he had to call Calvieri's bluff. It was too late to turn back, even if he was wrong. And God help him if he were. 'Our scientists have identified the compound as the virus. They didn't attempt to defuse the magnetic charge on the side of the metal cylinder, just in case you'd booby-trapped it. The vial's been removed from the cylinder for further tests. It's quite harmless now.'

Calvieri wiped the sweat out of his eyes. 'It's not over yet, Colonel. We still have one ace left to play. Sabrina. She's our ticket out of here. And don't underestimate us, we don't have anything left to lose. Not any more.'

'If anything happens to Sabrina—'

'It won't, as long as you do as we say. I'll call you back when we've decided on a plan of action. And don't try anything stupid like storming the room. You wouldn't want to have Sabrina's death on your conscience, would you?' Calvieri replaced the receiver and rubbed his hands over his face. He was devastated. He looked up at Ubrino. 'They found out about Helga.'

'How?' Ubrino replied. 'You said there was no way they could trace her.'

'I know what I said,' Calvieri snapped, raking his fingers through his hair. 'They found her name and number in an old address book under the floorboards in my flat. I don't remember putting it there. I thought I'd destroyed all my links with her. God, what have I done?'

'It's all collapsing around you and there isn't a damn thing you can do about it,' Sabrina said with a satisfied smile. 'You might as well give up now, Tony, you know you're finished. Nobody likes a failure, not even the Red Brigades.'

'*Sta zitta*!' Ubrino shouted, pulling the Beretta from his belt.

'Leave her,' Calvieri hissed and pushed the barrel of the gun towards the carpet. 'We need her in order to get out of here.'

'They could be stalling for time.'

Calvieri shook his head. 'Then they would have postponed the press conference. No, they don't intend to give in to our demands. That much is obvious.'

'Then press the button.'

Calvieri took the transmitter from his pocket and stared at it in the palm of his hand. 'The vial's already been removed for analysis. What's the use of blowing up an empty metal cylinder?'

'You only have their word for it. What if they're calling your bluff? Press the button. We have nothing left to lose. Press it.'

'No!' Calvieri yelled, his eyes blazing. 'You've been working with Zocchi for too long. Even if the vial is still inside the metal cylinder, what can we hope to achieve by killing millions of innocent people? Nothing. Absolutely nothing.'

Ubrino looked at Sabrina. 'She was right. You never intended to push it, did you?'

'Never,' Calvieri replied defiantly. 'But they didn't know that. If they had they wouldn't have agreed to our demands in the first place. It was psychological pressure. Can't you see that?'

'I believed in you, Tony. And this is how you repay my trust.' Ubrino levelled the Beretta at Calvieri. 'Give me the transmitter.'

'You'll have to kill me first,' Calvieri said in a challenging voice. 'And you can't do that, can you? You need me to get you out of here. You don't have the brains to do it by yourself.'

Ubrino thought for a few moments, then shoved the Beretta back into his belt. 'When this is over . . .'

'Then you'll kill me, sure,' Calvieri replied with an indifferent shrug, reaching for the telephone to call Philpott.

'What did he say, sir?' Whitlock asked after Philpott had replaced the receiver.

'He wants a helicopter ready in twenty minutes to fly them out. They're taking Sabrina as a hostage.' Philpott turned to Paluzzi. 'I want you and your men to clear the helipad. Only our helicopter must be there.' He gestured to Vlok. 'Dieter, I want you to go with them to make sure it all runs smoothly.'

Vlok agreed, then hurried out with Paluzzi and his men.

'Sergei, I want you and Mike to check the fifth floor. There shouldn't be anybody there, but it's best to be sure.'

Kolchinsky and Graham left the room.

Philpott turned to Kuhlmann. 'Reinhardt, I want you to commandeer one of the lifts then put a guard on each floor to make sure that Calvieri and Ubrino have safe passage to the helipad.'

'I'll see to it,' Kuhlmann said and went immediately to carry out the instruction.

'Which leaves me,' Whitlock said suspiciously. 'What do you want me to do?'

'Ever wanted to become a helicopter pilot?'

The telephone rang.

Calvieri answered it. 'You're three minutes late.'

'You made the conditions, not me,' Philpott replied.

'Is the helicopter ready?'

'It's ready.'

'And the lift?'

'It's been stopped on the fifth floor, as requested.'

'You make any move against us—'

'You'll kill Sabrina, you told me that before,' Philpott cut in.

'As long as we understand each other. She'll be released, unharmed, once we reach our final destination. I'll call you at the hotel tomorrow morning to tell you where to find her. Until then, *ciao*.' Calvieri replaced the receiver and turned to Ubrino. 'Bring her.'

'Why don't you bring her?' Ubrino retorted.

'Why don't I just bring myself?' Sabrina said, getting to her feet.

Ubrino grabbed her arm and pressed the Beretta against the side of her neck. Calvieri unlocked the door and eased it open. He then took hold of Sabrina's other arm and they led her out into the deserted corridor. All the doors were closed. The lift stood open at the end of the corridor. The silence was eerie. Ubrino dug his fingers into Sabrina's arm and guided her towards the lift. Calvieri kept his eyes on the doors behind them, his Beretta at the ready. Not that he thought Philpott would try anything. There was a touching loyalty amongst his kind. A loyalty that was foreign to someone like Calvieri. His loyalty lay with the cause, not with its protagonists. He glanced at Ubrino. Zocchi's militancy had obviously rubbed off on him over the past few years. Ubrino had suddenly become a dangerous liability. He would kill him the moment they were airborne. He couldn't afford to take any chances. But for the moment he needed Ubrino. Just as Ubrino needed him. A temporary bond was all that remained of a once close friendship.

Ubrino led Sabrina into the lift, the Beretta still pressed firmly against the side of her neck. Calvieri backed into the lift after them and closed the doors.

Whitlock sat behind the controls of the Lynx helicopter, Emile's peaked cap tugged over his head. He looked across at the lift doors. Where were they?

He thought about the briefing in Vlok's office. Philpott's instructions had been simple. Rescue Sabrina, unharmed. It meant he would have to kill at least one of them. Perhaps both. Ubrino was certainly the more dangerous of the two. A psychotic killer. Calvieri was less of a threat. Although he was always armed, he had never been known to use his gun. He left the killings to his *Brigatisti*. Whitlock touched the Browning in his belt and looked slowly around the deserted helipad. The landing lights were on as the darkness descended across Berne. He shivered in the light wind which had sprung up in the last hour and absently adjusted his cap as he turned his attention back to the lift doors. Where were they?

The doors suddenly parted and Calvieri stepped out

tentatively on to the helipad. He looked around slowly, then indicated for Ubrino to follow him. Ubrino emerged on to the helipad, Sabrina held tightly against him. Whitlock bit his lip anxiously. It was going to be a difficult shot. A mistake could cost Sabrina her life. That seemed to give him renewed confidence in himself.

Calvieri pointed to the rotors and turned his finger round in the air, indicating that he wanted Whitlock to start the engine. Whitlock remembered what Emile had shown him and pressed the starter switch. They were now less than ten yards away from the helicopter. He palmed the Browning from his belt. His hands were sweating. Calvieri reached the open door first and peered into the cabin. Satisfied it was empty, he clambered inside. Ubrino led Sabrina to the door and Calvieri grabbed her arm to help her up. Ubrino glanced around furtively, then gripped the door but as he pulled himself up Sabrina lashed out with her foot, catching him on the side of the head. He fell heavily on to the helipad, the Beretta spinning from his hand. Whitlock instinctively swung his Browning on Calvieri, then noticed out of the corner of his eye that Ubrino had got to his feet and was making for his fallen Beretta. For a split second Whitlock was caught in a dilemma. Then Sabrina shoulder-charged Calvieri, slamming him against the cabin wall. He grunted in pain and the Beretta slipped from his grasp. Whitlock kicked open the passenger door and shot Ubrino as he was aiming the Beretta at Sabrina's back. The bullet struck Ubrino in the head and he was dead before he hit the ground. Whitlock turned the Browning on Calvieri, giving Sabrina the chance to kick the Beretta out on to the helipad.

Graham and Paluzzi, alerted by the gunshot, emerged from behind a door leading on to the stairs and ran across to the helicopter. Philpott, Kolchinsky and Kuhlmann appeared behind them. Graham retrieved the two Berettas, then ordered Calvieri out of the helicopter. Calvieri jumped on to the helipad and slowly raised his hands above his head. Paluzzi frisked him and pocketed the transmitter. He found the key for Sabrina's handcuffs and unlocked them before helping her out of the helicopter. She took one of the Berettas from Graham and pushed it into her shoulder holster.

Whitlock cut the engine, then got out of the cockpit and looked across at Sabrina. 'Are you all right?'

'I'm fine,' she replied, massaging her wrists where the handcuffs had dug into her skin. 'Thanks, C.W.'

Whitlock smiled at her, then crossed to where Philpott was standing. 'Good work, C.W.'

'Thank you, sir.'

'Cuff him,' Philpott said, nodding towards Calvieri.

'Allow me,' Sabrina replied, then took the handcuffs from Paluzzi and snapped them around Calvieri's wrists.

'Have you got a cigarette?' Calvieri asked Kolchinsky. 'I haven't had one all afternoon.'

Kolchinsky took his cigarettes from his pocket, pushed one between Calvieri's lips, and lit it for him. Calvieri took a long drag then raised his manacled hands and took the cigarette from his lips. He exhaled deeply, then looked across at Philpott. 'I'm not taking this rap by myself. You'll find Nikki Karos at his house on Corfu.'

'Karos alive?' Paluzzi snorted. 'That's ridiculous. Mike and I were there when he was killed.'

'It was stage-managed for your benefit,' Calvieri said to Paluzzi.

'We've had the house under surveillance—'

'Don't you think he knows that?' Calvieri cut across Paluzzi. 'Why do you think Boudien dismissed the staff? To make it look as if Karos was dead.'

'We saw him die,' Graham snapped.

'I don't know how he faked it, but Nikki Karos *is* alive. I should know, I spoke to him on his private line this morning.'

Philpott turned to Graham. 'I want you and Sabrina to check it out. Emile can fly you there tonight.'

'I'll fly them over, Malcolm,' Kolchinsky said. 'Emile's a courier, not a combat pilot. If Karos is alive, we could come under fire.'

'Very well,' Philpott replied after a moment's thought.

He took Whitlock and Paluzzi to one side. 'Commissioner Kuhlmann has agreed to give us two hours with Calvieri before we have to hand him over to the local police. I want you to get as much out of him as you can before they take him away.'

'Where can we question him?' Paluzzi asked.

'Use Vlok's office.'

'What about Ubrino?' Whitlock asked, glancing at the body.

'The police will be here shortly. Commissioner Kuhlmann and I will stay here to tie up any loose ends. Now go on, get Calvieri out of here before they arrive.'

Whitlock and Paluzzi led Calvieri across the helipad and disappeared down the stairs.

Kolchinsky looked at his watch, then dropped his cigarette end and ground it underfoot. 'It's going to be a long haul. We'd better get started as soon as possible.'

'How long will it take us to reach Corfu?' Sabrina asked.

'You're my navigators, that's for you to work out.'

Graham and Sabrina exchanged an expressive look as they followed Kolchinsky to the helicopter.


'Sit down,' Whitlock said to Calvieri, indicating the chair behind Vlok's desk.

'What about these?' Calvieri asked, extending his manacled wrists towards Whitlock.

'They stay, for the moment.'

'So what's the deal?' Calvieri asked, sitting down.

'Deal?' Paluzzi asked suspiciously.

'Why am I here? Why haven't I been handed over to the local police?'

'You'll be handed over to them in two hours' time,' Whitlock told him. 'That's when you'll be officially booked.'

'And until then?'

'Hopefully you'll agree to cooperate with us,' Whitlock said. 'It would certainly benefit you in the long run if you did.'

'And what exactly does this "cooperation" entail?'

'A signed confession,' Paluzzi replied brusquely.

'And what's in it for me? I'm hardly going to be pardoned, am I?'

'A reduction in sentence,' Whitlock said.

Calvieri sat back and smiled to himself. 'So I'll get three life sentences instead of four. Not much of an incentive, is it?'

Paluzzi placed his hands on the desk and leaned forward, his eyes fixed on Calvieri's face. 'You're going to spend part of your sentence in an Italian jail. And that means you're going to need protection. All I have to do is make one phone call and all the Red Brigades prisoners will be transferred to other jails before you even get there. Can you imagine what those neo-fascist prisoners would do to you? And the warders won't lift a finger—'

'You've made your point.' There was fear in Calvieri's eyes. He chuckled nervously. 'You certainly know how to negotiate, Paluzzi.'

Paluzzi moved to the door. 'I'll get some paper from the other office.'

'Paluzzi?' Calvieri called out after him. 'I could use another cigarette.'

'I'll see what I can do,' Paluzzi replied as he closed the door behind him.

Whitlock sat on the sofa and looked at Calvieri. 'What made you team up with Karos? You two are complete opposites.'

'It was a case of us needing each other. I needed him to finance the operation and he needed the money to start a new life in some other part of the world. I don't know the whole story, but it seems there were several contracts out on his life. He knew it would only be a matter of time before he was hit.'

'So he orchestrated his own "death" in front of the authorities to make it seem all the more convincing?'

Calvieri nodded. 'He knew it would take the pressure off him, giving him the chance to start afresh away from Corfu.'

'What would his cut have been?'

'Twenty million.'

'Where would it have come from? You wanted the hundred million split between five terrorist groups . . .' Whitlock trailed off and nodded to himself. 'Of course, you only intended to give to four of them. The fifth was just a cover for Karos.'

'That's right. The Red Army Faction in West Germany were never in on the deal. Karos had his own contact in Berlin who would have collected the money for him.'

'Who hired the Francia brothers?' Whitlock asked.

'Karos. They'd worked for him before. I've never even met them. I spoke once to Carlo on the phone to stage the shooting in Venice, that's all. It helped to draw the suspicion away from me.'

Whitlock frowned. 'There's one thing I still don't understand. How did you manage to warn Ubrino that Mike, Sabrina and Fabio were on their way to the chalet?'

'I had a transmitter in my pocket which I carried with me at all times. Ubrino had the receiver in the chalet. We agreed that I would only use it in an emergency. He contacted the Francia brothers and, well, the rest you know.' Calvieri sat forward, his manacled hands clasped together on the desk. 'You were Anderson, weren't you? I knew it the moment I saw you properly on the helipad. The description matched perfectly. So who was Yardley?'

'I don't know what you're talking about,' Whitlock replied, holding Calvieri's stare.

'No, I suppose not,' Calvieri muttered, then slumped back in his chair.

When Paluzzi returned he placed a pad, a pack of cigarettes and a lighter on the desk in front of Calvieri. He then unlocked Calvieri's handcuffs and handed him a pen. 'Now start writing.'

# THIRTEEN

It took them five-and-a-half hours, including three fuel stops, to reach Corfu.

As Kolchinsky skimmed the helicopter low across the Khalikiopoulos Lagoon, Graham and Sabrina were smearing camouflage cream over their faces in the cabin behind him. They were both wearing black tracksuits, which they had got from the Test Centre in Zurich, and Sabrina also wore a black cap to hide her blonde hair.

'Are you ready?' Kolchinsky called out over his shoulder.

'Ready,' Sabrina replied, and pushed her Beretta into her shoulder holster.

Graham, too, loaded his Beretta and holstered it. 'How long before we deplane?'

'A couple of minutes,' Kolchinsky answered.

'And you're sure there are no guards?' Sabrina asked.

'That's what it says in the surveillance report,' Kolchinsky replied. 'Boudien's the only person who's been seen there in the last two days.'

Graham clipped the two-way radio on his belt. 'I still say we're on a wild-goose chase.'

'But what would Calvieri gain by that?' Sabrina asked.

'I know it doesn't make any sense but you'd understand my scepticism if you'd been there when Karos was shot. The guy was riddled with bullets even before he fell off the terrace. You don't just get up and walk away from that.'

Kolchinsky banked the helicopter in a wide arc to avoid flying over the house and landed on the helipad. He gave them a thumbs-up sign, the signal to deplane.

'If you haven't heard from us in thirty minutes you'll come in with guns blazing, right?' Graham said, standing in front of the closed cabin door.

'Just make sure I *do* hear from you,' Kolchinsky replied.

Graham pulled open the door and jumped out on to the helipad. Sabrina leapt out after him and closed the door behind her. The helicopter immediately rose into the sky and wheeled away towards a clearing on the edge of the lagoon where Kolchinsky would await their instructions.

They ignored the road leading up to the house. Instead they used the cover of the adjacent olive grove, dense trees with thick corded trunks. It would be impossible to see them from the house. The perfect approach. Graham put a hand lightly on Sabrina's arm when they reached the edge of the grove. The nearest of the four concrete pillars stood thirty yards away. Thirty yards of lawn. According to the surveillance report, the only way into the house was via the glass lift. Although the glass was bulletproof, it still made them feel uneasy. They would be trapped together in a confined space. And not only that, their progress could be monitored from inside the house. Graham had suggested climbing the pylons, using suction pads, but his idea was quickly scuppered when it turned out that the pylons were protected with razor-sharp pieces of glass embedded into the concrete. Sabrina had suggested using a length of rope to climb up to the terrace. The railing had an alarm built into it which would be activated the moment the grappling hook touched it. *If* the alarm was on. But they couldn't take that chance. Another idea discarded. There was no alternative; they would have to use the lift.

Graham broke cover and sprinted to the lift. Sabrina followed and took up a position on the other side. He pressed the call button and the lift arrived seconds later.

He pivoted round, Beretta extended, when the doors opened. It was empty. They stepped inside and he pushed the button for the first floor. They had agreed to cover the house, floor by floor, rather than risk any more time in the lift than was absolutely necessary. The doors closed and the lift rose slowly up the side of the house. They braced themselves to dive low out of the lift when it stopped on the first floor. It didn't stop. He hit the button for the second floor. It didn't stop there either. It slowed on nearing the third, the top, floor. Each was aware of the other's tension, and the sweat shone on both their faces.

The lift stopped and the doors opened. They dived low through the doorway, fanning the corridor with their Berettas. It was deserted. A closed-circuit television camera, mounted above the metal door at the end of the corridor, was monitoring their every move. The lift doors closed behind them. Graham got to his feet cautiously and was about to shoot out the camera lens when the metal doors suddenly slid open. They both trained their Berettas on the doorway. The room looked deserted. It had to be a trap. Sabrina stood up and covered Graham's back as he moved towards the open door.

They were both knocked off their feet as if hit by an invisible punch. Sabrina landed by the lift. Graham was slammed against the wall, winded. He fell, face forward, on to the carpet. The towering figure of Boudien appeared in the doorway, holding a CZ75 pistol in his hand. He disarmed them, then returned to the doorway and waited for them to recover.

Graham was the first to move. He rubbed his eyes, then pulled himself up on to one knee. He felt groggy. His whole body was tingling. He looked across at Sabrina. She lay motionless in front of the lift. For a horrifying moment he thought she was dead. Then she groaned and slowly eased herself up into a sitting position. She let Graham help her to her feet. Boudien gestured for them to enter the room.

It was a lounge. And Karos's obsession with snakes was evident everywhere. Prints and wood engravings lined the walls, bronze sculptures littered the sideboards, and even the carpet had snakes incorporated into its design.

Karos sat in one of the armchairs. 'Please, come in. Sit down,' he said, indicating the sofa opposite him.

Boudien waited until they were seated, then handed one of the Berettas to Karos and tucked the other into the back of his belt. He took up a position behind the sofa, his arms folded across his chest.

Karos placed the Beretta in his lap. 'I'm relieved that you both survived the shock. Gadgets have never been my strong point, I'm afraid. I was worried that I might have overdone it. My plans would have been thrown into complete disarray if the shock had proved fatal.'

'An electric shock? I thought as much,' Graham said, eyeing Karos contemptuously. 'What is it, some sort of metallic sensor?'

Karos picked up a remote control device from the coffee table next to the armchair. 'I find metallic sensors very unreliable. It's so difficult to set a level for it. It's either too high or too low. There really isn't a happy medium. This one works off a heat-seeking sensor built into the ceiling in the corridor. The sensor picks up the heat from a body and counters it with a charge of static electricity. It's part of my security system. Not that I've had to use it before. That's why I was worried about the strength of the charge.'

'I presume the remote also controls the lift and the door?' Sabrina said.

'And the closed-circuit television cameras,' Karos replied. 'That's how I was able to track you both from the moment you left the helicopter. My whole security system on one remote control. The wonders of science.'

'You knew we were coming?' Sabrina said.

'I realized something had gone wrong when Bellini didn't resign at five o'clock. I knew that if Calvieri had been taken alive he'd be sure to finger me. He wouldn't take the rap by himself. So I expected some sort of deputation, Miss Carver, either from your organization or from the *NOCS*.' Karos got to his feet and secured the Beretta under his belt. He gestured towards the drinks cabinet. 'Can I get you something? Brandy? Whisky? A bourbon, perhaps?'

'How did you manage to pull off your own death like that?' Graham asked, staring coldly at Karos.

'I wondered when you'd get round to that.' Karos poured himself a whisky. 'I've made a lot of enemies over the years and several of them have put out contracts on my life. Two attempts have been made to kill me in the last three months alone. Fortunately Boudien was on hand to thwart them. But I can't go on relying on Boudien to bail me out every time. I realized the only way to get the contracts lifted would be for me to "die". That would mean starting a new life away from Corfu. But I couldn't risk withdrawing large sums of money just prior to my "death". It would be too suspicious. So I went into league with Calvieri. I would cover the cost of the operation in return for a fifth of the ransom money. Well, that's how it should have worked.'

'You've told us why, not how,' Graham said.

'How? It's really very simple. Carlo and Tommaso Francia used to be stuntmen. They know the ins and outs of the film industry. They came up with the plan. The first hundred bullets in each of the helicopter's two machine-guns were actually blanks. I was rigged up with a series of small explosive charges hidden underneath my jacket. The charges were attached to sachets of blood. My own blood. It made it look more realistic. Boudien was in the control room with the detonator switch so all he had to do was activate the charges when Tommaso Francia opened fire. I fell off the terrace and landed on a safety net which was manned by four of my most trusted employees. He then sprayed the terrace with live rounds to keep you pinned down until the safety net had been rolled up and taken back into the house.

So by the time you and Paluzzi reached the railing it looked as though I had landed on the rocks. You both thought I was dead. What better witnesses could I have had?'

'Ingenious,' Graham said at length. 'But how did you know we would be there?'

'The bank statements in Dragotti's safe were the bait. I knew you would come sooner or later. So when Paluzzi called to say you were on your way we put the plan into action. As I said, it was really very simple.' Karos drank the whisky in one gulp and placed the glass on top of the drinks cabinet. 'Well, now that your curiosity's been satisfied, we can get down to business. Contact your pilot on the radio and tell him that Boudien and I have surrendered. Tell him to put down on the terrace to pick us up. It would be too risky trying to get us to the runway.'

'Then what?' Sabrina challenged. 'You'll kill us and have the pilot fly you two to a destination of your choice, then you'll kill him as well.'

'That's a little melodramatic, Miss Carver. I don't have any reason to kill any of you, as long as you do as I say. I'm only interested in getting away from Corfu.'

'And if I refuse?' Graham asked.

'Then Miss Carver will die,' Karos replied, indicating the gun in Boudien's hand.

Graham unclipped the two-way radio from his belt, switched it on, and put it to his lips. 'Graham to Emile, do you read me? Over.'

Sabrina was momentarily puzzled. Emile? Graham must be trying to warn Kolchinsky. But would it work?

There was a lengthy pause then the radio crackled into life. 'Emile to Graham, I read you. Over.' Sabrina felt a surge of relief.

'We've apprehended Boudien and Karos. Request that you put down on the terrace to take them aboard. Over.'

'Message received and understood. Am on my way. Over and out.'

'Perfect,' Karos said, then poured himself another whisky. 'Are you sure you won't join me?'

Graham and Sabrina remained silent.

'As you wish. It just seems a pity to waste such a fine whisky. I should have given it to the Francias the last time they were here. They appreciated it.' Karos turned the glass around thoughtfully in his hands. 'Tommaso's taken Carlo's death very badly. I had to take him off the assignment. He's become totally unreliable. All he talks about now is revenge. He'll find you, Miss Carver. You can be sure of that.'

'Unless I find him first,' Sabrina retorted.

Karos pondered the thought, then shrugged and took a sip of his drink.

The silence lingered until they heard the sound of the approaching helicopter. Karos activated the door on to the terrace and ordered Graham and Sabrina to their feet.

'What about the holdall?' Boudien asked.

'Bring it,' Karos answered.

Boudien picked up the white holdall at his feet, then jabbed Graham in the back with the CZ75. 'Put your hands on your head.'

Graham did as he was told.

'Now walk slowly to the door. And don't look round.'

Boudien kept his distance and followed Graham to the door. They disappeared out on to the floodlit terrace. Karos told Sabrina to put her hands on her head as well and, like Boudien, kept his distance, making it impossible for her to disarm him.

The helicopter was hovering close to the railing, facing the terrace. Kolchinsky had been alerted by Graham's coded warning but he couldn't do anything until he knew they were both safe. Then he could play his own ace. But it was all a matter of timing. He had to await his moment, then he would strike.

Karos stepped out on to the terrace behind Sabrina, his face screwed up against the noise of the helicopter's engine.

He gestured for Kolchinsky to land the helicopter. Kolchinsky kept it hovering.

'Tell him to land,' Boudien shouted to Graham.

Graham unclipped the two-way radio and tossed it into the swimming pool. Boudien hit Graham on the back of the head with the pistol butt. Graham stumbled forward but Boudien locked his arm around his throat before he could fall and pressed the CZ75 into his neck.

Kolchinsky, who was wearing an integrated helmet and display sighting system, turned his head towards the lift at the other end of the terrace to aim the single missile in the pod on the side of the helicopter. He fired. The lift, and part of the wall, disintegrated in a mass of glass, bricks and mortar which rained down on the terrace. Sabrina was the first to her feet and grabbed the Beretta which Karos had dropped in his panic to find cover. She aimed it at Karos, who was cowering in the entrance to the lounge. He slowly stood up and raised his hands above his head.

'Drop the gun!' Boudien snapped behind her.

She glanced at Boudien, the Beretta still trained on Karos. Boudien, with blood streaming down his face from a gash on his forehead, held the CZ75 on the motionless Graham who lay face down on the terrace. She knew that by surrendering her gun she would be breaking a fundamental UNACO principle, giving in to the demands of a criminal. But if she didn't, Boudien would kill Graham. She had no choice. Karos grabbed the gun from her hand and shoved her towards a set of stairs which led down to the garage at the foot of the house. Graham groaned and Boudien reached down to haul him to his feet. Graham, who had been feigning concussion, lashed out with his fist, catching Boudien on the side of the face. Boudien grabbed him as he tried to stand up and they both tumbled into the swimming pool, creating a cascade of spray.

Sabrina was about to swing round on Karos when she saw the King Cobra in the shadows at the top of the stairs.

It was at least fifteen feet in length. And it was raised up, its hooded head swaying mesmerizingly from side to side. Another few feet and it would be within striking distance. She pretended to stumble, then spun round and grabbed Karos's arm, propelling him towards the stairs. He saw the snake at the last moment. Its head shot forward, its fangs sinking into his leg. Sabrina remained motionless, ignoring Karos's pleading cries for help. The snake was still within striking distance. All she could do was wait.

Boudien was the strongest man Graham had ever fought. It was like hitting a brick wall. It was also like being hit by a brick wall. When he did manage to break free from Boudien's grip he made for the side of the pool but Boudien grabbed him from behind before he could climb out and yanked him back into the water. He cried out in pain as Boudien's elbow caught him on the side of the face, splitting open his stitches. Blood streamed down into the illuminated water. Boudien locked his arm around Graham's neck and forced his head under the water. Graham raked at Boudien's arm but he couldn't break the hold. He felt as if he were being crushed by a python. He was becoming increasingly dizzy. He felt he was losing consciousness. He made one last effort to break Boudien's grip. It was hopeless. Water seeped into his mouth. A thought suddenly flashed across his mind. Boudien had stuck the Beretta into the back of his belt. But would it still be there? His fingers raked at the back of Boudien's trousers. Nothing. It had to be there. He tried again. This time his fingers touched the butt but as he pulled it from Boudien's belt it slipped from his grasp. Darkness flooded over him.

Then there was a muffled thud, and another, and the pressure was gone from around his neck. He surfaced, coughing and spluttering, and grabbed on to the side of the pool. Boudien was floating face down in the water. There were two bullet holes in his back.

'Are you all right?' Sabrina asked anxiously, kneeling over him, the CZ75 still in her hand.

Graham sucked in several mouthfuls of air, then looked up at her. 'You took your time, didn't you?'

'So would you if you'd had a fifteen-foot Cobra in front of you,' she replied.

'What are you talking about?' he asked, his chest still heaving.

'The tank containing the two King Cobras was damaged in the explosion. One of them was killed, the other escaped.'

'Where is it now?' Graham asked, looking past her at the shattered tank.

'The last I saw it was disappearing down the stairs,' she said, then squinted up at the helicopter as it descended towards the terrace.

'And Karos?' he asked, pulling himself out of the water.

'Dead. Come on, we've got to get out of here. The whole island must have heard the explosion. It'll only be a matter of time before the police get here.'

He got to his feet unsteadily, but pushed her hand away when she tried to help him. He picked up the holdall and followed her to the helicopter which had landed at the end of the terrace.

'Michael, are you okay?' Kolchinsky shouted after Graham had climbed into the cabin.

'Yeah, I'm fine,' Graham replied, using his sleeve to wipe the blood from his face.

'I'm flying to Arta in Greece. I've got a friend there. An old KGB colleague. We can stay with him for the night then fly back to Switzerland in the morning. His wife's a nurse, she'll see to your stitches. Sabrina, put a dressing on the wound. It'll have to do until we get there.'

Graham unzipped the holdall and whistled softly to himself. Sabrina returned with the dressing and peered over his shoulder. The holdall was packed with bundles of notes. Hundreds of thousands of pounds sterling.

'That's some haul,' she said, flicking through one of the bundles.

'More than enough to start a new life,' he replied, taking the notes from her and replacing them in the holdall.

'Where do you suggest we go?' she asked with a mischievous grin.

'How about . . . Arta?'

She smiled, then dabbed some disinfectant on to a swab of cotton wool and began to wipe away the camouflage cream from around the wound.

The helicopter ascended into the night sky and headed out towards the Ionian Sea.

# FOURTEEN

*Friday*

Kolchinsky rang Philpott from Arta at two o'clock that morning to brief him on what had happened on Corfu. He didn't know when they would get back to Berne. Probably late afternoon. Philpott told him not to worry. Calvieri was due to appear at a preliminary hearing in Berne at three o'clock that afternoon. Whitlock and Paluzzi would be there.

The taxi pulled up a block away from the courthouse. The man in the back folded up the morning edition of the *International Herald Tribune*, placed it on the seat, then picked up his attaché case and climbed out of the taxi. The article he had been staring at for the duration of the journey lay face up on the seat. The headline read: TERRORIST LEADER ON MURDER CHARGES. He paid the fare and included a generous tip for getting him to his destination on time. The driver plucked the notes gratefully from the man's black-gloved hand, then slid the taxi into gear and drove off.

Richard Wiseman watched the taxi disappear into the traffic, then walked to the small hotel directly opposite the courthouse. It was the second time he had been to the hotel that morning. He had been there three hours earlier to reconnoitre the area. Now he knew exactly where to go.

He slipped into a narrow alley at the side of the hotel and paused at the foot of the fire escape to look around him. The alley was deserted. He climbed up the metal stairs to a flat roof. He glanced at his watch: 10.07 a.m. He still had a few minutes to spare before Calvieri was due to arrive at the courthouse.

His mind wandered back over the past two days. He had checked out of the Hassler-Villa Medici Hotel when Young had failed to call him from Berne and booked into the more modest Cesari Hotel under a false name. He had used the name ever since. The morning paper had carried the story of the two men who had been found dead in the martial arts centre opposite the Metropole Hotel in Berne. Neither man had been identified but he knew instinctively that one of them was Young.

He had flown to Berne the previous morning but was told by a receptionist at the Metropole Hotel that Calvieri had been out all day. He had rung the hotel at regular intervals throughout the afternoon but each time he had received the same reply. Calvieri wasn't there. Then, the previous evening, he had seen the report of Calvieri's arrest on one of the news bulletins. He had found out through one of his more reliable military contacts that although Calvieri was due to appear in court at three o'clock he would, in fact, be taken there secretly at ten o'clock to prevent any attempt by the Red Brigades to spring him. The security at the courthouse would be minimal in the morning and only increased for the decoy convoy that was due to arrive there at two o'clock in the afternoon. It had left him very little time . . .

He found himself staring absently at the narrow road running parallel to the side of the courthouse. The police van would stop there. He unlocked the attaché case and removed the specially designed detachable Vaime Super Silenced Rifle Mk2. It used subsonic ammunition and had a suppressor to cut the firing noise. It was one of Young's rifles which he had picked up from a locker at the station.

He snapped the ten-round box into place, then settled down to wait for Calvieri.

The police van swept through the open gates at the side of the courthouse at 10.24 a.m. Two police cars followed it in and the gates were immediately locked behind them. Whitlock and Paluzzi were riding in the second car.

The police van stopped beside a door at the side of the building. A policeman jumped out from the passenger side, walked to the back of the van, and unlocked the doors. He climbed inside and unlocked the cage nearest to the doors. Calvieri emerged from the cage, his hands manacled in front of him. He was the only prisoner in the van. He noticed Paluzzi standing beside the second police car, hands in pockets, and paused on the top step to smile disdainfully at him.

Wiseman's first bullet took Calvieri high in the shoulder, knocking him back against the open door. Paluzzi was still sprinting towards the van when the second bullet hit Calvieri full in the chest, punching him backwards into the van. The policemen scrambled for cover, shouting at each other in confusion as they scanned the rooftops for any sign of the gunman. A captain was quick to take charge and led a team of four men out into the street.

Whitlock hurried over to where Paluzzi was crouched beside Calvieri. 'The ambulance is on its way.'

'There's no rush,' Paluzzi said, and closed Calvieri's sightless eyes.

Whitlock punched the side of the van angrily.

Paluzzi stood up. 'Call Philpott, tell him what's happened. I'm going to see if they've found anything out there.'

Whitlock disappeared into the courthouse to phone Philpott at the hotel. The gate was unlocked again and Paluzzi slipped out into the street. All the activity was centred around the hotel. The two policemen there, one at the main door and the other at the entrance to the alley, were being questioned by the ever-increasing crowd of onlookers who were gathering in front of the hotel, jostling with each other in an attempt to satisfy their curiosity. Neither policeman was saying anything. A police car pulled up outside the courthouse and Paluzzi ordered the two policemen to clear the onlookers, who were already beginning to spill out on to the road. They scrambled from the car and began to disperse the crowd. Paluzzi showed his ID card to the policeman guarding the alley and was allowed to pass. He was told that the captain was on the roof. He climbed the fire escape to the flat roof and found the captain kneeling beside a discarded rifle.

The captain noticed Paluzzi behind him and got to his feet. 'The gunman got away,' he muttered through clenched teeth.

Paluzzi examined the rifle, then looked across to the courthouse yard at Calvieri's body, which had been covered with a grey blanket. He shook his head. 'I said there should be more security. But nobody listened. It wasn't my jurisdiction. It's certainly going to look good on Kuhlmann's record. Calvieri gunned down at a courthouse because he failed to sanction the proper security measures. The man's still living in the Middle Ages. The sooner he goes the better it will be for this country.'

'Commissioner Kuhlmann's a fine man,' the captain snapped. 'He did what he thought best under the circumstances.'

'And look at the result.' Paluzzi walked away then looked back at the captain as he reached the top of the stairs. 'I wonder if you'll still be singing his praises when the bombs start exploding in your cities. The Red Brigades won't take this lying down, you can be sure of that.'

Paluzzi descended the fire escape and emerged into the street, where he paused to look at the approaching ambulance.

Calvieri's death meant the Red Brigades would have to

appoint a new leader. There was only one real candidate. Luigi Bettinga. The *NOCS* mole.

Paluzzi dug his hands into his pockets and walked back slowly to the courthouse.

Kolchinsky, Graham and Sabrina arrived back in Berne at two-thirty that afternoon. It was three o'clock before they reached the hotel. Philpott immediately called a meeting in his room. Whitlock recounted the morning's events to them.

'Where is Fabio?' Sabrina asked, once Whitlock had finished speaking.

'Packing,' Philpott answered. 'He's been recalled to Rome. It seems they want some answers as well.'

Graham poured himself a second cup of coffee, then looked across at Philpott who was seated by the window. 'What's going to happen to Wiseman? C.W. seems certain he was the phantom gunman at the courthouse this morning.'

'Nothing,' Philpott replied, then took a sip of coffee and dabbed his mouth with a paper napkin.

'Nothing?' Sabrina repeated incredulously.

'We know he was in Berne this morning but he does have an alibi for the time of the shooting.'

'A prostitute he's paid to say she was with him,' she snorted.

'That may well be, but it's still an alibi. And we still don't have a single witness who could place him at the hotel this morning. Then there's the matter of the gun. We know he could have pulled the trigger with his middle finger, but try and explain that to a jury of housewives and accountants. They wouldn't buy it. The whole case would rest on circumstantial evidence. He'd never be convicted.'

'But C.W. can finger him as Young's paymaster,' Graham said. 'That's an accessory to murder charge at the very least.'

Philpott shook his head. 'And have it come out that we conspired with Scotland Yard's anti-terrorist squad to kidnap, and that's what it was, a prisoner on his way to court? We'd both be crucified. And you can be sure they'd never agree to work with us again. We can't risk that kind of hostility. They're our main ally in the UK.'

Graham gave a resigned shrug. Philpott was right.

'They've got enough trouble as it is with Alexander still on the run. They don't need us to add to it, especially as it was our plan in the first place to swop C.W. for him. No, the whole messy business is best left well alone as far as I'm concerned.'

'What about Conte and the Rietler woman?' Graham asked. 'What's going to happen to them?'

'Conte will stand trial for his part in the break-in at the plant,' Philpott replied. 'He'll be put away for a long stretch, the authorities will see to that. I've spoken to Commissioner Kuhlmann about Ute Rietler. He's agreed not to press charges.'

There was a knock at the door. Kolchinsky answered it.

'Paluzzi smiled at him. 'I've just come to say goodbye.'

'Come in,' Kolchinsky said, stepping aside.

'Are you off to face the music?' Whitlock said, looking up at him.

'Something like that. My plane leaves for Rome in an hour. I just came to say *ciao*.'

Philpott got to his feet and shook Paluzzi's hand. 'Thanks for all your help. We couldn't have done it without you and your men.'

'And we couldn't have done it without UNACO,' Paluzzi replied with a wry smile.

He shook hands with Kolchinsky and Whitlock, then turned to Graham and Sabrina and, putting his arms around their shoulders, led them to the door.

'You got a lift to the airport?' Graham asked.

'I've got the Audi. I have to leave it there anyway.' Paluzzi kissed Sabrina lightly on the cheek. '*Ciao, bella*.'

She hugged him. '*Ciao*, not *addio*.'

'That goes without saying.'

'What's the difference?' Graham asked.

'*Addio* is a final goodbye,' Paluzzi explained. '*Ciao* is more like a farewell.'

'Then *ciao*,' Graham said, shaking Paluzzi's hand. 'You look me up next time you're in New York. I'll take you to a game. You'll never be the same again.'

'You're on,' Paluzzi replied, then took a small gift-wrapped parcel from his jacket pocket and handed it to Graham.

'What's this?' Graham asked in disbelief.

'You can open it after I've gone. *Ciao*,' Paluzzi said, then waved at the others and left the room.

'Open it,' Sabrina said excitedly.

Graham tore off the paper. Sabrina burst out laughing.

'What is it?' Whitlock asked.

Graham smiled. 'An Italian phrase book.'

'I hope you take the hint,' Philpott said, jabbing the stem of his pipe at Graham. 'It'll be something for you to do while you're on leave.'

'We're back on leave?' Graham said.

'As from tomorrow,' Philpott told him. 'Naturally I still want your individual case reports on my desk as soon as possible.'

'Naturally,' Graham muttered.

'I won't count those few days you had off last week. You'll get a full three weeks' leave this time.'

'Thank you, sir.'

Philpott wasn't sure whether he had heard a hint of sarcasm in Graham's voice. He let it pass. 'I've provisionally booked five seats on a flight back to JFK tonight. I presume the three of you will be flying back with us?'

'I'm certainly looking forward to going home,' Whitlock said, automatically thinking of Carmen.

Sabrina shot Graham a sly glance, then turned back to Philpott. 'We thought we'd stay on here for a few days.

329

Do a bit of skiing, take in the sights, that sort of thing. Is that all right, sir?'

'I can cancel the bookings if that's what you mean.' Philpott lit his pipe and exhaled the smoke up towards the ceiling. 'Sergei, C.W., the shuttle leaves for Zurich at seven-thirty. Our flight to JFK leaves Zurich at ten. Now, if you'll excuse me, I've got a mound of paperwork to get through in the next couple of hours.'

They made for the door.

'Oh, Mike, Sabrina?' Philpott called out after them. He waited until Kolchinsky and Whitlock had left before taking a folder from his attaché case. 'You've got a thirty-six-hour clearance with the local police to find Tommaso Francia. And if you haven't managed to find him in that time, you're to pull out. I mean it. The first flight back to New York. Disregard my orders and you'll both be suspended. Do I make myself understood?'

They nodded.

'How did you know we were going after him, sir?' Sabrina asked.

'Instinct. And because he's after you.' Philpott took a sheet of paper from the folder and handed it to Sabrina. 'Those are his last known movements. He was staying in an apartment lent to him by an associate about half a mile from here but he managed to give our man the slip last night. You can be sure he's still in Berne, though. He wants you badly, that much *is* obvious.'

'If you knew he was on to me, sir, why didn't you tell me earlier?'

'I haven't had the chance. Our intelligence reports only came through yesterday morning.'

'Thank you, sir,' Sabrina said, holding up the sheet of paper.

'Thirty-six hours,' Philpott reminded them, then turned his attention to the folder in his lap. 'That's all,' he said without looking up.

Graham and Sabrina exchanged glances then left the room.

Tommaso Francia hadn't touched the glass of beer on the table in front of him. It had been there for the past twenty minutes. His eyes darted around the bar. It was small, dirty and almost empty. Two men played pool on the other side of the room. A couple of prostitutes sat at the counter. The barman looked suitably bored, occasionally glancing at the television screen at the end of the counter. It didn't hold his interest for more than a few seconds at a time.

Francia stubbed out his cigarette and immediately pushed a fresh one between his lips and lit it. He knew the authorities were on to him. Why else had the apartment been watched? Not that it bothered him. All he cared about was avenging Carlo's death. And he would, at any cost. Then he would kill himself. He would have nothing left to live for after that. A part of him had died when he had heard about Carlo's death on the mountain. He hadn't slept more than a few hours in the last couple of days. He was both mentally and physically drained but his obsession with revenge had kept him going. He had to kill the Carver woman. He owed it to Carlo. It would just be a question of choosing the right time.

'You got a light?'

He looked up sharply. It was one of the prostitutes. She was pretty but the excessive make-up marred her looks. He took a box of matches from his pocket and tossed them on to the table. She lit her cigarette and handed the matches back to him, her fingers lingering on the back of his hand. He pulled his hand away.

'You want to talk about it?' she asked, leaning closer to him. 'You've been sitting here for the last half an hour and you haven't even touched your beer. What's wrong?'

He clamped his hand around the glass. It shattered in his grip, splashing beer across the table. He opened his hand slowly and looked down at his palm. A four-inch shard of glass was embedded in his skin. H plucked it out and tossed it on to the table. He stood up, pocketed the matches, then wiped his bloodied hand on the back of his jeans and left the bar.

# FIFTEEN

*Saturday*

The weather didn't bode well for the weekend. Sombre, overcast skies and a chilly south-westerly blowing in off the Alps.

Not that it worried Francia. After putting a fresh bandage on his hand he dressed warmly, then packed the Mini-Uzi, four spare clips and the P220 automatic into his black holdall and left the apartment. He climbed behind the wheel of the hired Volkswagen Passat, started the engine, and drove to the Metropole Hotel. There was an empty parking space directly opposite the main entrance. It seemed like a good omen. He lit his first cigarette of the day and settled down to wait. He was in no rush.

Graham and Sabrina met for breakfast in his room at nine o'clock to run through the plan they had formulated the previous evening. Although they didn't know where Francia was hiding out, they were sure that he would be watching the hotel, waiting for an opportunity to strike. He had to be lured into the open. And Sabrina would be the bait. Their only concern was whether he would take the bait in the next twelve hours, which was all the time they had left before Philpott's deadline. It was time to put the plan into action.

Graham left first, using the fire escape to get to the car-park. He tugged his New York Yankees baseball cap over his head and put on a pair of sunglasses before crossing to the Volkswagen Jetta he had hired the previous evening. It was parked facing the road. He would be able to see if Sabrina was followed. He glanced at his watch. She would reach the street within a few minutes. He switched on the radio, found a music station, and began to tap his fingers to the beat on the steering wheel.

Sabrina slipped her Beretta into her shoulder holster, then pulled on a white down jacket and zipped it up to her neck. She flicked her ponytail outside the jacket, slipped on a pair of sunglasses and left the room, locking the door behind her. She took the lift to the foyer and told reception where she would be if anyone asked for her. She left her key on the counter and walked towards the entrance. A newspaper headline caught her eye as she passed the newsstand in the foyer. It was in Italian. VIETRI MORTO – ATTACCO CARDIACO. She bought a copy and read the accompanying story: Alberto Vietri, Italy's Deputy Prime Minister, had been found dead at his home the previous evening. He had apparently died of a heart attack. Her suspicions were confirmed when it went on to say that his body had been found by a member of the élite Italian anti-terrorist squad, the *NOCS*. She wondered what substance had been used to kill him. Probably hydrocyanic acid which, if fired directly into the face, causes paralysis of the heart; even the most experienced doctor would diagnose heart failure due to natural causes. The old tricks are still the best, she thought to herself, as she folded up the newspaper and left the building. She climbed behind the wheel of the hired Fiat Croma and drove away from the hotel.

Francia started up the Passat and followed her. Even at a distance of some yards, Graham recognized Francia from the photograph lying on the passenger seat and reversed out of the parking space. He let several cars pass, then swung into Zeughausgasse, tailing the Passat at a safe distance. He turned the photograph over. On the back was the number of Sabrina's carphone. He called her and gave her the registration number of Francia's Passat.

She replaced the receiver and glanced in her rear-view mirror. The Passat was two cars behind her. She smiled to herself. He had taken the bait. She drove to a small ski resort outside Berne and parked outside the hire shop. She went inside to get herself kitted out for the slopes. Francia parked in sight of the shop but remained in the car. Graham had to be content with a space beside a transit van. He couldn't see Francia's Passat from there.

Francia unzipped his holdall and slipped the Mini-Uzi inside his red and white padded ski jacket and zipped it up. He pocketed the P220 and the spare clips. He thought about shooting her as she emerged from the shop. No, he would wait until she was on the slopes. That was his territory. He made a mental note of her skis. A pair of red Volkl P9 SLs. At least she had good taste. He only used Volkl skis himself. She went straight to the ski lift, snapped on her skis, then climbed on to the pomma lift to transport her up the slope. He went to the hire shop and selected a similar kit for himself. He paid for them and hurried from the shop without waiting for his change.

He joined the queue for the next available cable car. It wasn't long in coming. Once inside he stood against the wall, the skis held in front of him to prevent anyone from bumping against the Mini-Uzi. He counted another twenty-seven people in the cable car. Its capacity was forty. That meant it would travel faster. He wouldn't be far behind her. Finding her wouldn't be difficult, for it was a small resort. It was just a question of time. And he had plenty of it.

He was one of the first to disembark when the cable

car docked. He climbed the steps to the exit and paused to scan the novice slopes directly in front of him. She was hardly going to be there. He had seen her ski. She was good. Very good. Someone bumped into him from behind and he instinctively clasped his hand over his midriff to prevent the Mini-Uzi from moving underneath his ski jacket. He glared at the woman, who mumbled an apology before stepping out on to the snow, unsure of herself on skis for the first time. The memories came flooding back. How many beginners like her had he and Carlo put through their paces on the novice slopes at the Stubai Glacier in Austria where they had been instructors for eight months after their life ban from competitive skiing? Hundreds certainly. And all lacking in confidence and technique.

He was jostled again, which snapped him out of his reverie. He stepped aside to let a party of skiers pass, then turned to the restaurant which was directly behind the cable car station. She was sitting by the window drinking coffee. Was it a trap? He had been toying with the idea ever since he began tailing her from the hotel. It was possible. Not that it bothered him, as long as he got her first. He entered the restaurant and bought a cup of coffee from the self-service counter, then sat down at a table within sight of the entrance. He was sure she hadn't recognized him. He looked like any other skier. He took a pack of cigarettes from his pocket. There was only one cigarette left in it. The condemned man's last smoke. He found the analogy amusing. He lit the cigarette, then sat back in the chair to wait.

He was right. She hadn't noticed him. Not that she was paying much attention to her fellow patrons. She was watching the beginners struggling to keep their balance on the novice slopes. Her introduction to the slopes had been at the age of four when her parents had taken her to Innsbruck on holiday. By the time she was fifteen she was already skiing the black runs, areas for expert skiers only. She loved the sport. It gave her a sense of freedom. And the more dangerous the black run, the more exhilarating it was for her. Whitlock was a good skier. And so was Kolchinsky, which had surprised her. He didn't seem the type. Graham was exceptionally good, which was remarkable considering that he hadn't started skiing until he joined Delta in his mid-twenties. He skied as if he had been doing it all his life. The thought of him brought her back guiltily to the present. She was supposed to be keeping an eye out for him. She saw him straight away. He was the only person there wearing a baseball cap. He was standing outside the restaurant rubbing his gloved hands together. She pushed the cup away from her, collected her skis, and walked to the door.

Francia slipped his hand into his pocket and his fingers curled around the P220. He had the perfect shot as she put on her skis. He held back. It would be too easy. He wanted her to know she was going to die, just as Carlo had known when he fell to his death. He took his hand off the gun as she skied away from the restaurant, heading for one of the off-piste black runs. He waited to see if she would be followed by any of her colleagues. Nobody went after her. Not that it surprised him. They were too professional to make that kind of mistake. They would wait for him to make the first move, if, in fact, it was a trap.

He stubbed out his cigarette, took his skis from the rack against the wall, and moved to the door. He snapped on the skis then propelled himself out on to the snow. He swerved sharply around the beginners group and headed towards the nearest of the black runs. The ski pole dug into the gash in his palm but he ignored the pain, it was irrelevant. By the time he reached the edge of the black run, demarcated with black poles, he could feel the blood trickling down the inside of his glove. He looked behind him. There was nobody in sight. Perhaps it wasn't a trap after all.

He followed the lone trail in the snow. It had to be her. He came across a cluster of trees and ducked into them, slewing to a stop out of sight of the slope. If she had any babysitters, he would be ready for them. He tried to flex his hand and a sharp pain shot up his arm. He inhaled sharply. At least it wasn't his gun hand. He unzipped his ski jacket and removed the Mini-Uzi. Then he saw a movement further up the slope. He had been right. It was a trap. He curled his finger around the trigger. A thought suddenly crossed his mind. The gunfire could not only alert her, it could also bring the police. He took his finger off the trigger. He would have to kill her colleague silently. He moved to the edge of the trees, the Mini-Uzi clenched in his hand like a club.

Graham only noticed the deviation in the tracks at the last moment. He was still slewing to a halt when Francia launched himself at him, catching him on the back of the head with the barrel of the Mini-Uzi. Graham fell back into the snow. Francia picked up the Beretta, ejected the magazine and threw them both into the trees. He crouched beside Graham and pressed the ski pole against his throat.

'Drop it!'

The voice startled him. He looked up slowly. Sabrina stood thirty yards in front of him, a Beretta held at arm's length. His eyes flickered towards the trees beside her. She had been in there waiting for him.

'I said drop it!'

Francia's fingers tightened on the Mini-Uzi in the snow beside him. He brought the gun up in one quick movement and she flung herself sideways as he fired. The bullets ripped into the trees. She searched frantically for her Beretta which had slipped from her grasp when she had hit the ground. It was lying in the clearing. She couldn't reach it without being hit. She scrambled to her feet and took off, zig-zagging through the trees in a desperate bid to outrun him. A volley of bullets tore into the trees to her left. She couldn't look behind her, she had to concentrate on carving between the trees. Then she reached a clearing which ended abruptly fifty yards further on with a vertical drop of twenty feet to the next slope. She dug her ski poles into the snow and launched herself down the fall line, her knees bent, her torso flexed, her pelvis thrust forward. She looked behind her. Francia had reached the edge of the clearing. He fired. The bullets peppered the snow behind her. She tensed herself to jump. He fired again, forcing her to swerve in the second before she launched herself through the air. She landed awkwardly, overbalanced, and tumbled headlong into the snow. Francia reached the edge of the ridge before she could get up. He aimed the Mini-Uzi at her. She opened her mouth to speak. Her throat was dry. She knew she was going to die.

Francia smiled faintly and trained the Mini-Uzi on her legs. He was going to make her suffer. And he was going to enjoy it. His finger tightened on the trigger. He saw a movement out of the corner of his eye and was still turning when Graham hit him with his shoulder. Graham's momentum sent them both over the edge of the ridge. Francia fired blindly as he fell. He hit the snow first. Graham landed within a few feet of him. They both lay face down in the snow. Neither of them moved. Sabrina grabbed the fallen Mini-Uzi and turned Francia over. She recoiled in horror. He had been impaled on one of his own ski poles. It jutted grotesquely from his stomach, the blood soaking the front of his jacket. She turned to Graham and turned him over on to his back. There was no blood. The bullets had missed him.

'Mike?' she said, shaking his shoulder. 'Mike, are you okay?'

He opened one eye, then the other. 'I feel like I've been sacked by "The Refrigerator".'

She smiled with relief. 'Can't you talk about anything but football?'

'How about baseball?' He eased himself into a sitting position and looked across at Francia. He screwed up his face. 'Rather him than me.'

'Thanks, Mike,' she said softly.

'Yeah, sure,' he said, shrugging his shoulders.

They heard the sound of the engine seconds before the police helicopter came into view. Graham sighed deeply, then picked up one of his red ski poles and began to wave it above his head to catch the pilot's attention.


New York was swathed in sunlight. Temperatures were exceptionally high for March. Not that it bothered Whitlock. He was used to the heat, having spent part of his childhood in the sultry Rift Valley region of Kenya. He stood on the balcony of his sixth-floor Manhattan apartment looking out across a packed Central Park. He was deep in thought. He had arrived back at the apartment at midnight, still dis-orientated by the six-hour time difference between Zurich and New York. Carmen had been there. She had returned the previous evening. She had been evasive when he questioned her on where she had been for the last five days. All she would say was that she had been staying at a hotel in the city. She had needed time alone to think about the future of their marriage. But she wouldn't be drawn on her conclusions. This had infuriated him and he had chosen to sleep in the spare room. They had hardly spoken to each other at breakfast and she had spent most of the morning in the kitchen baking for a local charity fête. He had spent the morning on the balcony, brooding. He was at his wits' end. How was he supposed to communicate with her when she refused to open up to him? It wasn't as if he was a stranger. They had been married for six years. But for how much longer?

The doorbell rang. Company was the last thing he needed. He decided to ignore the bell. Then it went again

340

and Carmen shouted to him to answer it. He cursed under his breath and strode across the lounge to the door. He opened it on the chain. His eyes widened in surprise. It was Philpott.

'Afternoon, sir,' Whitlock stammered, then unlocked the chain and opened the door. 'Please, come in.'

'Thank you,' Philpott replied, following Whitlock into the lounge. He looked around the room slowly and nodded his head in approval. 'Very nice, C.W.'

Whitlock smiled quickly. 'Won't you sit down, sir?'

Philpott eased himself into an armchair and took his pipe and tobacco pouch from his pocket. He held them up. 'May I?'

'Of course, there's an ashtray on the table. Can I get you a drink, sir?'

'A Scotch, if you have it.' Philpott tamped a wad of tobacco into the bowl of his pipe, then looked up as Whitlock crossed to the drinks cabinet in the corner of the room. 'Alexander's been rearrested. I thought you'd like to know.'

'That's a relief.' Whitlock poured out two whiskies. 'Ice, sir?'

'No ice. It seems he was quite relieved to have been finally caught. Life on the run wasn't much fun for him. Ah, thank you,' Philpott said, taking the tumbler.

Whitlock sat on the sofa. 'I'm sure you didn't come all this way just to tell me about Alexander.'

'Actually no.' Philpott was about to take a sip of his whisky when Carmen came in. He immediately got to his feet. 'Nice to see you again, Mrs Whitlock.'

Carmen shook Philpott's hand and sat on the sofa beside Whitlock.

'Again?' Whitlock said suspiciously, his eyes moving between Carmen and Philpott. 'You two know each other?'

'I went to see Colonel Philpott after I got back from Paris,' Carmen said.

'What?' Whitlock said in disbelief. 'You know the rules . . .' He trailed off when Philpott raised his hand.

'I'm not here because of that,' Philpott assured him. 'It was an exceptional case as far as I'm concerned. We had a long talk. I suggested she book into the Plaza. It was obvious she needed some time to herself, away from the pressures of family and friends.' He took a sip of whisky, then sat back in the chair. 'We don't want to lose you, C.W. And neither does Carmen. Only I couldn't give her any assurances about your future at UNACO. Not without clearing it first with the Secretary-General. I've spent most of the morning with him. He's agreed to let me speak to you both. Naturally what I'm going to tell you can't be repeated outside these four walls until it becomes official. Not to anybody.'

'I understand, sir,' Whitlock said hesitantly.

Philpott finished his whisky but declined Carmen's offer of a refill. 'There's been a lot of rumours circulating about who's going to replace who when I retire in four years' time. For a start, I'm not retiring in four years' time. I'm retiring at the end of the year. Doctor's orders. Jacques won't be taking my place as has been generally rumoured. He's too important to us in Zurich. He's built up an invaluable network of contacts across Europe which could be damaged if he were replaced. Sergei will take over from me when I retire. And *you* will become his deputy. But he'll only stay on as Director for a year. He wants to go back to Russia and settle there again now that Gorbachev's given new hope to the country. The Secretary-General doesn't want to lose him but naturally he won't stand in his way. That means you'll take over as Director when Sergei leaves.'

'Me, sir?' Whitlock stammered in disbelief. He had hoped for Rust's job at the most, but Director? He couldn't believe it.

'I recommended you to the Secretary-General because I

think you're the best man for the job. And you have the respect of all the field operatives. I know you'll do well.'

'Does Sergei know?'

'He seconded my recommendation. Jacques knows as well. He's thrilled at the idea. As I'm sure you are.'

'I am, sir,' Whitlock said, struggling to find the words. 'But what about Strike Force Three? Do you have a replacement in mind for me?'

'I've got just the man. Fabio Paluzzi.'

Whitlock grinned. 'He's coming over to us?'

'I spoke to him yesterday. He jumped at the chance. He'll be joining us next month. I'll put him with one of the other teams so that he can get some experience, then he'll be transferred to Strike Force Three when you come on to the management side in November.'

Philpott looked at Carmen. 'I hope that puts things in a clearer perspective for you, Mrs Whitlock. Naturally you'll want to discuss it by yourselves.' He took two airline tickets from his pocket and placed them on the table. 'Your flight leaves for Paris from La Guardia tomorrow afternoon. You'll find a confirmed booking at *your* hotel when you get there. Two weeks. The bill comes to us. And don't worry, Mrs Whitlock, we won't interrupt your holiday again by recalling C.W. You have my word on that.'

She smiled. It was obvious from her expression that she was far too emotional to speak.

'Well, I must be on my way.' Philpott reached for his cane and pulled himself to his feet. 'Enjoy yourselves.'

'Thank you, sir. For everything.'

Philpott nodded, then moved to the hall. They both accompanied him, and Whitlock opened the door.

'Thank you, Colonel,' Carmen said softly.

Philpott shook her hand. 'I only hope I've been of some help. Oh, and C.W., don't forget to send a postcard.'

Whitlock smiled and closed the door behind Philpott. He

turned back to Carmen. Her cheeks were streaked with tears.

'What's wrong?' he asked anxiously.

'Nothing,' she replied and kissed him lightly on the mouth. 'Not any more.'

# ALISTAIR MACLEAN'S

# UNAC🌐

## Death Train

## Alastair MacNeill

**When the mission looks impossible, the world calls upon UNACO**

Somewhere in Europe a train is carrying a deadly cargo of plutonium-IV packed in six reinforced steel kegs. But one of the kegs has been damaged . . .

UNACO's top unit is sent to track down the kegs – and find out how and why the plutonium was stolen in the first place. Agents Sabrina Carver, Mike Graham and C.W. Whitlock find themselves up against a powerful conspiracy of interests, including a sinister arms dealer and a highly placed business magnate.

Then comes the most frightening discovery of all: only five of the kegs contain plutonium. The contents of the sixth keg could have catastrophic results for the whole of Europe for generations to come.

And time isn't on their side . . .

ISBN 978 0 00 617650 3

# ALISTAIR MACLEAN'S

# UNACO

## Night Watch

## Alastair MacNeill

**When the mission looks impossible, the world calls upon UNACO**

After lengthy negotiations the Rijksmuseum in Amsterdam agrees to send its priceless Rembrandt, 'Night Watch', on a tour of the world's art galleries. Security is intensive. Even so, when the painting arrives in New York it is discovered to be a fake.

UNACO is immediately called into action. Agents Mike Graham, C.W. Whitlock and Sabrina Carver must find out who is responsible for the brilliant forgery and, most important, who now has the original in his private collection.

Speed and secrecy are vital. The hunt leads them to Rio de Janeiro at Carnival time, where their quarry is secure in his mountain fortress, high above the sea. Getting to him will be hard enough; getting out alive will be impossible . . .

ISBN 978 0 00 617743 2